DATE			

Motion
to
Dismiss

Books by Jonnie Jacobs

The Kali O'Brien Mysteries

SHADOW OF DOUBT
EVIDENCE OF GUILT
MOTION TO DISMISS

The Kate Austen Mysteries

MURDER AMONG NEIGHBORS
MURDER AMONG FRIENDS
MURDER AMONG US

Published by Kensington Books

JONNIE JACOBS

Motion to Dismiss

Kensington Books
http://www.kensingtonbooks.com

KENSINGTON BOOKS are published by

Kensington Publishing Corp.
850 Third Avenue
New York, NY 10022

Library of Congress Card Catalog Number: 98-067108
ISBN 1-57566-395-3

First Printing: March, 1999
10 9 8 7 6 5 4 3 2 1

Printed in the United States of America

For Valerie, Lora and Lee—
terrific people, valued friends

ACKNOWLEDGMENTS

I would like to thank Frances Kaminer for her insights into criminal defense work; Sandy Lauren, Linda Fairstein and Paul Bishop for their help with technical questions. All were gracious and generous in sharing their expertise.

Thanks also to Peggy Lucke, Lynn MacDonald, Penny Warner, Sandy Lauren (again) and my husband, Rod Jacobs, for their thoughtful comments on the manuscript. And a special note of appreciation to Dean James, for a good line.

Finally, although the locations in the book are real, this is a work of fiction. The characters and events exist only in my mind and on the pages of the book.

CHAPTER 1

The course of justice is rarely certain or swift. What's worse, it is often tedious.

Over the past seven days, I'd watched the jurors struggle to stay alert. Time and again, eyes glazed over, shoulders sagged, heads dropped. Juror number four had been known to snore—though he swore it was only heavy breathing—and juror number seven was close to finishing the baby blanket of creamy yellow she'd begun crocheting during voir dire. The faces, so sharp with anticipation in the beginning, were now masks of resignation.

I couldn't say that I blamed them. Business productivity and earnings analysis were simply not glitzy issues. Not when the money in question wasn't yours, at any rate.

But this afternoon, with the curvaceous Deborah Abbott on the stand, the jurors had perked up a bit. Particularly the male jurors. I'd taken her through the history of the company and an explanation of its present operations, which she managed to humanize despite opposing counsel's profusion of charts and graphs. Out of the corner of my eye, I could see the jurors nod and occasionally smile.

I'd saved Ms. Abbott for last. Not because her testimony would produce any bombshells, but because I hoped she'd be able to breathe life into a case that was about as exciting as a ride on a stone pony.

She'd more than lived up to my expectations.

The judge looked at me over the top of his glasses. "Any further witnesses, Ms. O'Brien?"

"No, Your Honor. The defense rests."

"Mr. Carson. Rebuttal?"

"No, Your Honor, we believe we've shown that the defendant company is in breach of—"

The judge cut him off. "This is not the time for closing arguments, Counselor. We'll take a thirty-minute recess. Save your remarks until court resumes. Hopefully we can finish before the end of the day."

When the jury had filed out, I found a pay phone and called Nina.

"Hi, it's Kali. I didn't wake you, did I?"

"No." Given the sleepy sound of her voice, I wasn't so sure.

"I thought you'd want to know that we've just finished with the final witness. Closing arguments begin after the break. Any last-minute thoughts?"

"Not really. You seem to have it well in hand."

"You did all the work. I'm only following the course you laid out."

"You've been a godsend, Kali, stepping in the way you have. On all my cases. I'm glad I don't have to worry about them." She paused. "On top of everything else." Her voice was thin, the last words barely audible.

"You okay, Nina?"

"I'm fine."

But we both knew she wasn't. Otherwise, she would have been in court trying her own cases, and I'd have been back in Silver Creek.

Nina Barrett and I had roomed together during our law school days at Boalt. I was maid of honor at her first wedding, and one of a handful of people present at her second. Until two years ago, when I'd left the San Francisco Bay Area to return to my hometown in the Sierra foothills, we'd met regularly for lunch and talked on the phone almost daily. We'd shared triumphs and failures, confidences and doubts, laughter and tears. What we were sharing now was entirely different.

Five months into her current pregnancy, Nina had gone into premature labor. After two weeks in the hospital, flat on her back, her veins filled with drugs, the doctors had been on the verge of sending her home to more bed rest, when they'd discovered a swollen lymph node. She'd been diagnosed with Hodgkin's disease shortly thereafter. The chemo and radiation treatments couldn't begin until the baby's lungs were mature enough that it could be "taken" by cesarean section. On both accounts, baby and mother, the doctors were hopeful—a term, Nina explained to me, that fell somewhat short of optimistic.

"You're coming by this evening, aren't you?" she asked.

"Are you sure you're up to it?"

"It will just be the four of us—you and Marc, Grady and myself. I have to commemorate my birthday in some way, after all. It won't be awkward, will it? You and Marc."

"No. We seem to be managing fine." I checked my watch. "I don't think you should push yourself, is all."

"It's not like I'm doing any of the preparation myself," she said.

That, I sometimes thought, was the saving grace in all this. With her marriage to Grady Barrett, Nina had entered the world of *money*. Big money—and all its trappings. She had plenty of hired help, including someone to look after Emily, her seven-year-old daughter from her first marriage.

"I'll be there," I told her. "But don't worry about canceling at the last minute if it turns out you're too tired."

"What I'm tired of is the waiting. And the worrying." She hesitated. "I think it's beginning to get on Grady's nerves too. Lately, he's seemed preoccupied. Like spending time with me is something he does out of a sense of duty rather than something he enjoys."

I mumbled encouragement of a generic sort. The truth was, I'd never found Grady Barrett to be a particularly warm person. He was gracious and witty, even helpful when the occasion warranted it, but not a man with whom I felt much rapport.

I watched the flow of people back into the courtroom. "I've got to run, Nina. I'll fill you in tonight."

The jurors' eyes had begun to glaze over again as Plaintiff's counsel droned on with the flat, dry delivery he'd used throughout the trial. It didn't help that he sprinkled his closing argument with yet more talk of percentages and ratios. When it was my turn, I tossed out half of what I'd prepared. I stood close to the jurors, looking them in the eyes, and tried to sound as though I were speaking from my heart. But mostly, I kept it short.

I'd stepped back a bit and was building up to my crowning argument, when I saw Marc Griffin come into the courtroom. He took a seat at the back near the door, acknowledging my glance with a quick nod.

His presence was a surprise, and it threw me off for a moment. Marc was Nina's law partner, and now, for an indeterminate amount of time, mine. He was also the reason I'd initially been hesitant about filling in for Nina.

Tall, sandy-haired, and suave, Marc was at his best orchestrating a complex transaction or crafting the terms of a tricky acquisition. He was a tenacious negotiator and an intimidating attorney, a man for whom the word *win* was a personal mantra. Marc and Nina's partnership was an interesting balance. One that suited Nina just fine but was less comfortable for me.

There was also the matter of our personal history. For three months during the spring of my second year in law school, Marc and I had been lovers. Unfortunately, he'd neglected to tell me that he was engaged to be married that June. By the time the marriage fell apart, four years later, I was past caring—but not enough past that the memory didn't sting. It still did.

Turning so that Marc was no longer in my line of vision, I concentrated on the faces in the jury box. Juror number three wouldn't look at me, but each of the others met my gaze. I couldn't tell what they were thinking though.

There was a lot of money on the table. If we lost, my client would be hard pressed to stay solvent. I recapped the main points and closed with what I hoped was an impassioned, memorable line about the integrity of the marketplace. Juror number four yawned.

I was in the hallway outside the courtroom when the plaintiff, a stocky man with a walrus mustache, approached me.

"You've got a lot of nerve, missy, talking about integrity." He leaned so close I could smell the garlic on his breath. "Your goddamn client ruined my business—and, in the process, my life."

"That's for the jury to decide. Now, if you'll—"

"How the hell are they supposed to decide if they don't know the truth?" His voice was loud and mean. "That little story you told in there just now was the Disney version of what happened, and you know it."

I could tell Sandborn was angry. On one level, I didn't blame him. The defense had clearly presented a better case. "You need to talk to your own lawyer," I told him. "Now, if you'll excuse me—"

He grabbed my arm. I could feel his fingers digging into my flesh through the soft fabric of my suit jacket. "It's your fault, missy. You're as much to blame as your client."

I looked him in the eye. "Let go of me."

Sandborn was breathing heavily in my face.

"Now," I demanded. I readied my briefcase to swing at his crotch in case he didn't.

A hand appeared from my left and grabbed Sandborn's shoulder roughly. "Move it, buddy," Marc said. "Before you get yourself in big trouble."

Sandborn released my arm with a snarl. "You'd better hope the jury sees through those fairy tales of yours." He stomped off, brushing rudely against an older woman on his way.

"You okay?" Marc asked.

I nodded. In truth, I was shaken, but I didn't especially like the idea of being rescued. "I didn't expect to see you in court," I said, intentionally omitting the thanks he no doubt anticipated.

"Yeah, well, I wasn't expecting to be here myself." Marc steered me off to the side of the crowded hallway.

"So what gives?"

He rubbed his chin. "We have a bit of a situation."

"What kind of situation?"

"The bad kind." He angled his body so the words stayed between us. "The police dropped by to see Grady this afternoon."

Grady Barrett, or more accurately Grady's company, ComTech Ltd. of Alameda, was one of Marc's biggest clients. I couldn't imagine what interest the police would have in a company that had developed a high-speed graphics chip.

"What about?" I asked.

Marc dropped his head a couple of inches, closing the conversational space between us. "Rape."

"Rape?" My voice was louder than I intended. Several heads turned our direction.

"Keep it down, will you?"

"You mean he's a . . ." It seemed ludicrous. "A suspect?"

Marc nodded.

"But why?"

His face was gray. "The woman says that's what he did."

I was dumbfounded. "What woman?"

"It's date rape," Marc offered. "Not, you know, the real thing. But from the sounds of it, he's going to need a lawyer."

"Date rape? You mean he's been seeing someone behind Nina's back?" I felt anger rise up in my chest.

Marc spread his hands, shrugged.

"Besides," I said testily, "date rape *is* the real thing. Rape is rape."

"You know what I mean. It's not like he broke into this woman's apartment and held her at knife point."

"What *did* he do?"

Marc shook his head. "I don't know. We didn't get much chance to talk. He's coming by the office about four. I'd like you to be there."

"The police haven't arrested him, then?"

"No. But I think we need to nip this early, before it turns into a media circus."

"Or a felony conviction," I added.

"I doubt there's anything to it."

"Does Nina know?"

"Not yet. Grady would like to keep it that way too."

I bet he would, I thought.

"I'm glad this trial is over, Kali. Grady's going to need help. He's got to be our first priority until we get this settled."

I nodded, fighting the uneasy feeling that had gripped me like a vise. The person I was most worried about wasn't Grady, however; it was Nina.

CHAPTER 2

Grady Barrett leaned forward, drumming his manicured fingers on the polished granite of the conference room table. His metal watchband knocked intermittently against the hard surface, producing a beat of its own.

Grady looked up. "We can keep this from Nina, can't we?" It wasn't so much a question as a statement.

Marc nodded. "We'll do our best. For her own good."

I shifted position and the chair squeaked, echoing the protest in my mind. I wasn't entirely comfortable withholding information from Nina, although I could understand the argument that we should. In any case, I wasn't at all certain we'd be able to keep it quiet.

"That's the most important thing right now." Grady's soft Southern drawl was more pronounced than usual, giving his words an edge of urgency.

"Absolutely." Marc nodded in agreement. "I'd feel the same way in your position."

Neither man looked at me. Irritation prickled my skin like a heat rash.

"You got anything to drink around here?" Grady asked with an abrupt halt to his drumming.

"Bourbon and water?" Marc was already out of his seat. He poured a glass for Grady and one for himself. "Kali?"

"No thanks."

Grady took a long swallow and sighed. He was a big man, over six feet in height, with a build that had helped secure him a football scholarship during his years at Stanford. Now, twenty-three years later, some of the muscle had turned soft. But Grady

Barrett was still an attractive man. He had a full head of hair, streaked by just the right amount of silver, and skin that was bronzed without being weathered. He was successful, smooth, and, I suppose, sexy, but I sometimes got the feeling that none of it went very deep.

Grady crinked his neck, then offered us the strained smile born of disbelief. "I gotta tell you, this is one headache I never thought I'd have."

"Why don't you tell us what's going on?" I suggested, since no one else seemed inclined to broach the subject.

He frowned into his glass. "First I knew about it was earlier today. A couple of policemen came by the office, wanted to talk to me about last Saturday. Seems there's a woman claims I . . . raped her." He stumbled slightly over the last few words.

"Who is she?"

"Her name is Deirdre. I didn't rape her," he said, raising his gaze and his voice. "No way, nohow. You've got to believe that."

Marc nodded.

I rubbed a finger across my chin and tried again. "Who is the woman?"

"Do I look like a rapist?" Grady was looking at Marc, not at me. "*Why* would I do something like that? Doesn't even make sense."

"So why is she claiming that you did?" I asked.

"How the hell should I know? Maybe she's feeling guilty or something."

"Guilty?" Now we were getting somewhere. "Am I correct in assuming that the two of you *did* have sex?"

Grady's brow furrowed. He had the decency to look uncomfortable. "She wanted it," he said, shifting sideways in the chair. "She was all over me from the start."

"And hard as you tried, you couldn't resist."

Marc shot me a warning glance, but Grady missed my point entirely.

"Maybe she set the whole thing up," Grady said. "For the publicity. She'll go on *Oprah,* write a book full of lies, and walk away a millionaire."

Marc cleared his throat. "Is she someone you're seeing?"

"Not exactly *seeing.*"

There was a sour feeling in my stomach I didn't much like. It wasn't that I rode a moral high-horse, or was insensitive to human frailty, but Nina was my friend. I wasn't sure I wanted to hear the details.

Grady drew a hand through the hair at his temples. "Christ, this is stupid. She's no one. Some woman I met at Caesar's." He sighed in frustration and slowed the tempo of his words. "I only met her that night. It was at the engagement party for Nick Moore." He'd been addressing Marc but turned to me to explain. "Nick works at ComTech."

"Does Deirdre work there was well?"

He shook his head. "I think it was one of those friend-of-a-friend kind of things. She didn't seem to know the others."

"And so you befriended her?" This time the disapproval in my tone was unmistakable. Marc shot me another look.

"She was wearing a tight dress. The kind that doesn't go much below the crotch and leaves nothing to imagination." This, too, was addressed to Marc. "We had a couple of drinks, danced some. I mean, it was that kind of party. People out to have some fun."

Never mind that one of those people had a wife who no longer knew the meaning of the word. "And after the dancing?" I asked.

"I gave her a ride home. Like I said, she was all over me."

I ran my hand along the smooth surface of the conference table. "Whose idea was the ride?"

"I can't remember. It just sort of evolved, I think. Hell, I should be the one accusing her of rape rather than the other way around."

Marc leaned forward. "So it was consensual?"

"Damn right. She enjoyed it too."

Like you'd know if she didn't, I thought, perhaps unfairly. "Do they have anything else against you? Bruises, signs that you used force?"

Grady gave me a look of disgust. Marc's expression wasn't much different.

"I told you, she was hot for it. I didn't force her to do anything."

"Tell us about the woman," Marc said. "Age, occupation, what she looks like."

"Late twenties, I'd say. Young but not youthful. Attractive, though it was clear she worked at it. A little too much makeup, a few pounds too heavy. Too much perfume."

And yet somehow irresistible. "Does she work?" I asked.

Grady shook his head, baffled. "Wait, something with the telephone, I think. Receptionist maybe."

If Deirdre had spent much time talking about herself, Grady hadn't been listening.

He pressed his fingertips to his temples, his brawny face suddenly slack. His eyes closed for a moment. "I screwed up," he said morosely. "I know that. I'm not saying I'm above reproach here. But I didn't rape her, for God's sake. If that's what she says, she's lying."

The distress in his voice was genuine. I felt the hard edge of anger soften.

"We've got to keep this from Nina. I never meant to hurt her. That's the last thing I want to do."

Marc rubbed his cheek. "What did you tell the police this afternoon?"

Grady shook his head again. "When they first mentioned the woman's name, I didn't even know who she was." He lifted his head, leaving faint pink imprints on his face where his fingers had been. "Do you think they'll go ahead with this?"

"Depends on whether they believe the woman's story," I told him.

"And whether the D.A. thinks a jury will believe it," Marc added. "It's your word against hers. It comes down to a question of credibility."

And that was where Grady might be in luck, I thought. He was good-looking, successful, and polished—with just a trace of vulnerability. No doubt he'd make a convincing witness.

But then, I hadn't met Deirdre yet.

CHAPTER 3

Nina was drinking ginger ale out of a champagne flute. The rest of us had filled ours with the real thing.

Marc raised his glass. "To the birthday girl."

"No longer a girl, I'm afraid." Nina smiled. She was stretched out on the sofa, her head and shoulders bolstered by floral chintz cushions. An afghan of rose-colored wool covered her legs and feet.

"But I'll drink to birthdays," she added. "I've recently come to appreciate that old adage that it's better to have them than not. I'll take as many as I can."

Nina's voice held the same wry cheerfulness she'd shown since being diagnosed, but I knew that it masked a sea of contradictory emotions. Emotions we'd all, at one time or another, endeavored to step around.

She looked at our strained faces and gave herself a theatrical slap on the mouth. "Oh, God, I'm sorry. I didn't mean to put a damper on the evening. It seems lately that whatever the conversation is about, it ultimately comes back to my health."

Nina's illness was not, however, the source of our discomfort that evening.

"In any event," Grady said smoothly. "Age becomes you. Every year you grow more beautiful."

Nina reached for her husband's hand, pulling it across the mound of her belly. She'd always been slender, and though her face was fuller now with the pregnancy, she didn't look as though she was into her sixth month.

"That's why I love you." Nina lifted his fingers and grazed

them with her lips. "To paraphrase Oscar Wilde, 'A good liar is not only a charmer, he's the very basis of civilized society.' "

Grady and I responded with stiff smiles. Marc laughed a trifle too eagerly.

I couldn't tell what Marc was feeling. He'd been Nina's friend almost as long as I had. But he was Grady's friend too, as well as legal counsel for ComTech, the company Grady had built from the ground up.

In truth, I wasn't so sure what I was feeling. Anger, for sure. But there was also a muted sadness that crept through my mind like wisps of fog.

"You're all so tense tonight," Nina said. "Come on, drink up. It's more than my birthday. There's good news to celebrate as well. Next week I start the medication that will mature the baby's lungs. After that, even if he's early, he should be able to breathe on his own."

"That's wonderful," I told her. Good news had been in short supply of late.

She nodded, eyes bright. "We're not there yet, but each day is like a milestone. We've finally started to think about names." This was something she'd refused to do before, feeling that it was tempting fate.

Grady poured more champagne, although his glass was the only one nearing empty.

"So, what do you think of Christopher?" Nina asked, addressing me and Marc.

"Great," Marc said with unwarranted enthusiasm.

"He'll end up being Chris," Grady grumbled. "I knew a Chris in high school, couldn't stand the guy."

"Grady's pushing for Mason, my maiden name. But I think Mason Barrett sounds like the line dividing the North and South during the Civil War. So far all we've managed to agree on is a sizable list of rejects."

Marc picked the book of baby names off the coffee table and started flipping through the pages. "Dilbert, Garfield, Knut, Tupper, Wirt, Zebulon." He closed the book and laughed. "Seems to me you could do worse than either Christopher or Mason."

"The family that lived next to us when I was young had three daughters," Nina said. "Their last name was Knight, and they named their daughters Windy, Stormy, and . . . believe it or not—Dayen."

"No?" Marc made a face. "That's child abuse."

Gradually, we were loosening up, like actors falling into their roles. Or maybe it was the champagne.

"How about Barrett?" I offered. "I knew a boy once named Thomas Thomas."

Marc groaned. "I never imagined being a parent was so complicated."

There was a creaking sound from the hallway. Emily shuffled into the room. She swung a bedraggled and threadbare stuffed dog in one hand.

Marc greeted her with a wide smile. "Hey, kiddo. How's Arf?"

"He's hungry." Emily glanced at her mother, then back to Marc, who pulled a handful of Hershey kisses out of his jacket pocket.

"He's got to show me his tricks first, remember?"

"Have you seen Arf's tricks?" she asked me, bubbling with anticipation.

I shook my head.

"Watch closely, okay?"

With Emily's help, Arf went through his repertoire of tricks, from rolling over and shaking to dancing a jig. Finally, he was rewarded with the coveted chocolates.

"Arf's quite the showman," I told her.

"He can do almost anything."

"Come here, honey," Nina said. "Give me a hug."

Emily put her arms around her mother's neck and kissed her cheek. Then she climbed into Grady's lap to eat her chocolates.

Watching Grady with his stepdaughter always warmed my heart, and tonight was no different. It was clear they adored each other. He might have his faults, I reminded myself, but he had many good points as well.

We were called to dinner by Simon, who, I suppose, is the modern-day equivalent of a butler. Nina, whose liberal roots were well established before her marriage to Grady, didn't refer to him in those terms, of course. It was usually just "Simon" or, in conjunction with his wife, "the couple who help us out."

When Nina and I had roomed together years ago, we'd shared our cramped, drafty flat with an endless stream of ants and the reverberation of arguments from the couple next door. It was always a bit of a shock to see her here in the midst of such opulence. But Nina had told me on more than one occasion that it wasn't difficult getting used to money.

With another hug for her parents, Emily departed with Arf to watch television. The rest of us ate in the wood-paneled dining room with a view of San Francisco Bay and the sparkling lights of the city beyond. We'd just finished our salads of winter greens garnished with pear and blue cheese, when the phone rang in the other room. Grady paused mid-sentence for a fraction of a beat and then continued with what he was saying. A moment later Simon appeared in the doorway.

"Sorry to bother you, sir. There's a man on the phone who wishes to speak with you."

"Didn't you tell him I was unavailable?"

"I tried. But he said it was important."

"Go tell him I can't be bothered."

Simon cleared his throat. "It has something to do with a police investigation, sir."

Nina was looking at Simon, so she missed the look that passed between Marc and myself, and the tightening of Grady's jaw.

Grady stood abruptly and pushed back his chair. "Must be that damn break-in at the plant last month. Maybe they've got a lead."

"What break-in?" Nina asked.

Marc made gesture with hand. "Nothing important. They made off with some, uh, office equipment."

I was glad that Marc had picked up on Grady's cover. I'm not sure I would have been as quick. My mind was too much on what the phone call might really mean.

"They probably recovered some of the stuff that was stolen and want Grady to verify it."

"At seven in the evening?"

Marc brushed the air with his hand. "You know how paperwork is. They have to catch up on it when they can." The nervous tapping of his legs made the comment seem ludicrous. "Hey, this is great salad. Really superb."

Nina gave him a curious look. "It's the same salad you thought was too froufrou when we served it at the Patterson closing last fall."

"Is it?" He laughed. "Guess my taste is maturing."

Nina sucked on her cheeks, her expression more perplexed than concerned. It dawned on me that she might suspect that our antics were part of some finely orchestrated birthday surprise.

Any thoughts she might have had in that direction were put to rest when Grady returned not long after, wearing a gray pallor that even his well-mannered apology couldn't disguise.

"Sorry for the interruption," he said.

"What was it?" Nina asked.

"Nothing." Grady's tone was sharp. He took a breath. "Nothing that I need to deal with at the moment." His forehead glistened with a band of perspiration.

"What the hell's going on? You've all three been tense as thieves the whole evening." Nina looked in my direction. "What do you know about this, Kali?"

Nothing. That was the word that bubbled to the surface of my brain. The answer I expected to give.

What I said instead was, "I think Grady should be the one to tell you."

Marc kicked me in the shin too late.

For a moment there was dead silence. Grady picked up his wineglass and took a sip. His hand trembled. "Let's talk about this after dinner, shall we?"

Nina shook her head. "I want to know. Now."

"Maybe we should leave," Marc said, starting to rise.

"No." Nina put a hand on his arm to restrain him. "You two already seem to know what this is about." Her voice was almost strident, her face flushed.

"Well?" When none of us answered, she grabbed the edge of the table, breathing hard. "Tell me, goddammit."

Grady sent her an imploring look. "I love you, Nina. You do know that, don't you?"

She rocked back as though she'd been slapped. "Oh, God. Don't tell me you're having an affair!"

"No, not that." Grady shook his head. "Never."

"Never again, you mean."

"Please, Nina. This is hard enough as it is."

"It's not another woman?" Her breathing became easier. "I'm sorry. It's just that I couldn't stand it. Not now."

Grady nodded. His elbows were on the table, hands folded

against his chin. I fought the urge to smack him hard between the eyes.

"Are you in some kind of trouble?" Nina asked, reaching for his hand. "Is that it?"

"Nina, sweetheart. I wanted to spare you this." He took a gulp of air. "I made an error in judgment. And now, well, things have gotten out of hand."

"Is it something with the company? Are there problems with the offering?"

"No, it's not that."

Nina waited. When Grady didn't continue, she turned to Marc. "Would somebody tell me what's going on?"

"Grady's been accused of sexual assault," Marc explained without inflection.

"Sexual . . ." Nina's expression was puzzled at first, then comprehension dawned. She pulled her hand from his. "You mean rape?"

"Date rape," Marc said.

There was a moment of heavy silence, before Nina spoke. "*Date rape?* What the fuck is that supposed to mean?"

"I didn't do it, Nina." Grady's voice cracked. He looked at her imploringly. "I swear."

"Then why's she accusing you?"

"I—"

Nina cut him off. "You *were* with a woman though?"

He nodded.

The tendons in Nina's neck rippled. "When?"

"Last Saturday. I met her at a bar."

"Who is she?"

"No one."

"What do you mean, no one. Everyone is someone."

"No one important, It's not like—"

"Jesus, Grady. Jesus fucking Christ." Her voice rose hysterically.

"I didn't do it, Nina." The pitch of Grady's voice matched Nina's.

I got out of my chair and went to Nina, touching her shoulder. "Try to stay calm. All this agitation can't be good for the baby."

Nina nodded, but her breathing was uneven, as though she

were sobbing without tears. She continued to rock back and forth in her chair, building momentum.

"But you were with her," Nina sputtered. "I'm flat on my back with your baby. I've got cancer eating away at me, cancer I can't begin to fight until the baby is born. And you had sex with some woman you met at a bar."

I wondered if Nina would ever forgive him.

"No." Grady spoke with the vehemence of one wrongly accused. He leaned across the table and met Nina's eye. "No, I did not. I didn't do anything wrong."

I looked at Grady. So did Marc. Then we exchanged a glance between ourselves.

"I gave her a ride home," Grady continued, "that's all. I swear to you. And now she's concocted some harebrained story."

"Why?" Nina stopped rocking, but her shoulders remained tight. "Why would she do that?"

"We intend to find out," Marc said, wading into the lie without a moment's pause. He looked at me, eyes narrowed. "Don't we?"

I hesitated, trying to put myself in Nina's place.

Simon appeared in the doorway just then, saving me from further moral debate.

Behind him were two uniformed police officers. "Mr. Barrett," one of them said, "we have a warrant here for your arrest."

CHAPTER 4

Marc followed Grady and the police downtown while I stayed with Nina. He and I met later that night at Olivetto's on College Avenue.

The café was crowded and noisy, and the table between us so small, we had to angle sideways to avoid touching knees. Although we'd never gotten beyond the salad course at dinner, we'd opted for late night coffee and dessert instead of a full meal.

"The press is going to have a field day with this," Marc said, scowling. "It's just the sort of dirty laundry they love." He dipped an edge of biscotti into his cappuccino and crunched down loudly.

"Maybe it will slip by them," I offered, not believing it for a minute.

He ignored me. "And right when the momentum is finally building on the stock offering. The price is going to take a nosedive because of this crap."

"So are a few people," I said pointedly.

Raising his eyes, Marc gave me one of those uneven smiles he's so good at. "I know that, Kali. I'm not completely heartless. Nina and Grady are my friends too, don't forget."

I smiled back, in spite of myself. It wasn't easy to resist Marc's charm, although when I'd agreed to help Nina out, I'd promised myself that I would. I'd managed so far by keeping my distance and reminding myself what a jerk he'd been ten years earlier.

"I feel sick about the whole thing," I said. "How could Grady do this to Nina?"

"I'm sure he's asking himself the same question."

"It's a little late for that." I poked at the apple tart with my fork. "Did they let you talk to him?"

Marc shook his head. "I might as well have not been there. How's Nina holding up?"

"She's angry, worried, confused." While she was clearly upset, hysterics were not Nina's style. She possessed an inner strength that always amazed me.

"You didn't tell her, did you?" Marc asked tersely.

"You mean about Grady's lie?" I put heavy emphasis on the last word.

Marc nodded.

I'd been tempted, but had decided against it. "No, I didn't tell her. I'm not so sure I won't at some point though."

Marc scooted his chair farther from the aisle to avoid the passing throng. "This is why I prefer corporate work. It's clean and neat."

"I've heard some pretty heated exchanges coming from the conference room. You can't convince me that some of your deals aren't emotional."

Another half-smile. "Impassioned maybe, but always with a sense of direction and purpose. There's none of this under-the-skin stuff."

I marveled again that Nina and Marc had ended up working together. Marc, who didn't let much of anything get close to him, and Nina, who embraced the world like a puppy on a picnic. It was a strange alliance.

"You'll be there tomorrow for the arraignment, won't you?" he asked.

"I don't think Grady needs us both."

Marc slid his hand around the coffee mug. "It would be a show of support."

I raised a brow.

"It's not going to help Nina any to have a husband in jail for rape," Marc added.

A valid point, but it didn't do much to ease my discomfort. "Even if he didn't rape the woman, he still cheated on Nina. Cheated on her when she was already down. And now he's lying about it."

"You'd rather rub her face in the fact that her husband slept with some woman he picked up at a bar? What purpose would that serve?"

Some vague principle of morality and truth, maybe. But we

were talking about Nina, not abstract principles. He was probably right. In this instance the truth was not going to help her.

"Sure, I can be there," I said finally. "The arraignment is the easy part. It's the next phase that's got me worried."

"You really think they'll go ahead with it?"

"My guess is that the police are working closely with the D.A.'s office on this. They wouldn't have arrested him unless they were planning on following through."

Marc licked his lower lip. "I bet somewhere down the line they drop it."

"We'll have a better idea how things look after the prelim. Prosecutors don't like to waste time or credibility on a losing case."

The furrows of tension between Marc's brows softened slightly. "Grady will make a hell of a good witness in his own defense. He's bound to come across better than the cupcake who's accusing him."

I leaned back and folded my arms. "What makes you so sure of that?"

"Look at him. He's a respected businessman. Educated, urbane—"

"Even if the"—I paused for emphasis—"*cupcake* is not equally educated and urbane, which we don't know for a fact, it won't necessarily work in Grady's favor. Not unless we end up with a jury of middle-aged male CEOs."

"I wasn't using the term in a derogatory sense." He sounded defensive.

"Of course not."

Marc started to say something more, then stopped and raised both hands. "Truce," he said. "I'm too tired to fight." He eyed what was left of the apple tart on my plate. "You're not going to eat the crust?"

I scooted it across the table in his direction. "It'll go straight to your waist."

He raised an eyebrow. "Since when are you worried about my midsection?"

"I was speaking in the abstract." Not that I hadn't, on occasion, given Marc's rugged frame a more than cursory glance. He'd filled out some in the years since law school, but he was still trim and firmly muscled. And still possessed of that goofy, boyish allure that had tempted me years ago.

"It's not just that I'm uncomfortable with Grady's lie," I said, sipping my coffee. "It may also prove to be a stumbling block in his defense."

"How's that?"

"If Grady will admit to having sex with the woman, then we have to argue only the issue of consent. But if he insists on sticking with this story he told Nina tonight—that he did nothing but give her a ride home—it's going to be a whole lot harder."

Marc lifted his shoulders in a shrug. "It *could* have happened that way."

"But it didn't."

"I'm just saying it's a possibility, is all. Isn't that what the defense is supposed to do?" He shifted forward. "It doesn't seem so far-fetched to me. Grady meets this woman." He cocked his head to make sure I caught the change of reference. No cupcake this time. "She's come to the party with a friend, so he gives her a ride home, to be helpful. She's taken with the guy, wants him to come in. When he shows no interest, she gets angry. Concocts this story of rape to get even."

I gave him a don't-take-me-for-a-sucker look. "Let's wait to see what the police have. And what this woman is actually like."

Marc finished off the rest of my tart and then slid the plate back in my direction.

He looked at me with narrowed eyes. "Grady's not a bad guy, you know."

"I never said he was."

Marc leaned over and poked a finger gently against my temple. "You don't have to say so. I can feel you thinking it."

CHAPTER 5

Grady's arraignment was scheduled for the two o'clock calendar the next afternoon. He was third up, after an armed robbery and a carjacking. The judge, mumbling in the same monotone he'd used with the two preceding cases, released Grady on his own recognizance. Arraignment is one of the rare stages in the justice system where things move briskly. Grady and I were in and out in under an hour, brushing past the cluster of reporters with a terse "no comment."

I was grateful to see that there were no cameras. For the time being, at least, we'd been spared the humiliation of a video clip on the courthouse steps.

"Where's Marc?" Grady asked when we were finally alone. He was in need of a shave, and his clothes were rumpled, but he came across looking as though he'd spent the night in a high-stakes negotiation rather than jail.

"At the office," I explained. For all his talk about showing support, Marc had decided at the last minute that only one of us was needed at the arraignment after all. "He'd like you to call him as soon as you get a chance. Something about nervous investors."

"If they're nervous now, just wait until they learn I've been arrested." Grady laughed without humor. "The timing of this thing couldn't be worse. When I screw up, I do it in neon, don't I?"

"I don't imagine there's ever a good time."

He rubbed his cheek. "How's Nina taking it?"

"She'll be happy to have you out of jail."

"Not half as happy as me. It was a sobering experience."

We stepped outside to a gray afternoon sky, but Grady lifted his face as though basking in the sun's warmth. He breathed deeply. "I never thought exhaust fumes would smell so sweet." He turned abruptly. "You can get the charges dropped, can't you?"

"I don't know. I haven't even seen the woman's statement yet."

"It's ludicrous that I have to be subjected to this nightmare solely on the basis of some cockamamie allegation."

We stopped at the corner and waited for the light to change. "I'm going to talk to the prosecutor later this afternoon," I told him. "I'll try my best to convince her to drop the case, but you'd best prepare yourself for a trial."

"Jesus. This could go on for months."

"Nobody's saying it's going to be easy."

"And meanwhile the bitch who started the whole thing gets to go about her business as usual." A spasm of irritation crossed his face. "She points the finger, cries foul, and that's the end of it as far as she's concerned. I could wring her goddamn neck."

"I wouldn't advise it."

Grady awarded me with a withering glance "It's not just me I'm thinking about here. Can you imagine what this is going to do to Nina?"

That, I thought, was something he should have considered before banging someone other than his wife. But Grady wasn't expecting an answer, so I kept my opinion to myself.

"I want her to believe me," he said solemnly. "That's very important, especially with . . . with everything else."

Again I bit my tongue—and bought a little more deeply into the lie.

"We'll know more how the case shapes up after I've had a chance to look over the police reports, particularly the statement given by the complaining witness."

"The complaining wit—"

Otherwise known as *the bitch.* "Deirdre," I said. "The woman making the complaint."

Grady looked glum. "She says I raped her. That's what people are going to remember."

* * *

I drove Grady home, dropping him off at the door without going in myself. I figured Nina and Grady had a lot of ground to cover in private.

"I'll come by this evening," I told him. "Fill you in on anything new I learn."

Then I headed back downtown to see Madelaine Rivera, the prosecutor assigned our case. Muni court, where we'd been earlier that afternoon, is housed in a boxlike building that also holds the city jail. The offices of the district attorney, along with superior court, are located in a historic and charming, if less well-appointed, building that actually looks like a courthouse.

I took the elevator to the ninth floor, passed through the D.A.'s reception area, and knocked on Madelaine's door. Our paths had crossed professionally in the past, and although I didn't know her well, we were on good terms.

"Hi, Maddy," I said leaning into the office. "You got a minute?"

She looked up and smiled briefly. "Three of them. But no more. I've got a hearing I need to prepare for."

Madelaine Rivera is shorter than I am, probably about five three, and thickly built. Her hair is dark, as are her eyes. She's not unattractive, but there's a harshness about her that, in my opinion, detracts from her appearance.

"Is this about the Barrett hearing?" she asked in her customary clipped tone.

I nodded, slipping in to take the seat across from her. "You really think you have a strong enough case to take this to trial?"

"I wouldn't have pushed for an arrest if I thought otherwise."

"It's my client's word against the woman's."

"It usually is."

I crossed my arms and leaned back. "Grady Barrett is going to be a strong witness." It was the same argument I'd discounted last evening with Marc. And I wasn't any more convinced now than I had been then. But Madelaine Rivera didn't have to know that.

She bunched a handful of wiry hair with her fist and pushed it off her face. "I know who he is. I saw that big writeup about him in the paper last week. One of the Bay Area's entrepreneurial hotshots. But that doesn't mean he's not human. Even priests and presidents screw up." She smiled. "Frequently by screwing around."

"I'm serious, Maddy. It's not just his reputation. Grady's a believable guy. He's got that charming, sincere demeanor that wins people over."

"Are you saying that good-looking guys shouldn't be held accountable?"

"He didn't rape her. The woman's story is going to unravel before your eyes."

"Now, where have I heard that before?" Her voice was thick with sarcasm.

There was a shuffling sound in the hallway. Madelaine turned and smiled at the lanky blond cop outside her door. "You waiting to see me?"

He gave her a look, something between a grin and a wink. "I'll catch you later."

She turned back to me and for just a moment I caught an unexpected softness in her eyes. Then it was gone.

"Guys like your client think they're above the law," she said, sounding as though she were winding up to address a political rally. "The way they see it, they don't have to answer to anyone. And if you ask me, they get away with it far too often. It's an opinion shared by a lot of folks out there, I might add."

"Is that why you're pushing this forward? To get even with guys who've managed to make it to the top?"

Madelaine rolled her pen between her palms. "What I'm doing is upholding the law."

"What about this complaining witness, Deirdre Nichols?" I heard the sneer in my voice, and I didn't like it. "How's she going to stack up against a guy like Grady?"

The corners of Madelaine's mouth twitched. "Better than you think."

"She let herself get picked up at a bar. How smart is that?"

"It was a private party, not that it matters. And Ms. Nichols isn't some simpleminded airhead. She's got a steady job and a young daughter. She does the mom thing for the kid's birthdays and holidays. Goes to church regularly, plus she's taking classes at night to get her degree."

Great. A regular Ms. Wholesome.

"Anyway, we've got more than just her complaint." Madelaine picked up a pen from her desk and clicked it a couple of times. "People at the party saw them together. Your client was drooling over her. Several people saw them leave together. And we have a witness who heard shrieks coming from her place that night."

"Shrieks?"

"Okay, heated sounds. But it's enough."

"So maybe they had sex. Two consenting adults and all." That wasn't the way Grady wanted to play it, but he might not have a choice.

"Then why would she suddenly change her mind and cry foul? It's not like she's some sixteen-year-old kid with a mother looking over her shoulder."

I shrugged. "Women sometimes feel guilty, even in these enlightened times."

"Besides," Madelaine said, brushing aside the pop psychology, "there were bruises on her arms. Big, ugly ones. And a nasty-looking abrasion on her cheek."

"Fresh?"

"You betcha." Madelaine held her pen eye level, as though sighting down the barrel of a gun. "Your client's going to pay for this, Kali. All his money and fancy house and club memberships won't help him one bit." She dropped the pen and smiled. "They may even work against him."

CHAPTER 6

Grady wasn't at home when I dropped by later that evening. "He's at the office," Simon told me, narrowing his eyes as though I'd been personally responsible for Grady's recent tribulations. "Would you like me to see if Mrs. Barrett is available?"

I nodded. "Please."

I'd brought along a briefcase containing copies of the police report and sworn statement of the complaining witness, as well as a yellow pad of notes from my conversation with Madelaine Rivera. I'd promised Grady an update, but I was just as happy he wasn't there. I much preferred to visit with Nina, who had been "asleep" both times I'd called earlier in the day.

Simon returned a moment later and invited me inside. "I'm glad you're here," he confided. "I think she could use some cheering up."

I wasn't so sure I was the right person for the job. Not under the present circumstances at any rate. I was uncomfortable with Grady's behavior, and even more uncomfortable with his lying to Nina. I felt sure she would sense some of my awkwardness.

I knocked on the open bedroom door. Nina was propped up in bed amid a cloud of soft down pillows—a position she'd once considered the height of luxury and had come, over the last month of forced bed rest, to detest.

"You up to some company?" I asked.

"Absolutely." Nina hit the remote, lowering the volume on the television. I didn't recognize the movie, but since it featured Cary Grant, it had to have been an old one. On the covers next to her lay an open book, spine out. The same biography she'd been reading for over a week.

I pulled the floral chintz chair closer to the bed. "How are you doing?"

"Truthfully?"

I nodded.

She picked at a thread of the comforter, then laughed. It was a harsh, almost hysterical sound devoid of any humor. I could see that her neck was red where she'd been scratching it, a nervous habit she'd had as long as I'd known her. "I think I'm about to lose my fucking mind. Aside from that, I'm feeling just dandy."

"You do have a lot coming at you all at once."

"Don't I though." Another stab at a laugh. "Funny thing is, before this stuff with Grady, I'd sort of made peace with the situation. I mean, we're almost out of the woods with the baby, and the other . . . well, I'm not looking forward to the chemo, but I figured I'd buy a wig, smoke some grass, and hope to hell the drugs massacre every damn one of those cancer cells. I'd even gotten to where I could think about something else on occasion. Something normal, like having the carpets cleaned or what I'd wear to Emily's ballet recital. And now this . . . this mess with Grady. I can't figure out whether I'm hurt, angry, or worried."

"You have every reason to be all three." I felt my throat growing tight, as it often did when we talked of Nina's troubles. It seemed unfair that fate had chosen to dump so many ills on such a good person.

"It's so hard to lie here, helpless. There's nothing normal at all about my life anymore."

"Someday all of it will be behind you. Look at the progress you've made with the baby. He's going to make it, Nina. And so are you." The words sounded hollow to my own ears, but I didn't know what else to say.

"The power of positive thinking. If only it were that easy." But Nina smiled, this time with genuine warmth. "I appreciate what you're trying to do, all the same."

She hugged herself and shifted her gaze to the window and the blue of the San Francisco Bay beyond. If you had to be confined to bed, you couldn't ask for a better view. "How's it look, Kali? The truth."

"I'm not sure I know enough yet to form an opinion."

"First impression, then."

"Better than I expected."

Based on the reports at least.

The woman had admitted that she'd been drinking, that she and Grady had been "flirting," as she put it, and dancing "close." She acknowledged that she'd invited him in after he'd given her a ride home. The fact that the alleged rape occurred on a Saturday and she hadn't reported it until Tuesday cut in our favor as well.

On the other hand, there were the bruises. They weren't as ugly as Madelaine Rivera had suggested, at least not in the photograph I'd been given, but they weren't the sort of thing you got bumping into an open door either.

"How come Marc wasn't there today?" she asked.

"He's got his hands full at ComTech. Damage control." I tried to make light of it, but I was irked that Marc had tossed it in my lap at the last minute. Rape defense attorney wasn't a title I much wanted.

Nina twisted her wedding ring. "Do you know anything about the woman?"

"Only what Grady told me. She apparently has a friend who works at ComTech." I hesitated a moment. "Did you ask him about her?"

"He says he can't even remember what she looks like. He met her at the office party and she asked for a ride home. End of story." There was a moment's pause, then Nina pulled herself straight and smacked her open hand against the bedcover. "How could Grady do this?"

I shrugged noncommittally. I didn't think she was looking for an answer.

"If nothing else, it's just plain stupid."

"I can't argue with that." Grady might be a hotshot in the world of computers and marketing, but that didn't mean he was immune to stupidity. Particularly male stupidity.

"In case you're wondering," Nina added, "I don't believe he raped her. Grady is a lot of things, but not that." She shook her head, as though to convince herself.

"I'm glad you're on his side," I told her. "He's going to need your support."

She shook her head again, more emphatically. "Don't misunderstand me. I don't think he raped the woman, but I'm not naive. There's more to this than the innocent lift home that Grady claims. You don't cry rape for nothing."

That's what troubled me. If the sex had been consensual, which I was inclined to believe it had been, why would she later say she was raped?

"If you don't mind my asking—" I hesitated, uncertain whether I was speaking as lawyer or friend. "You said something last night about Grady having had an affair."

Nina swallowed, then nodded. "It was a couple of years ago, right after you moved to Silver Creek. His secretary, of all things. I mean, how trite. She was practically young enough to be his daughter."

"You never said anything."

"I was numb. And as soon as I found out, Grady broke it off. He said he was sorry, stupid, ashamed. And I think he really was."

Nina's fingers grazed the comforter, tracing the outline of a pink rosebud. "I fell in love with Grady because he's generous, compassionate, intelligent, funny too—although that's a side of him most people don't see. He's someone I enjoyed being with, and I still do. But he's also someone who needs to have his ego indulged. He needs to know that he's *somebody*."

The intricacies of human relationships always amaze me. "So you forgave him," I said, thinking how difficult that must have been.

"I don't know that *forgave* is the right word, but we moved on. I was terribly hurt. He promised me it would never happen again."

Nina ran a hand through her hair, pulling the top section back in a knot. She looked at me. "Why? Do you think he was having another affair?"

This was the moment to come clean if I was going to. Tell her that *affair* might not be the right word, but that Grady had cheated on her. Get it out in the open. I could feel my pulse racing as I debated.

Finally, I shook my head. "Just asking."

With a sigh of exasperation Nina let the hair fall loose again. "What do you think really happened that night?"

Once again the friend in me warred with the lawyer. I hedged with a shrug.

We'd probably never know what actually transpired that night. Two people, two different versions of the evening's events. Most likely, one of them was embroidering the truth, at least a bit. Perhaps both of them. It was even possible that each honestly believed the evening had unfolded the way they claimed it had. The hardest thing of all was to predict which variant the jury would accept.

"On the bright side," I said, leaving the slippery slope of half-truth, "the jury in the Sandborn case came back today. We won. Sandborn didn't get a cent."

"Good work, Kali."

"You'd done all the work. All I had to do was follow the script."

The flickering television screen caught Nina's attention. She reached for the remote and turned up the volume. "I bet Grady made the evening news."

"Maybe you shouldn't—"

She glared in my direction. "Don't patronize me, Kali."

The arrest of Grady Barrett was, in fact, the evening's lead story. His picture—the same one I'd seen splashed across the business section on several occasions—flashed on the screen while the newscaster reeled off a summary of the arrest.

The screen cut away to footage of a woman. She was small-boned but amply rounded in the manner of an eighteenth-century beauty. Her face was dotted lightly with freckles and framed with waves of coppery red hair.

"A man shouldn't be allowed to get away with rape just because he's rich and influential," she was saying. "I'm a person too. I deserve respect. That's why we have laws, to even things out."

Nina rocked forward with a gasp. "Shit. That's Deirdre Nichols."

"You know her?"

She brushed the air with her hand, shushing me. But Deirdre Nichols had had her fifteen seconds of fame for the day. The station cut away to a car commercial. Nina aimed the remote and flipped off the television.

She looked at me as though the breath had been knocked from her lungs. "That's the woman who says Grady raped her?"

I nodded. "How do you know her?"

"Her daughter's in school with Emily."

"Deirdre Nichols lives in Piedmont?" The address she'd given the police was Oakland.

"Her sister lives here."

If that was an explanation, it fell somewhat short of its mark. "She lives with her sister?" I asked.

Nina shook her head. She seemed to be breathing again. "Deirdre uses her sister's address to get Adrianna into the local school. Not strictly kosher, but the girl usually spends a couple of nights a week with her aunt anyway. Deirdre stays there sometimes too."

"What's Deirdre like?" I asked, curious to know what sort of witness she'd make.

Nina flopped forcefully back against the bed pillows. "I don't know her very well, but she seems nice. She's a single mother. Not phony like a lot of the women in this town. She's kind of a lightweight in the smarts department, but she has a good heart."

A lot like Madelaine had described her. She'd probably tell a convincing story at trial.

Nina's fingers drew a pattern of fresh scratches across her neck. "I can't imagine why she'd make up a story about being raped if she wasn't."

CHAPTER 7

The six o'clock exercise class at the Y had been my goal for the past five evenings. Once again it carried on without me. I headed for the comforts of home instead of the rigors of health, unfortunately forgetting that Friday was bridge night.

I arrived home to a chorus of good-time howls and cackles echoing down the hallway from the kitchen. My kitchen.

"Is that you, Kali?" Bea called. "Come have some spanakopita. Not low-calorie by any means, but scrumptious."

Six women, average age close to seventy, were perched at various spots around the room, nibbling spanakopita as well as a variety of other delicious-looking finger foods.

"We're waiting for Helen," Dotty said, balancing her squat frame on the edge of a kitchen stool. "But we'll still be one short. We couldn't talk you into joining us, could we?"

"I don't play bridge, remember?"

"We'll teach you." The words sounded as a chorus, six voices speaking in unison.

Bea and Dotty had been renting my house in Berkeley while I was living in Silver Creek, three hours away. When I'd come back recently to fill in for Nina, I'd moved into the downstairs room—a subtenant in my own home. Surprisingly, it was an arrangement that worked well for all of us. But I usually tried to make myself scarce on bridge nights.

"Sorry," I said, sampling a triangle of golden brown puff pastry. "I've got work to do."

"You're always working," Dotty chided. "It's not healthy. You gotta learn to enjoy life."

"I do," I protested.

"Not enough." She scowled at me for emphasis.

"She goes more for *young* fun," Bea said, "not old fun like us. Besides, her work is interesting. No men's underwear for her." Bea was referring to her own part-time job with J. C. Penney.

"Such work," Dotty muttered, "defending rapists."

I spread sour cream on a wedge of roasted red potato. "How did you hear about that?" I asked.

"We heard all about it on the television," said one of the other ladies.

A second chimed in. "He doesn't look like a rapist, does he?"

"Maybe he's not," I offered.

"Well, dear, I certainly hope not. It can't be much fun taking the side of someone who's guilty."

I delivered the evening's civics lesson with a smile. "Representing someone is not, strictly speaking, the same as taking sides."

"What she meant," Bea explained, "is that it's harder to be a white knight under those circumstances."

Actually, I found it pretty hard to be a white knight in most situations. And the burden of representing someone who was truly innocent was heavy indeed.

"Anyway," I told them, "it's not really my case. I was just helping out because the actual attorney couldn't be at the bail hearing."

"Oh." They seemed oddly disappointed.

"You got a call a bit ago," Dotty said suddenly. "A Mr. Sandborn."

"Did he say what he wanted?"

She gave me a coy smile. "Only to wish you sweet dreams. Is he a new beau?"

"Hardly." I choked at the thought. "He was suing one of my clients. He lost."

"Oh, dear."

Bea poked her. "That means Kali won."

"Oh, well, that's wonderful . . ." Dotty smiled broadly, then looked confused. "Why is he calling with good wishes?"

"I imagine he's being sarcastic. He can't be happy about losing."

The ladies made another attempt at persuading me to join them. I ducked out with protests of work. Taking a sampling of food and a hefty glass of wine, I headed downstairs.

When I'd lived in the house as owner rather than subtenant, I'd used the two downstairs rooms primarily for storage and occasional out-of-town guests. But I was discovering they made a comfortable and cozy retreat.

Not that I was considering making the arrangement permanent. If I moved back to the Bay Area for good, and if I could afford to, I'd reclaim my house for myself. It was the "ifs" that were the stumbling blocks.

After years of belittling my childhood hometown of Silver Creek, I'd returned for my father's funeral. I found myself staying on, drawn by the same slower pace and small-town surroundings I'd run from more than a dozen years earlier. I'd set up my own law practice there, a practice I was now trying to keep alive long distance.

I'd also gotten involved in yet another not-so-smart relationship. It was because of Tom, as much as the town, that I'd decided to stay on initially. And now that part of the equation had changed. Tom and his wife had decided to reconcile.

Or, rather, she'd decided and he'd acquiesced.

I felt the familiar welling up of heartache and anger in my chest. It wasn't as if Tom and I had talked seriously of the future, or made any promises to each other. I'd known about Lynn from the beginning, and Tom's devotion to his kids. So why did it hurt so much?

Stop it, I told myself, dumping my briefcase onto the bed. Time to let go of what you can't change.

I set my plate and wineglass on the dresser and kicked off my shoes. Feeling guilty about the exercise class I'd skipped, I did a hundred sit-ups, thirty push-ups—women's variety—and touched my toes, barely. Then I plopped on the bed, picked up my wine, and called Marc.

"Did you happen to catch the evening news?" I asked without preliminaries.

"Yeah, I saw it."

"Quite a show, complete with footage of Ms. Deirdre Nicholas herself."

"They didn't waste any time, did they?" His voice sounded more nasal than usual, and he was breathing quickly, as though he'd been doing exercises himself.

"What did you think?" I asked.

"About the news? It was hardly unexpected."

"About Deirdre."

"She's a flake." Marc stared coughing and turned away from the phone so that his voice was faint.

"You got a cold?"

"Allergies."

"What makes you say she's a flake?"

"She just is. You saw her, she's not going to have any credibility at all next to a guy like Grady."

I wasn't sure I agreed. "Nina knows her. Turns out their daughters go to school together. Nina says Deirdre has a good heart."

"No offense, but Nina's not the best judge of character. She thinks everyone's a saint." A pause for sniffles. "How'd it go with Madelaine Rivera. You weren't by any chance able to convince her to drop the case?"

"Not a chance. No plea bargain either, but I'll try again. Maybe we can settle on sexual misconduct."

"Grady won't go for it. If the charges aren't dropped, he wants to go to trial. Clear his name."

Or wind up behind bars. "Did you talk to him this afternoon?"

"Yeah. I set up him up with Salmon & Sexton. They're nervous as hell over this."

Salmon & Sexton was the venture capital firm that had funded ComTech's most recent expansion. They stood to lose even more than Grady if the stock offering tanked.

"We're going to issue a press release aimed specifically at the investment community. Hopefully we can contain the damage by taking action up front."

"Did Grady say anything more about the rape charge?"

Another cough. "We didn't get around to that."

"What do you mean, didn't get around to it? Isn't he worried?"

"Right now he's more worried about the company." Marc's voice was throaty, as though he were congested.

"Maybe you should see an allergist," I suggested.

"It comes and goes. Why don't you tell me about Madelaine Rivera? I'll pass the word along to Grady."

I filled him in on my conversation, and on the contents of the police reports. "I'll go over things again tonight and get them in order for you. I've got a few ideas, avenues you might want to pursue. I'll get a summary to you by morning if I can."

There was a moment of dead air. I waited for another fit of coughing, but instead Marc's voice was smooth as silk.

"Actually, Kali, I was thinking it would be better if you took the lead on this."

"Me?"

"I'm going to be tied up with the Siefert case as well as running damage control on the ComTech offering."

"But I'm—"

"There's the woman angle to consider as well. Those things count, especially in a rape case."

"I'm not the right attorney for this. Nina is my friend."

"And you won't be helping her by keeping her husband out of jail?" He didn't wait for an answer. "With Madelaine Rivera on the other side, we need a visible female."

I started to protest again, but Marc cut me off.

"I'll help out. Give you all the support you need. But I think you should be the attorney of record."

There was pressure building above my right eye. I took another sip of wine. "Is that an order?"

"We're on the same side here, Kali. Don't make things difficult."

"Look who's talking."

"Hey, it's a marginal case at best. I can't believe they'll really go through with it."

"Rape is a serious crime."

"This wasn't rape. You know that as well as I do. Grady Barrett is an important name. That's the reason Ms. She-Bear Rivera is trying to make an issue of it."

I didn't like the snide edge to his tone, but in essence I agreed with him. "She does have a tendency to see things from her own perspective," I conceded. And to infuse them with passion.

"From what I've heard, fur is flying downtown. There's talk Madelaine's taking this on in order to show the cops who they're dealing with. She's pissed that they were pussyfooting around with the investigation."

"They were?"

"I doubt it. But the cops are steamed about something as well. I doubt she'll get much support from that quarter."

"Ought to make the prelim interesting."

"You think you'll be able to knock the wind out of her sails?"

I was beginning to feel the effects of the wine. And, the case *wasn't* airtight by any means. Grady's word against Deirdre's. Especially if he'd agree to let me argue consent.

"I just might," I told him smugly.

CHAPTER 8

For the day of the hearing, Madelaine Rivera had selected a
dark blue power suit with a light gray shell and simple silver
jewelry. I was favoring black and cream, without shoulder pads.
We were pretty evenly matched in terms of serious professional
attire.

By contrast, Deirdre Nichols was like a breath of spring. The
loose-fitting jumper of teal and lavender paisley did a remarkable
job of enhancing her soft femininity while hiding her generous
curves. The billowing red hair was tied at he nape of her neck
with a black grosgrain ribbon, and her makeup had been applied
with such a light touch that I could see the sprinkling of freckles
across her nose when I approached the witness box.

I offered her a smile, a trick I'd picked up early on in my career.
Deirdre returned it spontaneously. I knew that if the case went
to trial, which seemed at this point increasingly likely, Madelaine
would coach her to respond with more reserve in the presence
of "the enemy."

With each witness the prosecution had paraded to the stand
that morning, I'd felt the momentum of their case gathering. I
was sure that Grady, seated next to me, felt it as well. His posture
grew more rigid, his expression a little more hardened as the
morning progressed.

Officer Sylvester, who'd taken the initial report, spoke of Ms.
Nichols' highly charged emotional state at the time she'd reported
the crime. "As though she spoke from the heart," he said. A guest
at the Saturday night party had confirmed that Deirdre and Grady
had driven off together in his car. A neighbor had heard raised

voices around eleven. A woman's breathless, "Don't. Please," and a male voice that wasn't clear enough to understand.

To my dismay, Deirdre herself had made a surprisingly good witness, telling her story simply and believably as Madelaine led her through the evening's events. Now it was my turn. I doubted I'd be able to trip her up.

I cleared my throat with the trace of a nervous laugh. Like the smile, this was an attempt to put the witness at ease, to have her see me as a person rather than simply as an attorney. It was surprising how many times witnesses obliged by going out of their way to give you what you wanted.

"I'm going to take you through some of the testimony you gave earlier this morning," I told her. "I know it's going to seem terribly repetitive, but that doesn't mean I wasn't listening the first time. I just want to make sure I've got it right. Okay?" I loaded the word with all the empathy I could muster.

"I understand." Her eyes met mine as though we were old friends.

Judge Riley's gray head bobbed, though whether as a sign of approval or boredom, it was hard to tell. He'd been eyeing Deirdre Nichols as though she were the most captivating creature he'd seen in weeks, but at his age, even enchantment was no match for weariness.

"You testified earlier that you work as a receptionist at a hair salon called Rapunzel," I said. "And that you've worked there for approximately six months."

"Right."

"Where were you employed previously?"

"Well, I was out of a job for a while, but before I got laid off, I worked at a dress shop on Lakeshore Avenue." A flicker of a smile, a look in the eyes that said, *Am I doing okay?*

I nodded. "You also do house-sitting for additional income, is that right?"

"Yes. I stay in people's homes, take care of animals and watering, and generally keep an eye on the place while the owners are away."

"The night in question, you were living in a house in the Oakland hills?"

"I still am. The couple whose house it is are on an extended trip." She looked up at the judge and then back to me. "They have cockatoos that need to be cared for."

Out of the corner of my eye I caught a glimpse of Grady, eyes straight ahead, his expression still poker stiff. Turning back to the witness, I asked, "Do you have a home of your own?"

Deirdre licked her lips, adding extra luster to the soft pink mouth. "Not at the moment. In between house-sitting jobs I live with my sister in Piedmont."

"Now, Ms. Nichols—" I stopped myself mid-sentence. "Do you prefer Ms. or Mrs.?"

"Either one is fine."

"Nichols is your married name?"

She nodded.

"Are you currently married?" Not that it mattered, but stereotypes die hard, especially among the older judges. *Divorcee* has a different connotation than *virgin,* and I wanted to do what I could to paint Deirdre Nichols as other than the sweet young thing she was trying so hard to appear.

Deirdre shook her head to my question. "No, I'm not married at the present."

Point made. I added a mental check mark to the list in my head. As an afterthought I asked, "How long have you been divorced?"

Her eyes widened with ingenuous confusion. "Oh, I'm not divorced. I'm a widow."

Widow? Shit, just what we didn't need. More sympathy for the victim. And I'd walked right into it.

Judge Riley's brow crumpled with feeling. If he'd been conducting a symphony, we'd have had a crescendo of violins.

I turned and caught Madelaine's smirk. Without missing a beat I asked, "How long have you been widowed?"

"Almost five years. My husband died when Adrianna, that's my daughter, was two." Deirdre's green eyes clouded at the memory. She looked down at her hands. "I'm so glad Adrianna wasn't at the house the night Grady Barrett raped me."

"Ms. Nichols, simply answer the question." I spoke sharply, then backtracked. "Please." I softened it further with the hint of a smile.

Deirdre looked startled, like a child reprimanded for an unfamiliar wrong. "Sorry, I didn't mean to—"

Judge Riley leaned in the direction of the witness box. "You're doing fine," he said. "Just try to focus on the question."

Deirdre nodded. She glanced at Grady, then turned away, but I saw that hurt had clouded her expression.

I picked up again, reminding myself that I was doing this for Nina more than for Grady. "During these past five years I assume you've dated other men?"

Madelaine voiced an objection, which Riley overruled.

"Not at first," Deirdre said. "But then, yes."

As she'd done periodically throughout her testimony, Deirdre looked in the direction of a tall, angular woman seated in the visitors' section of the courtroom. I'd assumed at first that the woman was a court-appointed victims' advocate, but I'd learned during break that she was Deirdre's sister.

"Are you seeing anyone on a regular basis at the present time?" I asked.

Deirdre hesitated. "What do you mean by regular basis?"

"A steady boyfriend, someone you've been dating for a period of time, maybe exclusively."

Her gaze darted across the room again, but in a different direction. "Well, there's Tony," she said after a moment. "We were seeing each other for a while, but not so much anymore."

"You broke up?"

A small sigh. "It's complicated."

Madelaine jumped to her feet again. "I fail to see what any of this has to do with Ms. Nichols' testimony."

Judge Riley rubbed his cheek. "Is that an objection?"

"Yes, on the grounds that the question is irrelevant."

"Your Honor," I said, "the defense should be allowed latitude . . ."

Riley cleared his throat. "I know, I know. I will allow you to continue, Ms. O'Brien. For the moment."

I took advantage of the interruption to walk back to the defense table, ostensibly for a sip of water. In truth, I wanted to see who Deirdre had been looking at before she'd mentioned Tony's name.

The courtroom wasn't crowded. Despite the hoopla in the press over Grady Barrett's arrest, journalists had not shown up in droves—perhaps because Riley had refused to allow in cameras. My eyes scanned the quadrant where Deirdre's gaze had drifted.

There was a fair-haired man sitting alone near the rear, but I couldn't say for sure that he was the person she'd glanced at.

Turning back to address the witness, I asked, "For the record, can you state Tony's last name?"

She hesitated. "Rodale, I think."

"You *think?*"

"I mean, as far as I know. That's the name I know him by anyway. And it's the name on his driver's license." Her gaze again drifted to the rear section, where the fair-haired man was sitting. She licked her lips nervously.

"But you have some reason to doubt that's actually his name?"

Deirdre's fingers toyed nervously with the heart-shaped locket at her neck. "No, not really."

And yet her initial response had implied otherwise. I made note to find out more about Mr. Rodale, a man with whom Deirdre had a relationship that was, in her own words, complicated. Perhaps she'd fabricated the story of rape to get Tony's attention, or to defuse his jealousy. It wouldn't have been the first time a woman had used that ploy.

Approaching the witness box, I turned my attention to the night in question. "You testified that you met Grady Barrett at an office party you attended with a girlfriend. Correct?"

Once again her eyes flickered in Grady's direction. "Yes."

"You didn't know him prior to that evening?"

She frowned. "I thought he looked familiar, but I didn't know why. Now I realize that maybe I'd seen him at parents' night or something." She turned to the judge. "His stepdaughter attends school with my daughter."

"But you didn't remember that until later?"

"That's right."

"Was it before or after you filed a complaint with the police?"

Deirdre continued to finger the locket. "I'm not sure."

A fine answer, until she looked at the judge and added, "I'm sorry. It's just that I was so upset that things kind of blur in my mind."

The corners of Riley's eyes crinkled with a smile. "Just answer the questions the best you can, Ms. Nichols. That's all we can ask." If he'd been close enough, he'd probably have given her arm a reassuring pat.

"What was it," I asked, "that made you realize Mr. Barrett was someone you might have met in connection with your daughter's school?"

"I don't recall."

Keeping my tone conversational, I asked, "Could it have been his picture that appeared in Monday's business section?"

She bit her lower lip, giving the question serious consideration. "I doubt it. I don't have much use for the business section."

The corners of Riley's mouth tweaked in an avuncular smile.

Despite her avowed disinterest in business, I found the timing of Deirdre's complaint interesting, coming as it did the day after a major spread on Grady Barrett and ComTech, and three days after the alleged rape.

"I'd like to turn now to the party where you met Mr. Barrett. You weren't invited directly, but attended as a guest, correct?"

"Yes. But it wasn't like a formal party, or anything. Just some guys celebrating. My girlfriend works with one of them. He told her to come along and bring a friend."

"What is your girlfriend's name?"

"Judith Powers."

"Was it Judith who introduced you to Mr. Barrett?"

Deirdre gave me a wide-eyed look. "It wasn't the kind of party where people got *introduced*."

"I see." One of those parties. It might help us. "Who struck up the conversation first," I asked, "you or Mr. Barrett?"

The eyes dropped. "I don't remember."

Nor did she remember what they'd talked about, except that it wasn't "anything heavy." She spoke in a quiet, unwavering voice, answering my questions like a good student trying hard to please. Grady had bought her a couple of drinks—well, more than a couple, she conceded, and they'd danced some. Yes, they'd danced close, but it was that kind of music. And then they'd more or less drifted away from the rest of the party, finishing their last drinks "and stuff" in a booth at the back of the restaurant.

"What do you mean by 'stuff,' Ms. Nichols?"

She shrugged. "Conversation. Sometimes we just listened to the music."

"Did you ask him if he was married?" I pushed the image of Nina, pregnant and ridden with cancer, from my mind.

"He never mentioned it."

"What about the ring on his left hand?"

Her lips puckered like a pink rosebud. "I never thought to check."

Bullshit. But she carried it off convincingly.

"Did Mr. Barrett touch you at all while you were sitting there in the booth?" I asked.

I could feel Grady stir at the table behind me.

"Some."

"And did you ask him to stop?"

"It wasn't like that. It was just . . . touching."

I walked back to the defense table. She couldn't look in my direction without focusing on Grady as well. "Did Mr. Barrett offer you a ride home," I asked, "or did you ask for one?"

"I . . . I may have said something about not having a car there. But he offered."

"When you left the party, did he take you straight home?"

"Yes."

"And you invited him in?"

"I'm not saying I wasn't attracted to him," Deirdre said, sounding, for the first time, a bit testy. "He's an attractive man, and he seemed like a nice guy."

"Did you want him to kiss you?"

She looked at Grady and then quickly away. "I guess. Like I said, he *seemed* nice."

"So you didn't resist?"

"Not at first."

"You were having a good time?"

Deirdre leaned forward. Her eyes flashed with exasperation. "Look, I never said he jumped out of the bushes and raped me at knife point. Yes, we were having a good time. But then he crossed the line. I want him held accountable."

Grady snorted in disgust. I put a hand on his shoulder to quiet him. "Nonresponsive," I said to Judge Riley. "Move to strike."

Riley directed the court reporter to disregard the comment, then instructed the witness that she was to answer the question and nothing more. But I could tell from his tone that Deirdre Nichols had found a soft spot in the judicial armor.

"When you say, 'He crossed the line,' I take it you mean he forced you to have sex against your will?"

She lifted her chin. "Yes."

"After you made it patently clear that it was something you didn't want."

"Yes."

I led her, step by step, over the testimony she'd given on direct, eliciting from her an account of fairly steamy flirtation on her part. But she held firm on the issue of consent. She'd told Grady no and he had ignored her.

"What made you change your mind?" I asked.

Madelaine was on her feet again. "Objection. Assumes that witness initially intended to give consent."

"Sustained."

I rephrased the question. "Ms. Nichols, what did you expect would happen after this episode of kissing you've told us about?"

Deirdre shook her head, and a lock of red hair sprang from the ribbon at her neck. "We were clearly attracted to each other, but I thought . . . I thought it might be better to get to know one another first."

I checked my notes. "When Mr. Barrett persisted with his affections, despite the fact that you'd asked him to stop, is that when he grabbed you by the arm?"

"I think so. It's all kind of a blur."

Her fingers twisted a handkerchief embroidered with tiny purple flowers. I wondered if it was hers or Madelaine's. Not that Madelaine would ever have use for anything as dainty and lady-like herself, but I wouldn't have put it past her to have a stash of them for occasions such as this.

" 'All kind of a blur,' " I repeated. "Yet you're certain you told Mr. Barrett, 'Stop. Let go of me?' " This had been her testimony on direct.

"Yes."

They weren't the exact words the neighbor had heard, which might work to our benefit at trial.

"Certain you made it clear you weren't interested in having sexual relations with him?"

She hesitated, then nodded emphatically. "Yes, I'm certain."

"What did you do to resist?"

"I don't remember exactly." Tears sprang to her eyes. She dabbed them with embroidered white linen, lilacs facing out.

"Did you kick him?" I asked.

Madelaine rose. "Your Honor, Defense knows that the witness doesn't have to offer physical resistance."

"I'm just trying to determine what happened."

Riley nodded. "I'll allow it."

"I may have. I don't remember." Her voice wavered.

"How about bites? Or scratches?"

"I don't think so." She addressed her hands, which were folded in her lap. "He's so much bigger and stronger than I am. I was scared."

"So it's conceivable Mr. Barrett might have thought you weren't resisting at all?"

"He knew." She was crying harder now, but her voice no longer quivered with emotion. Anger had hardened it. "He knew how I felt, and he didn't care."

Grady squirmed in his chair. "Not true," he muttered under his breath.

"And afterward," I asked. "What then?"

She dabbed at her nose. "What do you mean?"

"What did you do after he'd . . . completed the act?"

Deirdre hugged herself, as if for reassurance. "I cried."

"Did you say anything to him?"

"Nothing important. It's like part of me couldn't believe what had happened."

"Did he say anything to you?"

She looked directly at Grady. Her eyes flashed anger and something else I couldn't read. "He just pulled up his pants and left. I've never in my whole life felt so . . . so devalued."

"When you finished crying," I said with a gentleness that wasn't entirely feigned, "what did you do then?"

Deirdre shook her head in confusion. "I don't understand. I cried off and on the whole night."

"Did you take a shower?"

"Not that night, no." Her tone was wary.

"Did you wash yourself?"

"I might have."

"But you don't remember for sure?" With most victims of rape, including date rape, there's a strong impulse to wash away the remnants of the crime. Even women who know they shouldn't destroy evidence succumb.

"I was upset," Deirdre said.

"Yet you waited until Tuesday to make a police report. Why is that?"

"I was ashamed, frightened. I tried to forget about it, but I couldn't."

"Did you tell anyone what had happened?"

She shook her head. "Maybe you don't know what it's like, Ms. O'Brien. Being raped is an awful experience. It makes you feel worthless. Humiliated. You can tell yourself that it's no reflection on you personally, but it doesn't matter. I didn't want to talk about it with anyone."

"Not even a friend? Your sister, perhaps?"

"No." A thin whisper of a word.

I stepped back. "I see."

My tone was skeptical, as I'd intended. But there was a part of me that found Deirdre's testimony disturbingly convincing. She might well have been lying through her teeth, but my suspicion was that there was some element of truth there as well. And I had the sinking feeling the judge felt it too.

CHAPTER 9

"You were too soft on her," Grady grumbled when we broke for afternoon recess. "You should have come down a lot harder, made her squirm."

"I explained before, what we're trying to do at this point is lock in her testimony. We can discredit it later, at trial."

He snorted in disgust. "If you'd nailed her today, we wouldn't have to *go* to trial."

"It's your word against hers. That's something for a jury to decide, not the hearing judge."

Grady shoved a hand into his pocket and jingled his keys. The tension he'd kept in check all morning had exploded now that we were no longer in the courtroom.

"You didn't even touch on the outfit she was wearing that night," he said. "I told you the skirt was skintight, and that little crop top was so flimsy she might as well not have been wearing anything."

I looked at him in disgust. "You're out of touch with the times if you think the she-was-asking-for-it defense still works."

"Well, she was." He caught my expression. "Not asking to be raped, but asking for a good time. Her story is nothing but a pack of lies."

"Except that you *did* have sex with her." It angered me that Grady took no responsibility for his role in setting events in motion.

Grady's expression was tight. "I told you, I don't want to use that."

"So what do we say about the bruises on her arm?"

"I was *not* the cause of those bruises, okay?" His voice was low and urgent. "I had nothing to do with that. Or the scrape on her cheek."

"What about the raised voices the neighbor heard?"

He shrugged. "Lots of people raise their voices. She's out to get me for some reason. That's what you should have focused on."

My mouth tasted bitter. "If you'd been home with your wife, we wouldn't be having this conversation."

"You trying to rub my nose in it?"

"I'm just trying to interject a little reality."

Grady sighed heavily. "Believe it or not, I know all too well what's real." He shoved a hand into his pocket and was silent a moment. "You really think it will go to trial?"

I nodded. I'd explained at the outset that the judge wasn't a trier of fact.

"I can't have this shit dragging on. I've got a business to run. A public offering in the works. A wife who is facing chemo and God knows what else. I don't want my name dragged through the mud on every goddamn front page and news hour for the foreseeable future."

"I'm afraid that's something you don't have a lot of control over at this point."

He stepped closer. "That's why you needed to pulverize her in there."

I turned away in disgust. "I've got to run to the ladies' room," I told him.

"Fine." His tone was as clipped as mine. "I have some phone calls to make. I'll meet you back here when court reconvenes." Grady turned to go.

"Don't forget to call Nina. I know she's waiting to hear how it's going."

He looked at me with reproach. "I don't think she needs *more* bad news."

It was clear he considered the bad news my fault.

I pushed open the heavy wooden door of the women's rest room and was glad to find it empty. After a day of being constantly onstage, even a moment's solitude was welcome.

I used the facilities, washed the afternoon's buildup of grime from my hands, and began to repair the damage to my makeup.

I was dabbing a blush of color on my cheeks when the door opened and Deirdre Nichols entered.

"Hi." She gave a self-conscious laugh.

I nodded in response. "I'll be through here in a minute." I figured Deirdre might be in need of some solitude herself. I've always found these rest room encounters somewhat awkward.

She didn't seem at all surprised to find me there, however. She glanced at the stalls, making sure we were alone. "I wanted to talk to you," she said, rubbing her hands over her upper arms as though to warm herself.

"I can't—"

"If you're busy, maybe later." She reached into her purse and pulled out one of those multipurpose calendar and address books.

I shook my head. "I meant, it's not a good idea. Not without your attorney present."

"You mean Madelaine Rivera?"

I nodded.

"She's not really *my* attorney."

"Not technically, but she's working on your behalf."

Her expression was skeptical. "Madelaine is part of the problem."

I wasn't sure I wanted to be a party to this. Both legally and ethically it was only asking for trouble. "You shouldn't be talking to me in any case," I told her.

Deirdre didn't appear particularly interested in what she should or shouldn't be doing. She sucked on her bottom lip a moment, studying me. "Madelaine says that you'll say bad things about me at the trial. That you'll try to make me look like a tramp, like someone who deserves what she got. She says you'll bring up all kinds of embarrassing stuff about me and say that I'm lying."

"It's my job to discredit your testimony." I didn't tell her that the dirt I could bring in was limited by law. "It's your word against my client's."

"Aren't you interested in what really happened?"

Curious as hell, but that wasn't my role as attorney. I shook my head. "Not really."

She frowned. "You seemed nice in there. Even when you were trying to make it look as though I wasn't really raped. You seemed like a real person, not just a lawyer. Like someone who had feelings. I thought you cared about the truth."

"Ms. Nichols, you need to remember that we've been assigned roles here. Personal qualities have nothing to do with it." I turned back to the mirror and finished applying my lipstick.

"Madelaine doesn't care either. She's taken over. She tells me how to dress, how to wear my hair, how to sit, what to say, and what not to say. All she wants is to win. It's like a game for her."

"Madelaine has got a job to do as well. But ultimately, she wants the same thing you do."

"All I want is some respect."

I recapped my lipstick.

"I'm a person too, you know. Not just something to be used and then discarded."

"Of course you are," I said, turning so that I was no longer addressing the mirror. I could understand Deirdre's frustration. Legal proceedings were driven by their own rules, which sometimes seemed very far removed from the emotionally charged event that triggered them.

Deirdre hugged her arms tighter across her chest. "I feel like I've been violated twice. Once by Grady Barrett and once by Madelaine Rivera."

"Have you tried telling that to Madelaine?"

Deirdre shook her head. "I know she's trying to help me. The police would never have done a thing if she hadn't given them a push."

Advising the complaining witness wasn't my role, but I couldn't help myself. "There are victims' advocates, you know. Rape counseling services, support groups. They're available to you without cost."

"Madelaine told me." She leaned against the wall and closed her eyes for a moment. Her lashes were long and soft, like brushstrokes against her creamy complexion. "The press will be covering the trial, won't they?"

"Probably. I doubt there will be cameras in the courtroom, if that's what you're worried about."

Deirdre pursed her lips in thought.

"Besides," I added, "you talked to news reporters the other day with no problem." It came out with a nastier edge than I'd intended.

Deirdre brushed at the skirt of her jumper. "I know I shouldn't have. It's just that I was angry."

Her tone was apologetic, as if Madelaine had chastised her for telling her story before the camera. That surprised me. It wasn't a bad move in terms of strategy. And Madelaine had never been one to shy away from the press.

"I take it Madelaine wasn't happy about the exposure."

"No, it was . . . something else." Deirdre sighed and tapped her heel against the ceramic tile at the base of the wall. "I don't know whether I want to go ahead with this," she said, her voice thin and thoughtful.

I held my breath. Looked away. Kept my expression impassive. Never let it be said that I tried to influence a witness. But inside I was delirious at the prospect that she might withdraw her complaint.

"I've got my daughter to consider," Deirdre said. "Among other things."

I dropped the lipstick into my purse.

"There's bound to be talk. Adrianna is smart. She'll pick up on it."

"You have to do what you think is right," I told her. I hoped the gods were watching, because I figured I'd earned a few bonus points for good conduct in the face of temptation.

"I don't know what to do," Deirdre lamented.

I glanced toward heaven and bit my tongue.

"I don't like to be treated like dirt. I'm a person too." It was the second time she'd used the phrase in less than five minutes.

I nodded.

"Men think they own the world."

No argument there.

She tucked a strand of loose hair behind her ear. "I really didn't know," she said after a moment. "I didn't know he was Emily's father, didn't know he had a lot of money and a big important job."

I didn't say anything.

Deirdre began crying softly, with the look of an injured child. "You think I'm lying about the whole thing, don't you?"

"You shouldn't concern yourself with what I think."

"Just because he's rich and educated and wears designer

suits—and I'm some dumb receptionist with bouncy hair and big tits, it doesn't mean he's right and I'm wrong."

There was something in her voice I couldn't ignore—a touch of real misery mixed with hurt and anger. "No," I said gently, "it doesn't."

She slouched against the bathroom wall. "I want him to know it was wrong to treat me the way he did. I want him to know how much it hurt." The words were capped with a pathetic whimper. "I'm a person too. I have feelings."

"I think you need to talk with Madelaine Rivera," I told her.

Deirdre nodded but made no move toward the door. I decided to skip the fresh mascara and leave. Whatever else the encounter had accomplished, it left me feeling oddly protective of a woman whose testimony I was supposed to tear to shreds.

I wondered, in passing, if that had been her intent.

CHAPTER 10

The cocktail waitress leaned low across the table so that her ample cleavage was not only at eye level but bountifully displayed. I was fascinated, but neither Grady nor Marc took notice. They were too deeply entrenched in some fine point of quarterly earnings and SEC filings.

The bar was noisy with Friday-night revelry. If you wanted to be heard, you had two choices—yell or huddle close to your companions. Marc and Grady were huddling. They weren't excluding me, but I'd grown tired of sitting forward in my chair and straining to hear. Instead, I sipped my wine leisurely and waited for them to finish.

Grady lifted the skewered onion from his martini and bit into it. Despite the intensity of the discussion, which I gathered focused on some less-than-favorable financial report, he was more relaxed than I'd seen him in the last few days.

The outcome of the hearing had come as no surprise. Judge Riley had issued a holding order Tuesday morning. We would proceed to trial.

I'd tried to prepare Grady for it, but the news had shaken him all the same. He'd been short with me then, and even more irritable later that afternoon when I'd tried to lay out the main issues of the case. His mood in the intervening days hadn't improved. But this evening he'd greeted me warmly, interrupting his conversation with Marc to include me, albeit only briefly.

My glass of wine was half empty when they paused again.

Marc offered me a smile that was both apologetic and conspiratorial. "Sorry to monopolize your client. I know you two were planning to go over pretrial strategy, but there were a couple of things that needed Grady's attention right away."

A perfect segue to my reason for being here. "How badly has the rape charge hurt the offering?" I asked.

"It hasn't helped," Marc said. "That's for sure. But it's too early to tell if there's permanent damage."

Grady snorted in disgust. "That's bullshit. There's *always* nervousness about an initial offering, especially in a volatile business like ours. This goddamn rape charge spells nothing but trouble. It's going to send the price into the toilet."

"If it's any help," I offered, "I think we stand a good chance of beating it at trial."

"It will be too late by then. Besides, *good chance* is far from a certainty."

I nodded. "True. But remember, the prelim was different. There, it wasn't a matter of assessing credibility or weighing the evidence. The judge was only looking to see if there was any basis for taking the case to trial. It's a fairly low standard."

"You can say that again." Grady made no attempt to disguise the bitterness in his voice.

I ignored it. "The big issue is going to be what defense we go with. I think consent is by far our best bet."

Grady shook his head. "I told you, that's not an option."

"Nina might understand—"

"It's ... not ... an ... option." He gave each word equal emphasis.

"You think the jury's going to believe that you simply gave Deirdre Nichols a ride home and that she made the rest of it up out of thin air?"

Grady leaned back in his chair and made a dismissive gesture with his hand. "Let's not get bogged down in technicalities just yet."

I was about to point out that defense strategy was hardly a technicality, but before I got the words out, I was momentarily blinded by the flash of a strobe. I blinked, and saw only green and blue.

Marc was on his feet in an instant. "What the hell ..." He yanked the photographer's collar and brought his face close. "What the hell do you think you're doing, buddy?"

The young man was shorter than Marc and had to stand on

tiptoe to keep his balance. A strand of straight blond hair fell across his forehead. He tried to brush it aside, but Marc batted his hand away.

"Hey, calm down," the young man said. He was probably in his late twenties, but there was a bright-eyed boyishness about him that made him appear younger. "I didn't mean to startle you."

Marc was breathing fast and hard, his eyes glazed with anger.

"I'm a reporter," the man said with a remarkably good-natured smile. "I've been researching a piece on the ComTech offering. When I saw you all sitting here, I thought I'd get a couple of informal shots."

"Well, you thought wrong."

"Marc, what's the problem?" It had taken me a minute to sort out what had happened.

Marc ignored me. He grabbed the camera with his free hand, releasing the young man, who looked startled and increasingly nervous.

"That's an expensive camera," he said warily.

"You think I give a shit?" Marc's eyes were cold, his expression hard. It was a look I'd not seen before.

Grady put a calming hand on Marc's shoulder, but Marc had already popped the back of the camera and unwound the roll of film, exposing it to light.

"What are you doing?" Fury strained the man's voice. "I've got practically a whole roll of pictures on there. A week's worth of work."

Marc handed the camera back, shoving it into the man's midsection. "Next time, ask first."

"This is a public place, you know. It's not like I was taking shots through your bedroom window. And I would have asked if you'd given me the chance."

"Yeah, sure."

"Marc—" I tried again, but he paid no attention.

The man rubbed his neck where a large red welt was taking shape. "I sell my stuff to respectable papers. We're not talking *National Enquirer* or anything."

"You ought to consider it," Marc said, straightening the sleeves of his jacket. "You'd fit right in."

The young man's face darkened with indignation. "You're a

real prick, you know that? The kind of guy who gives lawyers a bad name."

The bartender stepped between them, his sheer bulk providing a buffer. "What's the trouble here?"

"It's taken care of," Marc said affably.

The bartender looked to the young man for confirmation.

"I guess it's okay," he said after a moment. He turned and handed Grady his business card. "Maybe we could talk some-time—without the shark. You could probably use a little positive publicity." With a glare at Marc, he left.

"Jeez," I said when the man was gone. "Don't you think you overreacted a bit?"

Marc grinned, not quite sheepishly but close. "Maybe a little."

Grady drained what was left of his martini. "What got into you? You're supposed to keep me out of trouble, not create it."

"I kept your photo out of the paper, didn't I?"

"A lousy photo," I said. "They must have plenty of others in the archives."

"Publicity photos. There's a difference."

"What's so damaging about Grady's having a drink with his lawyers? This offering isn't based on the claim that Grady's a teetotaler, is it?"

Marc sucked his cheek, looking more amused than chastised. "I'll apologize, how's that?" He took the card from Grady's grasp. "Byron Spencer. God, with a name like that, the guy should have been a poet. Maybe journalist is the closest he could get."

"The sooner you apologize, the better," I said. "And try to sound sincere."

"Am I ever anything but?"

Grady looked at his watch. "Well, this was fun, boys and girls, but I've got to be going. I told Nina I'd be home before dinner."

"You're leaving? I thought we were going to talk about the case." That was the only reason I'd agreed to come. I was having a hard time fitting into Grady's schedule.

"I've got a handle on it. We can talk in a couple of days, okay?"

"Why not now?"

"Let's let the dust settle first."

I wasn't sure what dust he was talking about, and I wasn't sure I'd have any better luck pinning him down in the future. As

I watched him leave, I wondered once again how I'd ended up defending Grady Barrett on a rape charge.

Without asking me, Marc hailed the waitress and ordered another drink for both of us.

"So, do you think I'm a prick too?"

"Sometimes."

He grinned. "And the other times?"

If the truth be told, I didn't know what to make of Marc. And it wasn't just his behavior tonight. At times I felt myself drawn to him despite our past history. There was a chemistry between us I couldn't ignore. But other times he made me slightly uneasy. It was almost as though the face Marc presented to the world were artfully contrived to hide the real man beneath the skin.

I decided to sidestep the question. "Are you always that uptight about the press?"

Marc shrugged. "I guess I'm nervous about this offering. The talk in the investment community has been favorable so far, but that can change overnight." He frowned. "Which reminds me. I'll be in New York for a couple of days talking with investment bankers. You think you can manage the fort without me?"

I couldn't tell from his tone whether the question was posed in jest or not. Either way, I didn't think it warranted much of an answer.

"I figured as much," Marc said, reading my look. He gave me a disarming smile. "You seem to have things pretty much under control."

"Thanks."

"I like that."

"What?"

"A woman with a brain." He angled closer and spoke softly. "It's very sexy."

"You're verging on prickhood again."

He moved back to his own part of the table and grinned. "I'll work on fixing that."

When I got home, I checked the spiral notepad by the phone, where Bea and Dotty left my messages. There was one from a woman I'd worked with at Goldman and Latham, one from the gardening service, and none at all from the person whose name I most wanted to see there.

It wasn't that Tom never called me. He had phoned probably four or five times since I'd come back to Berkeley. Our conversations were always affable, and irritatingly light. Loretta, the springer spaniel I'd inherited from my father, provided safe ground for discourse. She was staying with Tom while I was away, and he recounted her antics for me at length. He filled me in on news of Silver Creek as well, and the people we knew in common, but he took pains not to mention Lynn unless I asked. And then he'd say something vague, like *she's trying hard to make it work.*

What the hell was that supposed to mean? The reconciliation had been her idea. The more important question, to my mind, was, what was Tom feeling? Unfortunately, feelings were something he didn't talk about much. Which I suspected was one of the reasons Lynn had moved out in first place.

I was running late Monday morning, so I didn't read the paper until I got to the office. Not that I made the connection even then. The article was short, on the inside page of the second section. A woman had fallen to her death from the deck of a home in the Oakland hills. No name or address was listed, and I gave the story only a passing glance, mentally adding it to the growing tally of tragic events that befall people every day.

It was only when Nina called a little after noon that my stomach curdled.

"Did you see this morning's *Chronicle?*" she asked.

"What about it?"

"The story about the woman who fell off her deck."

I knew then, before she said the name. "Deirdre Nichols?"

"One of the other second-grade mothers called me. She was in the office when Deirdre's sister phoned to say Adrianna wouldn't be at school." Nina's voice was faint, as though she were talking through spun cotton. "Poor Adrianna. To wake up and find her mother gone. She must have been so frightened. And then to find her lying in the dirt, bloody and broken . . ."

Nina's voice trailed off. I knew the specter of her own death and what that would mean for Emily weighed on Nina's mind, but that didn't fully account for the thin, quavery quality of her words.

"What happened? Do you know any of the details?"

"Only that Adrianna discovered the body. She was smart enough to call 911. God, the things we drill into our babies' heads." Nina paused for a breath. "I'm scared, Kali."

"Scared? Why?"

"After I heard, I called the police. Just to make sure." Another pause. "They've listed it as a suspicious death."

The sour feeling in my stomach rose to my throat. "Did they say why?"

"Only that they weren't ruling out foul play."

CHAPTER 11

"I'm worried," Nina said after a moment. I could hear her breathing into the phone.

I was worried too. Unless he had a rock-solid alibi, Grady Barrett would find himself the object of intense scrutiny—both from the police and from the public. Not to mention the investment bankers.

"Was Grady at home Saturday night?" I asked.

"He's never home anymore." Nina's tone was clipped. It was hard to separate the pique from the worry.

"Never?"

"I mean, he comes home, but late. Often after I'm asleep. It's this stock offering," she added. "It has him going twenty different ways at once."

"How about Saturday? Were you asleep when he got home?"

"I didn't hear him come in, if that's what you mean."

"What about Simon and Elsa?"

"I don't know. Their rooms are in the guest house in back, so it would be unusual for them to have heard him." She paused. "Grady's been so, so . . . I don't know, agitated lately. It worries me."

"As you mentioned, this offering has been on his mind."

There was a beat of silence. "Yeah, that's probably all it is."

"Deirdre Nichols' death may yet be ruled accidental," I reminded her. "*Suspicious* is a catch-all term for anything that needs looking into."

She sighed. "I realize that."

"Or it may turn out that the police might have another suspect in mind."

Nina wasn't reassured. "I hope to God," she said with quiet vehemence, "that Grady was meeting with someone that night. Someone who can vouch for him at the time of Deirdre's death."

My thoughts, though less impassioned, were similar.

After hanging up, I stepped to the front of the office and asked Rose, our all-purpose office hand, if she expected Marc to be calling in that afternoon.

"Probably not," she answered. "I talked with him this morning. Why?"

Deirdre's death was bound to put another hitch in the stock offering, among other things. I debated calling him, then decided to wait until I knew more. "Nothing important."

"He should be home Wednesday evening," she said without taking her eyes off the computer screen. Rose has never met a task she doesn't like, and she handles them all with the methodical, stony-faced efficiency of an army nurse.

Back in my office, which was still adorned with Nina's family photos and mementos, I sat for a good ten minutes, staring at the wall.

Grady Barrett was a successful and respected businessman. A soccer dad, a park commission official, and a member, if not regular attendee, of the community church. He might have over-stepped the bounds of morally decent behavior in his tryst with Deirdre Nichols, but that didn't make him a murderer. In fact, I reminded myself, murder wasn't even an issue at the moment.

Unfortunately, the logic of that argument did little to dispel the chill that had worked its way down my spine.

Let's let the dust settle, Grady had said when I'd pressed him about the rape charge. *I've got a handle on it. I can take care of it.*

Is that what he'd done? *Taken care of it?*

I wanted to hear from Grady himself.

Grady was in his private office when I arrived. He introduced me to the two men seated across the desk from him—detectives Flores and Newman from the Oakland police department. They were a Mutt and Jeff pairing of opposites. Flores was stocky and dark, Newman tall and fair. Neither seemed particularly happy to see me.

Grady, on the other hand, looked relieved. "I just called you," he said.

"And here I am. Must be ESP."

"Deirdre Nichols is dead. She fell from the deck of the house where she was staying." His face, though tanned, seemed paler than usual, and his voice faltered.

"I heard." Although the others were seated, I remained standing.

"Are you representing Mr. Barrett?" asked Newman.

Before I had a chance to frame a response, Grady nodded. "Yes, she is," he said emphatically. I left it at that for the moment.

"No need for an attorney, really." Flores pulled at an earlobe. "We're merely checking with people who knew Ms. Nichols, trying to piece together what might have happened the night she died."

Sure, and you just happened to start with Grady Barrett.

"Makes me wonder"—Newman nodded toward Grady—"why you're so eager to have an attorney present. You got something to be nervous about?"

Grady managed a stiff laugh. "I'm head of a major company in a competitive and cutthroat market. I've learned not to sneeze without an attorney present."

"That so?" The cop wasn't impressed. "An investigation like ours is a little different, see. We like to think we're all on the same side, just trying to find out what happened. Kind of raises my hackles when a citizen thinks he needs an attorney."

I leaned against the bookcase. "Cut the crap, Detective. If you have something to ask my client, go ahead and ask. Otherwise, you'll have to excuse us. He's a busy man."

"Yeah, I've heard he gets around." This was said with a pointed smirk.

Flores rocked back in his chair. "Before you arrived, we were asking about Mr. Barrett's activities Saturday evening. He claims he was here at the office, working late."

"Not unusual," I said.

"Unfortunately, there seems to be no one who can verify that."

I looked at Grady, who nodded imperceptibly. "As far as I know," he said, "the other offices were empty."

"I fail to see what my client's work habits have to do with your investigation of Ms. Nichols' death."

"Might be no connection at all." The cop turned his attention back to Grady. "Anyone call you that night?"

"No."

"Maybe you called out?"

Grady hesitated, thinking. "No, not that I recall."

"What kind of car do you drive, Mr. Barrett?"

No doubt they knew the answer already.

"I have two," Grady explained. "A Mercedes and a Suburban."

"And which were you driving Saturday night?"

"The Mercedes."

"What color is it?"

"Silver."

A smile pulled the cop's lips taut. "A convertible?"

Grady nodded.

"Ms. Nichols' little girl saw a silver convertible in the driveway sometime in the middle of the night."

Grady shrugged, but he wasn't quite able to pull off the show of indifference he was after. "Mine is hardly unique."

"She also saw a man in the driveway." The detective paused. " 'Course, if it wasn't you, I imagine she'll be able to tell us that."

I'd forgotten Deirdre's seven-year-old daughter was with her that night. Had she recognized Grady? Were the police withholding that critical piece of information in the hope of tripping him up?

I pushed the thought aside. If Adrianna had seen her mother fall from the deck, she wouldn't have waited until morning to call 911.

Unless she'd been scared, said the voice at the back of my mind. *Unless she'd been hiding.*

I rose and stepped between the cops and Grady. "This sounds like much more than a friendly discussion about Ms. Nichols' accident."

"Well, see, that's one of the things we're trying to find out. If it *was* an accident."

"Mr. Barrett has told you that he was at work Saturday night. That means he knows nothing that will help with your investigation. I suggest you leave now."

Newman stood and leaned forward, resting a hand on Grady's desk. "You don't have any plans to leave the area, I hope."

Grady shook his head.

"Good. We just might have a few more questions for you."

As soon as the detectives had gone, I crossed my arms and

turned toward Grady. "In case you don't realize it, you're in big trouble. You'd better get yourself a good attorney. And fast."

"I've got one."

"A criminal attorney. Marc's sharp, and he knows the business side of things, but we could well be talking a homicide investigation here."

Grady raised his eyebrows. "I was talking about you, not about Marc."

I shook my head.

"Why not?"

Because I don't trust you. "Because I'm not a criminal defense attorney either."

"What do you mean? You've handled criminal cases before, including murder. And you were doing all the work on the rape trial."

"This is different."

Grady's eyes narrowed with indignation. "I didn't kill her."

"I'm glad to hear it."

"You don't believe me, do you?"

"That's not really an issue."

"The hell it isn't. That's exactly why you don't want to be involved."

I shifted my weight to my other foot. "I have this awful feeling in the pit of my stomach, Grady. Three nights ago you as much as told me not to worry about the rape charges, that you'd take care of things."

"I didn't mean—"

"You're a winner there, you know. The D.A.'s office won't go forward without the complaining witness."

Grady's face grew flushed. "I didn't rape her either."

"So you said."

He pushed back his chair and stood, leaning forward over his desk. "Goddammit, I didn't do anything wrong. Hurtful to Nina, yes. Stupid, you bet. But criminally culpable, absolutely not."

"Maybe you'll get lucky and the police will see it that way too."

An exasperated sigh. "I don't have time for this nonsense. First the alleged rape, now these suspicions about Deirdre's death. The next couple of weeks are crucial if we're going to raise the kind of capital we need."

I crossed my arms and glared at him. "Life is what happens while you're making other plans."

Grady looked uncomfortable. He came around the desk and tentatively touched my shoulder. "Please, Kali." His voice had a quiet urgency to it, and a sincerity that surprised me. "If it comes to that—if it turns out Deirdre Nichols was murdered—I'd like you to represent me."

"Why?"

"Because you're conscientious, and you've handled this kind of case before."

I shook my head. "There are a lot—"

"But mostly because you care." He must have read the look on my face, because he was quick to clarify. "Not about me. I know that. You hold me at arm's length as much as possible. But you do care about Nina."

"You need an attorney you're comfortable with."

"I'm comfortable with you. Please. For Nina's sake."

I felt the beginnings of a headache. I pressed a palm against my forehead. "Let's hope it never becomes an issue."

There was a glint in his eye. I couldn't tell whether it reflected genuine need or simply the masterful "I got you" maneuver.

In either case, he was right about Nina.

CHAPTER 12

The afternoon sun, filtered by high clouds, bathed the hills in pale light. I drove through Montclair and into the wooded canyon where Deirdre had been living for the past month. I wound up and around, through a maze of hairpin turns and roads narrowed by erosion from the winter's heavy rains.

The house was shingled. It appeared to be newer than its neighbors, or maybe it had been remodeled more recently. It was set on the downslope, the kind of house that clings to the hill, descending three or four floors as it follows the terrain. I could tell, even from the vantage point of my car, that it would be a long drop from an upper deck to the ground.

Because of the narrow, winding streets, parking was always a problem in the hills. Deirdre's house was on a curve, which made it worse. I drove past, up the hill about a hundred yards, and parked in a wide spot near another house, then headed back down the road on foot.

When I got closer, I saw a strip of yellow police tape tacked diagonally across the front door. A moment later, a female officer in uniform emerged from the walkway to the side of the house. She had a pert nose, short blond hair, and a belt so loaded with weapons and other paraphernalia I didn't see how she had the strength to stand.

I nodded toward the tape. "Looks like you folks think her death wasn't an accident."

"There hasn't been a determination one way or another."

"Any idea when they'll release the scene?"

She squinted at me. "Are you a friend?"

For a second I considered going with it, then shook my head. "An attorney."

"You figuring there's a lawsuit in this somewhere?" Her tone was more amused than pointed.

I shook my head again. "Ms. Nichols was involved in a case I was working on."

The explanation was broad enough to cover a multitude of sins, and I'm sure she knew that, but she didn't ask me to elaborate.

"I don't imagine they'll want people tromping around the property for a day or two. Things like this take time. With it being outdoors and all, well, it's harder to make sure you've looked at everything you need to. That's why I came back here today, to check something for my report."

I peered around the side of the house and into the ravine in back. It was a sheer drop from the street-level deck to the ground. "Does anyone know yet how it happened?"

"Looks like she came off the deck. There were some abrasions on her legs embedded with wood splinters." She nodded toward the back of the house. "Like the redwood in the railing."

Not likely that she'd end up with scrapes and splinters if she'd jumped or fallen accidentally. I could understand why the police were being cautious.

"It must have been terrible for the little girl," I said. "I heard that she was here when it happened."

"I don't know how much she actually saw. I've been on cases where kids have witnessed some really awful stuff. Sometimes there's no one there to help them deal with it. Those cases break my heart."

I nodded. I'd been fourteen when I lost my own mother. Not a child, certainly, but it left an emptiness inside of me. A void that has never been filled.

"At least here the child has family," the officer said. "An aunt she's close to. That's who she called after she called 911."

It was a small consolation, but better than nothing. "Were you one of the officers who responded to the call?"

"Right. I got here a few minutes before the paramedics. But as soon as I saw the body, I knew she wouldn't be needing them." The cop paused. "It was almost surrealistic, like something out of those art movies. That head of coppery curls, the white of her nightgown, the spring grass such a lush green. There were even daffodils nearby."

"Nightgown?" I asked.

"Not the kind you sleep in. At least, not the kind I sleep in. It was one of those filmy ankle-length things. Maybe it's more like a robe than a nightgown." Her radio crackled just then and she stepped away to listen.

I wandered down the road a bit to eyeball the house from a different perspective. From where I stood, I could see most of the deck. It wasn't large, but it was wide enough to accommodate a chaise, barbecue, and a small table. It appeared also to be relatively private. There were no houses directly below that I could see, and the places to either side were angled in the opposite direction.

You seem like a real person, Deirdre had said to me that day in the rest room. *Like someone who has feelings.*

We'd been adversaries in the strict sense of the word, but that didn't stop me from liking her. I looked again at the precipitous drop off the deck to the ground and felt a wash of sadness at her death.

I was headed back up the road, when a man, laden with plastic grocery bags, emerged from a parked car. As he reached his front steps, one of the bags ripped, sending canned goods cascading down the hill. I crossed over to help.

"Thanks," he said.

"No problem. I dropped a bag of oranges once and they rolled forever, probably all the way to the bay. I was able to salvage only about half of them."

He laughed. "Been there myself. Some days you wonder why you bother to get out of bed." He stopped. " 'Course, compared to that poor woman up the road, I've got nothing to complain about. You heard what happened, didn't you?"

He'd obviously mistaken me for a neighbor, and I didn't bother to correct him. "Yeah, they said she fell from the back deck."

"From the looks of all the activity down there, I'd say they think there might be more to it than that." He nodded in the direction of his own house. "I was awake most of the night surfing the Net. Was probably sitting there at my desk when she went over. I keep thinking that maybe if I'd looked up, I'd have been able to help."

"You can see the back of her house from yours?"

"If I look. The road loops back on itself between here and her place."

But he apparently hadn't been looking. "How about sounds? Did you hear anything unusual that night?"

He shook his head. "I thought about that too. I keep the windows closed whenever there are people down in the canyon. The sound floats right up. Seems amplified almost. And I'm sensitive to noise."

I stuffed the last of the runaway cans into a bag. "Did you know her?"

Another shake of his head. "Don't think I've ever seen her, to tell the truth. How about you?"

"To say hello to. Nothing more."

"Only reason I even knew the Carsons were away and had someone staying in the house is because my son is their paperboy. You know the Carsons at all?"

I equivocated. "Not really."

"Funny couple. Didn't have a stick of furniture when they moved in. I thought they might have been burned out of their previous place, but my son says they just move around a lot."

After the 'ninety-one firestorm in the Oakland hills, there'd been a lot of people moving into new homes with literally nothing. It wasn't surprising the image stuck in our minds.

"I don't think I've said more than five words to them in the whole year they've been here. Every time I try to be friendly, they act kind of huffy and walk off." He hoisted the newly packed bags with both arms. "Well, I'd better get this all put away before the ice cream melts. Thanks again for the help."

As I drove back by the Carsons' house, I slowed, wondering where Adrianna had been standing when she saw the silver convertible in the driveway. And why Deirdre would have been dressed in a nightgown if there'd been someone else there. I'd spoken the truth when I told Grady I wanted nothing to do with this, yet I found myself, almost against my will, thinking how I would argue the evidence in court.

CHAPTER 13

"Jesus, can you believe this?" Marc sat forward on the edge of the couch, glaring at the television screen. He'd returned from New York several hours earlier, and we were at his place, watching the evening news. "The police haven't even listed it as a homicide, and already the press is primed to convict Grady."

I grabbed the remote from his marble-topped coffee table and kicked up the volume. A young Chicana reporter was recapping the highlights of the "Deirdre Nichols Investigation"—a term that had become almost a household word in the three days since her death. The newscaster spoke in clipped tones, touching on the alleged rape, Deirdre's fall from the deck under suspicious circumstances, and the continued questioning of Grady Barrett by police.

As she spoke, the camera cut away to footage of Grady and myself leaving the police station where we'd gone for further questioning that afternoon. We both looked haggard.

In conclusion she noted, "Mr. Barrett, speaking through his attorney, declined to comment."

"What the hell," Marc growled. "They make 'no comment' sound like an admission of guilt."

"It's not that bad."

"Well, it's certainly not good. Makes it sound like Grady's got something to hide." He turned to look at me. "Couldn't you have said something about your client's innocence? The media attention is inevitable. We might as well use it to our advantage."

"I wanted to get Grady out of there before he took a swing at somebody."

Although our forty minutes with the police had gone more smoothly than I'd expected, they'd made it clear they were scrutinizing Grady closely. Deirdre, it turned out, had made a call to Grady's office late on the afternoon she was killed. The police wanted to know why. When Grady claimed he'd never received the call, they scoffed, then pressed him again about the silver convertible, and the fact the little girl had seen a man near the side of the house.

For the first time, they'd also brought up the handkerchief they'd found in the house where Deirdre Nichols had been killed. A handkerchief monogrammed with Grady Barrett's initials.

They were no doubt hoping that Grady would crumble, or accidentally drop some incriminating bit of information. He'd done neither, but I hadn't been able to shake the feeling that the case against Grady Barrett was building with the momentum of an oncoming train.

And it wasn't only the police. Reporters had been hounding Grady, and my own phones—both at work and at home—had been ringing off the hook. Nina was close to falling apart at the seams. I was glad Marc was back in town, even if his agitation did little to quell my own.

He turned his attention back to the television and groaned. "This is terrific," he said sarcastically with a nod toward the new face on the screen. "How low will they stoop to get a story?"

I kicked him in the foot. "Shhh. I want to hear."

A gangling woman, identified by the reporter as Deirdre's sister, Sheila Barlow, was looking earnestly into the camera. I recognized her as the same woman I'd seen in court during the hearing on the rape charge. Like Deirdre, her coloring was fair, but there was little family resemblance beyond that. She looked to be a few years older, but that might have been attributable to her unbecomingly permed hair and whippet-thin stature.

"The police know my sister's death wasn't an accident." Sheila Barlow spoke softly, but with vehemence. "They know it was murder, and they know who did it."

The reporter, endeavoring to sound spontaneous, asked, "Can you tell us who that person is?"

"Absolutely." Sheila Barlow looked straight at the camera. "My sister's death came as a result of the rape charge she filed against computer tycoon Grady Barrett. He killed Deirdre to prevent her from testifying against him. I hope to God they're able to put together a tight enough case that he doesn't get away with it."

The camera panned to include the reporter. She tipped the microphone toward herself and said, "According to the police, there was no sign of forced entry. Would your sister have freely admitted the man she'd accused of raping her?"

"Finally," Marc grunted, "the woman uses her brain."

Sheila Barlow nodded her head in response to the reporter's question. "Deirdre wasn't mean-spirited at all. She was open and trusting. She never wanted to hurt anyone, even him. Ultimately, that was her downfall."

Sheila paused, then continued in a determined tone. "Grady Barrett got away with rape. The question now is whether he will get away with murder as well."

As the segment ended, the camera cut to a panoramic view of the Barrett home. With its stone construction, slate roof, and circular drive cutting through the broad expanse of lawn, the place looked like a French château.

In a voice-over the reporter concluded, "Grady Barrett has been questioned repeatedly by police, but to date has not been charged in the death of Deirdre Nichols."

Marc punched the seat cushion in disgust. "Story over truth. Anything to draw viewers. Don't these people have any integrity at all?"

"You'd rather do away with an independent press and rely on 'official' news broadcasts instead?"

"What I'd like is a news report that sticks to the facts."

"Your version of the facts, you mean."

He smiled and let go of some of the anger. "You have to admit this coverage was pretty lame."

I nodded. But I worried that it might also be more accurate than Marc wanted to admit.

Marc stood and flipped off the television. "You want another drink?"

He'd called me from the airport that afternoon to suggest that I pick up pizza and meet him at his place, where we could talk uninterrupted. As it turned out, I'd done most of the talking while Marc rolled his eyes, muttered about shoddy police work, and grew increasingly irritated. Two tumblers of scotch hadn't done much to relax him.

I'd had only one, but I was feeling the effects. "Make it weak," I said.

"That doesn't sound like you."

"I have a reputation as a lush?"

He grinned. "Used to be you managed to keep up anyway."

"I'm tired." I hadn't realized until just then how tired I was. I stretched out my legs the full length of the sofa and sank back against the soft leather seat cushion. "I've got to drive home, don't forget."

"You could stay here," Marc said from the kitchen. I couldn't tell by his tone whether this was an innocuous offhand comment or whether he meant something more by it. I passed it off by laughing.

Marc handed me my drink. "That wasn't a joke. You can even have the bed."

"How gallant."

"Only thing you have to decide is whether you'd rather sleep in it alone, or with me." His smile was disarming.

"I love the way men are so modest and unassuming."

He moved my feet aside so he could sit down again. "The voice of experience, I take it."

My response was noncommittal. I wasn't in any mood for witty repartee, and I certainly didn't want to discuss my romantic history with him.

"I'm not sure I'm up to this," I said after a moment's silence. Then, thinking he might misunderstand, I hastened to add, "I mean if Grady is arrested."

"You don't have to do it alone, remember. We'll both be involved."

I nodded. This was one of the things we'd discussed over dinner. Officially, I'd be lead counsel. But Marc would assist, devoting as much time and effort to the case as it took. That was what Grady wanted. Nina too. And there was a part of me eager for the challenge. But I still had misgivings.

"Besides," Marc added, "if they had an airtight case, they'd have done something by now."

I pulled myself to sitting position. "It's not the prosecution's case that bothers me. It's that I feel manipulated. And I don't trust Grady."

"You don't honestly think he killed that woman, do you?"

That woman. I hugged my knees and looked at him. Maybe it was men in general I didn't entirely trust.

"I know Grady seems brash and a little self-centered at times," Marc said. "But he's a good man."

"Maybe so. I don't think he's been completely honest with us about Deirdre Nichols though."

Marc brushed at his temples with his fingers. "He didn't kill her. At the moment, that's all we need to focus on."

If only it were that easy.

He pulled my feet into his lap and massaged the soles, a gesture that was familiar from our time together during law school. "Hopefully, the cops will turn their attention elsewhere fairly soon, and we can put this whole episode behind us."

With a murmur of agreement I leaned back again against the arm of the sofa and closed my eyes. Scotch and exhaustion had made my head light. The warmth of Marc's fingers sent a tingle down my spine.

Marc's hands moved to my calves, tracing an invisible pattern on my skin. I could feel relaxation spread to my entire body. "You never did say no," he reminded me softly.

"About what?"

"About spending the night."

Marc had hurt me once. I knew I didn't want to go through that again. I shook my head and answered, "No." The response didn't have the weight I'd intended.

"I missed you when I was away," he said.

I had no doubt that he was handing me a line as bogus as the news coverage we'd watched earlier. But it got to me all the same. Too many nights alone nursing a broken heart, I guess.

Marc leaned over and kissed me. Not a light kiss, but not a demanding one either. My resistance melted a little more. It would have been so easy to stay. Easy, and no doubt nice.

I was still weighing my options, when Marc surprised me by sitting back with a shrug.

"Okay," he said. "But don't let it go to your head that I tried."

You didn't try very hard, I thought to myself, surprised to find that I was disappointed.

Despite feeling exhausted, I didn't sleep well once I made it home. I was too unsettled by thoughts of Marc. Was he toying with me? His betrayal of our relationship during law school had left me hurt and humiliated. I'd gone into a tailspin of self-

confidence that I'd been a long time pulling out of. I was determined not to let it happen again. Why, then, had I felt myself being
pulled along, wishing that he'd been just a little more insistent that
I spend the night?

It was after four when I finally drifted off. I slept through my
alarm the next morning and got to work later than I'd intended.
Marc was already at the office when I arrived.

"We've been inundated with calls from the media," he said.

"I hope you stuck with the 'no comment' response."

"More or less."

"What's that supposed to mean?"

"One of the calls was from that kid with the camera last week."

I leaned against Marc's file cabinet. "Byron Spencer? The one
you were going to apologize to?"

"I did apologize. Wrote a nice note that Miss Manners would
have approved of. Sent him a check to cover his film, and then
some."

Trying to buy him off, more like it. But maybe I wasn't giving
Marc the credit he deserved. "You talked to him?"

"Briefly. I didn't think our standard brushoff would sit well
with him."

"How did he take the apology?"

Marc gave me a crooked smile. "Better than I deserved."

The phone rang and we waited for Rose to pick it up.

Marc kept his eye on the flashing light. "I finally told her not
to put anyone through until she checked with us first."

"Makes sense."

"What we really need is to hold a press conference of some
sort. Or at least issue a written release."

"Saying what?"

"That Grady didn't do it," he said, exasperated. "Let him
explain why he's innocent."

I shook my head. "At this point, the less we say, the better."

"I don't know about that. The investment bankers are talking
about withdrawing their endorsement. If the public offering is in
shambles, I'm not sure the company can survive. ComTech needs
the infusion of capital to keep going."

"You really think a press release proclaiming Grady's innocence is going to change all that?"

Marc rocked back, hands behind his head. "It just seems that

Grady should have a chance to tell his side. He hasn't even been charged and already they're raking him over the coals."

"If we start responding every time the media takes a potshot at him, we're only going to be fueling the fire. Grady will have a chance to tell his side in court. If it comes to that."

Rose knocked on the open door. "You two in conference, or are you taking calls?"

"Depends on who it is."

"Grady Barrett," she said.

Marc sat forward and picked up the phone. His end of the conversation was largely monosyllabic. When, where, hold on, and finally, we'll be right there.

When he'd hung up, he turned to me. "Looks like Grady's going to get that chance to tell his story after all. He's just been arrested."

CHAPTER 14

Marc and I waited almost two hours before they let us see Grady. We drank tasteless coffee from a vending machine and huddled in a corner away from the tide of other weary folks with police business. When we were finally ushered into the windowless, rank-smelling cubicle, there was little we could offer Grady in the way of solace.

He was hunched over in a wobbly, plastic chair. He raised his eyes and didn't even try for a smile. "How long until you can get me out of here?"

As angry as I was with him for cheating on Nina, and in spite of my doubts about his version of events, I couldn't help but feel a wash of compassion. The energy and confidence Grady generally wore like a second skin had deserted him. His jail-issue jump suit was tight through the shoulders and several inches too short in the legs, yet he seemed somehow diminished. There was a dazed, frightened look in his eyes.

"Can you do it today?" he asked, almost pleading.

"I'm not sure we can get you out at all." I took the empty chair to his left. Marc shuffled uncomfortably from foot to foot before taking the remaining chair.

Grady's eyes met mine. "What do you mean, you're not sure?"

"It depends on what they're charging you with. There's no guarantee you'll get bail."

His face, already drained of color, paled further. "You mean I might have to stay locked up until the trial?"

Or longer, I added silently before pushing the thought from my mind. "Why don't you tell us what happened?"

He ran a hand through his hair, leaving an errant tuft at his temple angling outward. "Nina called me at work to say the police were there to search the house. They had a warrant, and also one for my arrest. I'd barely gotten off the phone when one of them showed up at my office."

"They searched your house?" Marc asked. "What did they find?"

Grady shook his head, swallowed hard. "I don't know. I've been fingerprinted, photographed, strip-searched . . . humiliated beyond belief."

"Did you give them a statement?"

"No." His skin was pale and clammy. He looked like he might be sick. "I can't stay here. Please. You'll try to get me out?"

"We'll try," I told him, "but I have to tell you, the chances aren't good."

Grady was still, his gaze unfocused somewhere over my left shoulder. For a moment I wasn't even sure he was breathing.

"Are you okay?" Marc asked.

"God in heaven," Grady whispered. "How did this happen?"

It wasn't a question with a simple answer. For a moment none of us spoke.

"This could take months, couldn't it?" Grady asked. His voice was gruff with barely contained emotion.

"Let's take it one step at a time."

His face crumpled. "I can't bear to think what this will do to Nina."

Marc put a hand on Grady's shoulder. "Nina will be fine. She's stronger than you think."

"We'll take a look at the complaint," I told him. "And talk to the D.A. At that point we'll have a better idea where things stand."

Grady nodded numbly.

I hesitated a moment, then asked, "Is there anything you want to tell us?"

He looked puzzled.

"Monday you said you were working late the night Deirdre Nichols was killed. Nobody else was there."

"That's right."

"You sure there's nothing you want to add? Because now's the time to do it, so we know what we're dealing with up front."

He gave me a funny look. "You're asking if I want to change my story?"

Technically we were stuck with the story he'd told the police, but if he was going to add to it, better now than at trial. "I'm just trying to make sure there are no surprises waiting in the wings," I told him.

Grady sat straighter and shook his head vehemently. "I didn't kill Deirdre Nichols. I swear to it." His eyes flickered between mine and Marc's. "You believe me, don't you?"

"Of course," Marc said, speaking for both of us.

I didn't contradict him, but I didn't voice my agreement either.

Half an hour later I was seated once again across the desk from Madelaine Rivera, discussing a case in which Grady Barrett was the defendant. Only this time we were talking homicide rather than rape.

And as I'd predicted, she wasn't willing to recommend bail. Even for Nina's sake.

"I'm sorry," Madelaine said. "I understand how terrible this must be for her."

I wasn't sure she did. That any of us did, for that matter. "Grady Barrett isn't a danger to the community," I told her. "And he's not a flight risk."

"I'm not going to agree to bail."

I had a feeling the judge would follow her lead.

"But we might be able to cut a deal," she added.

"What sort of deal?"

Madelaine examined her nails. They were unpolished and cut close to the quick. "A confession would save us all a lot of time and grief. I think we could take that into account."

I looked at her. "You're crazy. No way would I recommend that."

"Look at the case, Kali. Our victim is a single mom struggling to make a life for her young child. Your guy is rich and successful, the kind who's used to throwing his weight around. First he rapes our victim, then he kills her so she won't testify against him. On top of that, it's the sweet and innocent seven-year-old daughter who discovers the body. The jury's going to love it."

"It's a nice story, but you're kind of short on evidence."

She shook her head. "I don't think so."

There was a knock at the doorway, the same blond policeman I'd seen in Madelaine's office on my last visit.

"Oops, sorry," he said with a quick smile. "Didn't know you had someone with you. I'll drop by later."

From his manner, I suspected his interest wasn't purely professional. "You two seeing each other?" I asked when he'd gone. The last conversation we'd had on the subject, several years earlier, we'd both been bemoaning the shortage of men who were straight, reasonably articulate, and not already spoken for.

Madelaine made a face, something between smugness and disavowal. "If you call a couple of dates 'seeing each other,' then, yeah, I guess maybe so." It was clear she hoped that was the case.

"Nice guy?"

"So far." She shrugged in what was no doubt intended as an offhand gesture. But there was a girlishness to it that made her appear for a moment almost ingenuous. It was a side of Madelaine I'd not seen before.

"What's his name?"

"Steve. Steve Henshaw." She let the name linger on her lips a moment before composing herself for business. "We wouldn't be bringing the case to trial," she continued, "if we didn't think we had a good chance of winning."

"And I wouldn't be defending this client if I thought I would lose."

She didn't smile.

"When am I going to get copies of the reports?"

"Soon. We're still processing some of the information."

"You want to give me the highlights? I'm assuming there's more to it than this alleged rape business."

This time she did smile. "Oh, yes. Much more." Madelaine seemed to be enjoying her role as master of suspense. "You know that Deirdre Nichols' daughter saw Grady's car in the driveway?"

"A car in some ways similar to the one he drives."

A shrug capped with a smirk. "And then there is the handkerchief monogrammed with Grady's initials. Matches one the police seized when they searched your client's house."

"Which Grady claims to have left at Ms. Nichols' the night of the alleged rape."

"And Deirdre just happened to keep it on the floor of the front hallway for two weeks? That's not going to play real well to any jury with half a brain."

She was right. I hadn't known they'd found the handkerchief in the hallway.

Madelaine pressed her fingertips together. "And I find it kind of interesting that the pants Grady was wearing the night in question ended up in the Salvation Army pickup two days later."

"What?" I felt my stomach knot, but I kept my expression flat.

"That's what he says. Their butler, or whatever he is, knew the pants Grady was wearing that night, and the cops didn't find them when they conducted their search." Madelaine ran a hand through her already rumpled hair.

"What *did* they find?"

She smiled. It was the smug expression of someone with the upper hand. "You'll get the whole picture when you read the report."

And then I'd have to have a long talk with Grady.

She leaned back in her chair. "You've got your work cut out for you, Kali."

On that point, unfortunately, we were in agreement.

As soon as I got back to the office, I called Nina. I told her that I'd seen Grady and that he was doing as well as could be expected. Then I turned the conversation to the search the police had conducted that morning.

"What did they take?" I asked her.

"I don't know. They spent most of their time in Grady's closet. They took some stuff. I'm not sure if that's significant, or if they were just covering all the bases." Nina was trying hard to stay calm, but I could hear the anxiety in the shallowness of her breathing. "Do you have any idea what's going on?"

"Not completely."

She listened in stoic silence while I told her what I knew; then she asked the question for which I wished I had an answer.

"How does it look for him?" Her voice was small, the words more breathed than spoken.

"I don't know yet. I'll have a better idea maybe after I see the police reports. Marc's working on getting them right now."

"It's amazing how one's life can change so abruptly." She let out a breath—a weary, forlorn sound that made my heart ache.

"It's probably not as bad as it seems, Nina." The assurance rang hollow in my ears, but I couldn't help myself.

"At least I have it easier than Grady." She paused. "He must be so scared."

"Everything will work out, I'm sure." Another empty platitude. Nina must have recognized it as such, because she didn't bother to respond. "I'm going to view the crime scene this afternoon," I told her. "I'll stop by to see you this evening."

"Kali?" She hesitated a moment.

"What?"

"Thanks. I don't know what we'd do if you weren't here."

"Try not to worry, okay."

A humorless laugh. "How do I do that?"

CHAPTER 15

Officer Duncan, the policeman assigned to be my escort at the crime scene, was a jowly man who took his gatekeeping duties seriously. From the start, it was clear that he wasn't about to turn me loose to poke and pry on my own.

"You want to begin inside or out?" he asked. His breath smelled of spearmint gum.

"Inside." I'd already eyeballed the deck from the street on my last visit, and since Deirdre and her killer had presumably been inside before stepping onto the deck, I thought it best to start there myself.

Duncan pulled a white-tagged key from his pocket and fiddled with the lock. Finally, he opened the door onto a tiled entry hall. I stepped inside. Duncan followed me like a shadow.

The kitchen was to the left; the living area, which stretched the length of the house, was straight ahead, with a wall of wide picture windows and a sliding glass door opening onto the deck. From where I stood, I could see above the treetops into the canyon below.

"Was the sliding glass door open or closed when the police got here?" I asked.

Officer Duncan shook his head. "Sorry, ma'am, I wouldn't know."

I took a notebook out of my purse and jotted a reminder to myself to check. When I moved into the living room, Officer Duncan was only half a step behind.

The house was nicely, but not elegantly, furnished. Two facing sofas in front of a fireplace, an easy chair and ottoman in the corner. They looked as though they'd come as a package deal from one of those modish showrooms where you can furnish a home in one easy trip.

The dining area, which was really an extension of the living room, contained a round oak table and matching chairs. There were no knickknacks, family pictures, or personal items to be seen. I wondered if the owners had packed them away before leaving on their trip, or if they lived as simply as it appeared.

Another thought struck me. "Have the people who live here been contacted yet?" I asked.

"Live here?"

"Deirdre Nichols was house-sitting for a couple who are on a trip. Do you know if the police have reached them about her death?"

"I'm afraid I don't know." His left hand rested on his belt buckle.

"I take it you weren't one of the officers who worked the scene initially."

"No, ma'am."

I opened the sliding glass door and moved onto the cantilevered deck. Below, I could see the yellow tape still marking the spot where Deirdre Nichols' body had fallen.

Why had she been outside on a chilly February night? Had her killer forced her onto the deck, or had she gone willingly? Looking around the house, I'd seen no sign of a struggle, yet I knew the police had found scratches on her body.

I moved into the kitchen with Duncan at my heels. His shoes squeaked on the linoleum floor.

The kitchen was a narrow room with an elevated eating bar at one end. It smelled of ripe garbage.

The coffeemaker was half full, and the counter was strewn with glasses and plates that hadn't made it into the dishwasher. At the far end were a ceramic mixing bowl, a cookie sheet dotted with unappetizing lumps of dough, and assorted baking ingredients—flour, sugar, a box of oats and one of raisins. Not messy exactly, but cast in that easy disarray of time caught short.

"You think it would taint the crime scene to clean up old food?"

Duncan looked around and shrugged. Maybe to him the stench and the crusty dishes weren't anything unusual.

As elsewhere in the house, I noticed the film of gray granules the police had used in looking for fingerprints. I wondered if they'd found any. Wondered if they had any physical evidence linking Grady to the house on the night of Deirdre Nichols' death.

I spotted a yellow notepad on the counter near the phone. A short shopping list of household staples was scrawled in pencil. I opened the drawer underneath. Pencils, tape, loose coins, and a telephone book.

Deirdre's straw bag hung on the doorknob. "May I?" I asked, gesturing to the purse.

Duncan nodded.

It was a jumble, like my own. But Deirdre's was a mother's purse. In addition to the customary makeup and wallet, it held a lavender Magic Marker, a half-eaten bag of M&Ms, a child's barrette in bright pink, and a can of Play-Doh. I felt a wash of sadness. I knew that the loss of her mother was something that would forever mark Adrianna's life.

I turned to Duncan. "Deirdre Nichols carried a Daytimer," I said. "Any idea what happened to it?"

"A what?"

"It's like an address book and calendar wrapped into one. Looks like a small loose-leaf notebook."

"Is that what they're called?" He smiled for the first time. "My daughter's got one of those. She's a hotshot architect up in Sacramento. Lots of building going on up there."

"I don't see it here," I told him, rifling through the bag a second time. "You think it was tagged into evidence?"

"Might have been. I couldn't say for sure."

Not that I'd really expected any other kind of answer. "I think the bedrooms are downstairs."

"You want to see the bedrooms?" He made it sound as though I intended something illicit.

I nodded and started for the stairs. Duncan, of course, was not far behind.

The house, like many built on the side of a hill, hugged the terrain for several levels. One flight down was a small bedroom that, from the looks of the stuffed animals on the bed, was probably Adrianna's. From the window I could see the carport, where Officer Duncan had parked, and the section of roadway where I'd pulled in. If the streetlights were bright enough, Adrianna would have had no trouble viewing the silver convertible as she claimed.

Down another flight of stairs were two larger bedrooms, which overlooked the yard, and a bathroom. I wondered if Adrianna had come downstairs looking for her mother, and instead seen her broken body in the yard beyond.

For a moment the room blurred. I shut my eyes. I'd been fourteen when my own mother committed suicide, and though now, years later, I often go months without reliving that day, there are times it rolls over me like a tidal wave. I can recall it as vividly as though it were yesterday, the shattering emotions of discovering her, slumped behind the wheel of the family car, and knowing instantly that she was dead. My heart went out to Adrianna.

Duncan checked his watch. "You about finished here?"

I blinked, forced my mind back to the work at hand. "I guess so."

We climbed back upstairs, where I took a second quick look around the interior, then Officer Duncan locked up the house and left. I remained near the front of the house for another moment, trying to etch the scene on my brain. I wanted to see in my mind's eye what might have happened that night, to view the unfolding events as though I were at a movie. But all I saw was a nondescript wooden house in need of paint and a yard that was close to being unkempt. Both as still and lifeless as the woman who'd once lived there.

CHAPTER 16

I spent the next half hour knocking on doors in the hope of finding a neighbor who had seen or heard something the night Deirdre Nichols was killed. For the most part, my knocks went unanswered, and the few people I did find home weren't able to help. Not that I expected anything different. How many people, after all, stay awake into the small hours of the night, peering out the window at their neighbors? Besides, I was certain the police had covered this ground before me.

I was ready to give up, when I saw a car pull into the driveway of the house I'd just left. In the interest of thoroughness, which I've learned over the years has its own rewards, I circled back. I reached the car just as a thickset middle-aged woman in khaki pants and a flannel shirt was emerging from the driver's door.

She was talking in animated fashion, as if she were in the middle of a conversation—although I saw no one else in the car. I hesitated. People who talk to themselves are not always harmless. Then she reached into the back and pulled out a cat carrier. I relaxed. Eccentric, maybe, but not totally out of touch with reality.

The woman looked up as I neared. "Hey, Sophie," she said, interrupting her own monologue. "We've got company."

Since she was looking at me, if not actually speaking to me, I took her comment as a greeting and introduced myself. "If you don't mind, I'd like to ask you a few questions about the woman who fell off the deck across the street."

"The way I heard it, she didn't fall. She was pushed."

"I was speaking generally."

"That's a problem these days; too many people do."

"Sorry." My high school English teacher would have loved this woman.

"I'd be happy to talk to you, but I don't know anything." She started for the walkway. "You'll have to come along though. Sophie can't stand being cooped up in this cage much longer."

I followed her to the house.

"What did you say your name was again?"

"Kali O'Brien."

"I'm Alice Morely. You're not allergic to cats, are you?"

I shook my head.

"Good. I've got six of them."

I knew immediately upon stepping inside that I was in the presence of cats. There was cat hair everywhere, and a strong feline odor. A large gray cat skittered down the hallway ahead of us.

"Like I told the police," Alice continued as though we hadn't digressed, "I go to bed early and sleep soundly. Most nights anyway. I didn't see anything, didn't hear anything."

She pulled Sophie out of the cat carrier and gave her a kiss. "Isn't that right, Sophikins? We sleep through most anything, even that horrible stuff kids today call music."

"From down in the canyon?" I asked. Several other neighbors had mentioned music the night Deirdre was killed. "Was there a party that night?"

"There's one nearly every Saturday night. Although I don't know that *party* is the right word. Young people mostly, carrying on. Drives some of the people up here crazy, but doesn't bother me. They never stay at it very late. And like I said, I can sleep through most anything."

Another cat appeared, thumping down from an open shelf onto the hardwood floor. He arched his back and yawned before meandering out through an open doorway.

"What about things you might have noticed before that night?" I asked. "Any strange cars in the area? Anything out of the ordinary? Or maybe there were workmen at the house."

Alice Morely shook her head. "It's pretty quiet over there most of the time. Just her and the little girl."

"Did you know Deirdre Nichols well?"

"The woman? Not really. She didn't live there, you know. She was house-sitting for the Carsons. Not that I knew them well either. I didn't even know they were away until she brought over a package the postman had delivered to that address by mistake."

A black cat emerged from the other room and hopped up on a chair and then onto the table, which was covered with file folders and papers.

"No, you don't, Samuel. You know better than that." Alice scooped him off the table and into her arm. "I can't have you messing up the wetlands petition. Or my other work. You know I have to get my talk ready."

She looked at me. "I'm what you'd call a community activist. I work for causes I believe in. That's what this country needs, you know, more people who are interested and involved."

I nodded, waiting for the moment when I could exit gracefully.

"Too many folks are quick to complain but not so willing to do much about changing things. That's something that really sticks in my craw, people who won't lift a hand to make this a better world. I'm talking basic stuff, like staying informed on local issues. Voting, even."

I moved toward the door, and Alice Morely followed.

"Take the Carsons for example. Neither one of them is registered to vote. I know, because I worked the precinct during the last election. I can't understand a person who won't take the time to vote. It's a privilege our forefathers fought and died for. Around the world people are dying still, trying to have their voices heard. And here we've got people who treat voting like a burden. You vote, don't you?"

"Absolutely."

"Good." She crossed her arms. "I hope you write your government officials too. Most people don't, you know. They forget that voting isn't the only way to make their voice heard."

I opened the door myself. "Thanks so much for your help, Mrs. Morely."

"Sorry I didn't see anything that night. I really like to do what I can."

I nodded.

"If more people took responsibility and spoke up, this country wouldn't be in the mess it is."

I took the stairs down to the street two at a time.

Back in the car, I checked my watch and debated my next move. I flipped on the radio, switching from the all-news station to a classical one. While I agreed with Alice Morely about the grating effects of some of the current rock tunes, good music was both soothing and uplifting. After the morning I'd had, I needed both.

As I wound down the narrow road toward town, my thoughts drifted to the raucous music that several neighbors had mentioned hearing the night Deirdre Nichols was killed. About halfway down the road, on my left, was an open area where the grade flattened. The shoulder was wide there. I pulled off and climbed out of the car. Close to the road, yet relatively secluded, it was an ideal place to party—except for the fact that sound, probably amplified by the terrain, would annoy the neighbors perched on the hillside above.

I looked up, trying to get my bearings. It was difficult to tell the houses apart, but I thought I could identify the one where Deirdre Nichols had been staying. From my current perspective, the third floor deck seemed even farther from the ground than it had earlier. My body tensed involuntarily as I envisioned her fall.

Had she known her killer and gone willingly to stand on the deck with him? Or had he dragged her there, struggling? And would she actually have welcomed Grady into her house in light of the charges she'd filed against him? It didn't make much sense to me, but then, lots of people do things I find hard to comprehend.

I wondered if anyone partying in the canyon that night had chanced to look up at the same time Deirdre was going over the railing. Of course, it had been dark, but the moon would have been almost full. You wouldn't be able to make out details under those conditions, but you might well have been able to see form and movement.

I wondered if the police talked to the kids who were there that night. And I wondered if they'd seen a man on the deck—a man of Grady's description and build.

I pulled into a gas station and used the pay phone to call work. "Is Marc around?" I asked Rose.

"He's come and gone. But he said to tell you that he's got a copy of the police report, and that he's working on the coroner."

It was good news that he had the report, bad news that he wasn't at the office, where I could look at it. "Can you leave him a message that I'd like to meet first thing tomorrow morning?"

"Sure. But if he doesn't call in again, he won't get your message until tomorrow anyway." I could hear the rustle of papers on Rose's end. "The press has been calling," she said. "Everyone wants a statement. What shall I tell them?"

"Tell them that Marc and I are both out."

I tried Marc's house next and got the answering machine. I left a similar message about meeting the following morning. There wasn't much I could do from the office, and I wanted to avoid running into anyone from the press, so instead of heading back to work, I drove to Rapunzel, the hair salon where Deirdre Nichols had been employed as a receptionist. I knew from news accounts that her coworkers were the last people known to have seen her alive.

The salon was near a busy intersection, sandwiched between a shoe outlet and a bagel shop. The storefront was modest, but the interior was a flashy array of bright lights, polished chrome, and shiny black lacquer. And mirrors. On every wall, floor to ceiling. The effect was dizzying.

To my left, three stylists were busy at work. The closest station belonged to a young woman in baggy white canvas pants, with a shaved head and so many body piercings, I lost count. Next to her was another woman, whose blond curls were secured haphazardly with colorful plastic clips. Neither looked as though she'd been to a hairdresser herself in years.

The stylist at the lead station was a man who looked to be in his mid-thirties, dressed all in black, including a heavy black five o'clock shadow, which I felt certain was cultivated rather than accidental. His hair was slicked back from his face, except where it was buzzed around the ears.

It was the man who addressed me. "What can we do for you?"

"You the owner?"

"That's me. Rick Bernard."

"I'd like to talk to you about Deirdre Nichols." When he didn't respond, I added, "She worked here, right?"

"Are you interested in her job?"

I shook my head. "I'm an attorney. I have a few questions."

He snipped a stray hair from the back of his client's head. "I'll be finished here in a minute, if you want to wait."

I sat, picked up a magazine, and tried to keep my eyes from drifting to the mirrored image of my own reflection, which jumped out at me from every direction. It was disconcerting, sort of like finding yourself suddenly cloned.

I scanned pages of fashion tips, makeup advice, and suggestions for finding and keeping the right man. God knows I could use help with all of them. The article that finally held my attention was a mother's loving essay about her grown daughter. Something that didn't apply to me at all. I felt a familiar longing stir within my chest. The chance to fashion an adult relationship with my mother is one of the things about her death that saddens me anew each time I think of it.

"Now, what can I do for you?" Rick Bernard asked, taking a seat beside me.

I closed the magazine and took a moment to shut down the memories as well. "To begin with," I told him, "I'm trying to get a sense of Deirdre Nichols. What her life was like, who her friends were, anybody she'd had trouble with, that sort of thing."

He ran a hand over his chin. "I'm afraid there isn't much I can tell you."

"Had she worked here long?"

"About five months, is all. We get a lot of turnover with receptionists. It's not exactly a career position."

"She was working out okay in the job?"

He shrugged. "She did her work, got along with people—both the customers and the stylists."

"How about her hobbies? Interests?"

"Money. Spending it, that is." Bernard laughed as though he'd delivered the punch line to a hugely entertaining joke. "I didn't get the impression she was so interested in earning it."

"Did she live extravagantly?" Certainly nothing I'd seen so far had suggested that.

"Not as extravagantly as she'd have liked." Another short laugh. "She had expensive tastes though." Bernard popped a breath mint into his mouth. "I think she may have had some once. Not lots, but enough that she lived better than she had recently."

"How about friends?"

"No one I can name." He turned to the two women. "Either of you know who Deirdre was friendly with?"

"She was friendly with everyone," said the blond with clips.

"Who she was friends with is what I mean."

"That's what you should have said, then."

He stuck out his tongue. "I thought you went to beauty school not teacher's college."

"The answer to your question is no." The woman went back to folding strands of hair in foil.

"Except for that guy," piped in the other stylist. "What's his name?"

"Tony?" I remembered the name from the rape charge hearing. The man with whom she'd had a relationship that was, in her own words, *complicated*.

"Yeah, that's the guy."

"Have you met him?"

"Unh-unh."

"He's a jerk though," the shaved head added. "She broke up with him once. I don't know why she went back."

Rick rolled his eyes. "Like I said, she appreciated the good life. Tony was rolling in the green stuff."

"What kind of jerk?" I asked.

The stylist with the shaved head answered. "The male kind. Big ego, small dick."

Rick Bernard laughed. "Not that you'd know big from small, Rachel. I'm not even convinced you know dick."

I cleared my throat to get their attention. "Am I right that Deirdre Nichols worked here the day she was killed?"

"Until six."

"Did she say anything about her plans for the evening?"

Another three-pointed conversation with the bottom line being, no, she hadn't dropped even a hint about her plans.

"Did she seem worried or upset that day?" I asked.

Rick shook his head. "In fact, she was in a pretty good mood, as I remember. Happier than she'd been for quite a while. It's a damn shame, her being killed."

I agreed that it was.

The telephone rang and Rick Bernard sprinted to the reception desk. As I waved my thanks and started for the door, he held up a hand.

"Wait, I think we might have Tony's phone number here, if you're interested." When he was off the phone, he rummaged through the drawer and pulled out a duplicate-copy message pad. He flipped a few pages. "Here it is."

I grabbed one of the pink and purple promotional pens from the counter and copied the number into my notebook. "Thanks."

"Come back for a haircut sometime."

It wasn't likely, but I nodded anyway.

"Keep the pen. Our phone number is on the side."

I glanced at it before dropping it into my purse. *Rapunzel, a full-service hair salon.* Accompanied by the phone number. "Thanks," I said again.

"Some hotshot salesman sold me on the idea," Rick said, pointing to the collection of pens. "Haven't seen any great upturn in business because of it."

I pulled out three business cards and left them on the counter. "If any of you remembers something more, I'd appreciate a call."

I wasn't going to hold my breath waiting.

CHAPTER 17

It wasn't yet seven when I got to Nina's. Simon, standing formally in the open doorway, informed me she'd already gone to bed for the night.

"Is she okay?" The words were out of my mouth before I realized what a dumb question it was. Cancer, a complicated pregnancy, and now a husband in jail awaiting trial for murder—how could she be okay?

"She said she had a headache."

"How did she seem, uh, otherwise?" I never quite knew how to approach Simon, who was privy to the intimate details of the Barretts' life, yet when all is said and done, an outsider.

Simon shook his head sadly. The glow of the front porch light gave his silver hair and white uniform an iridescent quality. "It is not easy for her, I'm sure."

An understatement if ever there was one. I wondered how Nina would ever get through the next months.

Just then Emily appeared from inside the house, one shoe off, hair hanging in her face, her thumb in her mouth. She slid past Simon and stood next to me, wrapping her free arm around my leg.

I don't have the gift of talking easily to children, but I could tell Emily was feeling unsettled.

"Hi, honey." I brushed the hair from her forehead. "How are you doing?"

She pressed against me without answering.

"Did you have a fun day at school?"

"We had a substitute."

"Ah." I dithered for a moment and then, unable to come up with a better topic, asked, "And after school?"

"I was supposed to go to gymnastics but we couldn't, because of the reporters were out front."

"They were here?" I looked at Simon.

"I wouldn't let them in, of course. But we thought it best if Emily stayed in the house."

Emily clutched my leg tighter. Tears welled up in her eyes. "I want my daddy."

"Now, now, missy, we'll have none of that." Simon's tone was gentle, but his reprimand struck me as unfair all the same. I had a feeling he was even more at a loss around kids than I was.

"I know your daddy misses you too," I told Emily, giving her a one-armed hug. I wondered how much she'd been told about Grady's arrest. "You could draw a picture for him. I bet he'd like that."

Emily was silent. She continued to hug my leg as though hanging on for dear life. Maybe she was.

"Have you eaten?" I asked her, an idea forming as I spoke. When she didn't answer, I added, "Would you like to go out for dinner?"

She looked up at me. "You mean McDonald's?"

I'd actually been thinking of something a bit more upscale, a place where I could get a salad of spring greens and a glass of wine, which goes to show that I really hadn't been thinking at all. "Is that where you'd like to go?" I asked.

She nodded. "Arf too. He's so lonely he's got a tummyache."

"Okay, Arf too."

Emily ordered chicken nuggets and fries. After scrutinizing the salads, I decided to join her. It wasn't the food, I reminded myself, that had brought me there.

After a few false starts I learned that Emily would talk if I stopped peppering her with questions and gave her the chance. In the course of the evening I learned about lizards—far more than I wanted to know, especially over food—pilgrims, Gretchen's new father—her third—and a boy named Fred who spit when he talked. And when we started making a list of truly disgusting foods, we both got the giggles.

We were having such a good time, in fact, that we went to

Fentons for ice cream afterward. It had been a long time since I'd had ice cream loaded with gooey chocolate sauce and whipped cream, and it wasn't, in truth, as good as I remembered. But Emily was in seventh heaven.

"I love chocolate," she said, spooning a dollop of the stuff into her mouth.

"I can tell. By the spoonful, no less."

"That's the way I take my medicine."

"With a spoon?"

She laughed. "Of course with a spoon. With chocolate sauce too. It hides the yucky taste."

The inventiveness of parents never ceases to amaze me.

"What did the pencil say to the paper?" she asked abruptly

"The pencil?" It took me a moment to realize Emily was setting up a joke.

I shook my head. "I don't know, what?"

"Take me to your ruler!" She grinned and shoveled another spoonful of ice cream into her mouth.

As we were finishing up, Emily waved to a friend—a skinny child with big, dark eyes. The girl came over to say hello

"This is Adrianna," Emily said, holding out a hand smeared with chocolate. "She goes to my school."

The name was familiar, and in the next instant I knew why. The narrow-shouldered woman Adrianna was with turned away from the counter just then and faced our direction. I recognized Deirdre Nichols' sister, Sheila Barlow.

Her expression darkened when she saw us. Her mouth thinned and her jaw tightened. Tucking her wallet into her purse, she approached. After the hostility she'd exhibited on the television newscast, I wasn't sure what to expect. I braced myself for a nasty scene.

Surprisingly, however, she was the model of good behavior. She introduced herself to me, chatted briefly with Emily, and didn't mention a word about Grady.

As she was leaving she paused, her pale eyes unexpectedly serious. "I think it might be a good idea if we talked sometime," she said.

Before I could answer, she took Adrianna's hand and led her away.

"Her other mommy died," Emily said solemnly.

I nodded, not sure what to say.

"Lucky for her, she had two."

"Two mommies?"

Emily licked her spoon and nodded.

I was happy for Adrianna's sake that she had an aunt she was close to, but I knew that no one could ever replace a mother.

CHAPTER 18

We held our first strategy session the next morning. Marc, myself, and Hal Fisher, an investigator I'd used when I'd worked at Goldman and Latham.

Hal is approaching fifty, a bit overweight, and scruffy-looking in the tradition of an aging hippie. He's also inclined to be a trifle more outspoken than is necessary.

Although they tried to hide it, I could tell the two men had taken an immediate dislike to each other.

"So, what have we got?" I asked Marc.

"Why are you looking at me?"

We were in his office, which is not only roomier than the one I was using, but neater. Marc was seated behind his wide wooden desk. Hal and I were sprawled in chairs across from him.

"You're the one who had the police report in your hot little hands all night." My tone was sharper than I'd intended, the fallout of an evening spent stewing when I wanted to be working. Despite repeated calls, I hadn't managed to reach him. "Where were you anyway?"

"Out." His expression was hard to read. Avoiding my eyes, he reached for a plastic portfolio. "Where do you want to start?"

"Let's look at the crime scene first," Hal said. He was eating granola from the box by the fistful, as though it were popcorn.

"Inside or out?" There was a contentious overtone to the question.

Hal crunched on his cereal. "Outside."

"Victim was found on a stone patio area directly under a third story deck. Body was twisted, on its side mostly. She was fully clothed, although not in street clothes." Marc skimmed his notes. "Here's something. There were bruises on her neck and upper arm. Probably the result of a violent confrontation prior to death—that's according to the cop who wrote out the initial report."

"Fingernail scrapings?" I asked.

"Taken, no results."

"Meaning the results aren't back yet or that there was nothing there?"

He looked again. "Doesn't say. But you'd think they'd know if they found anything."

"What they know and what they put down on paper aren't always one and the same," Hal said glibly.

Marc frowned. His lips barely moved when he spoke, and his voice was cool. "I wasn't born yesterday."

"How about a rape kit exam?" Hal asked.

The question took me by surprise. For some reason, rape hadn't occurred to me. And at this stage, the results could only hurt our case. If they'd pointed to someone other than Grady, the police wouldn't have arrested him.

Marc flipped through a couple of pages. "It doesn't say."

"We should find out," Hal noted. "It's fairly standard procedure these days."

"Anything else?" I made a grabbing gesture, and Hal handed me the granola box.

"Yeah. There were footprints in wet soil by the side of the house. Men's, size ten."

"Any idea what size shoe Grady wears?" I wondered if Grady's shoes were among items seized by the police in their search of the house.

"He's a size ten," Marc said. "But so are a lot of men, myself included. And they weren't Bruno Maglis—just running shoes."

Hal laughed. "There's no such thing as 'just shoes.' They've all got signature soles—shape, stitching, God knows what else. With enough detail, a shoe impression can be pretty precise."

"Well, without the detail it's meaningless," Marc shot back. "And I don't see anything here that makes it sound like this was a primo impression."

"What about hair?" I asked, mostly to stop the bickering. "Or fibers? Anything in the way of trace evidence?"

"Not outside," Marc said. He looked pointedly at Hal. "Is it okay if we move inside now?" Then, without waiting for an answer, he continued. "Most of the prints and hair collected around the house can be accounted for. Although it would help if they had a set of the Carsons' prints for comparison."

"Any that can't be accounted for?"

"There was a short gray hair found on the sofa." Marc looked up. "Could be Grady's, I suppose. But he was there the week earlier. Unless the evidence comes with a time stamp, we ought to be able to use his presence there the previous week to counter whatever they come up with in the way of physical evidence."

Nice in theory, but I wasn't banking on it. "What else?"

Marc went back to his notes. "Animal hair, some carpet fibers, a small pearl button."

"Stuff that might help us if we were trying to pin the murder on someone else," Hal said, "but nothing that's going to help us know who that person is." He pulled a grapefruit out of his tattered briefcase and began peeling it. The room filled with the scent of citrus.

Marc glared. "You forget to eat breakfast or something?"

Hal ignored him.

I rubbed my forehead. "The stuff might prove useful if we're able to identify another plausible suspect."

"We're a long way from that," Marc said, making no effort to hide his irritation.

"Okay," Hal said, prying a grapefruit section free. "Let's look at what the prosecution has. A motive, I'll grant you that. But nothing that directly links Grady to the crime. Only the handkerchief, the little girl's story about seeing a silver-color convertible in the driveway, and possibly the shoe print."

"And by their absence," I added, "the pants Grady wore the night of the murder."

Marc rocked back in his chair. "Unfortunately, there's also the phone call to Grady's office made from Deirdre Nichols' home phone at six forty-three that evening."

I nodded. "Grady says he never received the call though."

Marc flipped back a page in the report. "The record shows an eight-minute conversation."

That the cops hadn't told us. I was beginning to think Madelaine's offer to deal might not have been so far out of line.

"Maybe someone else at the office took the call," Hal suggested.

"Unh-unh." Marc's expression, directed Hal's way, was smug. "It's a separate line. No secretary, no switchboard. Goes directly to Grady's private office."

There was a moment of glum silence while we considered the possibilities.

Hal crossed his arms and lifted his feet to the chair opposite him. "Let's subpoena Ms. Nichols' phone records, see who else she talked to."

"And we should ask around at ComTech," I added. "There's always the chance someone else picked up the phone."

Marc resumed his reading. "There was no sign of forced entry," he said after a moment. "So presumably she knew her killer. Not so good for our case either."

A thought struck me. "Was the door locked when the sister arrived?"

Marc shuffled through the pages of the report. "Nothing here about it. I can't believe they didn't ask her."

Hal's laugh had a slightly superior edge to it. "Just because it's not in the report doesn't mean they didn't ask. They're not going to give you any more than they have to."

"But they *do* have to," Marc said, alluding to the rules of discovery.

"Only if you force them."

"How about the little girl," I asked, again jumping in to defuse the tension. "Do we have her full statement?"

"Just the summary. She apparently woke up when she heard someone knocking on the door. When she looked out the window, she saw a silver convertible. And she heard a man's voice."

"In the house?"

"That's not clear."

"Any idea of the time?"

"Ten. Or so she says. With a kid that age, though, who knows?"

Hal scratched his chin. "This is the digital era, don't forget."

"Did she get a look at the man?" I asked.

"Doesn't appear that way."

This, at least, was something in our favor. "What about other witnesses? Any of the neighbors see a man there?"

"The guy next door said he heard a dog start barking around ten-fifteen."

"Which could mean nothing more than a cat in the yard," Hal said. He offered us each a section of grapefruit. Marc declined, but I accepted.

"Yeah, but with the girl's statement about time . . ."

"Where does Grady say he was at ten that night?" Hal asked.

"Work."

"Alone," Marc added.

"Offhand, I don't know the number of silver convertibles in the Bay Area, but we ought to be able to find out. Unless she got a license number or something, there's no way they can say with certainty that it was Grady's car."

"What about the boyfriend?" I asked. "Tony Rodale. Did the police check what kind of car he drives?"

"She had a boyfriend?" Hal's interest was clearly piqued. "That bears looking into."

I nodded. "Especially in light of the fact that their relationship seemed unsettled."

Marc scowled. "I'm sure the cops already checked on him. They'd have followed up if there was anything there."

The look Hal gave Marc in return was pointed. "With cops you can't be sure of anything. Once they find their man, they kind of get tunnel vision, if you know what I mean." He turned back to me. "What do you know about this guy Tony?"

"He has money and he's a jerk."

"That narrows it down to a few thousand," Hal said, heavy on the sarcasm.

Marc didn't crack a smile.

I filled him in on what I'd learned from Deirdre's coworkers at Rapunzel. "And I have a phone number for him." I passed Hal the number. "I'll get you a copy of her testimony at the rape hearing. She said that the two of them had a 'complicated relationship,' if I'm remembering correctly. And there was some uncertainty about his name."

"Before you two get too far afield," Marc said, clearing his throat, "can we come back to the matter of Grady's defense?"

"There was a sort of party in the canyon below the house." I explained about the loud music several of the neighbors had heard. "It's possible someone saw what happened that night."

Marc looked through the report. "They haven't come forward yet."

Hal hedged. "That we're aware of."

The defense is supposed to get everything the prosecution does so there are no surprises at trial. But that doesn't mean everything gets handed over up front. A witness who could place Grady at the scene would just about sink our chances of acquittal.

"There's apparently a gathering there most Saturday nights," I said. "I think I'll drop by and ask around. Either of you gentlemen up for a hot date?"

Hal tossed the pile of grapefruit peels into the trash. "Unfortunately, I've already got one."

"Take her with you," Marc grumbled. "This is the kind of stuff that you should be doing, not Kali."

Hal sucked on his cheek. "It's a *him*, not a her, and I'm afraid we've got plans that can't be changed." He turned to me. "Marc's right though. I should be the one to follow up on this."

"Except if we don't do it this weekend, we have to wait another week. I don't mind going."

Marc muttered something indecipherable, then rocked forward. "Okay, *I'll* go."

He made a good martyr, but I wasn't so sure he'd make a good detective. "We'll both go," I said.

Marc shrugged. "I've got to tell you, I think you're stretching it a bit if you expect to find anyone who saw what happened."

"Speaking of stretching." Hal stood. "Are we about finished here?"

When he had gone, Marc tossed the report into my lap. "I can't believe you want to use that guy, Kali. This is a big case. Grady is a friend as well as a client. We can do better than some aging, ponytailed queer."

I shot him a nasty look. "He's a good investigator."

"He's a boor."

"Not everyone wants to look like Yves Saint Laurent."

"Grady's in deep shit, Kali. He's in jail for murder, his company is leveraged to the hilt, the investors have backed off. We've got to get this settled. Soon."

"Isn't that what we're working on?"

Marc sighed. He ran a hand through his hair and gave me a halfhearted smile. "Let's just make sure we do it."

CHAPTER 19

"Nina's on the phone," Rose said, poking her head into my office.

I pushed aside the police report, which I'd been going over in greater detail now that I was alone, and picked up the receiver.

"Hi, Nina. How are you feeling?"

She managed a small laugh. "I've been better."

"Is it the headache still or . . . or everything else?"

"The headache was just an excuse." Her voice was so thin I thought for a minute she was on the verge of tears, but she drew in a breath and continued. "I wanted to thank you for taking time with Emily last night."

"I enjoyed it."

"So did she. I felt so bad abandoning her to Simon and Elsa, but I just couldn't cope. The last thing she needed was to hang out with a mother who was falling apart at the seams."

I felt an ache in my throat thinking of what Nina must be going through.

"I keep reminding myself to take things a step at a time," Nina said.

"That's the only way to get through this."

She hesitated, then asked, "You haven't talked to Grady this morning, have you?"

"No." I felt a momentary alarm. "Why?"

"They won't let me speak to him," Nina said. She again sounded as though she were fighting to keep herself in control. "They said I had to come during regular visiting hours. I explained that I was confined to bed under doctor's orders, but it didn't seem to make any difference."

Alarm gave way to guilt. I should have thought to make arrangements for Nina to speak to Grady yesterday. "Let me see what I can do. I'm sure we'll be able to work something out."

Another deep breath. "Thanks. I'll feel better once I can talk to him."

I knew she'd be anxious, though, until Grady was back home. With luck, that might be only months, but it might also be a lifetime.

"Did you get a chance to see the police reports yet?" Nina asked.

"I was just looking at them."

"And?"

"And there's nothing there that we can't refute. The evidence is all circumstantial." My voice carried more conviction than I felt.

"No surprises?"

I thought of Grady's handkerchief in the hallway and the eight-minute conversation logged from Deirdre's phone to Grady's private number at ComTech. I decided Nina had enough to worry about already.

"Not really," I told her. "And there are a few angles the police may have overlooked. I've got Hal Fisher working on them."

"Hal? I haven't seen him in a couple of years. How is he?"

"A little grayer, a little heavier. As much of a free spirit as ever."

I'd introduced Hal to Nina when she was in the throes of divorcing her first husband, Jerry Allen. He'd managed to trace the assets Allen had hidden, and to get enough dirt on the guy that he hadn't followed through with his threat to contest custody.

"He and Marc didn't exactly hit it off," I added.

Nina laughed. "No, I imagine they wouldn't. It's funny how you can be so fond of two people and have them not get along at all."

"Seems to happen surprisingly often."

She sighed. "It does, doesn't it?"

I wondered if she was thinking of Grady and myself when she'd made the comment. Nina was quiet a moment. I couldn't tell if she was thinking or building up to a panic.

"He didn't do it," she said after a moment. "I know the question has got to be on your mind."

Technically, that wasn't an issue. Defense attorneys often represent clients they suspect might be guilty. She was right, though, that my doubts about Grady made me uneasy. For Nina's sake, I hoped I was wrong.

"It's something I try not to think about," I said, lying through my teeth.

"I know my husband," Nina said vehemently. "You don't live with a man without learning about his character. There's no way he killed Deirdre Nichols."

"I'm going to do my best to get him off, Nina. I promise."

"I know you will." She paused. "I'm counting on you, Kali."

I hung up the phone feeling, for the first time, the weight of what I'd agreed to take on. Nina's assurances aside, I wasn't convinced that Grady was leveling with us. And perhaps equally important, I was afraid that the friend in me might find herself at odds with the attorney.

Hal phoned the following afternoon when I was deep into reviewing the file on another matter.

"I told you we shouldn't be too quick to write off the boyfriend," he said. The words were embellished with a touch of good-humored self-righteousness.

With my mind still focused on the papers in front of me, it took me a moment to figure out what he was talking about. "You mean Tony Rodale?"

"That's the one. Turns out the police paid him a visit a couple of months ago, a domestic violence call. They hauled him in for assault, but his *assaultee*"—he gave the word emphasis with a phony accent—"the now-infamous Ms. Deirdre Nichols, refused to press charges. She had a black eye and a cut lip but insisted she got them walking into an open door."

I felt a ray of sunshine peeking out from the gloom. Pointing the finger is a time-honored defense strategy, and an abusive boyfriend could prove useful in deflecting guilt from Grady. "Any other incidents?"

"There's just that one in the system, but that doesn't mean he didn't go after her on other occasions as well. I'm on my way to pay him a visit right now. Want to come along?"

I glanced at the document I'd been reviewing, a book-length stack of papers with a story line only the most committed lawyer could love. I was only a third of the way through and already hopelessly lost in the tangle of minutiae. A change of pace held great appeal.

"Sure. When are you leaving?"

"I'll be by in about fifteen minutes. That okay with you?"

"Fine."

I was on my way out the door, when the phone rang again.

"Byron Spencer," Rose said, holding her hand over the mouthpiece. "You want to talk to him, or should I take a message?"

"Are you sure it's me he wants and not Marc?"

Spencer had not only accepted Marc's apology, but in true journalist fashion turned what might have been an ugly barroom scene into a valued contact. At least that's what Spencer seemed to be hoping. So far Marc had been less than forthcoming as an off-the-record source, but he seemed to dish out enough to keep Spencer coming back for more.

"He asked for you by name," Rose said.

"Take his number and I'll call him back when I get a chance."

I'd told Rose that I was meeting Hal, but I hadn't said a word to Marc. And I met Hal out front on the street rather than having him come into the office. The less Marc saw of Hal, the better, I thought. There was no point looking for contention.

"What do you know about this guy?" I asked Hal after I'd buckled myself into his Mazda and adjusted the air vents so they weren't directing heavy blasts of arctic air in my direction. I'd forgotten that Hal had a thing about fresh air.

"So far, not much. He's thirty-four years old, divorced. Has a clean record except for one DUI a couple of years back. He runs a small investment company—limited partnerships and that sort of thing. Lives well judging by his address and car registration. And he travels fairly frequently, always first class."

"How do you find this stuff?"

Hal smiled. "You don't want to know, trust me."

"Forget I even asked."

"Rodale grew up in Fresno. One of eight children. Went to the local community college, then transferred to Chico State. He never graduated though."

"How come?"

Hal gave me a sideways look. "Hey, I'm good, but I'm not a mind reader." He gunned the engine and switched lanes, squeezing into an opening in traffic that was only an inch longer than his car.

I braced myself. "You're not much of a driver either."

"I haven't had an accident in thirty years."

"Better thank your guardian angel."

Hal took his hands off the steering wheel and pressed them together in prayer.

"Not now!"

Hal grinned.

When he returned his hands to the wheel, I leaned back and started breathing again. "Anything on the Carsons yet?"

"The people Deirdre Nichols was house-sitting for? I haven't been able to trace them. From what I hear, the police haven't had any luck either. They're in the import business, and apparently went on one of their buying trips to the far corners of the world. The business phone is an answering machine; the address a post office box."

"Silly way to run a business."

Hal shrugged. "It's becoming more and more common." He was silent a moment. "I can cancel out of my date tomorrow night if you want me to check on those kids partying in the canyon for you."

"Thanks, but I don't want to impinge on your personal life."

"It's a relationship that's headed south anyway."

"Someone you still care about?"

"Someone I'm trying very hard *not* to care about." He tapped the wheel with his fingers. "So, how's it feel to be back in the Bay Area?"

"Wonderful and unsettling at the same time. Of course the situation itself is odd."

"I can imagine. Nina must be having a tough time of it."

I nodded. "She is. But it's not just Nina I was talking about." I hesitated before adding, "Marc and I were seeing each other for a while during law school."

"Uh-ooh." He glanced in my direction. "Painful breakup?"

"He was engaged to someone else at the time, and I didn't know it."

Hal clicked his tongue. "Such stellar behavior. When did you find out?"

It was a story not many people knew, but I'd always found Hal an easy person to talk to. "Marc had been away interviewing at firms in the East," I told him. "The day he was returning was his birthday, so I talked the apartment manager into letting me into his place to decorate. I put up banners and streamers, and taped big red hearts on all the mirrors and cupboards, even inside the refrigerator. All the places that Marc would normally look. And on every one of them I wrote in silver pen, 'I love you.' "

I swallowed. The raw shock of discovery was vivid still in my mind. "Janice called just as I was arranging candy hearts on his pillow. She left a long and rather passionate message on his answering machine."

"Janice?"

"His fiancée."

"Ouch. That's brutal."

"Yeah, it was. For a while anyway."

"What happened to the girl?"

"He married her. It lasted four years. I never knew her. Nina says I would have liked her."

"Must be weird working with the guy now. Is it going okay?"

"Yeah. Surprisingly, it is." Our working together hadn't been the problem I'd expected. What *was* a problem for me, or at least something of a puzzle, was the chemistry between us. Despite Marc's past sins and despite the fact that he sometimes irritated the hell out of me, I found myself attracted to him.

Hal looked at me, catching something in my expression. "You haven't been pining away for him ever since law school, have you?"

I laughed. "Hardly. But I seem to have a knack for getting involved with the wrong men."

"Easy to do."

"That's part of the reason I decided to come back here and help Nina. To give myself some distance from the guy I was seeing in Silver Creek."

"He turn out to be engaged too?"

"Married. He went back to his wife."

"And here I thought all the bad luck was mine."

"Guess I'm still looking for the right man."

Hal chuckled. "That makes two of us."

CHAPTER 20

Hal parked in front of Tony Rodale's home, a sprawling Mediterranean-style house situated near the Claremont Country Club. While much of the surrounding area to the east was still scarred by the devastation of the 'ninety-one firestorm, the stretch of streets surrounding Rodale's was lush with green foliage and mature trees.

"What makes you think he's home?" I asked.

"I called." Hal rubbed his chin. "Fancy digs. Rodale must have the golden touch with investments."

I nodded. Real estate near the country club was pricy, and his was one of the bigger houses on the street.

Rodale answered the door himself. He was about my height, with a thick, muscular build. He was wearing soft-drape wool slacks and a silk shirt open at the neck, revealing a chunky gold chain. His dark hair was thick and glossy, his eyes a little too small for the rest of his face. He wasn't unattractive, but neither was he the urbane financier I'd been expecting.

While Hal offered introductions and the reason for our visit, I handed over one of my cards. Rodale stuck it in his pocket without a glance.

"I'd be happy to help," he said with studied sincerity. "But I'm afraid there's very little I can tell you."

"We won't take long. Mind if we come in?" Hal had begun moving through the open doorway while he spoke. Inside, he whistled softly. "Nice place. Looks like something out of *Architectural Digest*."

I thought it looked more like something out of Hollywood for Wanna-bes. The couches and chairs were massive and upholstered in heavy black leather. The tables were ultramodern works of glass and chrome. A projection-style television screen covered the wall at the far end of the room. The remaining walls were hung with large abstract oil paintings favoring blobs and dribbles in bold primary colors.

"Guess you must have a green thumb for investments," Hal said.

Rodale laughed, flashing a set of perfect white teeth. "What can I say? I've been lucky. Can I get you a soda or something?"

I shook my head, but Hal was the one who spoke. "Sure, that sounds great."

Rodale went to the wet bar at the other side of the room, reached under the counter, and pulled out three cans of Diet Coke. He handed them to us, unopened. His sense of decorum was on a par with his decor.

Rodale took the slingback chair, leaving us the L-shaped sectional. He let his eyes run up and down my body for a moment before speaking, a move I suspected he intended as flattery.

"So," he said, popping the tab on his soda. "What is it you think I can help you with?"

"This allegation of rape Deirdre Nichols made against our client," Hal said. "Did you believe it?"

Rodale laughed uneasily. "I didn't have an opinion one way or the other. Not that it matters any more. I understand the charges were dropped."

"Did she talk to you about it?"

"Only in passing." He shifted in his chair. "Ours wasn't one of those bare-your-soul relationships."

Hal propped a foot on the glass surface of the coffee table. I wasn't sure if he'd done it intentionally to see how Rodale responded, or if he was simply, like many men, oblivious of such things.

"What kind of relationship *was* it?" Hal asked.

Rodale shrugged. "We had some good times."

"And some not-so-good times?"

Rodale gave another shrug. "Women, you know. Nothing's perfect."

"Had you known Deirdre long?" I asked.

"About six months. It was hot and heavy for a while, but never"—he paused, using the fingers of both hands to make quotation marks in the air—"never *serious*. I date a lot of women. That's the way I like it."

"Did she date other men?"

His smile was one of indifference. "I wouldn't know."

"So it wouldn't have bothered you if she did?"

"I never gave it much thought." Rodale leaned forward, elbows on his knees, fingertips pressed together steeple fashion. "What you gotta understand is, Deirdre was the one who got jealous. Not me. It was her that wanted things to be different between us."

Hal took a swig of soda. "Meaning she wanted more commitment?"

"Yeah. I'm no fool though. She liked the lifestyle I could give her, the presents I bought her, the kind of people I socialize with. She wanted that for keeps. Since I was part of the package, she wanted me too. But it was the package that got her attention."

I could understand how Deirdre might have been attracted at least as much by the accessories as the man. What surprised me, though, was the absence of any bitterness in Rodale's words. I wondered if he was being truthful.

He leaned back. "Deirdre was a good woman. You know, fun to be around. I felt bad for her about the rape, assuming that's what really happened, and I'm real sorry she's dead. But we weren't seeing all that much of each other there at the end. I kinda put a stop to it."

"When was the last time you talked to her?" I asked.

"That Saturday morning, the day she was killed. She'd heard I was taking Gabrielle to New Orleans with me, wanted to know if it was true."

"Who's Gabrielle?" I asked at the same time Hal said, "Was it?"

Rodale ignored my question. "Yes, I was planning to take her to New Orleans."

"Deirdre was upset?" Hal asked.

Rodale shrugged. "With women, who can tell?"

Hal pressed the soda can with his thumb. "I gather the police questioned you about Deirdre's death?"

"Of course."

"You have an alibi?"

"I was here. Fortunately for me, a neighbor saw my car in the driveway that evening." Rodale smiled at us. "I don't think I was ever a serious suspect."

"That so?" Hal drummed his fingers against his knee. "I'd have thought after the cops hauled you in for knocking Deirdre around, you'd be at the top of their list."

Rodale laughed uncomfortably. "That was all Deirdre's doing. I never touched her; she fell. But she was pissed at me because I wouldn't take her along when I was sailing down to Mexico with some friends. The charges were dropped anyway."

"Because she wouldn't testify."

"Guess she came to her senses."

Yeah, sure. Like all the other battered women who are afraid to speak out. But I didn't push it. Instead, I asked, "Do you have any idea who might have had reason to kill her?"

Another flash of white teeth. "Your client."

"Aside from Grady Barrett."

"His is the only name that comes to mind." Rodale stood. "Now you'll have to excuse me. I've got an important conference call scheduled."

He walked us to the door and promised to be in touch if he thought of anything else.

Hal was silent until we turned onto Broadway Terrace. "The guy sure went out of his way to make us believe Deirdre wasn't anything special to him."

"Maybe she wasn't. Rodale strikes me as the kind of guy for whom no one is special."

"Except that he likes to be the one calling the shots."

I nodded. "It was interesting what he said about Gabrielle. According to Deirdre's coworkers, she was in good spirits the day she died. Happier than she'd been for weeks. Doesn't sound like a jealous woman."

Hal tugged on an earlobe. "I wonder why the police let Rodale off so easy?"

"I guess they found his alibi sufficient."

"Doesn't strike me as rock solid. But then, they were focusing their energy on Grady, so maybe they never looked too hard."

"Rodale isn't someone I'd go out of my way to be friends with," I said. "But I'm not sure we'll have much luck trying to cast him as the killer."

Hal frowned. "Maybe not. But there's something about him that doesn't ring true."

CHAPTER 21

"Remind me again why we have to do this," Marc grumbled as I slid onto the soft leather upholstery of his Lexus.

I buckled my seat belt. "*We* don't have to. *I* wanted to, and you insisted on coming along."

While I'd worn jeans and a turtleneck, Marc had dressed for the evening in a blue blazer, razor-pleat slacks, and white rayon shirt. However inappropriate his attire, he looked good. But he did not look happy.

"This is the kind of grunt work your friend Hal should be handling," he said.

"Hal is tied up tonight, remember?"

Marc was barely able to contain a snicker. "Into S and M, is he?"

I gave Marc a withering look, which he might have missed in the darkness of the night.

"Wouldn't surprise me." Marc gunned the engine pulling out of the parking spot.

"Enough, already. Hal's a friend of mine."

"You've made that clear. In fact, I get the feeling you two are pretty chummy." Marc looked over at me with a raised eyebrow. "He isn't bi, is he? Like maybe it's more than friends."

"We're friends, period. What's with you anyway?"

The hint of a smile softened Marc's expression. "Just checking."

"Anyway," I said, getting back to the evening's mission, "if Grady's serious about not waiving time, we've got less than two weeks before the hearing. We have to find the kids tonight. Next weekend will be too late."

"So while Hal's getting laid, we're crawling through the underbrush like the Hardy Boys. I still say there's something wrong with this picture."

"Think of it as an adventure," I suggested.

He made a pretense of sneering, but I caught the glimmer of a smile underneath. "On the bright side," Marc said after a moment, "I get to spend an evening with you."

I couldn't tell if he was teasing, so I let the comment pass.

We stopped at a red light. Marc sucked his cheek. "I'd rather be taking you to dinner though."

"There's always another night."

"You'd go out with me if I asked you?" He sounded surprised.

I rubbed my chin. "Depends on the restaurant."

"No joke, Kali. Would you?" There was a serious edge to his voice I didn't expect.

"I might."

The light changed and we pulled away in another stretch of silence.

"Back when we were in school—" He stopped and started again. "I never meant to hurt you."

The brittle anguish of betrayal had dulled over the years, but I felt anger rising in my throat anew. "How could I *not* be hurt? We were sleeping together. We told each other our secrets and our dreams. And you never bothered to tell me you were engaged to someone else?"

"It does sound stupid in retrospect."

"Damn right it does."

"But it's the truth. All those things I told you—I wasn't lying. My feelings for you were genuine."

"But not very deep."

He shook his head. "That's where you're wrong."

I gave a skeptical snort.

"I was confused. Young, scared—"

"And selfish," I added.

He offered an apologetic smile. "That too. Hell, I don't like the guy I was back then any more than you do. I'd redraw him in a minute if I could, but I'm stuck with him."

When I didn't say anything, Marc continued. "I think I knew then that Janice wasn't right for me. The fact that I got involved with you should certainly have made that clear."

"One would think so."

"But we'd been together so long. Our families were friends, had been for years. It just seemed like one of those things that *was*. It never dawned on me to question it."

"Nor did it stop you from playing around while she was back in Cincinnati, or wherever she lived, planning your wedding."

"Cleveland." He paused. "I'm sorry, Kali. I know that's too little too late. But I mean it. The older I get, the more I realize how vulnerable we all are. At the time, I thought it was just me."

I folded my arms and gave my head a casual toss. "If it's any consolation, none of the emotional scars were permanent." None that I'd admit to him, at any rate. Besides, I'd acquired plenty of others along the way to keep them company. I thought fleetingly of Tom before pushing the memory from my mind.

"You're lucky." Marc's tone made it clear he didn't believe me. "I've picked up quite a number of scars myself. All of them permanent. And all of them painful."

"What about now? Are you seeing someone?" I hadn't heard Nina mention a name, but that didn't mean much.

Marc shook his head. "Casual dates. Nothing remotely serious for several years." He took his foot off the accelerator as we neared the next light. "Is this the road?"

I nodded. "Take a left."

I guided him through several turns to the wide shoulder where I'd parked the day before. Tonight, though, the space was occupied by a couple of pickup trucks and an older model sedan. We parked up the road a bit and walked through a tangle of leaves and scrub toward the clearing. Although I'd brought along a flashlight, it was still hard going. The ground was uneven and sometimes slippery.

As we got closer I could hear voices above the music, but I wasn't able to make out any words.

"This is it?" Marc asked.

"Right."

"Jesus, can't they find a better place to party?"

"It's private. And it's theirs. Didn't you have a similar place when you were a kid?"

"We'd sometimes sneak a beer under the maple between the sixth and seventh holes. But that's about it."

Marc's was a country club childhood, the product of a lifestyle most of us fantasized about when we were young. But he'd clearly missed some of the more memorable experiences that had been part of my own teenage years.

We stopped short of the partying. Through the bramble, about thirty yards ahead, we could see shadowy forms. Eight or ten males, each with a can in his hand. The pungent odor of marijuana filled the evening air.

"What now?" Marc whispered.

Before I could answer, a crackling noise from behind raised the hair on the back of my neck.

"Stay put and don't move." The voice was male and nasal, and raw enough that we obeyed instantly.

"You and your great ideas," Marc muttered.

"Shut up," ordered the voice.

I wondered whether our companion had a weapon, and whether he intended to use it.

"What's doing, Dirk?" A voice from the clearing called out in our direction.

"Hey, guys," Dirk called back, "we got company. Peeping Toms or something." He turned his attention to us again. "Okay, let's join the others."

"We were just leaving," Marc said, reaching for my hand.

"Yeah? Well, you've just had a change in plans." He put a hand on Marc's back and shoved. "Let's go."

As we inched toward the clearing, the cluster of young men moved in our direction. I'd been expecting kids, and the kind of spirited carousing of an after-game celebration. These may well have been kids—it was hard to tell—but there was a hardened, streetwise air about them that was a long way from high school football. I wondered if they were gang members—the kind who killed people as an initiation rite.

"Went to take a piss and stumbled on these two snooping around in the bushes," Dirk explained.

"We weren't snooping," I said, twisting to look for a gun. I couldn't see one.

"Yeah, well, you weren't on your way to the opera either."

A wiry little guy with dark hair edged to the front. "Hey, dudes, this is a private party. We kinda got this spot reserved, so to speak."

"And it's public property," slurred an unseen companion in

what, to my mind, was a complete nonsequitur. But several of his compatriots grunted agreement.

"Besides which," added another, "you ain't dressed right." He turned to me. "Not you, li'l lady. I'm talking about your friend here, Mr. Eddie Bauer." He flicked a finger under Marc's lapel.

Marc knocked the hand aside. "Get your hands off me, punk."

"Hey, the dude thinks he's tough." The wiry guy laughed as if he'd told a joke.

"Shut up, all of you." A broad-shouldered young man wearing a backward-facing baseball cap sauntered forward. The others grew quiet.

"You're not cops, right?"

"Right," I said. "And we're not here to crash your party either."

"We're attorneys," Marc said before I could stop him.

The young men seemed neither awed nor ready to laugh—the two reactions I'd anticipated. Apparently they didn't have much feeling one way or the other about attorneys.

"We're hoping to find someone who was here last Saturday," I explained.

"Who?"

"Anyone. I mean, we're not looking for a particular person. We'd just like to talk to people who were here."

Baseball cap crossed his arms. "How come?"

"A woman up the canyon was killed falling off her deck."

"Wow, she musta been really gassed," said the wiry boy with a giggle.

"Shut up," said the boy with the cap, who seemed to be the leader. He looked at me. "She didn't roll clear down here. Why you looking for people here?"

Over the past few minutes I'd felt some of the tension in my shoulders ease. If they were members of a gang, it didn't appear to be one bent on collecting scalps.

"Were any of you partying here that night?" Marc asked. "Maybe you saw something."

"What d'ya mean?"

"*See*," Marc said snidely. "You know, with your eyes." I could tell that he was growing impatient.

"Her house is up there," I said, pointing. "Above that stand of eucalyptus. The police think someone pushed her."

"Wasn't us."

"Nobody says it was. We just want to talk to anyone who was here that night."

"What's it worth?" asked Dirk.

Marc's anger was close to the surface. "All we're asking for is information. Maybe you should try cooperating simply for the novelty of contributing to the betterment of society."

"Save the civics lecture." Dirk rubbed his fingers and thumb together in the gesture of asking for money. "How much?"

"You know something?" Marc asked.

"Might be able to tell you who does."

"Ten dollars," I said. "If you can give us the name of someone who saw what happened that night."

"Ten?" His tone was derisive.

"Tell them," the wiry guy muttered. "We don't want to be standing here yakking all night."

"For twenty," Dirk said, "I'll give you a name."

Marc snorted in disgust. "Come on, Kali. Let's get out of here."

"Okay, twenty," I said.

Dirk held out his hand until I'd pulled out two tens and handed them to him. "Talk to Xavier."

"He saw something?" Marc asked.

"Says he did."

"Xavier says that?" It was a different kid this time. "He never told me that."

"That story about the angel, remember? You know how he could'n stop talking about her that night? Well, next day there it is on the news. That was the lady going over the railing. He called me up like he'd won at Lotto or something."

Marc shifted his weight. "So we'll need to talk to this fellow, Xavier."

"Good luck, man. Most days, Xavier don't know what he sees or what he says. His elevator stops short, if you know what I mean."

Unfortunately, I did. "Where do we find him?"

"Tonight?"

"Sure."

The young men looked at one another and shrugged. "Could be anywhere. If he's not here though, most likely he's hanging in Berkeley."

"Where in Berkeley?"

More shrugs.

"Where does he live?"

"Around."

"Around? You mean on the street?"

"His old man kicked him out last year. He lived over in Albany for a while with some chick."

"Do you know where?"

"He's not there anymore. Her parents got tired of feeding him. He still sees her sometimes though. She might know how to reach him."

We were finally able to pull an address of sorts from their combined expertise. The address was either 916 or 619. Or maybe 896. No one knew the street name, but it was one of those that ran south off Solano Avenue. The girl's name was Sara. Her last name began with *C* or maybe a *K*.

All in all, it wasn't a lot to go on.

CHAPTER 22

"Where to now?" Marc asked when we were back in the car.

"I guess it's too late to go calling on Sara's parents."

"Especially if we want their cooperation. Besides, we'd have to hit about fifty houses in the hope of getting the right one. Not a neighbor-friendly thing to do this time of night."

"No," I said, disappointed. "I guess not."

Marc leaned against the door and draped an arm over the back of the seat. "You want to go have a drink somewhere?"

A drink sounded good. "Sure."

Marc had been picking burrs off his trouser legs, and now he brushed them in disgust. "I'm going to have to send these to the cleaners."

"You should have worn jeans."

"I should have stayed home. What a zoo. No wonder people are worried about the future of our country."

"Hey, they told us what we wanted to know."

"For a price."

"So, they're steeped in the entrepreneurial spirit. That's the good old American way, isn't it?"

We wound up at Baywolf. The restaurant was filled with diners, as I'd known it would be, but we were able to get a table on the outside deck and an order of crab cakes to go with our wine. The evening was crisp, as it often is in early spring, but without any wind, the temperature wasn't uncomfortable. And the wine helped ward off the chill.

"This is more like it," Marc said, dotting salsa on a wedge of crab cake.

"All's well that ends well," I quipped.

"I was hoping we hadn't yet reached *the end* of our evening." He gave me an impish grin, which I ignored.

"I take it that's a 'no comment,' " he said.

"Right."

"You're a hard-hearted woman, Kali O'Brien."

"You'd better believe it."

Marc nudged the plate in my direction. "Do you really think this Xavier person saw Deirdre being pushed from the deck?"

"I know it's a long shot, but he might have. Until we talk to him, we won't know whether he saw, or heard, something that will prove useful. If we're able to uncover even one piece of evidence that isn't consistent with Grady's guilt, it might be enough to sway the jury."

"Like looking for a needle in a haystack."

"More or less. But the prosecution is going to put together a beautifully wrapped package, and we have to come up with some way to tug at a few of those ribbons."

"It's a pretty thin police report if you ask me." Marc frowned. "Almost like they wanted it to be Grady so they jumped from A to Z without spending a lot of time getting there."

That was often the case, but many times the cops were also right. When the available evidence was less than perfect, they filled in with intuition and experience. For my own peace of mind, I wished I knew if they were right about Grady.

"You're not convinced Grady is innocent, are you?" Marc asked, as if reading my mind.

"Not entirely, no. Are you?"

He nodded. "As sure as I would be about anyone."

Marc's fingers grazed the back of my hand. I felt the tingle all the way down my spine. I sipped my wine and pretended I hadn't noticed.

"You didn't see any reference to an address book or Day-Timer in the list of items seized by the police, did you?"

Another pass of the fingertips. "Not that I recall. Why?"

"I didn't find one at her house."

"You sure she had one?"

I nodded. "Deirdre talked to me the day of the rape hearing.

She pulled one of those leather-bound planners out of her purse to write down my number."

Marc retracted his hand, ran his finger around the edge of his plate instead. "You think the killer took it?"

"Someone did. Makes me think maybe there was something incriminating there."

He whistled under his breath. "If that's the case, good luck. It's gone for good."

"But if we figure out where it is, we may have a clue as to her killer."

Marc stared into his wineglass, swirling the deep red liquid before venturing a sip. He seemed lost in thought.

After a few beats of silence, I said, "I went to see Tony Rodale yesterday. The guy Deirdre was seeing."

Marc snapped to attention. "Why?"

"Hal learned that he'd beaten Deirdre in the past. She filed charges then refused to follow through."

"Shit."

"What's the matter?"

"Nothing. Just another loose end." He closed his eyes for a moment.

"I wondered if you knew him."

"Know him? Why would I?"

"He does something with investments."

"Yeah, well, that covers a lot of ground."

"I take it that's a no."

Marc ignored the comment. "Did you learn anything?"

"Not directly." I filled him in on the visit with Tony Rodale. "I doubt anything will come of it, but Hal has a couple of ideas he's going to follow up on."

Marc set the glass down with such force, the wine sloshed over the edge. "Shouldn't Hal be doing what *we* tell him to instead of going off on some half-baked scheme of his own?"

"He's been in the business a long time."

"All the more reason we shouldn't let him take over."

"He's not taking over." I leaned forward. "You don't like him, do you? Is it because he's gay?"

"I don't care one way or another what a person's sexual orientation is."

"Not in the abstract, maybe, but it makes you uncomfortable

in the flesh." In my experience, men seemed to have more trouble in this regard than women. Maybe because *maleness* is such an important part of their identity.

"You should have warned me, is all."

"Should I also have 'warned' you that he's Jewish and a vegetarian?"

"It's not the same." Marc cracked a conciliatory smile. "And it's not that I don't like him, just that I think he ought to remember that *he's* working for *us* and not the other way around."

On the way back to the car, Marc draped his arm casually around my shoulder. Although I didn't like acknowledging the fact, it felt nice. Better than nice, in truth. His touch brought a slow warmth to my whole body. I leaned a little in his direction, bringing us closer. Marc's hand squeezed my shoulder.

When we pulled into the driveway of his place, where I'd left my car, he turned to me. White moonlight filtered through the trees, casting a pattern, like lace, across his face and shirt. He reached for my hand.

"Spend the night with me, Kali."

Inside the car, the ethereal dappling of shadows gave the evening a feeling of unreality. A moment in time, without yesterdays or tomorrows. But deep inside, I knew that it was an illusion.

The yesterdays I could deal with, had been dealing with them for years. It was the tomorrows that had me worried.

"Not tonight," I told him. "But I won't say never."

He didn't push as I'd thought he might, but kissed me softly instead. "It's an open invitation."

When I got home, I lay awake in bed. Images of the path not taken flickered in my mind. What would it be like to be with Marc again? He'd treated me badly, but that was years ago. Let he who is without sin, I reminded myself. Besides, he'd admitted he was wrong. As he'd so aptly pointed out, you can't redraw the past.

As for the tomorrows—they had a way of working themselves out. Or not. Either way, they came and went, and we learned to bend with the weight of experience.

I turned on the light and punched the buttons on the phone.

What the hell. I was lonely. And tired of feeling that way. I felt again the tingle of Marc's fingers on my skin. There was no denying the sexual excitement I felt when I was around him.

I let the phone ring fifteen times before I gave up.

But I was awake for hours wondering where he'd gone to.

CHAPTER 23

Normally, I don't eat much breakfast. Coffee, always. A banana if I'm feeling virtuous, a piece of toast if I'm looking at a particularly busy day. Even on Sundays.

My tenants-cum-landlords took a different approach, however. Especially on Sundays.

That morning they'd persuaded me to join them. Fresh strawberries with cream, homemade Belgian waffles dripping with butter and syrup, a platter of thick cut Canadian bacon, and scrambled eggs laced with sun dried tomato. I didn't even try to count the calories.

"We heard you come in last night," Dotty said, dunking a piece of waffle into the syrup puddled on her plate.

I set my cup on the table. "Sorry, I didn't mean to wake you."

"No, no. Don't worry about that." A look crossed between them, then a pause. Finally, Bea explained. "We thought you might be staying out all night. At your boyfriend's."

"My boyfriend?"

Dotty nodded. "We took bets, in fact. Bea said you wouldn't be back until after breakfast this morning."

"What?" I didn't know whether to laugh or be angry.

"There's nothing like a new love to make you forget the old, that's what I always say."

"I'm not—"

Bea reached for a strawberry. "We just wanted you to know we wouldn't be shocked or upset or anything if you *did* spend the night somewhere else."

"At a man's place, she means."

"We may be getting on in years," Bea explained, "but we keep up with the times as best we can."

Dotty giggled. "I'd keep up for real if I could find myself a willing man."

"It wasn't a date," I said emphatically. They'd heard me mention Marc's name over the past couple of weeks, but unless I'd been talking in my sleep, they'd built a romantic fantasy out of nothing.

"You were out with him on a Saturday night," Bea offered.

"We were working," I assured them. "On a case." In the cold light of morning I was actually thankful Marc hadn't answered my late night call.

"Some work."

I brushed the air with my hand. "Don't hold your breath if you're looking to me for excitement."

Bea scoffed. "We don't need you for excitement."

"We have a pretty full plate on our own."

"I wasn't trying to suggest you didn't."

"We're off to the RV and camper show today," Dotty said smugly. She speared a piece of waffle with her fork. "You're welcome to come along if you'd like."

I shook my head. "I didn't know you were in the market for a camper."

"We're not. Wouldn't be caught dead with one of those things. All cramped and tight. But the shows are fun. It's a way to get out and mingle."

"Besides," Dotty said. "It's a real bargain. Seniors get in free."

I suppressed a smile and offered to clean up the kitchen, which wasn't difficult given that they were the sort of cooks who cleaned up as they went. A very different breed of creature from myself.

When the hour was sufficient for Hal to have recovered from whatever late night excesses he'd indulged in, I called and passed along Xavier's name as well as the assortment of possible addresses.

"Find out if Xavier saw or heard *anything* that night. He apparently told some of his buddies a story about seeing an angel, so I have a feeling you're going to have to work at getting a coherent answer."

Hal grumbled. "It won't be the first time."

"You sound down today."

"I am."

"The relationship that's headed south?"

"It's not headed anymore. It's there."

"I'm sorry."

"Don't be. I'll get over it."

I called Nina next. "How are you doing?"

"Okay." She didn't sound as though she believed it herself.

"Did you get to talk to Grady? They said they'd let him call you."

"Yesterday. Thanks for setting it up."

"Once they understood the situation, it wasn't a problem."

"I've been so worried, Kali. Thinking about him all alone in that horrible place."

It had to be hell to have a loved one behind bars, no matter what the circumstances. The fact that Nina couldn't visit had to make the anxiety worse. As if she didn't have enough to worry about already.

"He's not used to being around the kind of men who end up in jail," Nina said.

"How did he seem?"

She took a breath. "He sounded miserable. But at least I know he's being treated fairly and hasn't been jumped by one of his cell mates."

"You sound miserable yourself. Would you like some company today?"

"Maybe later. I didn't sleep well last night. Emily's off to a friend's house for the day and I'm going to try to get some rest."

"It's going to work out, Nina. Grady's going to be fine."

"I want to believe that. I really do."

"I'll drop by this afternoon. If you think of anything I can do before then, give me a call."

After I hung up, I continued to stare at the phone, imagining the multitude of emotions and fears that must be waging battle in Nina's mind. And there was so little any of us could do.

I started to punch in Marc's number, then wondered if I'd wake him. Wondered if I really wanted to talk to him, even. Was what I felt anything more than physical desire? Not that sexual passion didn't have its own rewards, just that it was wisest to recognize it for what it was.

Disgruntled, I nibbled the remaining square of waffle in spite of the fact that I was already stuffed, and tried to sort through my feelings.

When the phone rang, I jumped, then reached to answer, hoping it was Marc. Instead, it was Sheila Barlow, Deirdre's sister.

"I hope you don't mind my calling you at home," she said.

"I wasn't doing anything important."

"Or mind my calling you at all, for that matter."

"It *is* unusual."

"This whole situation is unusual." Her tone was clipped, betraying her impatience.

"Meaning?"

"Nina's husband. My sister. Adrianna and Emily being classmates. Our paths cross." She paused for a breath. "That's why we need to talk."

Actually, the situation wasn't as unusual as Sheila seemed to believe. Because victims frequently know their killers; overlap among friends and family is not uncommon. But there was no denying it was awkward.

"I don't know that talking will change anything," I told her. "But I'm willing to listen."

A moment of breathing on the other end, then she asked, "You aren't by any chance free right now, are you? The sooner I get through this the better."

"Now's fine with me."

"But not over the phone." She hesitated. "I know this is asking a lot, but could you come here? Say in about half an hour."

I gave half a moment's thought to the request being a setup. Sheila with a shotgun, waiting to blow me away the minute I walked through her door. It was a silly image, one born of too many evenings wasted on bad TV. But just to be on the safe side, I left a detailed note for Bea and Dotty before I went.

CHAPTER 24

Although Piedmont has a reputation as being an enclave for the rich and pampered, there are, in fact, a number of very modest homes in the city. Sheila Barlow lived in one of them. It was a square, single-story stucco, pleasantly kept but with none of the amenities that real estate agents refer to as *curb appeal*. I rang the bell and Sheila answered immediately. She must have been watching from the front window for my arrival.

"Thank you for coming. Especially on such short notice." Her tone was agreeable, but there was no welcoming smile in accompaniment. On the other hand, there was no shotgun either.

Sheila Barlow was taller than her sister by a couple of inches, and rawboned. Whereas Deirdre had been curvy, Sheila was angular. Her hair, which was cut short, was a lackluster brown rather than her sister's fiery red. But the family resemblance was clear, particularly through the eyes.

"Would you like some coffee?" Sheila asked.

"No thanks."

"I made a pot. It's fresh." There was just a hint of reprimand in her tone.

"Okay." I gave a hey-I'm-easy laugh. "Half a cup. Black."

Sheila marched off to the kitchen and left me standing by the door, which opened directly onto the living room. I sat on the sofa and waited for her return.

A picture of Adrianna, gap-toothed and grinning, was prominently displayed on the fireplace mantel. The coffee table was stacked with children's books as well as several guides to gardening. A knitting project of heathered teal hung over the arm of the chair to my left. The green walls and heavily draped windows rendered the room too dark for my taste, but there was a lived-in feeling about it I found appealing.

Another photo, in a silver frame, rested on the table across the room. I rose and was looking at it when Sheila returned a moment later with two hefty blue and white mugs. Despite my request for half a cup, the one she handed me was filled to the brim.

"You and Deirdre?" I asked, nodding at the photo.

"Almost ten years ago. It amazes me every time, how young we were."

"Who's the man? A brother?" He stood between the two women, a lanky, square-jawed man with ash-blond hair that hung over one eye. All three were mugging for the camera.

Sheila shook her head. "That's Frank Nichols. Adrianna's father." She gave a little laugh. "Though he wasn't yet her father when that was taken. In fact, that was the first time he'd met Deirdre."

"Looks like the three of you were having a good time."

She nodded, her eyes lingering on the photo. "We had a lot of good times."

I returned to my place on the gold-hued sofa. Sheila took a chair.

"I won't beat around the bush," she said in a tone that suggested she rarely did. "This is a distasteful and uncomfortable situation all the way around." She paused. "I include our present conversation in that assessment."

I took a sip of coffee and nodded in acknowledgment. It wasn't every day that a defense attorney was welcomed into the home of the victim's family.

Sheila cleared her throat. "My primary concern at this point is Adrianna. She's a gregarious, levelheaded little girl, but all the turmoil of this past week has taken its toll."

"It must be terrible for both of you."

Sheila wasn't interested in sympathy. "And then with all the talk at school and in the community," she continued, "not to mention the murder being the spotlight of the news . . . well, it's been very difficult."

"I'm sure it has."

"It's bad enough that she's lost her mother. I hate to have her dragged through it time and again."

Having lost my own mother under unnatural circumstances,

I knew only too well the stiff silences and uncomfortable stares that followed me in the months after her death. I couldn't imagine that murder was any less a topic for speculation than suicide.

"There's Emily Barrett to consider as well," Sheila continued. She clutched her mug with both hands. "I don't think it's right that innocent children should suffer because of their parents' mistakes."

I nodded again, unsure where she was headed.

"I loved my sister, but I know she was no saint. Especially when it came to men. Deirdre went after the wrong ones every time. And it seemed like the harder she went after them, the worse they treated her."

"I'm not sure I follow your point."

The furrows between Sheila's dark brows deepened. "The strain of a trial is what I'm worried about," she said, looking at me sharply. "Adrianna would be called as a witness. Ms. Rivera, the attorney in the D.A.'s office, said there was no way around that. My niece is an important part of their case."

"That's right."

"Ms. Rivera also said you'd have the right to cross-examine Adrianna. That you'd try to make it look like she doesn't know what she's talking about."

"That's what a defense attorney does." Although I had no illusion that heavy-handed questioning of a child witness would endear me, or my client, to the jury.

"It would be very hard on her," Sheila said.

"I wouldn't take pleasure in it myself."

She set her coffee on the spindle-legged table next to the chair. "And, of course, with a trial there'd be more coverage in the news, more talk around town. It could go on for months." Another pause. "I'm thinking of Emily as well, you understand."

I wouldn't have bet on that. But I thought I was beginning to see what it was she wanted.

Sheila leaned forward. "Sometimes it's best to put what's done behind you and move on with the healing, don't you agree?"

"Depends on the circumstances."

She stood and walked to the window. "I think it's possible that Grady Barrett didn't intend to kill my sister. He's a big man. A strong man. They might have been talking, perhaps heatedly.

Deirdre may have said something that upset him, and he reacted without thinking. Impulsively."

Sheila paused, closing her eyes for a moment to compose herself. "Perhaps he pushed her in a moment of anger. Pushed harder than he imagined. The railing isn't very high. It would be easy to lose one's balance and go over the edge."

"An accident?"

"No, the police are convinced it's more than that." Sheila returned to her chair. She reached for her coffee and stared at it without sipping. "Perhaps he did more than push her. Maybe they struggled first. My point is, that doesn't make Grady Barrett a cold-blooded killer. More like a man who succumbed to the heat of the moment. A decent man who made a mistake."

She replaced her coffee on the table, untouched, and folded her hands in her lap. When she continued, the words came in a rush. "If he were to plead guilty to that, I'd personally petition for leniency on his behalf. He'd get a lighter sentence, be able to resume his old life at some point. And he'd save Nina and Emily the ordeal of a public trial."

Finally, we'd come to the reason for our meeting. "You're asking my client to plead guilty to a lesser charge rather than stand trial for murder?"

She nodded with the barest of movements.

"I should think you'd want to see Grady Barrett put away for life."

"Deirdre is dead. Nothing is going to change that."

I studied her face, which was flushed but composed. "You're not angry, then?" I asked, unable to keep my amazement from showing.

"Oh, I'm quite angry." Sheila's voice was sharp. She took a breath. "But I'm practical too. Sometimes a bit too practical."

"What do you mean?"

She sat back in her chair with her arms crossed and gave me a rueful look. "I've always been the rock of the family. The one who followed the rules. I went to college, studied library science, found a job, while Deirdre played. Whenever things got tough, I was the one she came to for help. In fact, she and Adrianna had been more or less living with me for the past year."

"I thought she was staying at a house in the hills."

"Well, yes. She took long-term house-sitting jobs whenever she could, but when she needed someplace to stay in between, she came here. Not that I minded. Deirdre's liveliness was a nice change of pace." Sheila paused, then added a bit wistfully, "I've often wished I had a bit more of it myself."

"My sister and I are very different too," I said. "I think we'd both have been better off if the genes had been mixed a little more evenly."

"So you know what I'm talking about. Deirdre could certainly have used some of my sensible nature. I encouraged her to go to school, get some job training, start saving for her future, but that didn't interest her."

"What did interest her?"

"Having fun." Sheila sighed. "When our father died, he left us each a small inheritance. I banked mine, eventually bought this house. I still have some saved for a rainy day. Deirdre went through her money in a year. Travel, clothes, a new car—you name it. I could never convince her she ought to think beyond the pleasures of the moment."

"Was her husband that way as well?"

Sheila shook her head. "Not at all. In fact, it was a point of contention between them."

"It must have been hard on her when he died."

Something I couldn't interpret flickered in Sheila's eyes. "Yes, very hard." She paused. "It's been hard on Adrianna too, although she was too young when he died to actually miss him."

I couldn't imagine what it would be like for a seven-year-old child to have lost both parents. "What will happen to Adrianna now?" I asked.

"I'm seeking permanent custody. Eventually I'll adopt her. There isn't anyone else in the family except my mother's brother, whom we haven't seen in years." Sheila brushed her bangs with the back of her hand. "Adrianna is comfortable with me. I've been a part of her life from the day she was born. Yet you wouldn't believe the red tape. You'd think they could use common sense and save their precious policies and procedures for cases that warrant it."

"Dealing with bureaucracies is always frustrating."

She nodded emphatically. "It's one more reason I'd like to see this matter settled without a trial."

There we were again, the hidden agenda brought to the fore.

"I'm not insensitive to your concerns," I said, setting my mug on the coffee table. "But I think Grady Barrett has a good chance of beating this. He would walk away a free man."

"If he doesn't, though, he could be in prison for the rest of his life."

"It's a gamble, I admit. But I don't think the prosecution has a strong case. They're hanging a lot on the testimony of a seven-year-old child."

Sheila reached for a pack of cigarettes and lit one. "There's other evidence as well."

I nodded. "Nothing that can't be explained away though."

Sheila exhaled a lungful of smoke and then waved a hand in the air to clear it. "I'm sorry, I didn't ask if you minded."

"It's your house, but to be honest, I'd prefer if you waited until I left."

"Deirdre was the same way." Sheila took another drag on the cigarette and then crushed it out. She fiddled with the ashtray for a moment, then looked at me. "I heard him threaten her," she said quietly.

"Grady?"

"He left a message on Deirdre's answering machine. Said that if she didn't withdraw the rape complaint, she'd live to regret it. *But not for long.* Those were his exact words."

A death threat. One that sounded as though it came straight out of Hollywood. The jury would love it. "Do you have the tape?" I asked.

She shook her head. "It was Deirdre's. I doubt she saved it."

"When was this?"

"A couple of days before she died."

About the time Grady had told me not to worry about the rape charges, that he had things under control. I felt uneasiness rising in my chest.

"You inferred earlier that you thought Grady was a decent man. That he'd given in to the heat of the moment. How could you think that after hearing the tape?"

Sheila took a breath. "I think he was probably scared. Decent isn't the same as perfect. And all I said was that it's *possible* he didn't mean to kill her."

I regarded Sheila Barlow for a moment in silence. She struck me as a straightforward woman. One who felt intensely about things that were dear to her and didn't let herself be sidetracked by irrelevant emotion. But to see her sister's killer get off with a minimal sentence . . . Would she really find that acceptable?

"You've told the police about the tape?" I asked.

Sheila nodded. "But I have yet to give a formal statement to Ms. Rivera. If the case goes to trial, I'll testify as to what I heard. If it doesn't . . ." She shrugged. "Then what I heard doesn't matter."

"I'll relay your concerns to my client," I told her.

And I'd definitely have to have another heart-to-heart with Grady.

CHAPTER 25

Monday brought rain, further dampening my already sodden spirits. Rain is fine in the winter, and even in the fall, but once the trees have begun to blossom and the scent of spring is in the air, I'm ready to be done with it.

The day also brought reams of paper, delivered in response to our request for discovery. I was now slowly working my way through it. Single sheets, stapled sheets, misaligned sheets—pages upon pages of unlabeled—and sometimes unreadable—photocopies. The prospect of fashioning some sort of order from the chaos did little to brighten my mood.

I made myself a cup of tea, added a hefty dose of artificial sweetener, and picked up the sheets listing Deirdre's phone records for the week leading up to her death. Grady's private number jumped out at me immediately. An eight-minute call early on the evening she was killed. Scanning the list, I noted that she'd called him two days earlier as well.

Deirdre's last call was to her sister at seven thirty-eight the evening of her death. They'd talked for less than four minutes. A quick question, or perhaps a simple reminder—the sort of everyday routine that passes without note. And now they would never talk again.

There was another call to the same number early the next morning. Adrianna's call to her aunt for help. It gave me a funny feeling to be tailing the course of personal tragedy through something as mundane as phone numbers.

I felt again a wash of sadness for a woman I'd barely known, and for her young daughter who would face the remainder of her life without a mother's love. Then I shook the ghosts from my mind and turned my attention once again to the phone log. Each number was followed by a name. Some had been annotated, the words "dentist" or "pharmacy" scrawled in the margin by someone in the D.A.'s office; others had not.

Aside from Grady and Sheila Barlow, the only name I recognized was Judith Powers, the friend from ComTech who'd invited Deirdre to the party where she'd first met Grady. It appeared, from phone records at any rate, that the two women were good friends. They'd talked several times during the week, including the afternoon of Deirdre's death. Pulling my memo pad from the drawer, I added Judith Powers to the list of people I wanted to speak with. I went through the remaining names and numbers another time, and wondered if it was worth the effort to have Hal check them. Probably, although I thought it unlikely we'd turn up anything.

Setting the phone list aside, I moved on to the photographs of the crime scene. I forced myself to look at the close-ups of the body, but it was the broader views of the site that I concentrated on, hoping to understand what might have happened the night of Deirdre's murder.

Nothing jumped out at me. The house looked pretty much as it had when I'd visited the crime scene myself, except that a few of the photos had caught the case detectives at work. I noted one particularly flattering image of Madelaine Rivera's friend, Steve Henshaw, and wondered if she'd pull a copy for herself. It was a petty thought and I gave myself a quick scolding.

There was nothing that struck me from the preliminary lab or toxicology reports either. Deirdre's body had shown no indication of alcohol or drugs. Analysis of her stomach contents revealed that she'd eaten dinner—a grilled cheese sandwich and salad—anywhere between two and four hours prior to her death.

I'd started separating the papers into piles—the first step of an organization plan—when I heard voices coming from the reception area.

A moment later Hal appeared, knocking and pushing open my door at the same time. He was dressed in his customary dark cords and blue denim shirt. And, as usual, he was eating.

"Am I interrupting?" he asked, offering me a Lifesaver from the pack in his hand.

"Nothing that doesn't beg for interruption anyway." I popped a lime Lifesaver into my mouth, leaned back in my chair, and gestured toward the mess on my desk. "The most recent round of discovery. I'm trying to organize it, and then I'll see about making sense of it."

He scratched his cheek, feigning puzzlement. "You mean it doesn't arrive in your office already tabbed and bound in those neat little folders?" It was an old joke arising from a particularly convoluted piece of litigation we'd worked on together at Goldman & Latham.

I tossed an eraser at him. "Did you come by to help or gloat?"

"Neither, actually. I came by to report. Marc around?"

"He's spending the day at ComTech. Damage control."

Hal ignored the soft-cushioned visitor's chair across the desk from me and instead pulled up the plastic one that sometimes served as coat rack and in-box, and when I was really desperate, coffee stand. He straddled it so that his arms rested across the back.

"You want the good news first or the bad?" he asked.

"Let's try the good."

"Tony Rodale rides a motorcycle."

I laughed. "Okay, tell me the punch line."

"That's it."

"Then tell me the joke."

"No joke. Neighbors saw the guy's car parked at his place the night Deirdre was killed, right? The cops, bless their pointy little heads, seem to take this as proof he couldn't have done the deed. But that car isn't Tony's only means of transportation. He owns a Kawasaki 750 as well. Rides it regularly."

I held up a hand. "Wait a minute. Are you suggesting he left his car in the driveway and rode the bike to Deirdre's, where he killed her?"

"I'm saying that's a possibility."

But not much on which to base a defense. "If that's your idea of good news, I'm not sure I want to hear the bad."

"The guy gives off ugly vibes, Kali. Sometimes you gotta trust your gut, or at least give it a little slack."

"Fine. But how the hell am I supposed to argue that to the jury?"

"I'm working on it. Got a few angles I want to explore." Hal took a pack of cinnamon chewing gum from his pocket. "You want some?"

Cinnamon and lime seemed like a lousy combination. I shook my head.

"Besides, there's more." He popped a stick of gum into his mouth. "Deirdre's not the only one to file charges against Tony. The guy was married once. His ex claims he hit her and kicked her on numerous occasions. Even knocked out a front tooth."

"You've talked to her?"

"Briefly. She says Tony has a temper, especially around women. And"—Hal paused for dramatic effect—"he wears a size ten shoe."

The same size the police had found at the crime scene.

"Okay," I said begrudgingly. "It's good, at least for now. I'd like to be able to make a case for Grady's innocence, but if we can't do that, this will certainly help." When you're trying to convince the jury that your guy didn't do it, it's best if you can put a face on the *real* killer.

Hal grinned. "You're welcome." He pinched the chewing gum wrapper into a tight little ball and tossed it into the wastebasket. "How's it going for our client?"

"Casewise, I don't know yet. We're just beginning to see what we've got. But for Grady himself, not so well. Last I talked to him he was understandably glum."

"Maybe this stuff about Rodale will cheer him up."

"I'm afraid it's going to take more than that." I rolled my pen between my palms. "You want to give me the bad news now?"

Hal rocked back, stretched his arms straight. "I wouldn't get my hopes up about this Xavier fellow if I were you. I managed to track down the mother of the girl he was seeing. A woman by the name of Bryant. Marsha Bryant." He allowed a flicker of a smile. "No relation to Anita."

"You asked?"

"I'm sure I wasn't the first. Anyway, she hasn't seen Xavier in a couple of months. Hasn't seen much of her daughter either, but that's another story. According to Marsha Bryant, Xavier isn't the most reliable sort of guy. In fact, I got the impression that on a scale of one to ten, he'd be down in the decimal range. Something like .02"

"She's not likely to be his staunchest defender."

"True." Hal rubbed the back of his neck. "I left my number, and yours as well. She said she'd pass them on to her daughter when she saw her."

"Then the daughter's not with Xavier?"

"She's at some private youth camp. The mother had her locked up for being incorrigible."

When Hal left, I went back to sorting the papers on my desk. The record of telephone calls was on top of one of the stacks I'd made. I picked it up and examined it again. Pressing my fingers to my temples, I focused on the day of her death. Four calls. Grady Barrett, Sheila Barlow, Judith Powers, and the mother of one of Adrianna's friends. I could imagine what Madelaine Rivera would do with that. The dutiful mother and loving sister on the last afternoon of her life. It made a heartrending picture.

Out of curiosity, I picked up the receiver and punched the number listed in the phone log as Grady's private line at ComTech. If he hadn't received Deirdre's call, maybe it was because the police had misidentified the number.

A male voice picked up after two rings, catching me off guard.

"Who's calling?" he asked.

"Marc?" I thought I recognized his voice, but in my amazement at having the phone answered, I wasn't sure. "It's me, Kali."

"Hey, surprise. I was just thinking about you."

"You were?"

A soft chuckle. "I think about you a lot lately. How'd you know to try this number?"

"I didn't. I mean, I didn't know you'd answer. I was going through the calls Deirdre Nichols made the day she was killed. We got a sizable package of discovery material from the D.A.'s office today, including phone records."

"Any bombshells?"

"Not that I've seen so far. How's the damage control going at ComTech?"

He gave a snort of disgust. "The offering is on hold. Technically anyway. In truth, it's dead. The investors are nervous, the employees are walking on eggshells, and the business press is having a field day. But the company hasn't managed to self-destruct yet, so that's something."

"I'm heading out to Santa Rita in a bit to see Grady. You want to come along?"

He hesitated, then said, "Sorry. I'd love your company, but I've got too much to do here. Tell Grady we're working to keep it together. I'll bring him up-to-date as soon as I can."

I heard a voice in the background. Marc turned away from the phone and said, "Tell him to hold, I'll be there in a sec." Then he was back to me. "You going to be at the office later?"

"Probably."

"I'll be by about six. I'll help you go through the stuff from the D.A. Maybe we can get takeout and make an evening of it."

"Wow, the good life." The funny thing was, I found myself looking forward to it.

CHAPTER 26

The drive to the county jail at Santa Rita, where Grady had been moved following his arraignment, took me past mile upon mile of business parks and housing developments—all of which had sprung up in what ten years ago had been open pasture. Whole towns created anew, almost overnight.

The jail, once located in the hinterlands of the county, now sat on prime real estate. Not that it helped the prisoners any.

The rain had stopped but the sky was still gray and dark, casting the afternoon in a somber light. Water puddled in the parking lot, and I stepped carefully to avoid getting my feet soaked.

I checked in, then made my way down the long, airless corridor through a succession of double doors. You'd think I'd be used to it by now. But I found the journey just as unnerving as I had on previous occasions.

At each junction, I slowed as I waited for the automatic doors to swing open, then felt my stomach clench as they shut tight behind me. The metallic click of the lock sliding into place echoed in my ears. Despite the cameras that were mounted overhead, monitoring my progress, I felt utterly alone, afraid that I'd never find my way out again. It was frightening to be so much at the mercy of a faceless monolith.

Finally, I reached the interview room, then waited while the guard brought Grady through the door on the other side of the glass partition. The room was warm, almost steamy, and smelled of an unpleasantly heavy aftershave, but I imagined the odors on Grady's side were far worse.

Grady entered with his eyes lowered and took a seat. His face showed signs of fatigue, and his shoulders slumped forward like an old man's. The orange jump suit made him appear both ridiculous and pathetic. I was sorry I hadn't thought to ask for a contact room where I might at least have been able to offer the assurance of a touch.

I picked up the telephone, which was our sole means of communication. It was an uncomfortable way to relate to another human being, especially one who appeared so obviously in need of solace.

"You managing okay?" I asked.

"As well as can be expected." Despite his shrunken appearance, Grady's voice was strong.

I relayed Marc's message about ComTech. Grady nodded noncommittally, but I noticed his grip on the phone intensified.

"How much longer until the hearing?" he asked.

"It's set for a week from Wednesday."

"Good."

I didn't want to mislead him. "That's only one step in a long process though. Nothing is going to be resolved until trial."

Grady sat up straighter, shook his head. When he spoke, his voice had the ring of authority. "I can't wait that long. I need this cleared up now."

What he needed was a reality check. "I'm afraid the judicial system isn't overly concerned with a defendant's *needs*."

He shot me a quick look of surprise. "It is when the case is pure crap. That's what the preliminary hearing is about, isn't it? To throw out the cases that should never have been brought to begin with."

"In theory. But practically speaking it's rare—"

"I don't give a shit about the way things usually go." Grady's voice was intense. "I want this settled next week at the hearing."

"You don't understand!"

He cut me off again. "It's *you* who doesn't understand. I want you to sock it to them hard, you got that? Show the prosecution their case stinks."

The sympathy I'd been feeling moments earlier was clouded by rising irritation. "That's not the best way to handle it."

"Says who?"

"Me."

His mouth was tight. "I'm paying the bills here."

"But I'm the attorney." I took a breath and tried to explain.

"The more we give them at the prelim, the easier it will be for the D.A. to put together a winning case at trial. They'll be able to see how we're thinking, and what our line of defense will be. We don't want to show our hand before we have to."

Grady leaned forward so that his face was almost touching the glass. His eyes were narrowed and his forehead shone with a film of perspiration. "I can't afford to wait," he said brusquely.

"You can't afford to jeopardize your best shot at a winning defense either."

"That's for me to decide."

"You hired me to give you the best defense I can."

He shook his head. "With all due respect, there's no way in hell you know what's best for me."

"But I do know the way the system works."

"I don't give a fuck about the system. Nina needs me. I've got to get out of here."

Nina. I reminded myself that I was doing this for her. The thought helped quell my rising irritation. "I won't deny that it would be easier on her if none of this had happened, but Nina is a strong woman. She'll manage."

"She's having my baby, dammit. I want to be there for the birth of my son. And think about Emily. How strong is she? How well will she manage?"

"Don't you think it's better that they get along without you for a year, even a rough year, than for decades?"

Grady licked his lips. He rocked back in his chair and locked his arms across his chest. "The company needs me as well. If I don't get this turned around soon, the press will destroy me. I won't let that happen."

"We're talking fifteen to twenty-five years, Grady. Maybe life. Your freedom is at stake here, not just the damn company."

He bent forward again, clasping his hands between his knees. "You think I don't realize that?"

I rubbed my forehead. "Look, I know you're used to calling the shots. But this isn't something you can make go away just because it's a nuisance in your schedule."

"You're not listening. If the company goes down the tubes, I'm on the street. Everything I own is in the business. I'm leveraged to the hilt." His voice thickened. "Think about Nina. She's already got the pregnancy and cancer to contend with. You want to add poverty to the list?"

In my view, poverty with a loving husband at your side was preferable to poverty with a husband in prison, which seemed to be something Grady was overlooking.

"Their case can't be very strong," Grady urged. "Mostly it's that little girl's story about seeing a convertible parked in front of the house."

"That's damaging, Grady."

He waved a hand as if dismissing the thought. "You know how kids get confused. You ought to be able to tear her testimony to pieces."

"You're forgetting the size-ten shoe print at the side of the house, the phone call to your office, your clothes that are conveniently missing." I took a breath, reminded myself that Grady was my client, not my adversary. "And now there's a new development."

"What is it?" An edge of wariness had crept into Grady's tone.

"I spoke with Deirdre Nichols' sister yesterday. She apparently heard the message you left on Deirdre's machine.

A vein in Grady's temple throbbed and his gaze flattened, but his expression remained neutral. "Which message was that?"

"The one where you threatened her."

The look in his eyes was suddenly charged. "I *what?*"

"Threaten. As in drop the case or 'you'll live to regret it but not for long.' "

"She says I left *that* message?"

"You didn't?"

Grady shook his head in disbelief. "You think I'd be stupid enough to put something like that on tape?"

Nothing about being stupid enough to make a threat in the first place, I noticed.

"Does she have the tape?"

I shook my head. "Says she doesn't anyway."

"There you go. The woman has obviously made up her mind that I'm guilty. She'll say anything to see me put away."

"You think she's lying?"

"Damn right. I *know* she's lying. Or maybe it was someone else who left the message. Ever think of that?"

I wondered, not for the first time, why righteous indignation and outright falsehood often sound so much alike. I wondered which I was hearing in Grady's voice.

"Could be a lot of things," Grady added. "Like I said, she probably has it in for me."

"Actually," I told him, "she offered to speak out for leniency if you'd plead to a lesser charge. She's worried about the effects of a trial on Adrianna and Emily."

Grady shook his head emphatically. "Not a chance. No way am I going to end up in prison for something I didn't do."

"That's more or less what I told her. But still, it's an option you ought to consider. Going to trial is a gamble. You may end up with your freedom, but you could just as easily end up behind bars."

"But I didn't kill anyone." His voice arced.

"At this point, whether you did or not isn't the issue. The issue is whether the jury *believes* you did."

"That's outrageous."

"It's also reality."

Grady's shoulders sagged, and for the first time, I saw fear in his eyes. "God knows I've done some stupid things in my life," he said. "And I admit that I messed up royally by sleeping with Deirdre. It happened before I even thought about it. But I love Nina. I love her with all my heart, and I did *not* kill Deirdre Nichols. I swear to you, I didn't." His gaze met mine. His voice was barely audible. "You do believe me, don't you?"

I looked through the glass at Grady, a man I'd never really warmed to. A man who at times made me uncomfortable. Yet there was something genuine in his expression at that moment. Though I hadn't expected to, I found myself nodding.

"Yes, I believe you. And so does Nina."

Grady closed his eyes. "Thank you," he said.

CHAPTER 27

On the way back to the office, I stopped off at Stoneridge Mall, which was, aptly, only a stone's throw from the freeway. It wasn't so much that I was in the mood to shop, but I wasn't eager to return to the stacks of paper waiting on my desk either. More than anything, though, I simply wanted to immerse myself in the ordinary, to wash away the gloom of jail that clung to my skin like an invisible web.

I wandered the mall, bought some purple eyeliner I didn't need, and a pair of green suede pumps I needed even less. As I was leaving, I relinquished all claim to sanity and bought a Mrs. Field's oatmeal and raisin cookie to nibble on the way home. Two hundred calories, nine grams of fat—and worth every one of them, I thought, until I remembered that Deirdre had been making a similar type of cookie the night she was killed. That simple reminder of life caught short added to the gloom.

By the time I arrived back at the office, Rose had left for the day. I made myself a cup of coffee, went through my messages and returned a few phone calls, then got down to work. It was almost dark outside, and the rain had begun again.

Marc showed up a little before seven, lugging a pizza box and six-pack of beer along with his briefcase. Three flights of stairs and he wasn't even breathing hard.

He shut the outer door with his foot. "No anchovies, right?"

"Right."

His grin brought a twinkle to his eye. "All these years and I still remember." He set the box down on my desk. "Half with, half without."

Just like countless evenings we'd spent together during law school. Memories rolled over me like a wave and caught me by surprise. I felt an unexpected flutter in my chest.

"How'd it go with Grady this afternoon?" he asked, uncapping a bottle before handing it to me.

"He wants a full court press at the prelim. Doesn't want to wait until the trial to make his case."

Marc nodded. "It's a long, hard wait when you're sitting behind bars."

I moved aside the stack of papers I was working on and spread a double thickness of napkin on my desk. Then I pried a wedge from the section of pizza without anchovies. Between bites, I filled him in on my conversation with Grady.

"I think maybe I'm beginning to believe he didn't do it," I said in conclusion. Or maybe I just *wanted* to believe. I was still having trouble sorting it all out.

Marc made a vague acknowledging gesture." I've been telling you all along that he didn't."

"Are things at ComTech really as shaky as Grady says?" I asked.

"You mean financially?"

I nodded, wiping my finger on a clean napkin.

"A company that's growing like ComTech has to invest huge amounts of money and resources. The payoff comes down the line, usually by taking it public. That's where they are now, at the break point. ComTech needs an infusion of capital from new investors to keep afloat."

"What will happen if they don't get it?"

Marc took a swallow of beer. "The venture capitalists will pull out—they're not about to throw good money after bad—and the company will fold."

"Sounds heartless."

He laughed. "People don't invest in a start-up company out of social conscience."

"If ComTech doesn't make it, what does that mean for Grady?"

"He's borrowed against everything he owns and poured it into the company. He stands to make a bundle if things go right, but he'll lose his shirt if they don't." Marc paused. "A lot of us stand to lose if the offering doesn't go through."

"You've invested in ComTech yourself?"

"Small potatoes really, but it's a lot to me." He rocked back in the chair, using the wastebasket as a footstool, and took another long swallow of beer. His fingers worked the label, peeling it away in strips. "Remember all those long discussions we used to have about money?"

"Vividly."

He smiled. "You were such an idealist."

"And you, on the other hand, thought the road to happiness was paved with dollar bills."

"I still do. But now it's not the money I care about so much as financial security. How about you? Didn't you ever find yourself distracted by dollar signs?"

I shrugged. My youthful ideals hadn't fared well against the realities of student loans and the cost of living in the Bay Area. After almost three years in the D.A.'s office, I'd jumped ship for private practice in one of San Francisco's fast-track firms. Six years later, when the firm dissolved, I'd found myself back at the starting gate. I'd played the game straight and by the rules, but I was a long way from financial security.

Marc regarded me thoughtfully. "You know what else I remember? Those nights we'd drink champagne in the Jacuzzi, by candlelight."

Again, that flutter in my chest. Glimmerings from the past that I'd worked hard to banish from my mind. "How come you're spending so much time on memory lane tonight?"

"They were good times. I miss them."

I about choked. *Miss them?* That was something like murdering your parents and then begging for mercy because you were an orphan.

"Don't forget," I said tersely. "It was you who brought those 'good times' to an abrupt close."

Marc's eyes met mine. His expression was unreadable. "I haven't forgotten." Then he rocked forward, sending his feet to the floor with an abrupt thud. "Guess we'd better get to work. Anywhere in particular you want me to start?"

I surveyed the numerous mounds of paper, now restacked on the credenza behind me. I picked one at random. "Take this. I haven't had a chance to go through it yet, but it should contain stuff from Madelaine relating to the crime scene. See if you can put it in some kind of order, then make a summary sheet."

As Marc returned to his own office, I was still trying to wipe the pizza sauce from my hands. I suspected that my office would smell like anchovies and grease for days to come.

An hour and a half later he was back. The disorderly pile of papers I'd given him was neatly fastened with a heavy black clip. "I thought you said Deirdre Nichols' date book was missing."

"It is. At any rate, it wasn't booked into evidence."

He tossed the bundle on my desk in disgust. "Sloppy police work. They took it, all right. They just never bothered to log it in. Who knows what else they've overlooked?"

"You mean it's here?"

"A photocopy."

"Did you have a chance to look at it?"

He nodded. "Skimmed it anyway."

I found the relevant pages and flipped through them. "Doesn't look like anything is missing."

"That was my take on it too."

I checked the pages of the calendar, and then names in the address book. Adrianna's school, dentists and doctors, a couple of restaurants, and a lot of names I didn't recognize. Tony's number was listed, as well as Grady's private line.

"Nothing there that jumps out at me," Marc said. "How about you?"

I shook my head.

"Scratch *that* defense scenario," he said. "Too bad, I kind of liked it." His voice took on an element of melodrama. "A woman with secret, high-profile connections. Or low-life connections if you prefer," he added parenthetically. "Killed for what, or whom, she knew."

I cut him short. "We'd have had trouble arguing that in court, however. Not without corroborating evidence."

"Nonetheless, it was a theory ripe with possibilities."

"Madelaine knew I'd asked about the date book." I placed the clipped bundle on my desk and frowned. "I wonder why she didn't say anything?"

Marc laughed. "She probably hasn't gotten around to looking at her own stuff. Besides, she's not going to help you any more than she has to."

"Maybe," I said, not altogether convinced. The rules of discovery require prosecuting attorneys to make case documents available to the defense, and in my experience they've generally been pretty good about it. But a prosecutor who wanted to play hardball could easily stall or forget to include a particular item.

"If Madelaine was trying to be difficult though," I added after a moment's reflection, "she would have withheld the date book until we asked for it rather than sending it along with the other discovery materials. Especially since it was never logged into evidence."

Marc shrugged. "Maybe she's simply disorganized." He checked his watch. "You up for some ice cream?"

Another ritual from our days together during law school. I wasn't sure how much of this *old times* stuff I could handle. "I still have work to do."

He leaned across the desk and touched my chin. "I'll go out and bring some back, how's that? You still into coffee ice cream with fudge sauce and whipped cream?"

Not for years. But suddenly it sounded wonderful. "Okay, you've talked me into it. Make sure you carry it right side up."

"I haven't made that mistake ever again." Marc traced a finger across my lips. "I won't be long."

I went back to my evidence chart, marking possible arguments next to each item I thought Madelaine would introduce. I was lost in thought, trying not to overlook any of the tiny, telling details that might make a world of difference, so the first brush of cool air registered only in the back of my mind. Then I felt a stronger draft and heard the stairway door click shut.

"That was fast," I called out. "What happened, did you forget your umbrella?"

There was a shuffling sound at the far end of the hallway, then nothing. No response, no footsteps.

"Marc? Is that you?"

Silence.

I felt a prickly sensation at the back of my neck. Through the open door of my office I could see into the firm's empty, but lighted, reception area. Beyond that was the dimly lit hallway leading to the stairs.

I stopped breathing and listened. Not a sound. Outside, the sky was dark. I could see my reflection in the rain-spattered glass. I'd just about decided my imagination was playing tricks on me, when the lights went off, plunging the office into darkness.

Fear shot through me like an electric current. For a moment I couldn't move. Then, with a swell of terror, reason returned. I groped blindly on my desk for the phone, knocking the cordless receiver to the floor with a deafening crash.

Footsteps now. Slow and hollow. I wasn't able to tell in which direction they were moving.

Trying to stay quiet, I got down on my hands and knees to look for the phone. My fingers skimmed the soft pile of the carpeting, finding loose paper clips and dust balls, a gluey glob that felt like pizza, and the dried-up remains of what I thought was probably a spider. But the phone was nowhere to be found.

I heard shuffling sounds coming from Marc's office, drawers being opened and shut.

Out of the corner of my eye, I caught a beam of light sliding across the floor of the outer office. It moved erratically for several minutes, and then more purposefully in the direction of my office.

My heart raced. Panic compressed my lungs. Like some beached sea creature, I crawled backward into the corner, my eye fixed on the sweep of light. With effort, I was able to squeeze between the end of the credenza and the wall. I knew I wasn't completely hidden. One pass with the flashlight and I'd be obvious as hell. But I didn't see that I had any options.

The figure was shadowy, but appeared to be male. The only things I could make out with certainty were a pair of heavy, thick-soled shoes and dark trouser legs. He moved into the office, pausing near my desk, so close I was certain he could hear my breathing. I pulled back like a snail in a shell, willed myself into paralysis.

Suddenly, from downstairs, the squeak of a door followed by a thud as it shut. Footsteps accompanied by cheerful whistling. And then, seeing the dark upper hallway, silence.

"Kali?" I recognized Marc's voice. "What happened? Did a fuse blow?"

The flashlight went dark. Quickly, the intruder moved toward the door, pressing himself flat against the inside wall.

"Kali? Are you there?" Marc's voice betrayed growing anxiety.

Watch out, Marc. Turn back. Call for help. My throat burned with the unspoken words.

A moment's hesitation, then Marc took a few tentative steps closer. "Kali?"

Blood pounded in my ears. My body was soaked in sweat. If I tried to warn Marc, I'd give myself away. But if I didn't, we'd both be trapped.

A cry rose up in my throat of its own accord. "Run!" I screamed. "Get out, get help. There's someone here."

In an instant, the flashlight was on again. It swung in my direction and caught me in the eye, blinding me.

The figure started toward me, and I felt myself freeze, like an animal caught in the path of an oncoming car.

And then his foot found the phone I'd dropped. He tripped, and the light tumbled to the floor.

With a surge of adrenaline I jumped to my feet and ran for the doorway, flying headlong through the dark. I struck my shoulder against the doorjamb and nicked my shin on a table in the reception area.

Using the hallway wall as a guide, I bolted for the stairway at the other end.

And then bumped headlong into another human. Frantic, I screamed and punched and scratched with everything I had.

"Holy shit, Kali. It's me, Marc."

Behind us, footsteps. And then the flashlight beam caught us dimly in its sweep. A gunshot exploded, and then another.

Marc grabbed my hand and we charged down the stairs with the intruder in hot pursuit. When we reached the ground floor, I started for the door.

"It's locked," Marc reminded me in a whisper. "We have to go out through the garage."

I nodded numbly.

"We'll take the stairs to the garage," Marc bellowed, and then pulled me into the men's rest room just as the rapid-fire footsteps behind us reached the landing.

We flattened ourselves against the wall, our breathing labored. I could feel the pounding of Marc's heart through his shirt. I held my breath until I heard the clatter of feet heading down the metal stairs toward the garage.

"He'll find out we're not there and come looking for us," I said.

"Who is it?"

I shook my head. "A man, that's all I could tell. He came in right after you left."

"Just one?"

"I think so."

The echo of footsteps again, up the stairs this time.

"Shit," Marc said.

"I told you we wouldn't fool him."

The steps were slower now. The man was moving methodically, testing doors along the ground floor hallway. It was only a matter of time until he found us.

I looked around the rest room for something to use as a weapon. Even a broom or a mop would have been welcome. There was nothing but an overflowing trash can.

"Shit," Marc said again before heading for the farthest of the two stalls.

I wondered for a moment if he meant it literally.

"It might work," he mumbled, tugging at the heavy trash can. "Help me get this in front of the door."

"It's not going to hold him for long."

"Long enough, I hope."

When we'd set the can against the door, Marc dragged me to the last stall and gestured to the small window above. Even for him, it was a stretch to reach the window frame.

"I'll boost you up," he said.

"It's a long drop to the ground on the other side."

"You got another idea?"

I swallowed hard. I wasn't sure I could pull myself to the window, even with Marc's help, let alone fit through it.

There was movement in the hallway just outside the rest room door.

"It's stuck," Marc said, frantically trying to raise the window. "It won't open. Give me your sweater." He wrapped my black cardigan around his hand. "Stand back."

Several sharp blows, and the glass shattered. Marc punched at the remaining jagged fragments, knocking them loose. Then he bent over and clasped his hands, making a foothold.

"Come on. Give me your leg. I'll help you up. When you hit the ground, take off running. Don't wait for me."

Tiny shards of glass still protruded from the edges of the window frame. Not a lot of it, but enough to do damage. I could feel myself shrink in protest.

And then the door to the rest room rattled as someone pushed against it from the outside.

I stepped into Marc's cupped hands and scrambled to reach the window. He pushed at my backside, stuffing me through like a down bag into its sack. I twisted around and dropped into the alley at the side of the building, landing awkwardly. My left foot hit first and my ankle gave, sending a shock of pain up my leg. I wasn't sure I could have run even if I'd wanted to.

But I wasn't about to abandon Marc. I looked around for help. The area was deserted.

Hobbling out to the street, I waved at a passing car. The driver swung wide and drove past without slowing. A spray of cold, oil-slick water struck me in the face.

Another gunshot rang out from inside the building. My heart rose into my throat. *No, please. Not Marc.* I felt as though I were going to be sick. Another shot, and then Marc's brown leather loafer slid through the open window, followed by his leg. He hauled the other leg through and hurtled himself to the ground beside me.

CHAPTER 28

Marc's bathroom mirror was tiny, so I caught only a glimpse of his bowed head as he picked slivers of glass from my back. I hugged the towel to my chest and tried to think of something pleasant.

It didn't work.

"Ouch!" I yelped. "That hurts."

"I'm trying to be careful."

"Well, try harder."

"Maybe I should take you to a doctor."

I shook my head. "At this time of night we'd have to go to the emergency room, and you know what that means."

"Yeah," he quipped. "It means you'd get medical attention."

"Only after hours of paperwork and waiting. I'm not in mortal danger, just pain."

"Maybe you need more scotch."

"I haven't finished what I have yet."

"Drink up. It will help."

I took another sip, on doctor's orders. The scotch was smooth as silk. And it *was* helping—just not enough. I'd finally stopped shaking, but my ankle throbbed, my back and legs were scraped raw, and my insides felt like Jell-O.

"You really didn't get a look at him?" Marc asked for probably the tenth time.

"Only as a shadow in the dark."

Marc hadn't been able to give the police much of a description either. Medium height, medium build, dark hair and complexion. He'd been concentrating on getting away from the guy, he said, not committing his features to memory.

"The only thing clear in *my* mind," Marc muttered, "is the gun. I couldn't focus on anything else."

It had gone off during their struggle, but miraculously, Marc had managed to escape unscathed. "If you hadn't momentarily knocked the wind out of him . . ." I swallowed the sour taste that accompanied the thought. "I can't bear to think what might have happened."

"Yeah. That makes two of us." Marc worked another sliver loose. "You think the cops will find any prints?"

"I have a sinking feeling the guy was too smart for that."

"I wish I knew what he was after," Marc said, also for the tenth time.

I nodded in agreement. We'd called the police from a pay phone several blocks away, then hung around only long enough to give a statement and walk them through the office. If there was anything missing, it wasn't obvious. But we hadn't taken time to go through all the files yet.

"It almost has to be connected to Grady," I said, thinking out loud.

"But how? There's nothing significant in those files. And nothing we can't replace."

"Maybe the guy thought we had something we didn't," I suggested.

"Like what?"

"You think I know?" I reached for my glass of scotch, then gave another yelp.

"Hold still."

"I thought you wanted me to drink this stuff." I took a double gulp, then held my breath while he worked on another sliver.

Marc worked in silence for a few minutes.

"All done, I think." Marc took a ball of cotton and dabbed at my back with antiseptic. I shivered as the cold liquid touched my skin.

He leaned closer and kissed my shoulder lightly.

"What are you doing?"

"What's it feel like I'm doing?" The words were mumbled somewhere in the vicinity of my left ear and were punctuated with more kisses.

I shivered again, but not with the cold.

Marc slipped his hands around my middle, then up under the

towel to my breasts. His fingers were as soft and warm as his touch.

"I'm sore, Marc."

"This will help. Better even than scotch." Easing my body against his chest, he cradled me in his arms. His lips brushed my neck and shoulders.

He was right, I could feel the pain receding.

"Tell me if I hurt you, okay?" His hand slid across my abdomen, dipped into the waist of my jeans.

I heard a voice in my head warning me to be careful. Do you know what you're doing? she called. Are you sure it's what you really want?

But I wasn't listening. Cocooned against time, I no longer cared about the past or the future, about who or what had come before. I wanted to be held. I wanted to feel the warmth and comfort of another body. And I was surprised to realize how much I wanted that body to be Marc's.

We wound up in bed, although I'm not entirely sure how we got there. I remember Marc peeling back the covers, and finding myself smiling inwardly because he's the only man I've even known to make his bed on a daily basis.

I remember him running a finger along the nape of my neck and feeling pleasure all the way down my spine. The warmth of his breath near my ear, the feathery softness of his tongue on my skin. The sound of my name on his lips.

And then only the rising swells of sexual longing that blotted out the pain. No footsteps echoing in my mind, no tightly wound fear in my chest, no awareness of the red-hot fire across my back.

Afterward, I rolled onto my side and nestled against Marc's shoulder.

With a satisfied sigh he traced a finger along the inside of my arm. "Just like old times," he murmured.

I pulled his hand to my cheek. "I hope not."

He laughed. "Right, me too. How's the ankle?"

I kissed his shoulder contentedly. "What ankle?"

Another soft laugh, and then he was quiet. I thought maybe he'd drifted off to sleep until he propped himself up on an elbow. "Kali?"

"What?"

His gaze shifted to the window, where the treetops were illuminated by white moonlight. I saw a tremor pass through the muscle in his cheek. Then he picked up my hand and kissed my fingertips.

"I'm glad you're here tonight," he said finally.

"Me too."

I awoke the next morning feeling as though I'd been run through a meat grinder. My back was stiff and sore, my arm ached, and my ankle throbbed. Every movement caused my skin to pull and sting.

Marc was still sleeping soundly when I hobbled out of bed and into the bathroom. My face had escaped unscathed, and what I could see of my back didn't look nearly as bad as it felt. But my hair was a mess and the remnants of yesterday's mascara had left black smudges under my eyes. I wanted a shower—in my own bathroom. And I needed to brush my teeth and change into clean clothes.

I splashed water on my face and did the old toothpaste-on-the-finger routine for my teeth. I pulled on my pants, borrowed a T-shirt of Marc's, and rattled around the bedroom in the hope that he might wake up. We'd taken his car home last night, leaving mine at the office, so I was at the mercy of someone else's wheels.

Asleep, sprawled at a diagonal across the bed, Marc had an appealing boyishness that wasn't part of his waking demeanor. His skin seemed smoother, his expression more relaxed. The faintest hint of a smile pulled at the corners of his mouth. I felt a tingle of pleasure as I remembered the sensation of his lips on my skin.

Last night had been good. And it had seemed right at the time. But my feelings for Marc were confused, and in the cold light of morning I wondered if I'd just taken the first step down a very slippery slope.

But I wasn't ready yet to think about what it meant—or what it was I actually wanted.

For the moment, what I wanted was coffee. Marc's kitchen was equipped with all the latest gadgets money could buy. The cappuccino maker caught my eye, but since it had enough knobs and buttons to launch a missile, I was afraid to touch it. I settled for the kettle and a filter cone, and more noise. When Marc still showed no signs of waking, I called a cab.

As I sipped my coffee, I tried to think of some witty, sophisticated message to leave him. Something with just the right tone to let him know that it had been nice, but I wasn't about to let him break my heart a second time. A souped-up version of, "Hey, it was fun but no big deal."

I found a piece of paper and a pen, then stared at the blank page. The right words eluded me. Finally, I scribbled a note saying I'd taken a cab home and would see him later at the office. As I finished, I happened to glance at the pen I was using. Purple with pink lettering. The words RAPUNZEL, A FULL-SERVICE HAIR SALON were stamped along the side.

What was Marc doing with a promotional pen from the salon where Deirdre Nichols worked?

The question, which began with a flicker of idle curiosity, gained momentum the longer I thought about it. Most local salons offered cuts for both men and women, so it might well be happenstance. But it felt funny, like a grain of sand inside your sock.

I finished the note, and my coffee, then gathered my stuff and headed for the door. I got as far as the security chain, then went back into the bedroom and shook Marc awake.

He grimaced. "Do they have the names yet?" he mumbled, his voice thick with sleep.

"Wake up."

I shook him again and he turned with a start. "Huh?"

"Marc, it's morning."

He extracted his arm from under the covers and pulled me closer. "You leaving already?"

"It's almost eight. I want a shower and some clean clothes."

He mumbled something about a car.

"I already called a cab. We should probably call Rose too, and warn her that the office is a mess."

"I'll do it." He reached for my hand and kissed my fingers. "How do you feel this morning?"

"Sore, and still a little shaky." I sat on the edge of the bed, close enough to feel the warmth of his body. "Marc, where do you get your hair cut?"

He propped himself up on an elbow, touched the top of his head. "My hair? Does it look that bad?"

"It looks fine. I was just curious."

"A place near the gym. Why?"

"Not Rapunzel?"

He laughed. "With a name like that? Hardly."

"I found this by your phone." I held up the pen, feeling again the vertigo of uncertainty. "It's from the salon where Deirdre Nichols worked."

There was a slight change in Marc's expression. A tightening of the jaw maybe, or something through the eyes. I couldn't tell for sure what it was or what it meant.

"How'd it wind up here?" I asked.

He shrugged. "I don't know. I must have picked it up somewhere."

"But where?" An impatient tone had crept into my voice.

"Who can tell? You know how it is with pens."

"It's odd though. Where would—"

Marc pulled himself fully upright. "Can't we talk about this later? I'll give it some thought, but right now I need to use the bathroom."

The blast of a car horn sounded out front.

"There's my cab. I'll see you later at the office." I stood and started to leave.

"No kiss?" he asked.

I blew him one from the doorway.

I'd hoped to sneak into my house unnoticed, but Dotty was out front watering the roses when the cab pulled up.

"What happened to your car?" she asked over her shoulder. Then she saw me hobbling up the path. "More important, what happened to you? Are you okay?"

"I'll be fine, but it may take a couple of days."

She turned off the water and rushed to assist me. "Was it an auto accident? Were you in the hospital?" She looped a hand under my elbow as though I were feeble. "Oh, dear. And here we thought you'd spent the night with Marc."

"I did."

"Don't tell me *he* did this to you?"

I shook my head, then I explained about the intruder and our escape through the bathroom window.

When I'd finished, Dotty clasped her hands over her heart. "Marc saved your life, then?"

Or maybe I saved his, I added silently

She sighed. "How romantic."

* * *

A long, hot shower, fresh clothes, and a second cup of coffee worked wonders. And with my physical discomforts addressed, I was eager to deal with the uncertainties that awaited me at the office.

Marc was already at his desk when I arrived. "Someone was definitely here," he said, looking up from the files he was busily sorting.

"No shit, Sherlock. We met him."

He gave me a pained look. "That was meant more as a conversational greeting than deep analysis."

"Is anything missing?"

Marc rose and pulled me close for a kiss. "That's better." He brushed the hair away from my face. "You're not having regrets, are you?"

"No regrets." That much was true. I didn't tell him it was the *what next?* that troubled me.

"Good. Me either." His hands rested on the small of my back. "You were in such a hurry to get out of there this morning, I wondered."

"Just anxious about getting to the office."

Marc looked around. "It gives me the creeps to think of some guy prowling around in here."

I nodded. "I sure wish I knew what it was all about. Did he take anything?"

"Not that I've been able to determine so far. But it's clear he went through things. You want some help checking your office?"

I shook my head. "I think it will be easier to check everything myself. One of us should call Nina though." I hated to add to her burden, but I thought she needed to know.

"I'll take care of it. And Rose can check the inactive files against the master log sheet to see if any of them are missing."

"Good idea." I bit my lip, remembering the terror I'd felt last night. Searching for missing files might have been therapeutic, but I wasn't sure anything could erase the memory.

Generally, I try to limit myself to two cups of coffee a day, but I thought this was an ideal day for making an exception. I poured a cup from the carafe in the small conference room, then set to work.

The files in my office seemed untouched. As far as I could tell, the intruder hadn't even opened the desk drawer. I was less sure about the papers on my desk, but I couldn't say for certain that anything was missing.

As I was going through the Barrett file, I remembered the pages from Deirdre Nichols' date book. I picked up the phone and called Madelaine.

"Remember my asking you about Deirdre Nichols' Day-Timer?" I asked.

"Vaguely. You wanted to know if it had been logged into evidence."

"Right, and it hadn't."

She chuckled. "So you're going to try to build your defense around the missing Day-Timer, huh?"

"That would be hard to do. It was in the stack of discovery materials we got from you the other day."

Madelaine hesitated. "Are you kidding?"

"You didn't know?"

"I haven't had time to go through things in much detail yet." She paused. "I honestly didn't know it was there. I'm not playing games with you, Kali."

"No?" In this instance I didn't actually think she was, but only because I couldn't imagine what advantage it would have given her.

"The guys in Evidence aren't always as careful as they should be," she explained. "Sometimes things get collected but not noted. Or they get lumped into some generic category, like 'contents of kitchen drawer.' "

I rubbed my thumb against the smooth plastic of my pen. "Maybe you ought to find time to go through everything and let me know if there are any other surprises. It won't look good if it comes out at trial that the D.A.'s office isn't being straight with the defense."

"And you'd be just the one to make an issue of it, wouldn't you?" There was an unexpected sharpness to her tone.

"Hey, I was just—"

"I know, I know." She gave a disgruntled sigh. "We've each got a job to do."

"What's the matter? You sound ticked about something."

"Sorry, it's not you. Guess I was taking the message out on the messenger."

"The no-longer-missing date book?"

Another sigh. "My job would be a whole lot easier if the cops would simply follow procedure."

CHAPTER 29

I'd just hung up the phone from talking to Madelaine, when Hal poked his head into the office. "Got a minute for me?"

"Always. In fact, I was going to give you a call."

He took a seat, sprawling diagonally with a leg draped over the arm of the chair, foot dangling. His brown loafers were scuffed, and the stitching was so loose at the toe, I thought he might have trouble walking.

"What's up?" Hal asked.

I told him about the break-in last night, and our narrow escape.

"Jesus. What do the police think?"

"Not much so far." Unfortunately, break-ins, burglaries, even gunshots weren't uncommon in the area. Oakland had more than enough crime to keep the cops busy.

Hal scratched his cheek. "You think it's tied in somehow with this murder case?"

"I don't know. It's got me worried though. And frightened."

He nodded. "Getting shot at is no fun."

More than the shots even, it was the stark terror of hearing the intruder approach and finding myself cornered. My skin felt clammy at the memory.

"The guy waited until Marc left," Hal added after a moment's thought. "He probably didn't know you were in the building. It might be something Marc's working on that got his interest."

"I thought about that too." Especially after I'd discovered the pen from Rapunzel by Marc's phone. I couldn't help wonder if there was a connection between Marc and the case that I wasn't aware of. "Anyway, you dropped by to see me. What's up?"

Hal frowned. "I don't suppose you've heard from Xavier?"

I shook my head.

"Me neither." He tapped his fingers on his knee. "I've been doing some more digging on Deirdre Nichols though."

"And?"

"And nothing. A big, fat zippo. No disputes, no jealousies, no one who's going to profit from her death." Hal pulled a bag of M&Ms from his pocket, offered me some, and then popped a fistful into his mouth. "I checked into the other thing as well."

"What other thing?" It seemed to me I'd mentioned more than one avenue that warranted further investigation.

"Contractors, workmen, service people ... Nothing there either." Hal was referring to our persistent quest for another possible killer. "Of course, I haven't been able to reach the owners to double-check with them. When the Carsons travel, they apparently want to leave the cares of home far behind. No one seems to know how to reach them."

"That doesn't give us much to work with, does it?"

Hal picked out a single yellow M&M and bit it in half. "You ask me, I think Tony Rodale looks pretty good for the role. The guy's got a history of abusing women, including Deirdre. And the fact that a neighbor saw his car at home doesn't mean squat. Rodale owns a motorcycle as well as a Lexus. What's more, I have a witness who heard a cycle near Deirdre's place the night she was killed."

As well as every other night of the week, I was willing to bet. "You're forgetting that Adrianna saw a silver convertible."

"She thinks." Hal tugged on an earlobe. "Besides, you have any idea how many silver convertibles there are in the Bay Area? It's not exactly an exclusive club."

"The same can be said for motorcycles."

Hal smiled and popped another candy. "Our friend Tony called Deirdre Nichols at work the day she was killed. A short conversation, according to one of Deirdre's coworkers, but tense. And no one heard her say a word about Gabrielle or any other woman he might be taking on a trip. He wasn't being straight with us."

"Okay, so it's got possibilities."

Hal swung his leg to the floor and leaned forward. "Something else you might find interesting. There's a lot of rumors floating around about Tony."

"Rumors? What kind of rumors?"

"Shady friends, shady deals. Speculation that maybe he's into something besides apple pie and legitimate business."

"Such as?"

"Could be any number of things." Hal pressed his hands together, knuckles against palm. "I'm working on it."

"The more we can dredge up, the better," I told him. "As far as I can tell, the police wrote Rodale off as a suspect early on. We might be able to argue that they conducted a half-baked investigation, pinned the thing on Grady because it was easy."

Hal sucked on his cheek. "Or that they did it intentionally."

I looked at him. "What do you mean?"

"I'm not sure. But I get the feeling there's some connection between Rodale and a couple of the guys on the force."

That was a surprise. "Do you have anything to back it up?"

"Not yet."

Just then Marc dropped by with some files. He nodded in Hal's direction with only a trace of friendliness.

"Guess I'll be going," Hal said, standing. "Talk to you later, Kali." His eyes held a glint of amusement. "You too, Marc."

"What did he want?" Marc asked when we were alone.

"Just bringing me up-to-date."

"Anything new?"

I relayed the highlights of our conversation.

Marc shook his head in disbelief. "What's with this guy that he's harping on Rodale? Does he have an overactive imagination or something?"

"He's looking for whatever angle he can find."

"Yeah? Well, he's squandering valuable time and money if you ask me."

I shook my head. "I agree that it probably won't pan out, but if we're going to give Grady his best shot at a winning defense, we're going to need something different. Something a little bit flashy."

"We can't simply concoct a story out of thin air." Marc's voice rose with agitation. "It will backfire. We'll end up making ourselves look desperate."

"Calm down, nobody's—"

"Calm down? You seem to be giving an awful lot of credence to some hippie P.I. with a *hunch*. Maybe Hal's got eyes for Tony or something."

"Marc, you're being—"

He held up a hand. "I know, Hal's a friend of yours."

"Even if he weren't, you're being a jerk about this."

Marc drew in a breath, raked a hand through his hair. Finally, he gave me a quirky smile. "I am, aren't I? Sorry. I guess I'm a little on edge."

"More than a little."

"Okay, a lot on edge." He stood behind my chair. Pulling my hair up into a loose ponytail, he kissed my neck. "I don't want to fight with you, Kali. Especially after last night."

I sighed. "We're both on edge, I guess."

"With reason." Marc sat on the edge of my desk, facing me. He cocked his head. "I want to go about this right, so tell me, did you stay last night because you were scared or because you wanted to?"

"Probably a little of both."

"And what are you feeling now?"

I gave a noncommittal shake of my head. "Confused maybe."

"About me?"

I smiled. "About you, yes. But about me too. And what I'm letting myself in for. I wasn't being truthful when I told you the other night that what happened in law school didn't leave scars."

He touched my cheek. "I know that. But it's not going to happen again."

Maybe, I thought. But there are lots of ways to be hurt.

I'd set up an appointment that afternoon with Judith Powers, Deirdre's friend at ComTech. As I was leaving the office, I ran into Byron Spencer on the street in front of the building.

"Hey, I was just coming to see you," he said, pulling a business card from the pocket of his leather jacket. "I've been trying to reach you."

I took the card and nodded. I'd returned his call Friday morning, only to miss it again that afternoon. "I'm on my way out though."

"I can see." He fell into step beside me. "I heard about the break-in at your office."

I did a double take. "How'd you know about that?"

"I keep my eye on the crime report." He grinned. "Always looking for a good story. Anything taken?"

"You think I'd tell you if there was?"

Another gap-toothed grin. "I'm not the enemy, you know."

"There's a lot of territory between friend and enemy."

"Guess that means you don't consider me a friend either."

There was a goofy, guileless quality about Byron Spencer that made it hard to dislike him, but that was a long way from friend. "Maybe you should be talking to Marc," I said. "I thought you and he were tight."

"Sometimes. Depends on his mood."

I'd reached my car, and the end of my interest in pleasantry. "What is it you want?"

"Barter."

"Barter?"

"A deal. Quid pro quo. I help you with the Grady Barrett trial, in return for which you give me an exclusive."

"And just what do you propose to do by way of *help?*"

He shrugged. "I don't know yet. But would you be interested if I found a way?"

I laughed. It was hard to remain stern with someone who reminded me of a St. Bernard puppy. "You bring me something useful and then we'll talk."

CHAPTER 30

ComTech occupied the first floor of a four-story building in the Harbor Bay section of Alameda, an area replete with well-kept office and industrial parks. Immediately inside was a reception area, and beyond that a maze of modestly appointed cubicles.

The woman at the reception desk found my name on the visitor's list, handed me a temporary badge, and pointed me in the right direction. There was little activity that I could see, and I wondered if this was normal or the fallout of Grady's arrest and the company's financial instability.

Judith Powers was seated at her desk in front of a large-screen computer. She looked up when I entered the partitioned space that served as her office.

"The receptionist told me to come through," I told her, and then introduced myself. "I'm a bit early. I don't mind waiting."

"That's okay. Have a seat. I'm just about finished here."

Belying her name, Judith Powers was petite, probably not over five feet, with smooth, creamy skin and eyes the color of spring moss. She punched the keyboard a few times, and I heard the computer kick into processing phase.

She turned to face me. "You wanted to talk about Deirdre Nichols, right?"

I nodded. "You were one of the last people she talked to before she was killed."

"I know, the police told me. It kind of gives me the creeps to think about it." Judith pushed back her chair. "You want a soda or something? We can talk in the lounge."

"Sure, that sounds good."

She led me past the receptionist again and down a long hallway to a room with vending machines, a microwave, and half a dozen mismatched sofas and chairs. Sliding glass doors opened onto a small patio, where an acne-faced young man sat with his nose buried in a book. We had the inside to ourselves.

"My treat," I said, pulling change from my purse.

"Thanks."

We both opted for Diet Dr Pepper.

When we'd settled in, I asked, "Do you remember what you and Deirdre talked about the night she died?"

"The usual *what's-new, not-much*. We made plans to go out for a drink the next evening. It was a very brief conversation."

"Deirdre called you?"

"That's right."

"Did she mention Grady Barrett at all? Or the lawsuit?"

Judith shook her head. "I tried real hard to stay away from all that. It was awkward—my working here at ComTech, and Deirdre claiming Grady Barrett had raped her. She's my friend; he's my boss."

"I can see how that might be awkward."

"Awkward doesn't begin to cover it." Judith paused. "It's even worse," she added, "because I was the one who invited her to the party where she met Grady. So in some sense, I guess, I set the whole thing in motion."

"You're not blaming yourself, are you?"

"It's one of those things you can't help think about." She took a sip of soda, tucked a leg up under her body. "Of course, maybe if Marc had stuck around, things would have been different too."

"Marc?"

"Griffin." Judith cocked her head. "You work with him, don't you?"

I nodded. "It's just that I didn't know he was at the party that night." Since he spent a good deal of time at ComTech, it wasn't surprising that he'd have been included.

"He wasn't there for long. But Deirdre had her eye on him."

That I found more surprising. But maybe it explained how he'd wound up with a pen from Rapunzel. "They talked?" I asked.

Judith shook her head. "He left before she managed that. I got the impression she knew him."

"Knew him how?"

"I don't know. Maybe she'd just seen him before."

An enormous orange cat meandered through the patio doors and leapt up on the sofa next to Judith. "Hello, Alley," she said, stroking his fur. "No food today, I'm afraid. Only soda." She turned to me. "Alley's a stray we've kind of adopted here at ComTech."

"Looks like he eats well." He was, in fact, one of the largest cats I'd seen.

"He eats a lot anyway. None of it's probably very good for him."

I turned the conversation back to the reason for my visit. "Do you think Deirdre was telling the truth about the rape?" I asked.

"I don't know. Honestly. And I guess I don't really *want* to know either."

"How about the murder charge against Grady Barrett?"

Her green eyes darkened. "I suppose anything is possible."

It wasn't the ringing endorsement of innocence I'd been hoping for. "How do you get along with Grady?" I asked.

"I don't have much to do with him directly, but he's always been nice to me. Most people here feel the same way. We're all kind of in a state of shock right now."

"You'd say he's a decent man to work for?"

She nodded. "He's fair and honest and willing to listen. That's true whether you're going to see him about a complaint or some far-out new idea."

But he was still used to calling the shots, I reminded myself. And Deirdre Nichols' rape charge had changed that.

Setting my soda on the Formica tabletop, I asked, "How long had you known Deirdre?"

"A little over a year. We met in exercise class. We're actually quite different, but we got along well and we enjoyed a lot of the same things."

"Like what?"

Judith smiled, looking slightly abashed. "Parties, meeting new people." She stroked the top of Alley's rust-colored head. "But I'm serious about my job too, and about building a career. Deirdre didn't like to think too far beyond the moment, and she had no sense of money at all. She went through it like it was tissue."

The same thing Sheila had said. "What did she spend it on?"

"You name it. Clothes, restaurants, doodads. Her credit cards were always maxed out." Judith shook her head in disbelief. "I'm careful with money, always looking for a bargain. I put as much as the law allows in my 401(k). I deposit a regular amount into savings each month as well. But some people don't have that kind of control."

"Maybe they don't have the money to do that either."

She ran a finger along the seam of her soda can. "Deirdre's salary wasn't much, but she could have found a better job. Or gone back to school to get her degree. Her sister offered to help out."

"Why didn't she?"

Judith shrugged. "Deirdre wasn't one to look at the big picture. Although you'd think she'd have learned after being burned once before."

Alley stretched, then left Judith's side and joined me. I shifted position to make room for him, and he curled up with his back against my legs. "What do you mean about being burned once before?"

"Deirdre had to declare bankruptcy after her husband died."

I hadn't known that.

"Although she never told me so directly, I got the feeling that's maybe why he killed himself. Because of all the debts."

I hadn't known this either. "Her husband committed suicide?"

"Shot himself. Deirdre didn't talk about it a lot. I don't blame her. It must be a pretty painful memory to carry around all the time."

It was. I knew that from personal experience. "Do you think Deirdre was close to bankruptcy again?"

"I couldn't say for sure. It seemed she usually managed to bail herself out just when things were looking really bad. Money couldn't have been too tight, though, because she was planning a trip to Florida."

"When?"

"I don't know. Soon. She happened to mention it in passing a few days before she died."

"Why Florida? Was she going alone?"

Judith held up a hand to stop the questions. "I don't know any more than that. But I think she was going to take Adrianna, because she mentioned Disney World."

A trip to Florida. It wasn't such an odd thing in itself, but a bit surprising for someone who had trouble making ends meet.

I ran a hand along the cat's smooth fur. "Was there anything else unusual that came up the last few times the two of you talked? Disputes at work, or with neighbors, maybe? Any new men she'd been seeing?"

"Nothing that I can recall. The police asked me the same question."

That was too bad. It would make it harder to argue that the police had latched on to Grady without conducting a real investigation.

Judith leaned back, held her soda with both hands. "I wish I knew something that could help Grady. In my heart, I can't believe he really killed Deirdre. But I don't know who else might have either."

"How about Tony Rodale? Do you know him?"

"The guy Deirdre was seeing? I never met him, but I heard her talk about him. He's apparently one of those men who's into control—big time. He wanted her to be what he wanted her to be. Didn't like it when she showed any signs of being her own person at all."

"That didn't bother her?"

Judith laughed. "Oh, it bothered her all right. That's why she talked about him so much. But she liked the things he could give her too. He travels a lot, and he'd take her along. Seems like he was always buying her stuff. Deirdre was pulling back though. She'd just about decided to dump him. Said the fun wasn't worth the price."

Interesting, that wasn't the story Tony Rodale had told us. "Getting ready to dump him, or had dumped him?" I asked.

"She never said she'd done it." Judith paused. "But come to think of it, she did say she was ready to celebrate her independence."

"When was that?"

"The night we talked. That's why we were going out for drinks next day. To celebrate."

"She didn't elaborate?"

"I asked, but she said she'd tell me about it when we met."

Had Deirdre recently broken off with Tony? And if so, had it angered him enough that he killed her? Maybe Hal was onto something after all.

CHAPTER 31

"**D**o you always walk this fast?" Hal grumbled. We'd barely begun our trek around Lake Merritt and already he was winded.

"You were the one who suggested a walk," I told him.

"I should have specified a *leisurely walk.*"

From a distance, Lake Merritt glistens like a jewel in the center of Oakland. A diamond in the midst of steel and concrete. Up close, the lake looks, and smells, a lot less pristine. Nonetheless, its three-mile perimeter and the surrounding parklands are a favorite with everyone from joggers to Rollerbladers.

I slowed my pace. "If you'd give up cigarettes and junk food, you'd be able to keep up."

"No offense, Kali, but I *prefer* leisurely walks. If God meant us to scamper everywhere, he'd have given us four legs."

I laughed. "On this point, intelligent people can disagree." I didn't bother to tell him that with the cuts on my back and legs still smarting, I'd already slowed from my usual pace. "Now, what was it you wanted to see me about?"

"The Carsons." He paused, breathing heavily. "You know, the people Deirdre Nichols was house-sitting for."

Each word came as a separate puff. When I stopped to let him catch his breath, we were almost mowed down by two women runners pushing baby strollers.

Hal glared at them. "What is it with women these days? I thought this was a park, not a track."

"Fitness," I told him, giving him a gentle nudge in the shoulder. "A word that's not part of your vocabulary." When I thought

Hal had rested long enough to speak in more than one-word increments, I asked about the Carsons.

"They'd been having some problems with a guy by the name of Eric Simpson," Hal said. "He was apparently harassing them. They got a restraining order against him about eighteen months ago. I guess maybe it didn't do much good, because last June they just up and left their home in New Hampshire."

"They moved?"

"Moved, but without the usual forwarding address and such. Left their furniture and car. And their phone number here in the Bay Area is unlisted."

"I remember one of their neighbors telling me they weren't registered to vote."

Hal nodded. "I believe it. They've kept a low profile. On purpose, I suspect. That may explain why they've taken off without a word to anyone. Maybe Simpson found out where they were living."

We started to walk again, at a decidedly slower pace. "Do you know anything about this guy? Why was he harassing them?"

"The Carsons were in an auto accident a few years back in which Simpson's wife was killed. According to the report, it wasn't their fault. But Simpson apparently blames them. He's kind of gone off the deep end about it."

"And you think he traced them here?"

"It's a possibility." Hal paused. "Makes me wonder if Mrs. Carson looks anything like Deirdre Nichols. He might have gotten the two of them confused."

"But he'd have to have been standing right next to her to push her over the railing. Wouldn't he have known it wasn't Mrs. Carson?"

"It's just a theory. According to a neighbor I talked with, the two women had a similar build."

"Why would Deirdre have let him in?"

Hal shrugged. "He could have said he was with the telephone company or something. Or maybe it wasn't a case of mistaken identity. Maybe the guy simply lost it. Deirdre couldn't tell him where the Carsons were, and he thought she was holding out."

As Hal had said, it was just a theory. A fairly far-out one at that. But I felt a flicker of excitement all the same. Sometimes a theory was all you needed. Plant the seeds of doubt in the jurors' minds and let their imagination do the rest.

"Where was Simpson last seen? How do we get a line on this guy?"

"Calm down. I'm working on it. He's not in New Hampshire anymore, left there about four months ago. No one seems to know where he is at the moment."

"Do we know what he looks like? We could ask the Carsons' neighbors, see if anyone has noticed him around."

"I thought of that. I don't have a picture yet, but according to his driver's license, he's six foot two, two hundred and ten pounds."

"Big guy."

"And probably strong. He works construction."

"You'll keep on top of this?" I asked. I could hear the eagerness in my voice.

"You bet." Despite the slowed pace, Hal was dragging. "Can we sit for a minute?" he asked. "My knee is killing me."

"You've got a bad knee?"

"Yeah."

"A bad knee, easily winded. Why did you suggest we take a walk?"

"I wanted to talk in private."

I looked around at all the joggers. "This isn't exactly private."

"Private enough."

We sat on a bench looking out toward the lake, where colorful sails billowed in the wind and crew sculls glided across the water in silence. When Hal still hadn't said anything after several minutes, I turned to him. "What was it you wanted to talk about?"

"I get the feeling you and Marc are . . . well, if not involved, getting there."

I felt a slow-forming smile. "Not that it's any business of yours, but yes, I'd say we are." Getting there, at any rate. It had been only two days since I'd spent the night with him, but there was a definite change in our relationship.

Hal pulled out a pack of red licorice and offered me a piece. I bit into it and chewed off a strip. It was practically tasteless.

Hal, however, seemed to like it just fine. He finished the first piece and peeled off a second. "I'd go slow if I were you," he said at last.

"With Marc?"

He nodded.

I laughed. "Since when did you trade places with Ann Landers?"

"I was afraid that would be your reaction."

"What's the problem?" I gave him an impish grin. "You're not jealous, are you?" And then a thought struck me. I turned serious. "Marc's not gay, is he? I mean, bi?"

"Not that I'm aware of."

I heaved a dramatic sigh of relief, but Hal didn't smile.

He chewed on a piece of licorice. "I'm not sure you know him as well as you imagine."

"I know enough."

"I just think you should be careful, is all."

That wasn't like Hal. "What are you getting at?"

"I'm not sure myself." He paused to toss tiny pieces of candy to the pigeons at our feet. "As you know, I've been keeping an eye on Tony Rodale."

I nodded. That reminded me that I'd meant to tell Hal about my conversation with Judith Powers.

"I told you I got a no-good feeling about him," Hal added.

"Right, you did. And I'm thinking maybe you're onto something."

He looked at me and sighed. "Last night I thought I saw Marc's car pull into Rodale's driveway."

"You *thought* you saw it?"

"I'm not absolutely, positively sure. But ninety-nine percent there."

My response was automatic. "So?" But even as I said it, I had trouble coming up with an explanation.

"So it seems odd."

"Maybe Marc wanted to question Rodale himself," I said.

"At ten o'clock in the evening?"

"Well, then, you must be mistaken." I didn't realize how lame the words sounded until I said them aloud.

"Could be," Hal said, clearly not convinced.

"Why would Marc hang out with a guy like Tony Rodale?"

Hal rubbed a finger along his chin and gazed pensively at the drab gray of the lake. "That's what I'd like to know."

* * *

The office was empty when I returned, but Rose had left a handful of message slips on my desk. Two on other legal matters, one from Nina, and one saying that Xavier had called. My pulse jumped when I saw the name. Unfortunately, there was no message, and no return number.

The elusive Xavier. A young man who might, or might not, have seen events unfolding on the deck the night Deirdre Nichols was killed. I cursed my luck at missing the call.

As I was punching in the number to return one of my other calls, I noticed the timing of the messages. Xavier's call had come in last.

Hanging up, I waited a moment, then picked up the phone again and hit *69. The wonders of modern technology. If his was truly the last call, I could reach him even without knowing the number.

After fifteen rings, I was ready to give up. On the sixteenth, a male voice with a heavy Chinese accent picked up.

"I'm trying to reach Xavier," I said.

"He give you this number?" the man asked.

I lied. "Yes."

"Must be mistake. This grocery pay phone."

"Which grocery?"

"Sam Wong Grocery. You want vegetable, fish, good duck. We the best."

"In Oakland?"

"Best anywhere."

I wrote the name on a slip of paper. "No, I meant, where are you located?"

"Eighth Street. Oakland."

"Mr. Wong, was there a young man in your store about half an hour ago? Someone who used the pay phone."

"People use all time. Public phone."

"I wouldn't bother you, Mr. Wong, but this is important. I need to talk to the teenage boy who called me from your phone about half an hour ago."

"Public phone. Many people use."

"But do you remember a teenager?"

"All time. Kids buy candy, soda, use phone."

I tried again. "Is it the same kids every time?"

"Some same, some different. It public phone. Sam Wong grocery very popular."

I thanked him and hung up. At least I knew that Xavier had gotten Hal's message. He'd tried to reach me once. I hoped he'd try again.

After returning the other calls, I phoned the detective who'd been assigned the investigation of our recent break-in. The police had come up with no clear prints and had no leads at all, but the detective assured me the case would remain open and active until there was some sort of resolution. It wasn't an encouraging response. I figured the Oakland police had to have hundreds of open and active cases.

Rather than calling Nina, I decided to drop by in person, stopping at Just Desserts on the way to pick up coffee and two slices of carrot cake. We hadn't talked since Monday, when I'd phoned to report on my visit with Grady. I could tell by the strain in her voice that her husband's arrest was taking its toll.

As I rounded the corner near Nina's, the first thing that caught my eye was the ambulance pulling away from the Barretts' driveway, lights flashing.

CHAPTER 32

"You just missed her," Simon said hurriedly. "She's on the way to the hospital."

I swallowed hard. "What's wrong?"

"She was having labor pains."

"But she still has three months to go." A cold foreboding clutched my chest. Was she going to lose the baby on top of everything else?

Elsa joined us in the doorway, wiping her hands on her apron. "We are praying. The doctor says she needs to go to the hospital for stronger medicine. She stay there three, four days. Maybe longer."

"But the ambulance . . . I thought . . ." Slowly my pulse was returning to normal. "There's hope still?"

Elsa nodded. "The doctor say she has to lie down. All the time lie down. No walk, no sit, only lie down."

"That's why I couldn't drive her," Simon added. "The doctor wanted her to stay flat on her back."

"Did anyone go with her?"

"She said it wasn't necessary," Simon explained, though I could tell from his tone he didn't agree.

And neither did I.

When I got to the hospital, the woman at the front desk told me that Nina was still in the process of being admitted. I wasn't sure what, exactly, that meant, except that her room number wasn't posted. I headed for Emergency, where I fared no better. It was more than an hour before the powers that be let me see her.

Finally, I took an elevator to the fourth floor and knocked on the open door. Nina had managed to land a private room, but it was stark and stuffy. The air was heavy with a medicinal smell layered upon the lingering odor of cafeteria food.

"Hi," I said, entering.

Nina lay on her back, staring at the ceiling. She was wrapped in a faded blue floral-print hospital gown that made her pale skin seem almost translucent. An IV needle was taped to one arm.

She turned to greet me, her face wet with silent tears. Then a wan smile touched the corners of her mouth. "This is really shitty."

"Yeah, it is." I pulled the plastic chair from the foot of the bed around to the side. "What does the doctor say?"

"Not much. He's got me on some heavy-duty medicine to stop the contractions. And I have to stay flat. I can't even get up to pee."

"Fun."

"He's not even sure it will work." Nina gave me a look, something crumpled and sad. "I feel like I'm holding on by my fingernails, Kali. Like I'm slipping a little each day. I don't think I can make it."

"Yes, you can." I squeezed her free hand. "Each week the baby's chances get better. Each day, in fact. It's going to work out."

"Since when have you become such a Pollyanna?"

It was a tenuous conversion, born of worry and uncertainty. And I was sure Nina recognized it.

"I know it's got to be awful to lie there," I told her. "With nothing to do but wait. But you've got to remember that you're getting closer to the end all the time." And then I bit my tongue, remembering that death was another end she might be facing.

"It's easy for you to talk. You're not the one going through this." I could detect a hint of anger in her voice.

"You're right, I'm not."

"So cut the cheerfulness, okay?"

"I'm trying to help, Nina. I don't always know what's right. What to say to show support."

"Maybe I don't want support," she snapped. "Maybe I want someone to be sad with. I feel like everyone is pulling back. Yeah, they're sorry, but they're also glad it's not them. They mumble words of sympathy, then go on with their own lives."

"Oh, Nina." I leaned across the bed and hugged her. "I *am* sad. And I feel so helpless."

She hugged me back, then brushed a loose strand of hair from her face, the anger defused. "It's not just the baby, you know. It's what comes after. How am I going to give him the love and attention he needs when I'm struggling with the effects of chemotherapy?"

"Chemo is only twelve weeks." The voice of optimism again, but I couldn't help it.

She was silent a moment. "And what if I don't make it?" Her voice was soft and faint, as though she'd had to squeeze the words from somewhere deep inside her. "What if the treatment doesn't kill the cancer?"

Even Pollyanna didn't have an answer to that one. I shook my head and gripped Nina's hand harder. The nurse bustled in just then and shooed me out. I left reluctantly.

Wandering down to the cafeteria, I bought a frozen yogurt and ate it without tasting a bite. When half an hour had elapsed, I went back to check on Nina. She was still flat on her back, but I could tell that her deep blue mood had passed, at least for the moment.

"You didn't have to hang around," she said with a valiant attempt at a smile.

"I wanted to make sure you were okay."

"I am. Really. I didn't mean to get mad at you. I just gave in to a moment of panic."

I pulled up a chair and sat where she could see me without straining. "I wish I could do something to help."

"You are. You're here, for one thing. And you're handling Grady's defense. I'm so glad you're doing it, Kali. I'd worry if it were anyone else."

I knew she was plenty worried as it was. "How about Emily? Is she going to be okay while you're in the hospital?"

Nina nodded. "Simon and Elsa will look after her. She's comfortable with them. They're not a lot of fun though. If you have time, maybe you could stop by and see her."

"Sure. I'd love to. She's a neat kid."

Nina was silent a moment, watching the colorless solution drip into her arm through the IV. "Is the preliminary hearing still set for next week?"

"Wednesday." A week from today.

"How's it look?"

"Fine." I tossed off the word too quickly.

Nina sighed. "That bad, huh?"

I looked her in the eyes. "Actually, it's neither good nor bad. But Grady wants a full court press at the hearing. He'd like the charges dropped, and that's not going to happen."

"You haven't stumbled onto any lucky breaks, I take it."

"None that have panned out." I told her about Eric Simpson's vendetta against the Carsons, and about Xavier.

"You ought to be able to get some mileage out of the fact that the police don't seem to have looked into either."

I nodded. "But it will go further at trial than at the hearing. There's another angle they never looked at as well."

"What's that?"

"Did Deirdre Nichols ever talk to you about the guy she was dating, Tony Rodale?" In the depths of my brain I felt a niggle of worry when I remembered Hal's story about seeing Marc's car at Tony's. I tried to ignore it.

"I didn't know Deirdre very well," Nina said. "I saw more of her sister, Sheila. Adrianna and Emily were on the same soccer team last fall, and it was Sheila who came to most of the games."

"I don't suppose Sheila ever mentioned anyone her sister was involved with?"

Nina shook her head. "For the most part, the only thing we talked about was the kids. It's too bad Sheila never had children of her own. She's the sort who would make motherhood her life's work."

"Was she ever married?"

Nina's expression darkened. "She was engaged once. Or almost engaged. She never told me the details, but I got the impression she never really got over him. He died a couple of years ago and she sometimes acts like she's his widow."

I debated the wisdom of telling Nina about my recent conversation with Sheila, and decided against it. Although I had trouble believing Grady had been foolish enough to leave a threatening message on Deirdre's answering machine, I hadn't totally discounted the notion.

"She came to see me a couple of days ago," Nina said after a moment.

"Who did?"

"Sheila. She wanted me to persuade Grady to accept some sort of plea bargain. In the interest of the kids."

So much for protecting Nina. "She tried to get me to do the same thing too," I told her.

Nina gave me a long look. "You weren't going to tell me, were you?" She spoke fast and breathlessly. "You were worried it might upset me."

"You've got a lot—"

"Kali, it's hard enough being physically out of commission. Don't treat me like my mind is gone too."

"You know it's not that."

"I know nothing of the sort. You've been trying to shield me since the moment Deirdre first cried rape." Her voice spiraled. She pulled her hand from mine. "I *know* only what you choose to tell me, which isn't a whole hell of a lot."

She was right, of course. And I felt torn. How did you draw the line between brutal honesty and reassuring empathy where friendship was concerned?

"You've got enough to contend with right now," I told her.

"That doesn't mean I've had a lapse of judgment. My brain is one of the few parts of my body that's working just fine."

"I know that, Nina."

"Funny, you don't act like it." Anger flickered in her words.

"You're under a lot of stress. I only—"

She cut me off. "What gives you the right to decide what I can handle and what I can't?"

We were both silent. Nina closed her eyes, took several deep breaths. "Don't shut me out, Kali."

"If that's really what you want."

"I do." She seemed to hesitate, then turned her gaze in my direction. "From now on anything we say is privileged communication. Okay? Conversation between counsel. We're partners on this."

I gave her a questioning look. "Okay."

Another deep breath. "I think Sheila is wrong about the tape. For one thing, Grady wouldn't have made such a theatrical threat. It's not his style."

I nodded.

"But I'm sure he was up to something. I can pick up on stuff like that."

"What do you mean?"

"I don't know exactly. But there were a couple of secretive phone calls in the days before Deirdre was killed. Grady was acting jumpy as well. If there's any truth at all to what Sheila says and it comes out at trial, you'll be broadsided. Juries love stuff like that."

My stomach churned. "Are you suggesting we go along with what Sheila is asking? You want Grady to plead guilty to a lesser charge?"

"I don't know what I want, except that I want you to be careful, Kali. Grady's a good man, and I love him with all my heart. But he's not perfect."

CHAPTER 33

By Saturday the medicine had kicked in enough that Nina's doctor pronounced her stable. She had to remain in the hospital and wasn't allowed up, but the contractions had stopped.

I took Emily by the hospital for a visit that afternoon, then we picked up Marc and went on an excursion to the Oakland zoo.

The day was glorious. Clear and warm, but still fresh with the scent of early spring. Emily, who'd been rather subdued in the hospital, sprang to life once she was free to run around. With Marc close on her heels, she scampered excitedly from one exhibit to the next. They called to the baboons, had imaginary conversations with the tigers and bears, and spent half an hour feeding the llamas in the petting zoo. When we'd completed our tour of the animals, we headed for the rides. I passed on the roller coaster, although Emily and Marc assured me it was nothing, but I joined them on the train and the carousel.

I chose to ride a pink pig—not because I thought he was cute, which was Emily's criterion, but because I wanted to sit behind her and Marc so that I could watch them together. Marc had an easy way with Emily, a silliness that matched her own. It was a side of him I'd not seen before, and one I found oddly appealing.

Nonetheless, I was aware of a nagging tickle in the back of my mind, an uneasiness brought on by Hal's comment about seeing Marc with Tony Rodale. It made no sense, and when I'd asked Marc, he'd shrugged it off saying Hal must have been mistaken. That was my conclusion too, but the tickle persisted.

As I turned to give the carousel operator my ticket, I caught sight of a man near the exit, a familiar face I couldn't quite place. I looked for him again on our second swoop around, but he was gone. It wasn't until we were on our way to the refreshment stand that I remembered who he was. The cop Madelaine Rivera was dating. Somehow I hadn't imagined her falling for a guy with kids.

We bought hot dogs and took them to an empty table away from the bustle of a birthday party in progress.

"You having fun?" Marc asked Emily.

Her mouth was full, but she nodded vigorously.

He turned to me. "How about you?"

"More fun than I've had in months." The answer was only partially in jest. I didn't know where our relationship was headed, or where I wanted it to head even, but I knew that we'd crossed the invisible line of simple friendship.

Under the table, Marc's hand slid intimately up my thigh. He raised a brow and grinned. "Really? The most fun in *months?*"

"Really."

Marc gave me a playful pinch. "I hope that's a slight exaggeration. I seem to remember a night that was kind of fun too."

Emily poked a straw at her soda. "I wish my daddy was here though."

"Me too, honey." Marc stroked her head. "And I know that's what he'd like as well."

"Simon says it might be a long time before he comes home. Maybe never."

I wanted to give Simon a good shake.

Marc tucked a wayward strand of hair behind her ear. "Don't listen to Simon, sugar. Your dad's coming home. We're going to make sure that he does."

Simon wasn't the only one who needed a shaking. I kicked Marc under the table. It was one thing to be optimistic, but I wasn't comfortable with empty promises. And I didn't have the foggiest idea how you explained the difference to a seven-year-old.

"We're going to try," I told Emily. "We're going to try very, very hard. But it's not really up to us, or your dad. If it was, he'd be with you right this minute."

"How are you going to try?" she asked.

That was something I'd been wondering myself. But Emily's question was of a different nature. "Some people have accused your daddy of doing a bad thing," I explained.

She nodded knowingly. "They say he got mad at Adrianna's mommy and pushed her. She hit her head and died."

I wondered if this was the distilled wisdom of a seven-year-old or an explanation carefully constructed by Nina. "He says he didn't though," I told her. "I believe him, and so does your mom."

"Me too," Marc added. He opened a plastic packet of catsup and squeezed it onto his French fries.

"So why can't he come home?" Emily asked.

"Because it's not up to us. We are going to tell our side of the story—why we think your dad didn't do it. And the other side will tell the reasons they think he did. A group of people called a jury decides who they believe."

Although Emily nodded, I wasn't sure how much she understood. Nonetheless, the answer seemed to satisfy her. She reached for a handful of Marc's fries.

"Your mom will be home before long too." I added.

Another nod. "As soon as my baby brother is born."

"Maybe sooner, even." The baby wasn't due for another three months.

"Except then she's going to be very sick," Emily said solemnly.

I realized how confusing all this must be for someone her age.

Marc swung his legs over the bench we were sitting on and stood. "How about an ice cream cone?" he asked Emily.

"With sprinkles."

"Absolutely." He turned to me. "How about you?"

My eyes were focused elsewhere. I'd caught sight of Madelaine's friend again, pouring creamer into a container of coffee. I waited for him to join one of the tables of children, but instead he walked off in the other direction.

Marc turned to follow my gaze. "What is it?"

I shook my head. "Nothing really. I saw someone who looked familiar. A cop Madelaine Rivera is dating."

Marc strained to see where I was looking.

"He turned left at the gate," I said. "You can't see him from here."

Marc licked his lower lip. "What kind of cop?"

"Homicide, I think." I spoke softly, above Emily's head. The man had, after all, been investigating the scene of the crime for which her father was facing trial. Then I shrugged. "It's not important."

Marc frowned. "What's he look like?"

"Athletic build, blond hair cut close to the scalp, a slight scar on his chin."

Marc crumpled our hot dog wrappers and paper cups, then dumped them in the trash. "She's dating a cop, huh?"

"They went out once or twice at any rate. I think she'd like it to be a regular thing."

Marc laughed, but I thought I detected a darkening in his expression. If I hadn't known him better, I might have suspected he was secretly enamored of Madelaine Rivera. Or perhaps I didn't know him as well as I thought. I remembered Hal saying that very thing.

"You two ready to head home?" Marc asked, already moving in the direction of the exit.

Emily hung back. "Aren't we going to get ice cream?"

"Sure. We'll eat it in the car."

"I thought we were going to ride the bumper cars," she protested.

Marc ruffled her hair. "Not today."

He appeared distracted on the way home—no longer joking with Emily, and seemingly oblivious of my presence. Although I'd hoped we might spend the evening together, Marc asked to be dropped off first, before I took Emily home. I tried to hide my disappointment.

"Is something wrong?" I asked when we reached his place.

Marc shook his head, offering me an apologetic smile. "Sorry, I've got a headache. I think it was too much sun."

"If you feel better later this evening, you want to take in a movie?"

He looked at me for a moment, then touched a finger to my cheek. "I've got work to do. But if I had my druthers, I'd choose to be with you any day." He turned to Emily in the backseat. "You too, sport. I had great fun today. We'll do it again sometime."

He got out of the car with a wave to both of us.

I had work to do too, so I told myself that maybe it was just as well. Still, I couldn't help feeling a little hurt. I wondered if I'd done something to make him angry.

After taking Emily home, I went by the grocery and picked up salad fixings for dinner. Then I hit the bakery section and added a fresh apple strudel to my basket. If I was going to spend Saturday night alone, working, I figured I deserved some consolation.

Bea had left me a note saying that Hal had called twice. He would try again later or reach me at the office. After I'd put the groceries away, I tried calling him back. No answer. I tried again after dinner, but he was still out. Obviously Hal had a more active social life than I did.

Since I had the house to myself for the evening, I worked at the dining room table, which offered better light and more space than my cramped desk downstairs. I turned on the stereo and slipped in a Miles Davis CD. Then, kicking off my shoes, I got down to work.

With the hearing only four days away, I needed to transform my rambling notes and thoughts into something concise and compelling. It wasn't going to be easy.

Whatever small hope I'd had of finding a major flaw in the prosecution's case had pretty much evaporated—and with it, our chances of getting the case dismissed pretrial. While the evidence against Grady wasn't overwhelming, it was strong enough. There was no doubt in my mind that if I offered only a routine challenge to the state's case, the judge would find probable cause to try Grady for murder.

I'd been clinging to the hope that Hal might come through with something solid about Tony Rodale or Eric Simpson. Or that Xavier would come forward with an eyewitness account that exonerated Grady.

They were all long shots, and I'd just about given up. Hal's call today was encouraging. He wouldn't have phoned on a Saturday if it wasn't important.

Some days I wake up exhausted. For no particular reason, I feel spent and oddly out of sorts. As though my body had been dismantled during the night and reassembled with a slightly different fit.

Sunday was like that. My jaw ached from grinding my teeth,

my head was filled with vague memories of an unsettling dream, and my neck was stiff.

I've learned from experience that it's best to try to shake the feeling by ignoring it. So after breakfast I forced myself down to the gym, where I walked the treadmill and rode a stationary bicycle for five totally uninteresting miles, and then put my muscles through the wringer at exercise class. When I felt I'd had about as much as I could handle, I took a shower and drove to Sam Wong's grocery in the hope of locating Xavier.

By the time I parked, half a block from the store, I realized that a warm Sunday in early spring was probably not the optimal day for finding teenage boys at the local grocery. Nonetheless, I did stumble across a handful of them sitting on the sidewalk outside, smoking. They had shaved heads, multiple facial piercings, and the vacant stares of misspent youth.

Two knew Xavier. But they didn't know where he was right then or where to find him. They promised to tell him that I wanted to talk with him. I didn't think they'd remember for longer than five minutes.

"You got a call," Bea said when I got home. "Someone from the police department. I wrote his name on the pad by the phone."

On a Sunday? I was surprised. Maybe they'd found a suspect in our break-in. It would certainly be a relief to have that off my mind.

I dialed the number Bea had written down, then waited to be connected with Sergeant Fogerty.

"Are you acquainted with a Harold Fisher?" he asked without preliminaries.

Hal. I felt it in my chest, like a rolling blast of thunder. Bad news of the worst kind. "Yes," I managed to say. "He's a friend of mine." My voice sounded foreign to my own ears.

"I'm sorry to have to tell you that Mr. Fisher was killed last evening."

I sucked in a lungful of air, feeling suddenly as though I were suffocating. "Killed?"

"He had your card in his pocket," Fogerty continued.

When I didn't say anything, he continued. "I realize this is painful for you, but we need a positive in-person identification.

Do you think you could help us with that? I can send someone over for you."

My mind was several beats behind the sergeant's. "Killed?" I repeated. "How? Was there an accident?"

Sergeant Fogerty cleared his throat. "He was shot, ma'am."

CHAPTER 34

The morgue is not a comfortable place to spend time, even on a lovely spring afternoon. Or maybe especially then, when the contrast between life and death is underscored so starkly.

Sergeant Fogerty was kind, though, and patient. He didn't try to hurry me, and he didn't turn gruff, or paternal, the way some men do when confronted with an emotional situation.

"You ever done this before?" he asked, leading me into a small room at the end of a downstairs hallway.

I shook my head.

"We use closed-circuit TV these days. It helps a little. Still, it's not pleasant. You going to be okay?"

"I think so." I was grateful I didn't have to stand close to the actual body.

Fogerty darkened the room and angled a television on a metal cart so that I could see it.

"You ready?"

I nodded.

The screen flickered and then settled on what looked to be a sheet. After a moment, two rubber-gloved hands raised the sheet just enough to accommodate viewing. Steeling myself, I lowered my eyes to look, tentatively at first, the way you test the temperature of hot water. I turned away quickly and then, when the initial shock had worn off, looked back again. Hal's skin was colorless, his expression frozen, but his face was unmarked and clearly recognizable.

I nodded. "It's him." Where the sheet angled up, I could see the upper portion of Hal's skinny shoulder and pale, hairless chest. He seemed much frailer in death than he had in life.

"You're sure?" Fogerty asked.

I nodded again.

He touched my arm and turned on the light. "Thank you."

"That's it?"

He nodded. "All we needed was a positive identification."

"Do you know what happened?" I asked. "Or why?"

Fogerty led me back upstairs. "Not really, certainly not the 'why' part. A couple out walking their dog found the body late last night. Your friend was slumped over the steering wheel of his car. Shot. Had probably been dead for several hours by then."

The image of Hal bleeding and crumpled in pain while I was at home waxing envious about his social life loomed large at the back of my mind. I tried to ignore it.

"Where'd they find him?" I was still reeling from the news of Hal's death, trying to fit the pieces so that they made sense.

"The car was on Belleview," Fogerty said. "By the lake."

I leaned against the wall. "Is that where he was killed?"

"Looks that way."

"Any leads?"

Fogerty shook his head. "It's most likely a case of being in the wrong place at the wrong time, but we won't know for sure until we get further into the investigation." He paused and looked at me kindly. "No offense, but did your friend by any chance do drugs?"

"No. At least I'm pretty sure he didn't." Not unless you were counting tobacco and sugar. Hal wasn't even much of a drinker. "Why? Did you find something that makes you think he did?"

"Just wondering, is all. That's most often what's behind this type of crime. He have any family?"

"He has a brother," I said, trying to remember what Hal had told me about him. "Same last name. He teaches at one of the schools back east. Amherst maybe, or Williams. As far as I know, Hal didn't have any other family."

"We'll try to reach the brother." Fogerty shook my hand, touching my shoulder at the same time. "Thanks for your help. I know it wasn't easy for you."

From downtown I drove to Lake Merritt, five minutes away, and parked near the spot where Hal had been killed. The afternoon sun was still bright, and the sky unclouded. But the day seemed dulled by a haze of my own coloring. Only a few days earlier, Hal and I had walked the perimeter of the lake. And now Hal was dead. It didn't seem possible.

Sorrow swelled in my chest. I closed my eyes and let the tears come. After fighting them so long, it felt good to let loose and cry.

I remembered meeting Hal for the first time when I was fresh out of law school. We'd been on opposite sides of a case then, but he'd taken me to lunch anyway and given me an hour's briefing on the unwritten rules and behind-the-scenes politics of the D.A.'s office. We'd remained friends even when the client he was working for got sent away for thirty years.

A host of images paraded through my mind like pages in a photo album. Nearly ten years of memories during which Hal had been there for me as a friend, as well as someone I counted on in my work.

For a while, the sadness in my heart was so intense, I felt I couldn't breathe. But gradually grief gave way to numbness. I wondered how Hal had ended up, to use Fogerty's words, in the wrong place at the wrong time.

Or if the answer was really that simple.

I knew I should tell the police what I could about Hal's life. That he was gay, that he'd had a string of failed relationships, and probably a series of one-nighters and attempted relationships as well. Hal might have been searching for Mr. Right, but I knew he wasn't putting his life on hold while he looked.

Was that what had led to his death? A lover's quarrel, or perhaps the wrong choice for an evening's companion?

Or could his death be connected in some way to his work as a private investigator? He'd called me yesterday, twice. Was he killed because of his investigation of the Barrett case? With that thought came a new wave of sorrow, intensified by guilt. I knew I'd have to tell the police about that too.

Finally, I started the car and drove to Marc's. Although I was still feeling hurt by his sudden indifference yesterday afternoon, I didn't want to be alone.

Marc answered the door looking half dazed. He was wearing a rumpled shirt and jeans that showed signs of having been donned hastily. His hair was sticking up on one side and his eyes were bloodshot.

"Sorry," I said. "I didn't expect you to be asleep still." It was already past noon.

He shook his head, as much to clear his mind, I suspect, as in response to my apology. "It's not a problem."

"Are you alone?" I felt suddenly uncomfortable at the prospect of what I might have interrupted. No wonder he hadn't wanted my company last night.

Marc apparently read my mind, because he responded with a twisted smile. "No one's here. I was just resting."

For a moment we stood awkwardly in the open doorway. And then, surprisingly, the tears started flowing again. Damn, I'd thought that part was past.

"What is it?" Marc's face registered concern. He no longer seemed half asleep. "What's the matter, Kali? What's wrong?" He pulled me close and encircled me in his arms.

I pressed my face against his chest. "Hal was killed last night," I said tearfully. "Somebody shot him."

"*What?*"

"He was in his car, by the lake."

"Shot? Jesus. Did they get the guy who did it?"

I shook my head. "I know you didn't like him much, but he was a sweet guy. Honest and funny and generous beyond belief."

"Liking has nothing to do with it," Marc said. His voice was scratchy with emotion. "I certainly didn't wish him any harm. Hal was a friend of yours, someone you cared about."

"I can't believe he's really dead."

"Jesus, what a shock." Marc stepped back. "Come on, I'll make some coffee. You look like you could use it."

I followed him to the kitchen.

"Do you know how it happened?" he asked, measuring grounds into the filter.

I relayed the few details of Hal's death that I knew. "I'm worried," I said, swallowing hard to hold back a fresh round of tears, "that it might be my fault. That maybe Hal was killed because he was working on Grady's defense."

"Sounds to me like you're looking to beat yourself up."

"No, I think it's a real possibility." What had started as simple supposition had now taken hold in my mind. And I was troubled.

"But why?" Marc handed me a mug of coffee.

"Hal was suspicious of Tony Rodale."

Marc raised an eyebrow.

"He said there were rumors circulating about him."

"What kind of rumors?"

"He didn't know exactly. But he was digging to see if he couldn't find out more."

Marc was visibly shaken. "And you think he found something on Rodale?"

"Maybe. Hal said Rodale might have had police connections as well."

Marc sank into the leather sling chair. "Jesus. Why didn't you say something about this before?"

"There was nothing to tell, really." A half-truth of sorts. I wondered if Marc recognized that.

We sat at the glass-topped dining table and sipped our coffee as though it were a task that required full concentration.

"There's also Eric Simpson," I said after a moment. "The guy who was hounding the Carsons. Hal was looking into that too. He was digging in a lot of different directions, in fact. It could be any of them."

"Or none." Marc rubbed the back of his neck. "Street crime is usually random, don't forget. Rotten luck as opposed to sinister motives."

But what had Hal been doing down by the lake in the first place?

"I take it his wallet wasn't missing?" Marc said.

"I don't know. I didn't ask." I wished now that I'd pressed Fogerty for more information. But the shock of Hal's death had been too fresh for clear thinking. "The sergeant I spoke with asked me if Hal did drugs."

Marc's face registered surprise. "What made him ask that?"

"I guess it's one of the first things that comes to mind in a situation like this."

"Did he?"

"I don't think so."

Marc leaned forward, elbows on the table, his head in his hands. He was still for a moment. Then he stood abruptly and walked to the window. "Maybe now isn't the time to mention this, but if your theory is correct, you might be in danger yourself."

"Me?"

"And me," he added wryly. "If that makes it any better."

A cold chill worked its way down my spine. "What happened to your street-crime-is-usually-random argument?"

"It's still floating around out there. This is an alternative." Marc sat again, turning his chair so that he faced me. "Think about it. If Hal was killed because of something he discovered about Deirdre Nichols' death, then the killer might think we know also."

I stared at my cup, not at all comfortable with the direction my mind was taking. "There was the break-in at our office," I said, thinking aloud.

Marc nodded.

"You really think . . ."

"I don't pretend to understand it," he said. "But I know I don't like it. In fact, it scares the hell out of me."

It scared the hell out of me too.

CHAPTER 35

I ended up staying at Marc's for dinner and then through the night. I couldn't face being alone, and I think Marc felt the same way. He seemed almost as unsettled by the news of Hal's death as I was—a reaction I found both surprising and endearing.

We watched the news at six and again at eleven, but there was no mention of Hal's murder. Without celebrity status or an overlay of tantalizing circumstances, life cut short by violence was apparently too prevalent to be newsworthy.

Monday morning I awoke early, before the sun was fully up. While Marc slept, I slipped quietly out of the house and drove home for a shower and change of clothes. I was at my office desk by seven-thirty.

I'd stopped for a latte on my way to work. I sipped it while I checked the answering machine. There were three messages: two late Friday afternoon from investment bankers wanting to speak with Marc, and one on Saturday, from Hal.

Kali, give me a call as soon as you can. I'm onto something, babe. I've got information on Tony Rodale and Deirdre that might just save Grady's ass. You're going to love it. Hal's words were punctuated with a chuckle. *Didn't I tell you I had a bad feeling about that guy?*

Hal's familiar voice brought a sudden ache to my throat. But his message sent a chill down my spine.

What had been, last night, only speculation now faced me in bare, bold relief. It couldn't be happenstance that Hal had been killed just as he'd discovered something suspicious about Tony Rodale.

When Marc came in later that morning, I started to play the tape for him. Then, with an uncomfortable thought that floated in from out of nowhere and lodged itself squarely in my mind, I decided not to. Hal had been right about Rodale. Had he been right in warning me about Marc as well?

My stomach felt sour. I'd been sure that Hal was mistaken in thinking he'd seen Marc with Tony Rodale. And Marc himself had denied it. I still thought Hal must have been wrong. But there was enough doubt in my mind to make me hesitate.

I remembered the pen from Rapunzel I'd found in Marc's kitchen. Had he known Deirdre as well as Tony? Was Marc somehow implicated in a web of deceit that went to the heart of our case? These were not thoughts I welcomed, but I couldn't ignore them. Once the seed of suspicion is planted, it takes root very quickly.

I spent an uncomfortable morning trying to prepare for the preliminary hearing while niggling thoughts about Marc intruded. Twice I headed for his office with the message tape, and twice I turned back.

After lunch I called downtown to check on the investigation of Hal's death.

"Nothing new," Sergeant Fogerty told me. "But we managed to reach his brother. Thanks for your help with that."

"I might be able to help some more." I told him about Tony Rodale as well as the other angles Hal had been pursuing in connection with Grady's upcoming trial.

If the system were truly efficient, word would get back to Madelaine and she'd have the inside scoop on our defense strategy. I was banking on the fact that bureaucracies are rarely efficient.

Fogerty listened, but without the enthusiasm I'd hoped for.

"I can make you a copy of the tape," I said.

"I don't think that will be necessary."

"But you'll follow up on Rodale?"

"I'll relay your message to the detectives in charge."

"Tell them he called on Saturday, the day he was killed. The timing might be important."

When I again turned my attention to preparations for Wednesday's hearing, I had trouble concentrating on anything but the slender folder I'd labeled TONY RODALE. Inside were my notes from the visit Hal and I had paid him ten days before, along with the status report from Hal concerning Tony's alleged abuse of both Deirdre and his ex-wife.

What had Hal wanted to tell me? He'd discovered something he thought would be useful in Grady's defense. If I could figure out what it was, the police might be able to find Hal's killer. And I might be able to get Grady acquitted of murder.

Hal had listed two phone numbers for the ex-wife, both in Los Angeles. I tried them with no luck. Not even a machine where I could leave a message.

He hadn't included a business number for Rodale, but I found a listing in the white pages for Rodale Investment Management and dialed. The woman who answered had a thin, chirpy voice.

"I'd like some information about investments and financial planning," I told her. "Is there someone there who could help me?"

"I'd be happy to send you one of our brochures."

"I was hoping I could speak with someone in person."

"Mr. Rodale is out of the office at the moment. May I have him return your call?"

I didn't want to talk to Tony Rodale himself; I wanted to speak with someone who knew him. "There's no one else?" I asked.

"No, not really."

"It's a very small company, then?"

"In terms of personnel. But the investment assets are quite substantial."

"Who handles the paperwork?"

This stumped her for a moment. "I do some of it. Most of it Mr. Rodale takes care of himself."

"I see." I was sure Hal would have done better. "What sort of investments does Mr. Rodale handle?"

"It would be best if you talked to him directly. It's a very personalized service."

Best for those who were actually looking to invest, maybe. But not for my purposes. "Has he been in the business long?" I asked, not willing to be put off.

"Seven years. Ma'am, why don't I send you a brochure?" I sensed her growing impatience.

"Yes, of course. But I have a few more questions first. What is Mr. Rodale like?"

"What's he like?" It was obvious this wasn't the sort of question she usually fielded.

"It's important to me to know something about the person handling my finances. It has to be someone with whom I'm, uh, compatible."

"I suggest you make an appointment, ma'am. There's no charge for an initial visit."

"I will, if I decide to go forward. But, you see, it's difficult . . . that is, well, I have limited mobility." Play on her sense of compassion and hope God didn't inflict me with some terrible disease by way of punishment. "It's not easy for me to get out and around."

"My mother uses a walker," the woman said sympathetically. "The simplest errands take her forever."

"So you understand why I'd like to know a bit about Mr. Rodale before deciding whether or not to follow up with an appointment."

"Well, he's easy enough to work for," she said, her voice having lost a good deal of its chirpiness. "And his clients seem to like him. I can tell you that. He's quite friendly with some of them."

"Does he strike you as a man of principle?"

"Principle?"

It was apparently not a word that got a lot of play around Rodale's company. "Integrity," I explained. "Is he somebody I should trust with my money?"

She gave a breathless little laugh. "Well, those who *have* trusted him have done rather well financially. But you'd have to make that assessment yourself."

She had her lines down perfectly.

"I really think you should read the brochure," she added. "As a first step."

I fingered the tape with Hal's message, then scooted sideways to my office door and closed it. "You know," I said as though the thought had suddenly struck me, "I'm not even sure I have the correct company. A friend gave me the name, but I've got such a bad memory. . . . There were a couple of listings in the phone book that might have been it. Maybe you could tell me if a Marc Griffin is a client of Mr. Rodale's. Then I'd know I have the right place."

"I'm sorry, I can't divulge names of our clients. But Mr. Rodale can supply you with references once you've talked with him. You really should start with the brochure, however."

If nothing else, it would be interesting to see how Rodale presented himself on paper. I gave her my address, but used my sister Sabrina's name. The phone number I recited was the office number with two digits transposed. I certainly didn't want him calling me back.

A little after five, Marc knocked on my open door. "You want to grab some dinner a bit later?" he asked.

I did, and I didn't. Where had this feeling of distrust come from? I wondered. Yesterday I'd turned to Marc for comfort— something he'd provided amply and without hesitation. And today I felt the need to keep my distance. Or at least to keep my thoughts to myself.

I shook my head. "I've got work to do."

"You need to eat, regardless."

"I can munch while I work."

"We'll keep it simple and quick," Marc prodded. "I promise. We can discuss the points for the prelim at the same time."

I shook my head again. "I just don't feel up to it."

He came around the desk and hugged me from behind. "It's not healthy to grieve in isolation, Kali. You're sad, you're worried, you feel guilty. It's going to eat away at you if you let it."

I could smell the scent of soap on his skin, could feel the warmth of his body through my blouse. For a moment the veil of doubt lifted. Marc was my friend. My lover, in fact. He was also Nina's law partner and my cocounsel. What possible connection could he have with Tony Rodale or Deirdre Nichols?

I held his hand against my cheek. "I know you're trying to be helpful."

"I care about you, Kali. And I know you're hurting. You've always been so independent, as though it were a failing to let people close to you."

"It's not that," I told him.

"Is it me? Have I done something to upset you? If so, I'm sorry."

I hesitated, then turned to look at him. "Hal left a message for me Friday before he was killed. He said he'd discovered something about Tony Rodale that might save Grady. He mentioned Deirdre also."

"Did he say what it was?"

Had I imagined it, or had Marc's body really tensed when I told him about the tape? That was the trouble with suspicion. It clouded and befuddled your judgment.

I shook my head. "No, he didn't say."

A flicker of something in Marc's expression. Disappointment or relief?

"You've been holed up in here all day," he said. "Like you were avoiding me. I thought maybe you were angry with me."

"No, I'm not angry." With mixed feelings I let go of his hand. As much as I wanted it to be otherwise, I couldn't ignore the sense of unease that was tugging at me. "I just feel like being alone."

Marc kissed the top of my head. "I'll be home tonight if you change your mind."

It was almost eight when I left work. I stopped at McDonald's and picked up a grilled chicken sandwich, fries, and diet soda, then drove up Broadway Terrace to Tony Rodale's house. I parked across the street and down several houses, away from the streetlamp. I didn't know what I expected to discover, but I was sure that at some point Hal had done the same thing. Besides, I was plum out of ideas of my own.

What, I wondered for the zillionth time, had Hal discovered about Tony Rodale? Had it cost Hal his life? And might its absence in our case cost Grady his? Hal, Grady, Marc. Rodale seemed to be at the heart of it all.

I turned on the radio and ate my dinner in the dark. Except for the flickering light from the television, Rodale's house was quiet. No one came or went, and I saw no human activity inside.

Within an hour, I was bored out of my mind. After two hours, I felt an overwhelming urge to brush my teeth. And finally, three hours into my stakeout, I had to go to the bathroom so badly, I left.

As I was pulling out, I noticed a black car parked several spaces ahead up the road. The driver looked up as I passed, and

I recognized the cop I'd seen at the zoo the other day. The one Madelaine Rivera was dating.

Despite his unenthusiastic response, Fogerty had apparently passed along my message. And those in charge had listened. With a sense of relief I waved at the cop and drove home to prepare for tomorrow's interview with Grady.

CHAPTER 36

"How's Nina doing?" Grady asked even before he was seated at the table in the interview room. He looked tired, and his flesh appeared looser, as though his large frame had shrunk from within. "Is she really okay?"

Was anyone with cancer, the threat of premature labor, and a husband in jail ever okay? But I figured *okay* was a relative concept. At least the contractions had stopped.

"She's doing well," I told him. "The medicine is making her a little jumpy, and she hates having to stay flat, but all things considered, she's doing remarkably."

"And the baby?"

"He appears to be fine." I was thankful that I'd remembered to request a contact meeting this time. Face-to-face assurances carried more weight than those offered through glass. "They did another sonogram and everything is normal. Another month and his lungs will be developed enough that he should be healthy, even if he's early."

"He'll be able to breathe on his own?"

"Looks that way." I reached into my purse. "Here, I brought you a picture."

Ultrasound photography wasn't the same as shooting with Kodak. When Nina had first showed me the picture, it looked like nothing but wavy lines, reminding me of the patterns made by magnetic filings in high school physics. But when she'd pointed out the head and limbs, I was actually able to discern the shape of a baby. It was pretty exciting stuff, and I wasn't even directly involved.

"See," I said, leaning across the table and tracing the contour Nina had shown me. "He's sucking his thumb."

Grady stared at the picture for several moments. The lines around his eyes eased and his face brightened. "This is my son," he said with awe. "Isn't it incredible?"

I gave a nod of agreement.

He looked up. "I want to be there when he's born. I want to hold him."

"I know you do."

"I want to be there for him, and for Nina. You can't imagine how awful it is not to be with her right now, when she needs me most."

"It must be hard for both of you."

Grady tapped his fingers against the plastic tabletop. "You're going to get me out of here, aren't you? Soon?"

It's never pleasant being the bearer of bad news. I tried to put a favorable spin on it. "The state's case has a lot of holes in it. I think our chances at trial are good, but I wouldn't expect any miracles tomorrow."

He blinked. "What are you saying?"

"The burden of proof at the preliminary hearing is very low," I reminded him. "All they have to do is show that a crime was committed and that it's likely you committed it."

Grady slumped forward, rubbing his temples with his fingertips. "But I didn't."

"That's the issue that gets settled at trial."

He shook his head. "I can't wait for the trial. Don't you understand that?"

"It's not the—"

He sat back and glared at me through narrowed eyes. "I'm not worried about tipping our hand, or whatever you call it. I want you to do what you can to get me off. I want it done at the hearing so I can get out of here and put this nightmare behind me."

We'd been over this ground before. My advice was to do nothing more than defendants usually did at this stage, namely, trying to expose as much as possible of the prosecution's case.

"I don't want to reveal the strength or direction of our defense," I told Grady. "Not now, not when the chances we'll prevail are close to zero."

"Then why have a hearing at all?" he snapped. "It's supposed to test the prosecution's case, right?" He didn't wait for an answer. "The logical extension is that sometimes the judge finds the evidence *doesn't* support the charges."

"Rarely."

"You told me yourself that the defense is allowed to present evidence."

"Allowed, but—"

"You said that it was different from a grand jury indictment, which is strictly the prosecution's show." His tone was intense. He punctuated each point with an angry thrust of his finger. "You said you were glad we were getting a hearing, that it was better for us."

I nodded. "Better because we can see more of the D.A.'s case. But the bottom line is that it's a lot easier to convince a jury than a hearing judge. You really need to convince only one out of the twelve that the state hasn't proved its case. But more important, the burden of proof is so different at trial."

Grady folded his arms in disgust. "And meanwhile, I'm sitting in jail. My wife is in the hospital, my baby son won't know his father, and the company I've worked my whole life to build is down the tubes."

I tried to keep the irritation from my own voice. "You need to realize that this is more than an inconvenience. More, even, than a major annoyance. You're charged with murder, Grady. Murder."

"Are you're trying to tell me that I'm likely to be convicted?"

"The D.A. isn't doing this for fun."

"Jesus," he exploded. "I didn't do it. Isn't there any room for truth in the system?"

"If I start down the path you want at the hearing, I have to destroy Madelaine's case. Otherwise you'll be worse off. The publicity will affect the jurors, and we'll have given the prosecutor, and her witnesses, our line of attack at trial. We'll have locked ourselves into stances we might later wish we hadn't."

"I don't give a damn," he said hotly. "It's a gamble I'm willing to take."

I wasn't so sure that I was. "Let's go over the evidence," I said with a sigh. I pulled my notes from my briefcase.

"We've done that."

"And now we're going to do it again."

Grady rolled his shoulders and huffed in exasperation. But he sat square in his chair and looked at me. "Okay, let's do it, then."

"They've set the time of death for somewhere between eight and midnight," I said. "During this time you were at work, right?"

Grady nodded.

"You didn't see or talk to anyone?"

"No. I don't even know for sure what time I left."

"A neighbor saw your car pull into the driveway a little before midnight. That sound reasonable to you?"

"I guess."

"You left work and drove straight home?"

Grady was staring at his thumbs.

I waited.

"Yeah, as far as I can remember." He didn't look at me.

"They're going to use the little girl's testimony, you know. She saw a silver convertible in the driveway at ten. She heard a man's voice."

"She's a kid."

Children's testimony was sometimes unreliable, but not always. "A child witness can evoke juror sympathy," I told him. "She can come across as entirely believable."

"Isn't it your job to discredit the prosecution's witnesses? A kid ought to be easy."

"Not as easy as you might think." In fact, dealing with a child witness was a tricky proposition. I had to discredit Adrianna without turning the jurors against me, and therefore against Grady.

"Anyway," Grady continued, "she only *heard* a man; she didn't see him, did she?"

I shook my head.

"And there was nothing distinctive about the car she saw, right? Mine isn't the only silver convertible in the Bay Area."

"Still, it would be better for us if you drove a station wagon or a minivan."

"The best thing," Grady said with disgust, "would be if I'd never laid eyes on Deirdre Nichols."

"That wasn't what got you into trouble." I was still angered by his betrayal of Nina. "What you should have done," I said, "is kept your pants zipped."

Grady looked at me for a moment with a tight expression, as though he were ready to explode. Then he shook his head and sighed. "You're right. But I didn't. We have to deal with what we've got."

"Adrianna and the car," I said, recapping. "There's also the shoe print. We can handle that the same way we do the car. Nike is a popular brand, and ten is a common size."

Grady nodded vigorously.

"Only thing is, it strains credibility that you just happened to donate the pants you were wearing to the Salvation Army two days later."

"Monday was the pickup. I always go through my closet the night before and toss things that are getting old."

If we could substantiate that Grady's custom was actually that, it might help. But I wasn't sure it would alleviate suspicion entirely. I made a note to check with Simon about routine pickups by the Salvation Army and other charities, then moved on to the next item.

"We also have to contend with the fact that your handkerchief was found in Deirdre Nichols's front hallway."

"I told you, I left it there the night I gave her a ride home."

"The night of the alleged rape."

He nodded.

I rocked back and looked him in the eye. "Why?"

"Why what?

"Why did you leave it there?"

He backpedaled. "I didn't *leave* it exactly. I handed it to her. In the car. She must have kept it."

"Interesting that she kept it on her hallway floor."

He shrugged. "Some people aren't all that neat."

Like everything else about Grady's story, it was plausible but not very convincing.

"One of the best things we have going for us," I said, "is that the cops never looked at other possibilities. But if I bring this up at the hearing, we'll lose the advantage of surprise at trial. And the truth is, a jury is going to be a lot more receptive to this approach than the hearing judge."

Grady rocked forward. "Didn't I just tell you I can't wait until trial? Whose side are you on anyway?"

I ignored the pique that had worked its way into his voice.

"There's something you should know. The investigator we had working on the case was killed two nights ago. Murdered."

Grady's anger dissipated. "My God. You think there's a connection?"

"The day he was killed, he left a message on my answering machine about the guy Deirdre had been seeing. He said he'd discovered something that might help your case."

A glimmer of excitement crept into Grady's expression. "Like what?"

"At this point I don't know any more than I've told you. If I raise the issue at the hearing, though, and it's not enough to sway the judge, then we've lost it. By the time we go to trial, the prosecution will have found a way to defuse the impact. It's much better to catch them off guard when the jury's present."

"The investigator didn't give you any idea at all?" Grady's tone was impatient.

I snapped at him. "He wasn't planning on getting killed before we had a chance to talk."

Grady held up a hand in surrender. "Sorry."

I swallowed hard. It was still difficult for me to talk about Hal without feeling a sweeping grief. "I was hoping Deirdre might have mentioned him to you. His name is Tony Rodale. He runs some sort of investment fund."

Grady shook his head.

"Think hard, Grady."

"I am, dammit. I'd tell you if I knew."

I leaned back, took a breath, and dipped my toe into waters of a different sort. "The investigator also told me he saw Marc with this fellow Rodale. I'm thinking Rodale's in investments, Marc's handling your stock offering, the company needs an infusion of capital ... I'm wondering if it isn't all tied together." Although I was damned if I could figure out how.

Grady appeared honestly perplexed. "Marc? He's a straight arrow when it comes to accounting and securities matters. And I've never heard of Tony Rodale. I wouldn't worry about that being an issue."

It was the answer I wanted to hear, although it didn't completely dispel the doubts lingering at the back of my mind. Not about Marc. And not about Grady either. Or my complicity in Hal's death.

"The press will be at the hearing tomorrow," I told him. "It's important you look confident but not cocky. You want to show concern—there's been a tragic death after all—but you want to come across like a man in command. Think you can manage that?"

He nodded. "Of course I can."

I wasn't really worried about Grady's demeanor in court. It was the kind of role he played naturally. "If you think of something during the hearing, write it down on a slip of paper and pass it to me. Without any theatrics. If the press asks for a comment, keep your mouth shut. We'll hold a brief press conference at the conclusion of the hearing. You got all that?"

"Just promise me you'll try to get the case thrown out."

"I'll try, Grady. Honestly, I will. I understand how you feel. But I'm not going to commit malpractice by jeopardizing the case for a one-in-a-million chance of seeing charges dropped at the prelim."

Grady fingered the ultrasound image of his unborn son. "Who is going to care for him while Nina goes through chemo if I'm still in jail? Who's going to be there for Emily? This is my family we're talking about, goddammit. I need to get the charges dropped."

On my way back to the office, I stopped off downtown to see if I could learn anything new about Hal's death. Fogerty was on his way out as I entered, but he recognized me and stopped short of the doorway.

"You coming to see me?" he asked.

"I was hoping there'd been some progress."

He shook his head. "Sorry to say, there hasn't been. Not for lack of effort, you understand. We've had officers combing the area for witnesses. Had the car towed and let the forensic guys go through it close up. The brother is flying out today or tomorrow. If you don't mind, he'd probably like the chance to talk with you."

"Feel free to give him my number. I'd like to meet him."

Fogerty checked his watch and again started for the door.

I turned to follow. "I take it nothing's turned up with Tony Rodale either."

Fogerty looked at me blankly.

"The phone message. Remember? I told you yesterday that

Hal had been working on a case for me, that he'd left a message on my machine saying he'd discovered something that might implicate Rodale."

"Oh, that. Right. I passed along the information, like I said I would. But the boss calls the shots. He didn't think it was worth pursuing."

That was a shock. "What do you mean? You had a man there last night."

"There?"

"Outside Rodale's house."

Fogerty shrugged. "News to me. But, hey, I only work here."

"The man you called 'the boss,' what's his name?"

"Gibson. Cedric Gibson."

"Thanks."

I pushed through the double door and headed for the elevator. Gibson was tied up in a meeting, so I tried the front desk instead. Chances were, I'd get more out of a detective working the investigation anyway.

"I'm looking for a detective who works homicide. He's tall, blond, mid-thirties. Has a slight scar on his chin."

"You know his name?"

Sure, but I'm playing twenty questions for the fun of it. "I've forgotten it," I explained.

The desk sergeant scratched his cheek. "Blond, with a scar on his chin. Only guy I know of who fits that's description is Steve Henshaw."

Bingo. I recognized the name. "That's him, thanks. Is he around?"

The desk sergeant changed sides and scratched the other cheek. "Only thing is, Henshaw doesn't work homicide. Never has. In any event, he's off today."

CHAPTER 37

"What do you mean he doesn't work homicide?" I asked the desk sergeant.

He'd turned away to talk to a fellow police officer, and now looked back, surprised to find me still standing there. "Sorry, were you talking to me?"

"What division is Henshaw with?"

"He's on special assignment."

"What kind of special assignment?"

The sergeant pulled on his lower lip, scowling. "If you've got questions, you should talk to Henshaw himself."

Only thing was, Henshaw wasn't in.

I returned to Gibson's office and waited forty minutes until he was free. Although he agreed to see me, it was clear he considered my visit an intrusion, even before he knew why I was there.

Cedric Gibson was a jowly man with deep-set eyes and a stern expression. When I mentioned Steve Henshaw's name, the fixed glower became almost reproachful.

"You must be mistaken," Gibson said when I'd finished explaining my interest in the matter. He folded his hands on his desk, thumbs pressed together.

"No, I saw him parked off Broadway Terrace, near Tony Rodale's house."

Gibson's shoulders twitched in a half-shrug. "Must have been someone who looked like him."

I shook my head and feigned certainty. "I'm sure that it was Henshaw I saw."

"Maybe he was simply in the neighborhood. I know for a fact

that Detective Henshaw isn't involved in any homicide investigations."

"What *is* he involved in?"

"Sorry, that's information we like to keep within the department." Gibson drew his hands back into his lap. "I can assure you, however, that his investigation has no bearing on the charges against your client."

"What about the murder of Hal Fisher. Does it have bearing on that?"

Gibson shrugged, like *who-knows*. "The investigation is moving forward, but we've still got a long way to go."

"Any progress?"

"We're working a number of things."

Things that he clearly had no intention of sharing with me. I tried an end run. "You're telling me no one from the department is keeping an eye on Tony Rodale?"

Gibson's eyes narrowed. "Why should we be?"

"Because there's a good chance he's implicated in Deirdre Nichols' death. And maybe Hal Fisher's as well."

Although I'd been assured that Hal's last message to me had been relayed to Gibson, maybe it hadn't been. Not fully anyway. Or maybe it hadn't been presented in the right context. I laid it out for him again, explaining that Hal had discovered something about Rodale and Deirdre Nichols that pointed to a killer other than Grady.

Gibson leaned back in his chair and frowned. "We'd hardly authorize a stakeout on something that flimsy."

"Are you telling me you're not going to pursue this?" I could hear my voice rising in volume. "Hal Fisher left word for me that he'd discovered something tying Rodale to Deirdre Nichols' murder. That same day Hal himself was murdered. You think that's flimsy?"

"What I think," he said not unkindly, "is that you're emotionally involved in your friend's death. And understandably upset."

A smile flickered on his lips. A gesture no doubt meant to establish rapport, but the effect was quite the opposite. I was growing increasingly irritated.

"If Henshaw's not involved in any homicide investigations," I prodded, "what was he doing at the crime scene the morning Deirdre Nichols' body was discovered?"

The smile faded. "What makes you think he was?"

"I saw him. Or, rather, I saw photos of him. They were part of the discovery materials I received from the D.A.'s office."

"He must have been in the area," Gibson said with an off-handed shrug. "Probably needed to get a message to a fellow officer."

"One who just happened to be at a crime scene?"

Gibson glared at me. "As I'm sure you realize, detectives cover a lot of territory in the course of a given day."

It wasn't, I thought, all that different from the explanation he'd given me for Henshaw's presence outside Rodale's house.

"None of this feels right to me," I said after a moment.

"With all due respect, Ms. O'Brien, it's not your problem."

"It is if it impacts my client's case."

"But I just told you, it doesn't."

I stood. "It will be interesting to see what Officer Henshaw has to say. Under oath."

Gibson stood as well. "You'll have a hard time getting a subpoena to go on a fishing expedition."

Probably true, but I wasn't about to admit it. "We'll see about that."

Gibson's mouth was tight. "Take my advice, and drop this line of inquiry. It's not going to help your client in the least."

I didn't slam the door on my way out, but I wanted to. I gave myself a mental pat on the back for exercising restraint in the face of such overwhelming temptation.

On the drive to the office, however, my anger subsided, diluted by doubt and suspicion. Was I mistaken? Had I seen a police officer on a stakeout because that's what I *wanted* to see?

But if I was right, and the police weren't keeping an eye on Rodale because of Hal's message, why *were* they watching him?

I was at my desk later that afternoon, fine-tuning my opening statement, when Marc returned from a meeting. He knocked on my office door.

"How's it going?" he asked, draping himself against the door frame. He'd removed his tie and unbuttoned the collar of his shirt.

"So-so."

"Anything new on Hal's death?"

"They're looking at a number of things," I told him, mimicking Gibson.

"They know Hal was working for us?"

"I told them, but I don't think they were much interested."

"Figures." Marc moved behind me and started massaging my neck and shoulders. "The chances are, you know, they're right."

"What do you mean?"

"That Hal's death had nothing to do with this case. He had to have been working other cases as well."

I lowered my chin and leaned forward, giving Marc more room to work my back. "I just want them to find whoever did it," I said, although I knew the chances of that were slim.

I also wanted to know what Hal had discovered about Tony Rodale that might help Grady—and whether Marc was implicated. The chances of that, I thought, might be equally slim.

"Try taking a few deep breaths," Marc said, running a thumb along my shoulder blades. "You're tight as a wire."

As Marc worked tiny circles along the vertebrae of my spine, I tried breathing deeply, in and out. I could feel my body begging to relax, but the knot inside me wouldn't let go. The confusion and doubt were too deeply rooted.

"I know you're upset, Kali. But you've got to put Hal's death aside for the moment and focus on tomorrow's hearing." Marc's fingers moved to the muscles at the back of my neck, kneading them softly.

Finally, in spite of myself, I began to relax. For a short while we were quiet, each of us lost in our own thoughts.

"How's it look for the hearing?" Marc asked, breaking the silence.

"Aside from the fact that Grady wants me to present a full-blown defense, not too bad. I'm looking forward to finally being able to question some of the prosecution's witnesses."

Marc's hands stopped their kneading. "I'm afraid I've got some bad news on the other-suspect front."

I turned to look at him. "What do you mean?"

He leaned against the desk, facing me. "Remember Eric Simpson?"

I nodded. "The guy hassling the Carsons." I'd been hoping we could find him before the hearing, and maybe find some way to connect him to Deirdre Nichols' murder.

"He's not going to work into your alternate-scenario plan."

"Why not?"

Marc looked glum. "He's in jail. He's been there since the end of last month. No way he could have killed Deirdre Nichols."

My heart sank. "You sure?"

He nodded. "I just found out this morning. It's definitely the same guy."

"Damn."

"Better to find out now than get shot down after you've raised the idea in court."

Better not to get shot down at all.

"That doesn't leave us with much," Marc said slowly.

"Except Tony Rodale. But he comes into play only if we get into a finger-pointing mode, and only if we need to point to a specific face."

"That's kind of the name of the game, isn't it?"

"Depends on how desperate we are."

Marc picked up the pen on my desk and rolled it between his fingers. "Still no idea what Hal was hinting at in his message?"

I shook my head, wondering if I dared to be completely frank with him. I turned to look Marc in the eye. "How do you know Rodale?" I asked casually.

Something flashed in Marc's eyes, but his face was largely unreadable. "What do you mean?"

"You *do* know him, right?"

"Of course. He's the guy Deirdre Nichols was dating."

"I mean outside of this case." I could feel my heart pounding in my chest. Hear the rush of blood in my ears. "You have some other connection with him, am I right?"

Marc frowned. "What makes you think that?"

"Just answer the question."

A moment's pause, and then Marc shook his head. "Why would I?" His tone was earnest, his expression one of confusion.

"Is that a no?" The words were sharp, but I couldn't help it.

Marc nodded.

I swallowed, trying the answer on for size. Maybe Hal had been wrong after all. "You've never met him?" I asked.

Marc shook his head again.

"How about Deirdre Nichols? Did you know her before she filed rape charges against Grady?"

The confusion on Marc's face deepened. "What are you suggesting?"

"Did you?"

He crossed his arms, glared at me. "No, I did not."

"How about after? Did you meet with her after she accused Grady?"

Marc looked ready to explode. His eyes were narrow and dark, and his expression stony. "You're the one who skated on ethical thin ice by meeting with her privately," he snapped. "Not me."

"She followed me into the rest room."

"Well, she didn't follow me, and I didn't talk to her." He paused, collecting himself, then continued in a calmer voice. "Now, you want to tell me what this is all about?"

I wasn't so sure myself. Why was I making such a big deal about something Hal had uttered almost in passing? *Go slow,* he told me. *You may not know Marc as well as you think.* There was nothing substantive about the comment.

But Hal had also said he'd seen Marc with Tony Rodale. Thought he'd seen, I corrected myself. Even Hal had admitted he wasn't certain. I'd misread Marc once ten years ago. Was that coloring my thinking now?

I hedged. "I saw a cop outside Tony Rodale's house the other night."

"A cop?"

"The guy Madelaine Rivera is dating. It looked like he was on a stakeout. I assumed they were watching Rodale in connection with Hal's death. But it turns out the guy's not even in homicide. He's on special assignment."

A muscle in Marc's jaw pulsed erratically. "What kind of special assignment?"

I shook my head. "Nobody would say. I hate to offer up Rodale as an alternate suspect without knowing all the details."

"Then don't do it. I've said that all along. Chances are it will backfire."

"It may be our only hope."

Marc went to the window, locked his fingers behind the bar of his neck. "You think Hal kept notes of his investigation?"

"Not anything that would help us. Hal's approach was to file things mentally until he was ready to pass along the information. He wasn't big on the intermediary steps."

"No kind of record at all?"

"I doubt it."

Marc turned back into the room, favoring me with a weary smile. "Too bad."

I nodded agreement.

He sat on the edge of the desk, facing me. "Now, you want to tell me what's with all the questions about whether I knew Tony Rodale or Deirdre Nichols?"

There we were again. I wanted to tell him, to open up and get it off my chest. I wanted to hear him cast the doubt from my mind. But still, I hesitated.

"Hal thought he saw you with Rodale," I said. "Remember?"

"Seems to me we covered that before. Hal was mistaken."

"There's also the pen from Rapunzel."

Marc's smile widened. "We already covered that one too."

"You haven't remembered how you got it?"

"What's the big deal? You've never inadvertently walked off with a pen that wasn't yours?" Marc shook his head, bemused. "Happens to me all the time. A couple of people at ComTech have taken to taping their names on their pens when I'm around."

His explanation *was* plausible. Judith Powers worked at Com-Tech and was Deirdre's friend. She might have had the pen sitting on her desk. It was even plausible that one of the other employees patronized the salon.

Marc reached for my hand. "You're worried about Grady's trial and you're upset about Hal. It's hard not to let other stuff build and grow out of proportion."

"I guess so."

"After the hearing is over, let's get away for a few days. Just the two of us. There's probably still fairly decent snow in the mountains. We could get in some skiing. Or we could head north to Sea Ranch. I've got a friend who has a house there we could use."

"I don't think—"

"I'm not asking you to make a life commitment, Kali. I only want you to give me another chance." He paused. "To give *us* a chance." His voice caught on the last few words.

Maybe that's all we needed, time to get to know each other again. Time to erase the doubts and to learn trust.

"Please say yes."

I gave his hand a squeeze. "No promises," I told him. "But I'll think about it."

I worked at the office until almost seven. Rose came in before she left to make sure I was properly equipped with paper and pens as well as a cellophane sack of throat mints. I'd never figured out whether it was nerves or the air inside the courthouse, but my throat always gave out about midway through a day at trial.

Before leaving, I called Nina. I could tell the tension was getting to her, because she was in a foul mood.

"Emily was in a fight at school today," she said. "The teacher called, and then the principal. What am I supposed to do? I can't even talk to Emily except by phone."

"Surely they must understand—"

"Oh, they know the circumstances, if that's what you mean. Me in the hospital and Grady in jail. I'm sure that's part of the reason for the call. Nobody knows quite what to do with us."

"Did they say who started the fight?"

"They say it was Emily. She says it was the other little girl." Nina sighed. "It doesn't really matter. Emily apparently gave the girl a bloody nose and pushed her so hard, she fell down."

My heart went out to Emily, who was probably the most vulnerable of the Barretts. She had to be feeling the stress of her parents' troubles, and trying to find her way pretty much on her own.

"I wish I were freer to spend time with her," I said.

"Grady and this trial need your attention at the moment. And I do have people who are helping with Emily. Thank God. I couldn't bear it if I thought she had to rely solely on Simon and Elsa, as lovely as they are."

"It's good to have friends you can count on."

Nina was silent a moment. "I do have some wonderful friends, you foremost among them. But I've discovered there are also a lot of people I thought were my friends who are now delighting in the gossip." Her laugh was bitter. "The numbers are weighted heavily into the latter camp."

"I bet people care more than you think."

"Don't bank on it." Her tone was bleak. "And there's plenty for them to feast on. As if coverage in the local press wasn't bad enough, there was a piece about Grady in Monday's *Wall Street Journal*. One of my neighbors sent me a copy."

"About the trial?" With all that was going on, I hadn't been reading the *Journal* recently.

"About Deirdre, the trial, the falling fortunes of ComTech. What was she trying to do, rub my nose in it?"

"Maybe she saw Grady's name and didn't bother to read the article." It sounded lame, but I didn't know what else to say.

Another humorless laugh, which wound down to a sort of mewing sound. "I hate this, Kali. I fucking hate everything about life right now. *Everything.*"

The pain in her voice sent a rattle through my chest. It's a terrible thing to watch someone you care about hurting. It's even worse when you're unable to help.

I offered reassurance, but the words rang hollow in my own ears. "I know things seem pretty bleak right now, but they'll turn around."

"Not soon enough, I'm afraid." Her voice faltered. "Or far enough."

"You're strong, Nina. A fighter. You always have been. Now's not the time to give up."

"I've got news for you, Kali—hope doesn't always spring eternal."

I knew in Nina's place I'd feel the same way.

"You'll call me tomorrow at the end of court?" she asked after a moment.

"You know I will."

"And you'll tell me the truth, no matter how bad it looks?"

I hesitated for only a second, but she jumped on me.

"Promise me, Kali."

"I promise."

Bea had fixed homemade soup for dinner, and she and Dotty talked me into sharing it with them. I was grateful. Both for the soup, a delicious chicken vegetable with curry, and for the conversation, which was about nothing heavier than restaurants that failed to live up to their reputation. My two companions had quite a list, and they expounded on it for a good part of the meal.

When we'd finished eating, I fixed myself a cup of coffee and went downstairs to work. About ten-thirty the phone rang.

Bea called down. "It's for you."

I picked up the receiver. The voice on the other end was scratchy and faint.

"Kali?"

"Is that you, Marc?"

He coughed, a ratchety, wheezing sound as though he were having trouble getting enough air.

"Marc? Are you okay?"

"I need help, Kali. Will you help me?"

CHAPTER 38

"I need help," Marc said again.

Fear clutched my chest. "What's wrong?"

"I'm hurt."

"Hurt? How?" I could hear panic edging its way into my voice. Marc was not one to readily admit need.

Silence, accompanied by labored breathing.

"Should I call an ambulance?"

"No ambulance." The words were thin and frayed. "It's not that bad."

Maybe not, but it sounded close.

"Please, just come get me. I'll explain when you get here."

"Where are you? At work?" I thought maybe our attacker from the other night had returned.

"No, I'm—" He paused. "I'm a couple of streets south of Alcatraz. Near a church, close to Sacramento Street." There was a shuffling noise on the other end, another audible breath. "Look for a blue house. I'll be in front."

"You're sure you don't need an ambulance?"

"Positive."

"Should I call the police?"

"No." His response was vehement. "I'm okay, honest. I'll explain when I see you. Just hurry."

"I'm on my way."

I drove above the speed limit, but not nearly as fast as the frightened voice in my head urged. Each stop sign was exasperating. Each curve in the road pushed the limits of my patience. Red lights lasted forever.

Had there been an auto accident? Or maybe a biking accident?

I knew Marc was a biker. Maybe he'd taken a bad spill. My mind filled with other visions as well. I thought of Hal, dead. Of the man who'd broken into our office. I gave a silent prayer, hoping for a simple biking injury.

I turned onto the first street south of Alcatraz. Small houses, barred windows. Some boarded and abandoned. It was not a prosperous part of the city.

The neighborhood was dark, the streetlights few and far between. The sliver moon, low on the horizon, was no help. Shadow and stillness, broken only by an occasional gust of wind that sent dry leaves across the roadway like scampering rodents.

I could feel my heart pounding in my chest, my blood pulsing in my ears. I wondered fleetingly if I was walking into a trap, if someone was using Marc to lure me into danger. I'd grabbed my can of pepper spray before leaving the house, but it wouldn't be of much use against a gun. I wished I'd thought to tell Bea and Dotty where I was going.

I slowed at each corner to read the street signs, many of which were missing or obscured by low-hanging foliage. When I passed a church, I slowed the car to a crawl and kept my eyes on the houses to either side of the street. It was too dark to tell blue from any other color. I struggled instead to find Marc, but with cars parked along the curb I found it difficult to see onto the sidewalk.

It was a glint of white—a shirt reflected in the car's headlights—that first caught my attention. And then my eyes made out a form slouched against a tree near the curb. Marc was sitting on the ground, bent over, clutching his stomach, swaying slightly from left to right.

I stopped the car without taking time to park it and jumped out. As I got closer, I saw that his shirt was torn across the shoulder and that there were dark stains down the front. Marc's face was scraped and swollen. He held his left arm close to his chest.

"My God, Marc. What happened?"

He looked at me with one eye and groaned.

"We need to get you to the hospital," I said.

"It's not as bad as it looks."

Even if it was half as bad, I thought a visit to the emergency room was in order.

Marc tried to straighten, and was only partially successful. "They gave me a bloody nose—that's what makes it look so bad."

"Who hit you? What happened?"

"Two guys." He winced, as though talking hurt. "They jumped me."

"Why?"

"Creeps like that don't need a why. They took my wallet and watch."

"You're lucky they didn't kill you."

"I think they may have tried. Fortunately a car drove by and scared them off."

In my mind's eye I saw Hal's lifeless body laid out in the morgue. Had the same two men gotten to him? If the car hadn't driven by when it did, would Marc have ended up dead as well?

Fear closed my throat, making it difficult to speak. "Can you walk?" I managed to ask.

"I could a bit ago. I used the car phone to call you." He started to get up, but it clearly hurt to move. "You've got so much on your mind right now. I hated to bother you."

"Don't worry about it." I put an arm around his middle.

"Careful. They kicked me in the stomach and ribs. I think that's where most of the damage is."

Moving an inch at a time, we finally got Marc into the car. He closed his eyes and gritted his teeth as I buckled the seat belt around him. I drove slowly so as not to joggle him any more than necessary.

"What were you doing in that neighborhood anyway?" I asked when it became clear Marc wasn't going to volunteer a full explanation.

"I went to see a guy."

"What guy?"

Marc closed his eyes again. "I got a call from someone telling me to meet him there. He said he had some information about the case."

"And you went?" The full force of my anxiety was embedded in my words. I practically screamed at him.

"It was stupid, I know. But it was the only way I could think of to hear what the guy had to say."

"Which was what?"

Marc shook his head. "He never showed."

"Unless the two thugs who attacked you made the call. Did you think of that?"

"It crossed my mind."

"You could at least have told someone where you were going," I said with a note of annoyance. Not that I'd bothered to do so myself.

"Don't be angry with me, Kali. Please. Not tonight. I feel shitty enough as is." His voice wavered, and I wondered for moment if he was close to tears.

"I'm not angry," I said softly. "I'm worried."

Getting Marc out of the car was a bit easier than getting him in, but not by much. His forehead was damp with perspiration by the time I got him settled in his own bed. He let me wash the cuts and scrapes on his face, but he was too uncomfortable to even think about removing his shirt. He was shaking, and breathing unevenly. I tried again to persuade him to go to the hospital.

"Tomorrow, if I'm not better."

"How about the police? I'll call them for you."

"It won't do any good."

"You should report it, Marc."

"They'll never find the two guys."

"They might."

He leaned his head back against the pillow. "Just let me rest, okay?"

I poured us both a glass of scotch. Marc barely touched his. "How about some ginger ale or something?"

"There isn't any."

"I can go to the store."

He shook his head, barely moving it from side to side. "Just stay with me for a little while. Can you do that?"

"Of course."

Marc's skin was pale and clammy, and I worried that he might have a concussion or some internal bleeding. There was no way I was going to leave him alone. I rinsed out the washcloth with cold water and pressed it against his forehead.

Marc closed his eyes. "I'm afraid I'm not going to be much use at the hearing tomorrow."

"Don't worry about it."

He took in a gulp of air. "I'm sorry, Kali. So terribly sorry." There were tears on his cheeks.

I wanted to cradle him in my arms, to comfort him like a baby, but he was too broken and bruised for that. I reached for his hand instead, and held it in my own.

"I wanted a fresh start for us," he said unevenly. "I wanted a chance to do things right."

"Shhh," I whispered. "Try to rest. We'll talk tomorrow."

"I'm so sorry," he mumbled again. And then again. Until finally he drifted off to a troubled sleep.

I pulled a chair up next to the bed and covered myself with Marc's robe. My own slumber, when it eventually came, was as troubled as his.

CHAPTER 39

"Where's Marc?" Grady asked the next morning, taking a seat beside me at the defense table near the front of the courtroom.

Dressed in a dark blue suit and freshly pressed shirt, Grady looked almost the picture of his former self. Hardy, handsome, and self-assured. Since he was a man who thrived on challenge, I suspected he would find the contention of the courtroom preferable to the helpless waiting of jail.

"Marc's not feeling well," I explained.

"What's wrong with him?"

I shrugged it off. "One of those things."

"Nothing serious, I hope."

That made two of us.

I'd stayed the night at Marc's, sleeping fitfully in a chair next to his bed. Before sunrise I'd checked on him one last time and then driven home to shower and change for court. It wasn't the best preparation for on-your-toes thinking, but surprisingly, the lack of a solid night's sleep had yet to catch up with me. I could only hope that my luck held until court adjourned for the day.

My eyes scanned the room, sizing up the crowd that packed the area set aside for spectators. No cameras, thanks to an earlier judicial ruling, but the media was there in force. For the last half hour they'd been mingling in twos and threes, like customers waiting for the doors to open at Macy's after-Christmas sale.

I'd seen Madelaine stop and exchange pleasantries with several of the groups on her way in. Next time I'd have to do the same or she'd win the war before we even fought the first battle.

Grady leaned toward me and whispered, "You're going to push for a dismissal, right?"

"I'm going to try. It's a long shot though."

"My family needs me," he said. "Just remember that."

As if I could forget. The thought had been weighing heavily on my mind these last few days. Very heavily. It wasn't just Grady's future in my hands, but Nina's and Emily's as well. My nerves were frayed from worrying.

Grady's fingers drummed the table silently. I felt my own anxiety straining every fiber of my body. Finally, the appointed hour arrived. We rose as the deputy pronounced court in session and called our case.

"People versus Grady Barrett."

I could feel Grady stiffen as the words rang out. No matter how much a defendant professes to have come to terms with being caught in the judicial system, it always comes as a cold slap of reality to hear his own name called out in such an official context.

"You may be seated," the deputy said.

There was a general rustle in the crowded courtroom as people returned to their seats and got comfortable. Grady sat rigidly with his hands folded on the table. I touched his sleeve lightly in a gesture of support.

We'd drawn Edith Atwood as our judge for the hearing. Although I'd never met her, I was familiar with her reputation. A veteran of almost a decade on the bench, Judge Atwood was known for her no-nonsense approach to moving cases through the system as efficiently as possible. It was a quality I found admirable in theory, but a bit offputting now that I was going to be on the receiving end of her judicial whip.

According to rumor, she was in the midst of a nasty divorce that had further sapped her reserves of patience. Her rulings often reflected this.

Judge Atwood took a seat behind the bench and donned a pair of tortoiseshell reading glasses. Petite, with birdlike features and short, wispy hair that was more salt than pepper, she looked like a woman not given to easy smiles or aimless banter. Not on the job, at any rate.

In words taken almost verbatim from the penal code, Judge Atwood delivered a perfunctory admonishment about the purposes and limitations of the preliminary hearing. "This is not a trial," she concluded, "and you are not playing to a jury. All we need to determine at this stage is whether there is reason to believe a felony has been committed, and that Mr. Barrett is the person who committed it." She looked over her glasses at Madelaine. "How long do you propose to take, counselor?"

"Two days should do it, Your Honor."

Judge Atwood nodded and made a notation on the sheet in front of her.

I spoke up. "The defense may need additional time."

Her eyes showed surprise. "You intend to put on a case, Ms. O'Brien?"

"I may, Your Honor, depending on how the prosecution's case goes."

Although it was clear that Judge Atwood wasn't pleased with my announcement, there was nothing she could do about it but scowl. The law allows defendants to put on a defense if they wish.

"How many days do you anticipate needing?" she asked.

I had no idea. "Two."

She sighed and made another notation.

Beside me Grady whispered, "Will that be enough time?"

About one and a half days more than I could possibly fill. I nodded.

"Are the People ready?" Judge Atwood asked.

Madelaine rose. "Yes, Your Honor."

Her opening remarks were thorough if not inspired, and pretty much what I'd been expecting. As a prelude to showing motive, Madelaine began by addressing the rape charge and the case against Grady that had been dropped following Deirdre Nichols' death. She then proceeded to lay out the case against Grady, piece by piece. Adrianna's statement about having seen a silver convertible and hearing a man's voice. The handkerchief, shoe print, and missing slacks Grady claimed to have donated to the Salvation Army.

No surprises until she mentioned a name I'd not heard before. Charles Berger.

I scratched a note to Grady. "Who's he?"

Grady answered with a nervous shrug.

Shit. This was the kind of stuff that wasn't supposed to happen.

That's what the rules of discovery were all about. I shot Madelaine a questioning look, though it did me little good.

"Is defense counsel ready to proceed?" asked Judge Atwood when Madelaine had concluded her remarks.

"Yes, Your Honor," I said, standing.

"Good. Please, don't feel you need to belabor points already raised by the prosecution. Bear in mind, this is only the preliminary hearing."

"Yes, Your Honor."

"And I don't want to hear a lot of unnecessary rhetoric. Even though we've been graced with the presence of the press"—here she paused to nod toward the chairs at the back of the room, and when she continued, her voice took on a sardonic edge—"in spite of their interest, we'd like to proceed as though our eyes were on justice rather than on the media."

I nodded, took a calming breath, and began.

"Your Honor, the prosecution's case is based entirely on circumstantial evidence. In order to prevail in this situation at trial, the People need to show that the evidence points only to the defendant and to no one else. We intend to show that such a scenario does not stand up to logic. This is a case where the police, in their zeal to apprehend a culprit, jumped to an immediate and erroneous conclusion about who committed the murder. It's incumbent on you to dismiss the case."

I paused for a sip of water. Out of the corner of my eye, I could see Grady. He looked alert and interested, but confident—the model of a defendant buoyed by his own innocence. Turning back to the judge, I continued.

"The defense will show that each and every point raised by the prosecution is open to a different interpretation. What's more, we intend to show that the police overlooked at least one, and possibly several, other logical avenues of investigation. They were aware of additional suspects and simply chose to ignore them."

Judge Atwood didn't blink, but there was a murmuring from the rear of the courtroom. With luck, tomorrow morning's headlines would allude to alternative suspects and defense surprises. I only hoped I could deliver.

I talked for nearly fifteen minutes, reconstructing the crime step by step, even though Judge Atwood had told me it wasn't necessary. What I said or didn't say in my opening statement wasn't going to change her decision one iota, but my words would be repeated in papers and newscasts, and I wasn't about to give up my chance to spin the tale the way I wanted it told.

I tried not to get carried away, but made sure I used words like *innocent* and *groundless* and *rush to judgment* enough that the press would pick up on them.

When I sat down, Grady touched my sleeve. "That was very good," he said, sounding almost surprised. "Everything you said made absolute sense."

Of course, Grady was hardly an impartial audience.

The state's first witness was the female police officer who'd responded to the 911 call placed by Adrianna. I recognized her from my visit to the crime scene the Monday following Deirdre's death.

After the officer was sworn in, Madelaine asked that she state her name and occupation for the record.

"Janet Morrison, patrol division with the Oakland police department."

Madelaine took her through a few preliminaries, then asked about the discovery of Deirdre Nichols' body. Officer Morrison explained that she'd arrived at the scene just after Deirdre's sister, Sheila Barlow. She'd tried to calm both the girl and her aunt while at the same time preserving the crime scene. She'd been grateful when backup help arrived. Morrison had kids of her own, she explained, and she'd found Adrianna's distress upsetting on a personal level.

I took her through much of the same territory on cross. I wanted to see if any of the details changed. They didn't. Some police officers are very good at testifying, while others get nervous and fumble for words or trip over details. These inconsistencies can serve as fodder for the defense. Unfortunately for us, Officer Morrison was a pro.

Next up was the coroner. He acknowledged that the time of death could not be determined with precision, even in conjunction with extrinsic evidence. He was, however, able to say with confidence that Deirdre Nichols' death took place sometime between eight P.M. and midnight. It was his determination that there'd been a brief struggle and then Deirdre Nichols had been pushed to her death.

I'd given a copy of the autopsy report to a forensic pathologist

I'd used as an expert witness on previous occasions. If we went to trial, I would undoubtedly call him, but he'd found little in the report to quibble with.

Detective Hawkins, the lead investigator on the case, took the stand as we neared morning recess. Because the Best Evidence Rule is not applicable to preliminary hearings, the investigating officer can make use of reports and other information that would be inadmissable as hearsay at trial. As a result, Madelaine was able to cover a lot of ground with a single witness. The physical evidence from the crime scene, the results of the search of Grady's house, and the absence of any verifiable alibi on Grady's part. She hit them all, then graced me with a smug smile as she returned to her seat.

"Your witness," she said with grave formality.

Before I could begin my cross examination, Judge Atwood called for morning recess.

"How does it look so far?" Grady asked as the courtroom emptied.

"We've barely begun."

"I don't like that judge." He was fidgeting in the seat beside me, twisting his watchband and pulling at his cuffs. "She doesn't seem very friendly."

"It's not her job to be friendly."

The bailiff came to escort Grady to the rest room. I looked around for Madelaine to see if I could get some background on Charles Berger. When I couldn't find her, I found a pay phone and called Marc at home. I didn't get an answer there, so I tried the office next.

Rose picked up on the first ring. "How's it going in the battle zone?" she asked.

"So far, so good. Is Marc free?"

"He's not in yet."

"Not in?" I felt a rush of anxiety.

"He called though," she added. "Said he'd had a bad night and was going to sleep late. He told me that you already knew."

"Right, just checking." I was relieved to know that he hadn't taken a turn for the worse after I left. "How did he sound?"

"Like somebody just ran over his cat."

Close, I thought.

When I got off the phone, I was surprised to find Byron Spencer standing behind me. He smiled broadly. As usual, his good cheer was as bountiful as a puppy's.

"And so it begins," he said dramatically. "Another revolution for the wheels of justice."

"So it does."

We moved across the hallway.

"I didn't see you in the back of the courtroom this morning," I told him.

"I got here a little late, but I saw most of it." He stuck a hand in his pocket. "Where's your other half?"

"Marc?"

He nodded.

"He's not in court today. Why?"

"Just asking." A pause. "Remember our deal?"

"What deal?"

"You told me when I'd found something to let you know. Barter, remember? Quid pro quo."

Spencer's help in return for an exclusive. I'd assumed it was loose talk on his part, pie-in-the-sky dreaming by a kid who'd read too many detective novels. But I certainly wasn't about to rule out help in whatever form it took.

"Meet me for lunch," he said, lowering his voice to a conspiratorial level. "I have something I think you might find interesting."

I slung my purse over my shoulder. "I don't have time for lunch."

"I was talking hot dogs from a street vendor. Something quick and quiet. I think we need to be discreet."

I bit back a smile. Definitely too many crime novels. "Okay. As long as we can be quick."

"Noon recess," he said. "Tenth and Jefferson. I'll bring something for us to eat."

CHAPTER 40

Judge Atwood poured herself a glass of water from the brown plastic pitcher on her right, and reminded the witness that he was still under oath. Then she looked at me. "Counselor?"

Checking the collar of my gray silk blouse, I stood for cross. "Detective Hawkins, you stated that you arrived at the scene within an hour of the first patrol officer, is that correct?"

"Yes."

"And what was the first thing you did after you arrived?"

"The first—"

"In terms of assessing the evidence."

Hawkins' dark eyes narrowed as he tried to decipher the question for hidden tricks. He was wasting his time; I wasn't setting any traps just yet. It was more like I was scrounging for bait.

Finally, he cleared his throat and ventured an answer. "I took a verbal report from the patrol officer."

"And what did you do after that?"

"I talked to the EMT in charge, and then to Ms. Barlow, the deceased's sister."

"You didn't talk to the little girl, Adrianna?"

"Not right then, no. That was several hours later."

I moved closer. "What did you do next?"

"I made an assessment of the crime scene."

"Did you begin your inspection of the scene outside in the yard or inside the house?"

Hawkins folded his hands. "Outside, where Ms. Nichols' body was."

"You stated that the victim was wearing a white gown."

"That's correct."

"Can you describe this gown?"

He mustered a bemused expression. "I'm no fashion expert." This drew titters from the journalists in the room.

"Just describe it as best you can."

"Well, I know it was white, and long. And made of some kind of filmy material."

"The kind of thing someone might wear for entertaining?"

Hawkins shook his head. "More like at home. Loungewear, I think that's what they call it."

I gave him a quick smile. "You know more about fashion than you give yourself credit for, Detective." Another ripple of laughter, cut short by a stern glance from Judge Atwood.

"Wouldn't you say it was an odd thing for Ms. Nichols to be wearing, if, as the prosecution suggests, she was expecting a visit from the man she accused of raping her?"

"Objection." Madelaine rose to address the judge. "The detective's opinions on appropriate attire are not relevant, Your Honor."

Judge Atwood propped her chin on one hand. "There's no jury present, Ms. Rivera. Let's save the objections for things that matter."

In any event, Detective Hawkins sidestepped the issue by having no opinion one way or another.

"You also testified about shoe impressions in the soil at the side of the house." I paused. "I take it there was more than one?"

"Yes. Most were partials and not very clear, but one was fairly decent. It was in a flower bed. The loose, damp soil took the impression easily."

"The other prints were less clear?"

"Right."

"So you can't say with certainty that all the prints were made by the same pair of shoes, can you?"

"Not with one hundred percent certainty, no. But the clear print was a size ten Nike Pegasus, and there was nothing about any of the other prints inconsistent with that shoe."

"You testified that the prints were found on the north side of the house, in this general vicinity, here." I pointed to the drawing of the house that Hawkins had used during his testimony on direct. "Some were leading toward the rear yard, where the body was found, and some leading away."

"Correct."

"And you believe it likely they all came from the same pair of shoes."

"I just said that, yes."

"Just this single set of impressions."

Hawkins rolled his eyes, annoyed. "Yes."

"So the EMTs didn't leave any shoe impressions when they examined the body?"

Hawkins shifted in his seat. "Well, yes, but I assumed you meant in addition to those."

"And were those prints pristine, or less clear?"

"A little of both."

"So, actually, there were quite a number of prints. Some partials, some very clear. One was a size ten Nike Pegasus, many were not. Is that correct?"

"Yes, but—"

"You've answered the question, Detective. Let's focus on the clear Nike print for a moment. It was found here, is that correct?" I pointed again to the drawing. "Near the street entrance to the side yard, well away from where the body was found?"

"That particular print, yes."

"You testified that it was a left shoe print, with wear patterns similar to the left Nike Pegasus seized from Mr. Barrett's home."

"Correct."

"Can you say with certainty that it's a perfect match?"

At the defense table, Grady stirred. I saw his jaw grow stiff and his hands clench.

Hawkins licked his lips. "Not with absolute certainty, no. The print wasn't clear enough for that degree of accuracy."

I waited a moment, allowing members of the press to absorb his words, then continued. "All right, let's move on to the house now. It's your contention that Ms. Nichols fell from the deck, is that correct?"

Hawkins leaned back in the witness stand. "I'd say pushed rather than fell. But, yes, she appears to have come off the deck after a struggle. As I mentioned earlier, there were markings on the railing of the balcony, and fibers from her gown were caught in the wood there. An aluminum deck chair had been knocked over as well."

"Anything else to indicate a struggle?"

"The coroner found scratches and abrasions on Ms. Nichols' body that weren't consistent with a fall."

I walked back to the defense table. "When you questioned Mr. Barrett in conjunction with your investigation, did you examine him for scratches or other markings that might indicate a struggle?"

"Yes, we did."

"And did you find any?"

Hawkins hesitated. "Mr. Barrett is a large man. He'd easily be able to overpower a woman of Ms. Nichols' build."

"That was not my question, Detective." I turned to the judge. "Your Honor, I request that Detective Hawkins' response be stricken as nonresponsive."

"This is a prelim, for goodness' sake," she said to me. Her tone verged on being sharp. Then she turned to the witness. "Detective Hawkins, you know how we do this. Just answer the question."

Hawkins sighed. "No," he said without elaboration.

"Thank you." I checked my notes. "Now, moving on. Your report indicates that you dusted for prints at the crime scene, both inside and out."

"That's correct."

"Did you find any of Mr. Barrett's prints there?"

Hawkins glanced in Madelaine's direction. "No."

Early on, I'd been ready to explain away Grady's prints by virtue of his presence at Deirdre's house the week earlier. But we'd gotten lucky. Deirdre Nichols had been a meticulous housekeeper. Now I could simply reverse the argument.

"If, as the prosecution suggests, Grady Barrett was in the house the night of the murder, wouldn't you expect to find at least one print you could identify as his?"

"Depends on what he touched and whether he wore gloves."

If we were in front of a jury, I'd have pushed it, painting a ludicrous picture of Grady making a social call in a pair of gloves. Under the circumstances, I was trusting that Judge Atwood could see things clearly on her own.

"Did you inspect the rest of the house?" I asked Hawkins.

"Yes, I went through every room in the house myself."

"Was there any sign of a disturbance other than on the deck?"

"No, not really."

"So it was all very neat and tidy."

He smiled. "Well, the kitchen was kind of messy. But lived-in messy, if you know what I mean."

I feigned ignorance. "Not really."

"There were dirty dishes from dinner next to the sink, and Ms. Nichols had apparently been baking cookies, so there was baking stuff around."

"Baking stuff? Can you be more specific?"

He gave a fractional shrug. "A bowl still partially full of batter, raisins, chocolate syrup, cookie sheets, a measuring cup. There was probably more, but I can't remember offhand."

"But no signs of a struggle in the kitchen?"

"No."

I paused for a sip of water and checked my notes again. "The handkerchief that you found in the hallway. You testified that it was monogrammed with the defendant's initials and that it matched others found during a search of Mr. Barrett's home."

"That's right. The handkerchief is a specialty item, imported from England."

"But you can't say with absolute certainty that it belongs to the defendant, can you?"

He scoffed. "It pushes the limits of plausibility to think that two men with identical initials and handkerchiefs had reason to kill Ms. Nichols."

"Your Honor—" A quick glance at Judge Atwood's scowling face prompted my retreat. I sighed. "Never mind."

Turning back to Hawkins, I took a different tack. "Assuming for the moment that it was Mr. Barrett's handkerchief, isn't it possible that he dropped it when he was at Ms. Nichols' house a week earlier?"

"Possible, I suppose."

"There are no tests you can run, no way of determining how long the handkerchief had been at the house. Is that correct?"

"Not really, but it's unlikely—"

"Thank you, Detective. Now, on the morning the body was discovered, did you have any idea as to the killer's identity?"

"No, not then."

"What was it that led you to Mr. Barrett?"

Hawkins shifted in his seat, crossing his legs. "It was a lot of things. The handkerchief, the little girl's statement about seeing a silver convertible and hearing a man's voice, and then the next day we found a record of the call between Ms. Nichols and the defendant. It didn't take much to put two and two together."

Especially if you preferred simple arithmetic to more complex reasoning. "So you determined fairly early on that Grady Barrett was the principal suspect in the case?"

"The evidence was there. We couldn't ignore it."

"In fact, you were fairly certain Grady Barrett was your man when you first questioned him, weren't you?"

"Not at all," Hawkins said, thereby skirting the issue of Miranda warnings. "We were just gathering information at that point."

Sure, and I've got a bridge I could sell you.

"At what point did Mr. Barrett become your prime suspect?"

Hawkins glanced at Madelaine. "That's not an easy question to answer. Sometimes these things just evolve."

"So there was no one, single piece of evidence that convinced you Grady Barrett was your killer?"

Hawkins looked uncomfortable. "No, not one piece alone."

"Aside from the handkerchief and the single shoe print, was there any physical evidence from the crime scene that pointed to Mr. Barrett?"

"From the crime scene itself, no."

"And when you searched Mr. Barrett's house, you found no hair, no fibers, no blood—no evidence at all that could be traced to Ms. Nichols, is that correct?"

"That's true with regard to the items we seized. But the slacks he was wearing the evening she was killed are missing."

"Given away as part of a scheduled pickup, is that correct?"

"The pickup was scheduled, but I don't know about that particular pair of pants. Seems awfully convenient to my mind."

"Your Honor—"

She cut me off. "Same as I said before, Ms. O'Brien. I'm capable of separating the wheat from the chaff."

I directed my attention once again to the witness. "Detective Hawkins, did you question anyone else in connection with Ms. Nichols' murder?"

He pulled himself up straight. "We talked to a number of people."

"Did you question anyone else as a potential suspect?"

"Grady Barrett was our best suspect."

"He was your only suspect, wasn't he?"

"The evidence pointed to the defendant."

"Is that because you chose to interpret it that way?"

Madelaine jumped to her feet. "Objection, Your Honor. Asked and answered."

"Sustained. Ms. O'Brien, let's move along. You've made your point."

I took a moment to regroup, then stepped forward to address Hawkins. "Let me make sure I understand what evidence we're talking about, Detective. The handkerchief, which could have been there from an earlier visit. The impression of a shoe, which could have been made by *any* size ten Nike Pegasus and was only one of many prints made by various shoes. And finally, the car Adrianna saw—a silver convertible."

"Yes, in addition to the missing pants—"

I cut him off. "Detective Hawkins, certainly you aren't saying that there's anything unusual about people donating items of used clothing to charity?"

His brow furrowed. "No, not in general."

"And I'm sure you don't mean to imply that Grady Barrett is the only man with a size ten foot who drives a silver convertible?"

He glared at me and muttered, "No."

I managed an incredulous face. "Thank you, Detective Hawkins. I have no further questions."

CHAPTER 41

The last of the morning's witnesses was Charles Berger, the name Madelaine had sprung on me in her opening statement. I rose to voice my objection to Judge Atwood.

"Your Honor, Mr. Berger's name was not included on the witness list we were given. This morning was the first I heard of him."

Madelaine was all sincerity. "The People weren't aware of his existence, either, until late yesterday. I didn't finish meeting with him myself until almost ten last night."

"You couldn't have tried to reach Ms. O'Brien?" Judge Atwood asked.

"I did try, Your Honor. I called Ms. O'Brien at her home as well as at her office. She didn't answer at either number." Madelaine made that in itself sound suspicious.

I wasn't about to explain where I'd been. "The defense requests time to prepare for cross," I said, more upset about sabotage than any real preparation. "We ask that the witness not be allowed to testify at this time."

"The witness is here today," Madelaine urged.

"He can come another day as well, can't he?"

Judge Atwood frowned. "This is a hearing, not a jury trial. Let's see what we've got. Then, Ms. O'Brien, if you think you need more time to prepare, we can bring him back."

With a sigh I slid into my chair at the defense table and leaned to whisper in Grady's ear. "It's the best we could reasonably expect."

"Why didn't you pick up the phone last night?" He sounded testy.

I ignored him. In truth, twelve hours' notice wouldn't have helped much. "You sure you don't recognize the name?"

Grady shook his head.

Madelaine called Charles Berger to the stand. He was a skinny, acne-faced kid of about eighteen. Dressed in tan slacks and a too-small jacket, he looked like a young boy being dragged off to church on Sunday morning.

Grady sucked in his breath. He may not have recognized the name, but it was clear to me that he knew the face. And that he wasn't happy to see Berger in court. It was too late to ask for an explanation.

After Berger was sworn in, Madelaine took him through the preliminaries. He worked as a bagger at the Safeway in Montclair, about five minutes from the house where Deirdre Nichols was killed.

"And were you working there the night of February twenty-eighth?" she asked

"Yes, I was."

Madelaine walked back to the prosecution table and extracted a set of head-shot photos from her file. "I'd like to have these photographs entered as People's Exhibit A." She whisked them in front of my eyes and then past the deputy and judge.

"Objection, Your Honor. I haven't had time to examine the photos."

"I'll have another set made for the defense at the close of court today."

Business taken care of, she approached the witness. "Mr. Berger, did the police show you these photographs?"

He examined them briefly. "Yes."

"And were you able to identify one of them as a man you saw at the Montclair Safeway on the night of Friday, February twenty-eighth?"

"Yes."

"Tell us please, do you see that man in court today?"

"Yes, I do." He pointed to Grady, who was sitting as still as stone, eyes straight ahead. "That's him, there."

Uneasiness prickled my skin.

"Let the record reflect that the witness has pointed to the defendant," Madelaine said, then turned again to address Berger.

"Do you recall what time it was on the night in question when you saw the defendant?"

"Yes. It was about . . ." His voice squeaked and tried again. "A little before ten."

There were murmurs from the gallery. Next to me, Grady froze. I felt my own stomach knot. He clearly hadn't been working as late that evening as he'd claimed.

"You're sure it was the defendant?" Madelaine asked.

"Positive. I recognized him from when I did a report on Com-Tech in high school."

"So you knew it was Mr. Barrett at the time you saw him, even before the police questioned you?"

"Yes, I did."

Madelaine rocked forward on her toes. "Did you speak to him?"

"I think I said, 'Nice evening,' or something. The store manager likes for us to act friendly with the customers."

"Can you tell us what transpired?"

"I was getting carts from the lot. I saw Mr. Barrett pull up, park his car, and go into the store."

"What kind of car was he driving, do you recall?"

Berger glanced at Grady. "A silver Mercedes convertible. With the top down."

Another wave of murmurs from the back of the courtroom.

Madelaine let a moment pass. "And you said this was about ten in the evening?"

"That's right."

"Are you sure of the time?"

"I could be off by ten minutes in either direction, but not much more. I'd come back from my break at nine-thirty, and I know that I was bagging again by ten-fifteen."

She cocked her head. "So you saw Mr. Barrett go into the store at about ten?"

"Yes."

"Did you see him come out again?"

"Yes, just a few minutes later. He was opening a pack of gum."

Madelaine acted surprised. "That was it? No other groceries?"

"None that I could see."

Grady's leg was bouncing nervously under the table. I put my hand on his knee to quiet him.

"How did he seem?" Madelaine asked.

"Objection," I said, standing. "With all due respect to the witness's social acumen, he's not qualified to judge Mr. Barrett's mood.

Judge Atwood frowned. "Ms. Rivera is merely asking the witness to share his observations. She isn't requesting an evaluation of the defendant's feelings or thoughts."

But that, by implication, was what Madelaine was after.

Judge Atwood addressed the witness. "You may answer the question."

Berger looked at Grady and then lowered his eyes. "He seemed kind of nervous."

"What gave you that impression?" Madelaine asked.

"Little stuff. He kept looking over his shoulder, jiggling the change in his pocket. I don't know how to describe it exactly, but he looked tense and jittery." Berger paused and hazarded a smile. "Kind of like I feel right now."

Madelaine acknowledge his candor with a smile of her own. "Thank you, Mr. Berger." She turned to me. "Your witness."

"May I have a minute, Your Honor?"

"Take five." Nary the flicker of a smile.

Seething, I turned to huddle with Grady. "You want to tell me what this is all about?"

"I stopped at the store."

"A store practically in Deirdre Nichols' backyard. It's not exactly on the way home from your office."

A small shrug, which was more stiff than casual. "It's a store we go to."

"For gum?" I was barely able to contain my anger. Courtroom surprises were exactly what I'd wanted to avoid. "You could have stopped at the convenience store half a mile from your house," I told him.

"But I didn't." Grady's voice was flat.

Fighting the urge to scream at him, I whispered, "Why didn't you tell me about this before?"

"I never thought of it."

He never thought of it. Grady was either lying or stupid, and I was pretty sure he wasn't stupid. "There's also the matter of time. You told me, and the police, that you were at work until after eleven."

He nodded, then swallowed hard. His face was pale. "I guess I misjudged the time."

Turning away, I pushed back my chair and addressed the judge. "May I approach the bench, Your Honor?"

Madelaine joined me in conference.

"This is outrageous," I said. "The prosecution can't wait until the last minute to come in with a witness this potentially damaging to the defense."

"She just did," Judge Atwood remarked coolly.

"What I mean is, I need time to prepare. This is a major prosecution witness whose identity was revealed to me only this morning."

Madelaine folded her arms. "I didn't set this up to deliberately sabotage you."

"It doesn't matter," I huffed. "The effect is the same."

Judge Atwood removed her glasses and rubbed the bridge of her nose. "Since this is not a trial, and since I'm the sole trier of fact, I don't see the addition of a last-minute witness as a major problem."

"If you—"

She looked at me sharply. "I'm not finished, Ms. O'Brien"

"Sorry, Your Honor."

"On the other hand, I can understand how an unexpected witness can throw you off." She paused and slipped the glasses back over her nose. "I'll excuse the witness at this time and allow you to recall him at a later date."

I let out a sigh of relief and returned to my seat at the defense table.

"We will take our lunch recess at this time," Judge Atwood said, addressing the courtroom. "Court will reconvene at one-thirty."

I was steaming. If I hadn't promised to meet Byron Spencer for lunch, I'd have used the time to berate Grady. Maybe even to punch him in the nose. Instead, I shoved back my chair and walked out of the courtroom without saying another word to him.

Spencer was waiting for me on a bench at a nearby city park. Or what had once been a park. Like so many open urban areas, it had become a haven for drug dealers, derelicts, and the homeless. The rest rooms were covered in graffiti and missing their doors, the sandbox smelled of urine, and the playground swings were nothing but knotted chains.

"I got us deli sandwiches," Spencer said. "And Cokes. One diet, one regular. Take your pick."

I went for the diet.

"I left early to pick up the food. Did I miss anything?"

Yeah, I thought, the floor just fell through. I shook my head. "Just the usual. One minute it looks good for the prosecution, the next minute for the defense."

Spencer unwrapped his turkey sandwich. "It's exciting watching this case unfold. Like television. Only better because it's the drama of real life." He sounded like a sixteen-year-old kid.

"What was it you wanted to tell me?" I was still irked at Grady, and it carried in my tone.

"You remember our deal—if I brought you something useful, you'd give me an exclusive when it's all over."

I nodded.

"Something substantial, none of these two-sentence quips. I want the real inside story."

"It depends on what you've got for me," I told him.

"Fair enough." He'd taken a bite of sandwich, and paused a moment to swallow it. He turned to face me. "Deirdre Nichols was working for the police."

"Wrong woman, Spencer. She worked at a hair salon."

He shook his head. "No, not working as in a job. Working with them as a snitch."

It was like being hit between the eyes with a sledgehammer. "A snitch?"

"An informant. You know, someone who feeds the cops information."

"I know what a snitch is. I'm just surprised. In fact, I'm dumbfounded."

He looked pleased. "So you didn't know?"

"Not at all. Any idea what it was about?"

"The cops are after a guy she was seeing."

"Tony Rodale?"

"Yeah, that's him. He's some kingpin of the drug world. They wanted to bring him in."

I felt as if the air had been squeezed from my chest. It was so far-fetched as to be ridiculous, but it also made sense. The pieces fit perfectly. "Do you have any proof?"

He shook his head again. "Not really."

"You must have *something*."

"I got this in strict confidence from someone who knows. Someone who doesn't blow hot air. I'm sure it's true."

"Jesus, Byron, you could have gotten it from the pope himself. But without proof it doesn't do me any good. It's just rumor."

"Her record's sealed," Spencer said. "But if you could find a way to check it, you'd discover two previous arrests on drug charges. The first was a slap on the wrist really, probation and counseling. The second one was about a year ago. A nothing sentence. This last one should have netted her some time, but the charge was dropped. That's because she agreed to cooperate with the cops."

I took a bite of my pickle. *Snitch. Drug deals.* It certainly opened up a wealth of possibilities with respect to her murder. Assuming it was true. "You don't have any information relating directly to her murder, do you? Anything pointing to someone besides Grady Barrett?"

"Afraid not. I'll keep looking though. I've got a couple of irons in the fire, so to speak."

"Good."

"See, I was thinking maybe her boyfriend found out about her being a snitch and all—and killed her. That's what they do in movies."

And in real life, I added silently.

It had potential, at least as a starting point. No wonder they'd been in such a hurry to arrest Grady; they wanted Rodale out of the loop. It would certainly buy us some mileage with the jury, even if it wasn't enough to swing things our way at the preliminary hearing. Finally, the defense had some ammunition.

And then it hit me.

Hal's discovery. Had he uncovered the same information? Was that what had killed him? I fought a wave of nausea.

"What's the matter?" Spencer asked.

"Listen, what you've told me is interesting. Better than that, even. But it could be dangerous as well." I told him about Hal's murder.

"You don't know for sure that's why he was killed though," Byron said.

"True, but it sure makes sense."

"I'll be careful." He spoke with bravado, perhaps unaware that his face had gone pale. "A reporter doesn't turn his back on a good story just because he fears for his own safety."

Byron Spencer sounded at that moment very young and naive. And very idealistic.

I liked him all the better for it.

CHAPTER 42

Sheila Barlow took the stand when court resumed after lunch. Her full gray skirt and crisply pressed white blouse accentuated the drabness of her appearance.

Madelaine requested that she state her name for the record, then asked, "What is your relationship to the deceased?"

"I'm her sister."

"Older or younger?"

"Older by six years."

Next to me, Grady sat with shoulders squared, pulling at his knuckles. As unobtrusively as possible, I put a hand on his wrist. He got the message and stopped.

"What is your occupation, Ms. Barlow?"

"I'm a librarian with the city."

"Are you married?"

"No."

"Have you ever been married?"

"No."

"Any children?"

Sheila smiled faintly, no doubt amused that she'd been asked about children despite never having been married. "No, I do not."

"Would you say that your relationship with your sister was a close one?"

Sheila nodded. "Very. Deirdre has lived with me off and on over the years, and she was living with me at the time of her death, although she had taken a temporary house-sitting job elsewhere."

At Madelaine's urging, Sheila described her sister in more detail. Deirdre had been full of life. People were drawn to her.

She was outgoing and trusting, and those qualities sometimes got her in trouble.

Although the words were laudatory, I thought I occasionally heard a tone of pique in Sheila's voice.

"On the morning of March first," Madelaine was saying, "did you receive a call from Adrianna?"

Sheila sat straighter, as if to brace herself against the memory of that day. "Yes."

"I'd like to turn now to that morning. What happened when Adrianna called you?"

"It was a little after six. She didn't chatter the way she usually does. She just said, 'Ema.' That's what she calls me," Sheila explained. " 'Ema, something's happened to Mommy.' Poor child, I could hear the fright in her voice."

"Did she say anything more?"

"I asked her where Deirdre was, and she said outside. On the ground." Sheila's voice quavered. "I told her to hang up the phone and go to her room. That I'd be right over."

Step by step, Madelaine led her through the events of the morning—how she'd reached the house, taken one look outside, and known that her sister was dead. The police and paramedics had arrived not long after. Sheila had remained with Adrianna, trying to comfort her.

When Sheila started to repeat Adrianna's story about seeing a silver convertible parked in front, I objected. "I would like to hear the account from the witness herself."

Sheila sucked in a breath as though she'd been physically struck. "For God's sake, the child has been through enough."

"Your Honor—"

Judge Atwood cut me off, then warned Sheila against further outbursts. She turned back to me. "Do you really feel it is necessary to bring the girl into court?"

Grady stirred beside me. I ignored him.

"Yes, Your Honor, I do. She is a crucial witness for the prosecution. Her remarks about seeing a car similar to one driven by my client, and about hearing a man's voice, are critical parts of the case against Mr. Barrett. It's essential that we be able to question her directly."

Madelaine approached the bench. "She's only seven years old, Your Honor, and she's just lost her mother. Detective Hawkins already testified as to the content of her statement. Surely Ms. O'Brien is not so heartless as to require the child to relive that terrible chain of events once again?"

"The last thing I want is to inflict more pain on Adrianna," I said. "But Grady Barrett is accused of a crime he didn't commit. He has the right to confront any witness against him."

Sheila Barlow's face reddened with resentment. She glared at me.

Judge Atwood removed her gray-framed glasses and rubbed her eyes. I knew that she wanted to keep the hearing as simple and short as possible. And I knew she believed that Adrianna's comments could be relayed adequately by others. I was sure that on a personal level her sympathies were with Adrianna as well. But she surprised me by taking my side on this one.

"Ms. Rivera," she said finally, "you may continue to question the witness about her conversation with her niece if you'd like, but defense counsel has the right to question Adrianna. You'll see that she's in court tomorrow?"

Madelaine's brow creased with annoyance. "Your Honor—"

"We'll do it in closed session."

Sheila Barlow looked ready to explode. The veins in her neck stood out in livid ridges and her mouth was contorted. "Can't you spare her this?"

Judge Atwood didn't admonish her for the outburst, but, rather, tried to explain. "I'll make every effort to make it a non-threatening experience for your niece. I don't relish the idea of taking her through it all again, either. But the law states that the defendant has a right to confront and question witnesses against him." She leaned back in her chair. "And rightly so. You may proceed, Ms. Rivera."

Madelaine resumed her questioning by changing direction. "Did you know that your sister had filed a rape complaint against the defendant?"

"Yes."

"Did she discuss the matter with you, particularly with respect to the then-upcoming trial?"

"Yes, she did." Sheila never looked at Grady.

"Can you tell us, please, what she was feeling in this regard in the days prior to her death."

Sheila nodded. "Deirdre felt that even though the trial was

going to be difficult for her, and for Adrianna and myself, it was important that she go through with it. She said people like Grady Barrett were used to getting their own way. They were the sort who took whatever they wanted and didn't care if others got hurt."

"Did your sister play for you an answering machine message she'd received from the defendant?"

Sheila licked her lips and spoke softly. "Yes, she did."

"And what was the gist of that message?"

I leapt to my feet. "Objection. Hearsay."

"Admission against interest," Madelaine shot back, targeting one of the exceptions to the hearsay rule.

"Your Honor, it's an admission against interest only if you give the rule a creative interpretation, and only if the words were spoken by my client."

Judge Atwood leaned forward. "Is the tape itself available?"

"We haven't been able to find it," Madelaine explained. "It was probably erased."

The judge pressed her fingertips together, frowning in thought. "I'll allow the testimony for now. Until I know what was said, I can't make a ruling. In any event, I'm sure the issue will be raised again at trial, assuming the case gets that far." She nodded toward Madelaine. "Would you repeat the question?"

"What was the gist of the message your sister played for you?"

Sheila lifted her chin. "Mr. Barrett was trying to convince Deirdre not to testify against him."

Grady began pulling at his fingers again. There were tiny drops of perspiration across his brow.

"How did you know that it was Mr. Barrett on the tape?" Madelaine asked.

"He said it was. And I recognized his voice."

"Do you recall the exact words he used?"

Sheila looked down at her hands. "He said that if Deirdre didn't recant her story, she'd 'live to regret it, but not for long.' Those were his words."

I could feel Grady tense. "Not true," he whispered through clenched teeth. "I never threatened her."

Madelaine tilted her head. "And *did* your sister consider retracting her complaint?"

"Never," Sheila said emphatically. "And the defendant knew

it." She shifted her gaze and looked directly at Grady. "That's why he killed her."

I jumped to my feet. "Your Honor."

"Yes, I know. I will disregard the last remark."

Madelaine nodded in my direction. "Your witness."

CHAPTER 43

I began where Madelaine had, with the sisters' relationship. I knew that Sheila was angry with me because I hadn't counseled Grady to plead the case out. And now, in addition, she was upset that I was forcing Adrianna to testify. She wasn't going to cooperate any more than she had to.

"Were you and your sister always close?" I asked, mindful that six years is a sizable age difference at certain stages.

"In recent years, yes."

"How about when you were younger."

"I was in high school when she was still a child," Sheila said. "Although we got along, I suppose we weren't *close*."

I wondered fleetingly what Sheila had been like at sixteen. Probably as somber and reserved as she was now. "But as you both grew older," I said, "the relationship became stronger, is that correct?"

"Yes. Particularly after Adrianna was born."

"Was your sister living with you at that time?"

"No. She and her husband were down in Palo Alto." Sheila's expression darkened for a moment, then she gathered herself back. "I visited them frequently, however, and I took care of Adrianna on any number of occasions when Deirdre and Frank wanted to get away. After he died, she and Adrianna moved in with me."

Would I gain anything by bringing out Deirdre's brush with bankruptcy? Probably not, especially at this stage.

"Frank was your brother-in-law?"

Sheila sucked on her bottom lip. "Yes."

"After she was widowed and moved in with you, did Deirdre live with you continuously until the present?"

Sheila took a sip of water. "No, she moved out several times. She tried to make it on her own, but . . . well, it's hard to raise a child as a single parent. Especially if you don't have much in the way of assets or income."

"So she moved back out of necessity."

Sheila looked at me sharply. "No, it wasn't out of necessity. At least not in the way you make it sound. I liked sharing my house with my sister and niece, and they liked sharing their life with me. We were close, all of us. A family."

I nodded, and moved on to the morning she'd learned of Deirdre's death. "You said that Adrianna called you a little after six A.M.?"

"That's correct."

"And you got to the house before the patrol officer, who arrived at six thirty-three?"

She thought for a moment. "Yes."

"So you left home immediately after receiving the call?"

"Yes, I was out the door in an instant. I knew something was terribly wrong."

I tapped my chin. "Were you asleep when Adrianna called?"

"No. I was already up for the day."

"And dressed?"

"Yes."

"Had you had breakfast?"

She gave me a puzzled look. "I'd had coffee. I don't normally eat breakfast."

"So as soon as you hung up the phone from talking to your niece, you grabbed the car keys and left?"

"Yes."

"And when you arrived at the house, did you render aid to your sister?"

Sheila dropped her gaze. "I could tell from looking at her that she was dead."

"You didn't check for a pulse just to make sure?"

"There was no need. And at that point I was more worried about Adrianna."

"You testified that you tried to comfort her. How did you do that?"

Sheila cleared her throat. "I held her, read to her a little. The police wouldn't let us leave, but I didn't want Adrianna to see all that was going on. We went into the den, where it was quiet."

"At what point did she tell you about seeing the silver convertible?"

"Not until the police were questioning her. They let me stay when they talked to her. Until then, I'd just assumed she'd slept through the night." Sheila took another sip of water.

"And when the police allowed you to leave, what then?"

"I took Adrianna home."

I stepped back to the defense table, standing near Grady. "Moving now to the answering machine tape. You stated earlier that Mr. Barrett gave his name when he left the message."

She nodded.

"Anyone could have given Mr. Barrett's name. Isn't that so?"

She hesitated. "I recognized the voice."

"After he'd said his name."

For a moment she looked flustered. "I know it was him. Deirdre told me. She said she wasn't going to cave in to him."

Grady exhaled loudly, shaking his head in denial. I shot him a warning glance.

"Ms. Barlow," I continued, "you heard a message that you believed was left by Mr. Barrett. Your sister assumed it was Mr. Barrett. But you don't know, with absolute certainty, that it *was* Mr. Barrett's voice you heard, do you?"

"It was him. I'm certain. I know his voice."

We'd see, come trial, if she knew his voice as well as she thought. And I could use her certainty here for impeachment purposes.

I shifted gears. "Your sister interpreted the message as a threat?"

Sheila relaxed, clearly glad to be off the matter of identification. "Yes."

"Was she scared?"

"Of course she was. Who wouldn't be?"

I moved closer to the witness box. "Then why didn't she contact the police?"

Sheila licked her lips. "I don't know. Maybe she thought it wouldn't do any good."

"And why would she open the door of her home to a man she was afraid of?"

"I don't know," she snapped. "Deirdre sometimes used bad judgment."

My shoulders were tight with tension. I stepped back to the defense table, thinking I might leave my questioning of Sheila Barlow at that. It was becoming clear there was no way we were going to get a dismissal. The case was going to trial.

But the lunchtime conversation with Byron Spencer had been churning in the back of my mind all afternoon. Abruptly, I swung around.

"Was your sister ever arrested?"

Madelaine was on her feet immediately. "What's that got to do with anything?"

Judge Atwood raised an eyebrow, looking in my direction.

"It goes to the existence of another suspect, Your Honor."

Madelaine crossed her arms. "It's the defendant who's the focus of this hearing, Your Honor. Our purpose is to determine if there is probable cause to believe that the defendant committed the crime in question. That's all we need look at."

"Your Honor, the case against my client is entirely circumstantial. It's our contention that the police moved in haste, without examining all the possibilities."

"You're saying that the evidence believably points to another suspect?"

I took a breath and threw caution to the wind. "Yes, Your Honor."

"You have a specific somebody in mind?"

"I might."

Judge Atwood rubbed her nose. "This is highly irregular."

"An innocent man has been arrested for murder, Your Honor. He's been deprived of his liberty, of the comfort of his family."

She held up a hand. "Let's see where it goes, Counselor. But I'm warning you, I don't want to be led off on some wild-goose chase."

I nodded, and repeated the question for the witness. "Was your sister ever arrested?"

Sheila hesitated. "Yes," she whispered, clearly uncomfortable with the question. "Twice."

"When was the first time?"

"Several years ago. I can't remember exactly. It was after Frank died."

"And what was she arrested for?"

"Hit and run, driving under the influence. She was having trouble coping with the loss of her husband."

"And the second arrest?"

"About eighteen months ago. She was found in possession of cocaine."

"These were her only two brushes with the law?"

"The only two I'm aware of." Sheila sighed. "Deirdre wasn't the most responsible person in the world. I'd be the first to admit that. But she was a good person. Someone with a kind heart. She just never thought through the consequences of her actions."

Either Sheila hadn't known about the most recent arrest, or she was covering for her sister. I wished I knew more of the details myself. But her answer had at least jibed with what Byron Spencer had told me. So far his information was accurate.

I tried coming at it from a different angle. "Was your sister romantically involved with anyone?"

"She always had a man."

"Was her most recent relationship a serious one?"

"That was something we didn't talk about much."

I pressed my fingertips together, eyeing her skeptically. "Even though you were close."

"We were close like sisters," she said tightly, "not like girl-friends."

"Does the name Tony Rodale mean anything to you?"

While I asked the question, I kept one eye on Madelaine, who showed no reaction to the name. Did that mean she wasn't aware of the drug connection and Deirdre's role as informant?

Sheila cleared her throat. "I believe he was a man Deirdre had been seeing."

"Thank you. No further questions."

Judge Atwood peered at me over the tops of her glasses. "That's it?"

"For now, Your Honor."

It was almost five o'clock by the time court adjourned for the day. I'd been hoping to catch Cedric Gibson, but I'd missed my chance. Not that I expected anything other than the stonewalling I'd encountered the other day. At least now I thought I understood why.

A drug sting. One that was probably close to going down. Months of undercover work setting things up, and now their informant was dead. The last thing the police wanted was to have the setup blown before they'd netted their prey.

I caught up with Madelaine outside the courthouse. "Good work today," I said by way of greeting.

"You too." She turned with a smile. "I really did try to reach you last night to tell you about Charles Berger. It was an honest-to-God instance of a witness turning up out of the blue."

"It happens." We stopped at the corner and waited for the light to change. "You still seeing Steve Henshaw?" I asked casually.

Madelaine laughed. "Don't tell me you're looking to see if he's available?"

"Just curious."

"We've gone out a couple of times. I don't think he's exactly swooning at my feet."

"I understand he's on special assignment."

She nodded.

"Undercover narcotics," I said.

She looked surprised. "Word gets around, doesn't it? That's what scares me about these undercover things. Seems to me that everybody and his brother knows what's going on."

Two for two. Sheila Barlow had confirmed Deirdre's arrest on drug-related charges, and now Madelaine had, by implication, verified that Rodale was under investigation. It was looking, increasingly, as though Spencer's information was accurate.

A lot of pieces were beginning to fall into place. I was willing to bet that Henshaw had been at Deirdre's house after the murder, checking to make sure there was nothing there that might give away her role as informant. He might have taken her date book and then slipped it, unnoticed, into the evidence room. That would explain why it had turned up but not been logged in.

The light changed and we crossed the street. "Must be hard," I said, "dating a man who can't talk about his work."

"I get the feeling he wants to keep that part of his life separate anyway." She turned at the garage entrance and grinned. "Besides, we're heavy into *nonverbal* communication."

CHAPTER 44

By the time I reached home I was feeling wrung out. I poured myself a glass of wine and called Marc. No answer. Not at his place or the office. I felt a thread of alarm work its way down my spine.

I reached Rose at home. "Did Marc ever call in again?" I asked.

"No, but I didn't expect him to. Why? You sound worried?"

"I am, a little. When I tried to reach him just now, there was no answer."

"Guess he's feeling better," she said with a laugh.

Easy for her to shrug it off; she didn't know about the beating he'd taken last night. On the other hand, she was probably right. I was wasting my energy worrying about him, when he'd no doubt slept the day away and then taken in an early movie or gone out for a bite to eat.

I thought about checking on him in person, just to be sure, but I was tired. And angry too. I'd gone out of my way to help, not to mention giving up a good night's sleep to keep an eye on him. I was irked that he hadn't had the common decency to call.

Bea and Dotty were out for the evening at their Italian cooking class. I put a pot of water on to boil for my own, much simpler Italian feast. While I chopped fresh tomato for the pasta and made a salad, I tried to systematically review the day in court. What kept popping to the fore of my mind, however, was Tony Rodale, and Deirdre's role as informant. It was interesting information—if only I could decide how to use it to our best advantage.

Nina phoned just as the water was starting to boil. "I thought you were going to call."

"You beat me to it." I turned the heat down to simmer and topped off my glass of wine.

"How did it go today?"

"Some good, some bad."

"I want the truth, Kali. None of this sugar-coated stuff." She paused. "The news report mentioned something about a witness who saw Grady in Montclair around the time Deirdre was killed."

I drew in a breath and let it out slowly. "That was the bad." I recapped Berger's testimony for her.

A long stretch of silence. "Do you think there's a chance the witness is confused?"

"He sounded certain." Reluctantly, I skipped the sugar coating. "And he comes across as credible."

"Jesus." Nina's voice wavered. "That places Grady within spitting distance of the crime rather than at work."

I tried to put a positive spin on it. "He was still five or ten minutes away. It's not the same as having a witness place him directly at the scene."

"What does Grady say?"

"That he was buying gum." I worked to keep my tone neutral.

Nina didn't respond immediately. Finally, she sighed, a broken whimper of a sound that I felt in my own belly.

"Lots of people were at the Safeway that evening," I told her, wanting to make things better. "It's hardly incontrovertible evidence against him."

"But it looks bad. You know that, don't pretend it doesn't."

"The prosecution's case always looks bad for the defendant."

"So what's the good news?" she asked bleakly.

I related the day's testimony, underscoring the positive. "But the most interesting development," I told her, "was what I learned outside of court." I went on to explain what Byron Spencer had told me.

"You think there's any truth to it?"

"Actually, I do."

"That's got to be the solution, then." Nina's voice rose as she strived for optimism. "Rodale must have found out Deirdre was working with the police, and killed her. You even said before that there'd been domestic violence charges filed against him."

"Filed and dropped."

Nina wasn't about to be dissuaded. "We both know how that works. Do you know what kind of car Rodale drives?"

"Unfortunately, not a silver convertible."

"He could have borrowed a car—assuming that Adrianna actually knows what she saw."

I sipped my wine. "I'm questioning her tomorrow. That's one of the things I intend to find out."

"Do you know if Rodale has an alibi for the night of the murder?" Nina asked.

"He says he was home, but to my knowledge there's no one who can verify that. And he does wear a size ten shoe."

"Kali, I think you're onto something." Nina's voice was tinged with excitement. She may not have wanted a watered-down version of the truth, but she was eager to grasp at anything that gave her hope.

"It also explains why Deirdre let her killer into the house," she continued. "That's always bothered me about the police scenario. It never seemed right to me that she'd open her door to a man she'd accused of rape. Especially if she thought he'd threatened her."

"I know. It's bothered me too." I wrapped the telephone cord around my finger. "If the killer was Rodale, though, how do we explain the message tape?"

"It must have been someone besides Grady. He wasn't the only one who wanted the rape charge dropped, you know. We're not the only people who will lose big time if this offering doesn't go through."

I hesitated before asking, "Is your financial situation really as bad as Grady claims?"

"Probably worse. Grady is one of those people who tend to see the glass as half full."

"Oh, Nina, I'm sorry." Her troubles seemed endless. "You've got so much to contend with. It's not fair."

"I've given up thinking about what's fair," she said curtly. And then added, "But there is some good news. The doctor says I can go home tomorrow."

"That's wonderful news!"

"Still confined to bed. Still harboring cancer cells. Still married to a man charged with murder. But all this at home again rather than in the hospital." She gave a thin laugh. "And we call that good news. It's funny how fast your perspective changes."

Even with the limited number of us present for Adrianna's testimony the next morning, the group was too large for the session to be held in chambers, as Judge Atwood had originally hoped. She'd ordered the courtroom closed to the press and public, however, and we'd forsaken tables and witness stand to gather informally, sitting in chairs grouped as though for classroom show-and-tell.

Adrianna was allowed a stuffed, floppy-eared bunny, but not her aunt. I'd seen to the latter. It wasn't that I thought Sheila Barlow would intentionally try to influence the child, but I knew that she was eager to shield Adrianna from the trauma of testifying. While I shared her concern, I wanted to hear Adrianna's story from her own lips.

Judge Atwood, dressed today in a skirt and blouse rather than her judicial robe, sat to Adrianna's left. A child psychologist appointed by the state of California sat to her right. Madelaine, Grady, and I completed the other half of the circle.

Judge Atwood began by addressing Adrianna. "Do you know why you're here today?" When she didn't get an answer, she continued. "We need you to tell us about the night your mommy was hurt. We will ask you questions and all you have to do is answer them. If you don't know or can't remember, that's okay."

Adrianna looked at the judge without acknowledgment. She was wearing a blue corduroy jumper with a white blouse, and a satin ribbon in her hair. Birthday party clothes, I was willing to bet.

"You think you can do that?" the judge asked.

Adrianna blinked several times in rapid succession and hugged the velour bunny against her chest.

Judge Atwood glanced at the psychologist, who shrugged noncommittally, then turned back to address Adrianna. "You ready to begin?" she asked.

This time the girl nodded, and Judge Atwood seemed relieved. She motioned for Madelaine to start.

It was clear that Madelaine was as uneasy with the situation as the rest of us. She spoke in a slow, sugary manner, with added inflection and an abundance of facial expression.

"Do you remember the night your mommy got hurt?" she asked.

Adrianna nodded.

"Tell us what you remember."

Adrianna hugged her bunny. "I had a dream."

Madelaine looked taken aback. That clearly wasn't what she wanted to hear. "A dream? That's nice, but why don't you tell us about the part when you woke up."

Adrianna looked at Grady with a flicker of a smile and then dropped her gaze. I felt my stomach turn over. Was she going to identify Grady as the man she'd seen?

"What made you wake up?" Madelaine asked after a moment's hesitation. I could tell she was uncomfortable in uncharted territory.

"A noise."

"What kind of noise?"

"I can't remember."

"But you remember hearing a noise?"

Adrianna patted the head of her rabbit. "At first I thought it was another dream, like with the chocolate. But it wasn't."

Madelaine pressed forward. It was clear she wasn't going to let herself be sidetracked by childhood banter. "Do you know what time it was when you woke up?"

Adrianna nodded intently, trying very hard to do what was expected of her.

"What time was it?"

She sat up straight. "Ten-o-one."

"That's very precise," Madelaine said, obviously surprised.

"It's a palindrome."

I remembered Emily making a similar remark. The second-grade teacher had done her job well.

But Madelaine appeared confused. "A palindrome?" she asked.

Adrianna nodded. "It's the same forwards and backwards."

"Ah." Madelaine leaned forward in her chair, elbows on her knees. "You woke up around ten o'clock when you heard a noise. Did you hear anything else?"

"I heard a man." She looked again, briefly, in Grady's direction.

His head dropped forward. He sat stone still, not looking at Adrianna.

"You heard the man talking?" Madelaine asked.

Adrianna nodded.

"Could you make out what he was saying?"

"My mommy's name—Deirdre." She dragged the name out into long syllables.

"Anything else?"

"Something like 'forget it.'" Adrianna shuffled her shoes against the hardwood floor. "And a very bad word."

"That's all?"

"I couldn't understand most of it."

Madelaine frowned. "Did you see the man?"

Grady still hadn't moved. I felt my own muscles freeze as Adrianna's eyes flickered again toward Grady.

She shook her head. "He was upstairs."

I could feel Grady relax.

Technically, I could have objected to the response. Adrianna didn't know where the man was if she couldn't see him. I was sure, though, that I'd gain nothing but the ire of the court by doing so.

"Did you see anything?" Madelaine asked.

"A car. In the driveway."

"What color was the car?"

"Silver."

"Was it a big car?" Here Madelaine stretched her hands, and her voice. "Or a little car?" She reversed the gesture and made her voice small.

"Medium," Adrianna said. "A convertible."

"Anything else about the car? Scratches, dents, decals . . ."

Adrianna twisted a finger in her hair and shook her head. "Except for the peace symbol."

Again Madelaine did a double take. "A peace symbol?"

I could see her thinking that no way would Grady Barrett drive around sporting a hippie bumper sticker, and that maybe an important part of her case had just collapsed.

But I had a sick feeling that I knew what Adrianna was talking about. So did Grady. I heard him groan under his breath.

"How do you know about the peace symbol?" Madelaine asked, trying to buy time while she figured out how to minimize the damage.

"They're on a lot of cars," Adrianna explained.

"I see."

"Tommy says it means the car cost lots of money. They put it up front, where the engine is."

"Up front?"

"And on the trunk too."

And then it dawned on Madelaine as well. She cast me a smug look and turned back to Adrianna. "A hood ornament, you mean. Like this?" She took out a sheet of paper and drew the Mercedes symbol.

Adrianna nodded, pleased to know that she'd done something right.

"I'd like the record to reflect that the witness has identified the car she saw the night her mother was killed as a silver *Mercedes* convertible." Madelaine turned to me, the shadow of a smile still on her lips. "Your witness."

Judge Atwood leaned toward Adrianna. "You doing okay, honey? We can take a short break if you'd like something to drink."

"I'm fine, thank you." The words were braver than the tone.

I swallowed, feeling the implications of Adrianna's testimony in the pit of my stomach. Unless I could show that she was confused, the prosection had moved one step closer to placing Grady at the crime scene.

"Now it's my turn to ask questions," I explained, scooting my chair so that I could address Adrianna face on.

Questioning a child witness is always tricky. There's no guarantee that the child even knows the difference between truth and fantasy, let alone that her testimony is accurate.

I took out a sheet of paper myself and drew the actual peace symbol. "Is this what you saw on the car?"

Her finger traced the corner of her mouth.

"Or how about this?" I said, sketching out what I recalled as the Toyota symbol.

Madelaine was fidgeting behind me. "Your Honor—"

Atwood sent her a silencing glance. "It seems like a perfectly reasonable line of inquiry to me." She nodded in my direction. "You may proceed."

By now Adrianna sensed that something was up. She wound a spiral of hair with her right hand and clutched her stuffed animal with the left.

"There's no right or wrong answer," I told her. "You just tell us what you saw. Do either of these look like the symbol you saw on the car in the driveway?"

Finally, Adrianna shook her head. "It was like the one the other lady showed me."

Score one for Adrianna.

I forced a smile, not wanting her to pick up on my disappointment, and moved on. "Okay, now we'll try a different question. Still about the car. It was dark outside, wasn't it?"

She nodded.

"So it must have been hard to see the color of the car."

"I could see because the front light was on."

"So you're sure it was silver, and not white or beige or gray?" I had no idea how I'd tell gray from silver myself.

"It was silver," she said emphatically.

I brought out the color brochures I'd picked up from car dealers over the last few days. "We're going to play kind of a game," I said. "I'll show you a color and you tell me what it is, okay?"

I showed her red, which she got, and then frost, which she called white, and then metallic blue.

She hesitated. "Pearly blue," she said at last.

A few questions later she picked out silver without a moment's uncertainty. And gray was gray. She was a girl who knew her colors.

Taken in conjunction with Berger's testimony about seeing Grady at the Safeway in Montclair, Adrianna's identification of the car was bound to carry weight. I felt anxiety coursing through my body.

"You said you'd woken from a dream."

She nodded.

I tried imagining that it was Emily I was talking to. Casual conversation. I didn't want Adrianna picking up on the apprehension I felt. "Can you remember what the dream was about?"

"Rabbits."

"Was it a scary dream?"

She smiled. "No. Rabbits aren't scary."

"So it was a comfortable dream?"

Adrianna nodded.

"Was there just that one dream?"

Her eyes scrunched tight in thought. "I had a different dream before. About chocolate syrup. Ema gave it to me."

"You dreamed she gave you chocolate syrup?"

Adrianna nodded. "Because she loves me."

"So that wasn't scary either?"

"No."

"So you had a couple of dreams, and then woke up when you heard a noise, is that right?"

Another nod.

"Do you think that maybe the noise and the man's voice were a dream too? They only seemed real because they were scary and your other dreams weren't?"

Her chin jutted out. "I wasn't scared. And it *was* real."

"But sometimes dreams can seem very real."

"It wasn't a dream." Adrianna was bouncing in her seat, growing agitated.

Judge Atwood leaned forward. "Are you nearly finished, Ms. O'Brien?"

I could tell by her tone that I was, whether I'd thought so or not. "Yes, Your Honor."

CHAPTER 45

"You want to tell me what's going on here?" I asked Grady. Only I didn't ask it so much as bellow it.

We were alone finally, in one of the tiny interview rooms reserved for attorneys and their clients. It was fortunate that Judge Atwood, with a commitment that required her attention for the afternoon, had declared court in recess until the next morning. Otherwise, I might have been shouting at Grady in open court. I was that mad.

I crossed my arms and glared at him. "You want to tell me how Adrianna saw a silver *Mercedes* convertible in the driveway the night her mother was killed?"

Grady rubbed the flesh of his cheek. He looked pale and uncomfortable.

"Saw it not ten minutes after another witness saw *you* in a similar car only minutes from the house where Deirdre Nichols was murdered?"

He closed his eyes for a moment.

"What kind of game are you playing? I'm your attorney, goddammit. You're suppose to tell me the truth."

Grady shifted in his chair and swallowed. "I was there," he mumbled. "At Deirdre Nichols' house."

"No shit, Sherlock. I know that, the judge knows that, and if we'd had a jury present, they would know it as well. Your goose would be cooked." And it wasn't any too far from that now.

"I didn't kill her."

"That's comforting to hear."

"I mean it," he said, looking me in the eye. "I didn't."

I crossed my arms and said nothing.

"She must have been dead already—that's why she never answered the door."

"Are you saying that you never saw her that night?"

Grady hunched forward. "I rang the bell, knocked on the door, even called her name a couple of times. That's probably what Adrianna heard. Deirdre never came to the door."

"So you just moseyed back to your car and left?" My voice dripped with sarcasm.

Grady nodded.

"You expect me to believe that?"

"It's the truth. I swear."

I snorted in disgust. "Truth is a concept that seems to elude you, Grady."

"Please, Kali. You've got to believe me." His voice cracked. There was a pleading quality to it that caught me by surprise.

"You were there at the house?" I asked skeptically. "There within the time frame of Deirdre's murder, but you didn't kill her?"

"Right."

"Or speak to her?"

"Right." He nodded eagerly and then his face folded. "It sounds ludicrous, doesn't it?"

"Right," I echoed.

"But it's the truth."

"Why didn't you tell me before this? I explained to you at the beginning that I didn't want any ugly surprises in court."

"I didn't think you'd believe me." His tone was apologetic. "I didn't think *anyone* would believe me."

"They're going to be a whole lot less inclined to believe you at this stage."

Grady looked miserable.

"I don't want a client who lies to me."

"Please. I need your help."

I sighed. "Why don't you tell me what happened that night. Only this time make it the truth and don't leave anything out."

Grady rubbed his knees. "I was at work, like I told you. I left about nine-thirty. Deirdre had said to come by about ten."

I opened my mouth to speak, but he held up a hand.

"We had a deal. She was going to recant her story about the rape, and I was going to pay her."

"You bribed the witness?" No wonder he hadn't been forth-coming with the whole truth. "Jesus, Grady. That's a crime in itself."

He shook his head. "No, it wasn't a bribe."

"No?"

"It was a business arrangement."

"Give me a break."

Grady ignored me. "I didn't rape her, in case you're interested. So it wasn't like I was paying her to lie."

"Why'd she claim you did, then?"

He pressed his knuckles together, and then his thumbs. "I wasn't the most gracious person that night. I think she was hurt and angry, and wanted to pay me back."

"So she cried rape."

He addressed his hands. "She said I used her. She said I treated her like dirt. Like she was nobody."

That was pretty much what Deirdre had told me herself the afternoon she'd followed me into the women's room during the rape hearing. I could only surmise that she'd been thinking romance, or something close to it, while he'd seen nothing more than available body parts.

Grady took a breath and looked up. "She said that it was the moral equivalent of rape."

"So you tried to buy her off?"

Another shake of his head. "No. I apologized."

"That was it?" My words rang with cynicism.

"It was a sincere apology."

"Must have been twenty-four karat." I brushed the air with my hand, disgusted. "You offered an apology and Deirdre agreed not to testify against you?"

"Well, she wanted money too. But that was her idea, not mine. She said she wanted to start over—move away, go back to school, try to make something of her life. I take it she'd been involved in a bad relationship, one she was eager to get away from. She needed money to do that."

"How much?"

"A hundred thousand."

"A *hundred* thousand?" That was more than money; it was a fortune.

"What could I do? I was worried about what the rape trial

would do to the ComTech offering. I stood to make a lot more than that if it went through."

My head was spinning. I'd asked for the truth. But the trouble with the truth is that sometimes it's unpleasant.

"So that's what you were doing at Deirdre's place the night she was killed," I said. "You went to pay her off?"

"Half of it. She was going to get the other half as soon as the rape charges were dropped."

I leaned back in my chair, more overwhelmed than angry. "The shoe print on the side of the house?"

"When Deirdre didn't answer, I started around the side of the house to see if I couldn't tap on a window or something. I heard music coming from the back and I thought maybe she hadn't heard the doorbell. But then a dog started barking. For all I knew, he was in the yard, ready to attack me. I decided to let it be. I'd call her in the morning."

"And the handkerchief?"

"I told you, I'd left it there the week before. She was going to return it that night. I told her it was no big deal, but she insisted."

"What about the pants you were wearing that night? The ones you said were part of a Salvation Army pickup."

"That's the truth," he said. "They were old and getting worn through the seat. It was one of those ironic twists that the pickup was that Monday."

I thought through the other evidence the D.A. had gathered against Grady. All of it was consistent with what he'd just told me.

"I grant you it's not the most believable explanation," I told him. "But it beats the hell out of the story you told initially, on which three witnesses have now tripped you up. I don't see why you didn't tell the truth from the start."

Grady looked sheepish. "Well, there's one other small part."

"What's that?"

"The money."

"What about it?"

"I don't have that much sitting around. I kind of borrowed it from the company."

His words sank in slowly. "Embezzled it?"

"Well, it *is* my company, or mine and the investment bankers'.

And I would have paid it back just as soon as the stock went public. It was more a securities violation than a crime."

A fine point. But any way you looked at it, it was certainly a lesser crime than murder.

"Jesus, Grady. You couldn't have dug a deeper hole for yourself if you'd tunneled clear through to China."

"You think I don't know that? You think I haven't sat here beating myself up for being stupid and shortsighted?"

"And selfish," I said without thinking.

"And selfish."

"Not to mention morally repugnant."

Grady leaned across the table and touched my hand. "I'd give anything to be able to rewrite these last couple of weeks. I know I've behaved badly. And I love Nina with all my heart. I can't bear to think of the pain I've caused her. But I can't go back and change what's done. The only thing I can do is go forward and try to make it right."

I pressed my fingers against the side of my face. "What a mess."

"I didn't kill Deirdre Nichols. That's what you need to deal with first and foremost."

For the first time since the morning I'd talked with Grady about the rape, I found myself truly believing him. But would I be able to convince anyone in a court of law?

CHAPTER 46

As I left the courthouse, I mulled over the prosecution's case against Grady. The evidence was strong enough to hold him for trial. About that there was no doubt in my mind. Our only real chance was to point the finger at someone else, and have it stick.

I headed toward police headquarters on Washington Street to pay another visit to Cedric Gibson. He was shuffling through the clutter of papers on his desk when I knocked on the open door of his office.

"Ms. O'Brien," he said, rocking back in his chair. "What can I do for you this time?"

"I know about your investigation of Tony Rodale," I told him without beating around the bush. "And I know that Deirdre Nichols was working with you as an informant."

Gibson neither confirmed nor denied it, but pressed his fingers together and regarded me silently.

I took a seat across from him. "I don't want to blow your operation. But Grady Barrett is charged with murder. He's facing trial for a crime he didn't commit."

Gibson brought his fingertips to his chin, making an indentation in the flesh. "The evidence is there."

I nodded, trying to avoid a confrontation. "At first blush it does appear as though Grady might have been involved. But all of the evidence is subject to another interpretation as well, and that's something the police never took the time to explore. They wanted a quick arrest, and they snagged Grady."

"We 'snagged,' to use your term, the man we believe committed the crime."

"The other suspects never got a second glance from your detectives."

"And that's what you think Rodale is, a possible suspect?"

"He wears a size ten shoe. He's someone Deirdre would have opened the door to late at night. He has a history of domestic abuse. If he'd got wind of the fact that she was cooperating with the police, he might well have killed her." I sat back. "There's also the fact that she was planning to break up with him. Maybe she told him it was over, and that's what made him snap."

Gibson raised his hands and gave me the time-out sign. "Can we talk unofficially for a moment?"

"We can start there."

"Tony Rodale was arrested this morning."

"On drug charges?"

He nodded. "You can make whatever you want of 'alternate scenarios,' but I can tell you that Rodale did not kill Deirdre Nichols."

"What makes you so sure?"

"One of our detectives has been working undercover. He was with Rodale the night of the murder."

I felt my heart sink. "Steve Henshaw?"

"Does it make a difference who it was?"

I flopped back in my chair. Disappointment flooded through me. Being in the company of a cop was a pretty good alibi. In fact, they didn't come much better.

"Maybe it was one of Rodale's henchmen," I said.

"I don't think so. We've had our eye on most of his associates. In any event, you'll have a hard time making the case in court."

"Deirdre Nichols was an informant. That alone ought to raise reasonable doubt about Grady's guilt in the mind of at least one juror." I was less certain that it would be enough to negate probable cause at the hearing.

Gibson stroked his cheek. "And once you make that preposterous assertion, how are you going to back it up? Don't think someone from this department is going to march into court and do it for you."

"You'd lie on the stand?"

"We'd try like the devil to avoid getting to that point." He looked me in the eye and his manner softened. "I'm not trying to one-up you, Ms. O'Brien. There is simply nothing to support the notion that Deirdre Nichols was killed because of a drug operation. It's a catchy Hollywood gimmick, but in this case it simply doesn't hold up under scrutiny."

It had to, I thought glumly. It was Grady's only chance.

"If it's any consolation," Gibson continued, "we've got a lead on two guys we suspect of killing your friend Hal Fisher. That's one homicide we just may be able to tie to Rodale."

"Because Hal found out about his drug connection?"

"Looks that way."

I closed my eyes for a moment, feeling the weight of Hal's death on my shoulders. I was glad they'd found his killers, but it was small consolation for loss of a life. Especially since I couldn't help thinking I'd set the whole thing in motion by asking him to work on the case. And it was all for naught. Grady was going to stand trial, and perhaps be convicted.

"I can't do anything with speculation," Gibson said. "But if you have anything concrete to bring me, I'll be happy to listen." He rose and ushered me to the door. "I don't like to see killers get away with murder."

"Or to see innocent men convicted?" I asked pointedly.

He offered a brief smile. "That too."

I returned to the office feeling discouraged. Without Tony Rodale to put forward as an alternate suspect, our options were limited. We were stuck with Grady's original story and little to offer by way of countering the evidence against him.

I stopped at Rose's desk to pick up my messages. "Any word from Marc?" I asked.

"Not a peep. Now I'm beginning to get worried."

"Did you try to call him?"

"Once this morning and twice this afternoon."

"I'll stop by his house after work. Maybe he's just not answering the phone."

"Yeah, I guess." I could tell that Rose didn't buy into that fiction any more than I did. But neither of us wanted to contemplate the other possibilities.

She handed me my message slips. "That boy Xavier called again," she said. "I told him to try you at four."

I looked at the clock. It was now a quarter to.

"I'm glad you made it back," Rose said. "I get the feeling he's not long on patience."

"I need to talk to him no matter what is going on. If I'm on the phone with someone else when he calls, get me anyway."

I opened the door to my own office, set my briefcase on the floor, and kicked off my shoes. Flopping into the chair at my desk, I closed my eyes for a moment and tried to ignore the worry that gnawed at me.

Hal had been making inquiries about Tony Rodale. Hal was now dead. He'd told me he'd seen Marc with Tony. Marc was missing. What did it mean?

My thoughts were broken by the jangle of the phone. I glanced at the clock. Three fifty-eight.

"Hello," I said into the receiver.

"You the lady wants to talk to me?"

"Xavier?"

"Yeah, is me."

"I appreciate your calling back."

"Is nothin. 'Sides, wanna see my picture on the front page."

"Your picture?"

"Yeah, see my name in print too. You's with some newspaper or somethin' the man says."

"I'm a lawyer," I explained, then hastened to add, "But I know someone with the newspaper."

"He gonna make me look good? I don't want none of those pictures what makes me look like ugly dog."

"Let's talk first. I'll put you in touch with the journalist, but I can't make any promises." I wasn't sure whether Byron Spencer would even talk to Xavier.

"They tell me you asking 'bout the flying angel."

"The flying angel?" I could tell this wasn't going to be easy.

"Yeah, that's what the man say."

"A couple of weeks ago a woman fell from the deck of a house above the canyon where you and some friends were partying. I understand you saw it happen."

"Yeah, was wild. All white and fluttery, like an angel. Not every day you see something like that."

"Did you see anyone else on the deck with her?"

"The force of evil, that's what was there. And her all in white."

"This evil ... force, can you describe it? Big frame or slender? Tall or short?"

"Didn't have no frame, lady. Was a force. A spirit."

I worked to keep my irritation from showing. "So you didn't actually *see* anyone with her?"

"I told you, evil. Red eye glowing like a burning ember."

"Its eye?"

"Like an ember."

"You saw a spark of red, like an ember?" My mind was churning, trying to give substance to his words.

"Not a spark. It was there, lurking."

"Did you see the ... the flying angel before she fell?"

"All in white."

"What about after she fell, did you see anyone on the deck then?"

"Evil, triumphant, slinking off into darkness."

I pressed my hand against my forehead, seeing my last line of defense slinking off into the darkness as well. "Xavier, is there a number where I can reach you? I might think of something else I need to ask."

"I'm here, I'm there. A number'd be no good."

"What if I need to talk to you again? Or my friend at the newspaper?"

"He gonna take my picture?"

"If that's what you want."

He seemed to think about it a minute. "I got your number. I'll be in touch."

I spent what was left of the afternoon preparing for tomorrow's day in court. I reviewed my notes, the police report, and other materials, seeing and feeling the events from a fresh perspective now that I knew Grady had been there. I was trying hard to imagine things as they might really have happened.

At six I packed up my briefcase and headed over to Nina's to welcome her home from the hospital. On the way, I stopped by Marc's. The house was dark, and his car was nowhere in sight. I rang the bell anyway, then pounded on the door. Nothing.

Anger had long since given way to worry, but the worry was now clouded by a new sort of uneasiness. Had Marc been honest with me about the circumstances of his beating? Tony, former kingpin of the drug world, was now in jail. If Hal had really seen Marc with Tony, what kind of trouble might Marc be in? By the time I reached Nina's, my head was spinning. But answers were in short supply.

Simon opened the door for me and Emily escorted me upstairs. "Mommy and I were playing go fish," she chirped. "Simon hates to play go fish."

"You must be happy to have your mom back home."

She nodded. "I wish my daddy was here too."

"I know you do, honey."

Emily pushed open the bedroom door.

"Hi," I said to Nina as Emily pulled me into the room.

Nina smiled. "I was hoping you'd come by." She looked pale and tired, but she made a valiant effort to sound upbeat.

I pulled an emerald velvet armchair closer to the bed and sat.

"God, I'm happy to be back home," she said. "Hospitals have got to be among the most depressing places on earth."

Next to prisons, I thought. "They serve a purpose though."

She nodded without conviction, then turned to Emily. "Why don't you go see if your dinner is ready, sweetie, while I talk to Kali. We'll keep the cards right where they are and finish the game after you eat."

"I'm not hungry."

"Kali and I need some grown-up time."

With great reluctance Emily left us, but not before giving her mother a smothering hug.

"How did it go at court today?" Nina asked when we were alone. "Did Adrianna say anything new?"

"She was a good witness," I began. "She seemed certain the car she saw was a convertible and that it was silver." I paused. "She also knew that it was a Mercedes."

"A Mer—" Nina lowered her head to her hand and closed her eyes. "Was it Grady's?" she whispered, then, without waiting, answered her own question. "Yes, of course. So he *was* there that night."

I couldn't tell her what Grady had told me in confidence, but I wanted to reassure her somehow. "He had nothing to do with Deirdre's death," I said. "I firmly believe that."

"But he *was* there that night, wasn't he?"

"He swears that he never saw her or spoke to her. That's all I can tell you. Grady will have to give you a fuller explanation."

"Dear God. It just keeps getting worse and worse, doesn't it?"

"He didn't kill her, Nina. We may not prevail at the hearing, but we'll beat the charges at trial."

"You hope. We both know that juries are unpredictable."

"We'll present a strong defense."

Nina drew in a breath. "You really think there's no chance it's going to be dismissed before trial?"

I hesitated. "The other day you asked me to skip the sugar coating. Is that the way you want it still?"

Her shoulders slumped. "It will be months, won't it? Maybe years."

"Six months at least," I said. My throat felt raw. "I'm sorry, Nina. I tried, but the prosecution's case is solid."

"The baby will be crawling by the time the case gets to trial. Maybe even walking. I'll be finished with chemo." She closed her eyes. "Assuming I'm still alive."

I reached for her hand.

"I can't face it alone, Kali. There must be *something* you can do. You can still put on a defense."

"I'd like to be able to do that, believe me. But I need something to work with."

"The state's case can't be airtight," Nina said.

"It isn't. And there are things that don't feel right to me—"

She leaned forward. "Like what?"

"I can't put my finger on them." It was like searching for a word that remained just outside your memory.

"What you need is a witness who saw someone else there that night."

"That's not going to happen. I've canvassed the neighborhood. So did Hal. And I finally spoke with the kid who claimed to have seen Deirdre fall. He's useless."

"He didn't see anything at all?"

"If he did, he sure can't communicate it." I filled her in on my conversation with Xavier. "I'm afraid we're stuck with simply picking away at the prosecution's evidence."

"And you don't think that will be enough?" Defeat was etched in her voice.

"I wish I could be more optimistic."

"What does Marc think?"

I hesitated, not happy about worrying Nina further. I decided, finally, that I had no choice. "You haven't heard from him the last couple of days, have you?"

"No. Why?"

I told her about the phone call that had lured Marc into the flatlands of Berkeley, and his subsequent beating. I also voiced my suspicions, starting with what Hal had told me and then tiptoeing around the terrible doubt at the core of my thinking.

Nina saw where I was headed immediately. "You don't seriously think he might have been involved in Hal's murder, do you?" Her tone was incredulous.

Gibson had told me they had two suspects in the case. But that didn't mean Marc wasn't somehow implicated. "When you look at the whole picture—"

She shook her head vehemently. "No, there's got to be another explanation. Have you checked with the hospitals?"

"It wasn't until this afternoon that I really began to worry."

"I can take care of the checking," she said. "Making phone calls is one of the few things I can do from bed. You focus on getting Grady's case dropped, and try not to worry about Marc. He's done this before."

"Disappeared?"

She nodded. "Not come into the office for a couple of days, at any rate."

"Without telling you where he is?" I felt a glimmer of hope.

Nina pulled her hair back from her face. "Marc is a good friend. Like most men, though, he keeps things to himself. Sometimes he'd call, but not always. I learned not to ask."

I didn't feel like eating dinner, so I nibbled on cheese and crackers instead, and washed them down with several glasses of merlot. I didn't feel like working either. I sat by the living room window and looked out at the twinkling lights across the bay.

"You look troubled," Bea said, coming to sit beside me. "Is the hearing going badly?"

I gave her a resigned smile. "You might say that."

"It must be so much harder for you when you're representing a friend."

I nodded. Even though Grady wasn't someone I'd initially have classed as a friend, he was the husband of one. And someone whose strengths I'd come to appreciate.

Grady, Nina, Marc, Hal—I couldn't shake the feeling that I'd let them all down.

"Sometimes," Bea said soothingly, "things really *are* beyond our control. You do what you can and try your best, but none of us is able to direct the course of events."

"Thanks." I squeezed her hand. "I'll try to remember that."

Taking the case file, along with another glass of merlot, I headed downstairs to work. I pulled out the police report and went over the crime scene step by step. I looked at my notes on the investigation and on the testimony to date. Once again I couldn't shake the feeling that the answer was there if only I could see it.

Finally, exhaustion caught up with me and I went to bed. Sleep eluded me, however. Instead, my mind replayed possible scenarios for the night of Deirdre's murder.

She'd been upbeat at work that day, made plans to meet her friend Judith the next evening to "celebrate her independence." I'd assumed she'd been talking about her breakup with Tony Rodale, but maybe it was Grady's payoff she was referring to. What did that tell me about her killer, or was it totally unrelated?

She'd come home, talked briefly with her sister, slipped out of her street clothes, and prepared a simple meal for herself and Adrianna. Then she'd busied herself baking cookies while waiting for Grady, whom she didn't expect until almost eleven.

Had she been expecting someone else as well? From the look of the kitchen, I thought she'd probably been caught unawares. But would she have opened the door to a stranger? Possibly. And that brought me back to the ultimate question—who might want Deirdre dead?

It was after three in the morning when I drifted off to sleep. By then the germ of an idea began to form. Did I dare risk voicing it in court?

CHAPTER 47

"The prosecution rests, your honor." Madelaine Rivera lifted her chin and walked purposefully to her table in front of the gallery railing. Although I didn't turn to look, I was willing to bet she made eye contact with members of the press.

It was only ten o'clock in the morning. Madelaine had wrapped things up quickly, so as not to undercut the strength of Adrianna's testimony at the close of court yesterday. It was a wise strategy. I'd have done the same.

Next to me, Grady was looking agitated. He leaned close. "Are you going to have me testify?"

"Not at this stage, for sure."

"But it's the only way to explain what really happened."

"Trust me on this."

"I need the case dismissed." Grady's voice was a low whisper, almost a hiss.

Judge Atwood gave us a cool look. "Are you ready, Counselor?"

"Yes, Your Honor." I shuffled papers and then stood slowly. "The defense would like to recall Sheila Barlow."

Judge Atwood's frown deepened. "You want to *start* by recalling a prosecution witness?"

"We would, Your Honor."

There was a rustling sound at the back of the courtroom. The media folks smelled something unusual in the wind.

"And we request that she be called as a hostile witness," I added.

Another wave of reaction from the courtroom. *Hostile witness* is an ominous-sounding term, but in legal parlance it means that the attorney can ask leading questions, as befitting cross examination. Nonetheless, there was a palpable buzz from the back of the room.

As Sheila Barlow took the stand, I had a moment's doubt about the path I was about to lead us down. Although my sleep last night had been uneasy, and tangled with wakefulness, I'd woken this morning with a clear sense of what had been bothering me about the case all along. And now I was about to gamble on a hunch.

I approached the witness stand, hoping to put Sheila at ease. "I'd like to go over a few things from your earlier testimony, to make sure I understand it."

Sheila nodded.

"You testified that on the morning Adrianna called you to say that her mother was hurt, you were already up and had had your coffee."

"That's correct."

"So you got up that morning around, what, five-thirty, six?"

"Sounds about right. I don't recall exactly."

"Can you tell me why you were up at that hour?"

She adjusted the silver brooch at her throat. "I'm often up early."

"Even on Sundays?"

She looked at Madelaine, then away. "Sometimes."

"Did you set the alarm to wake you that morning?"

"I . . . I don't remember."

Madelaine was on her feet. "Your Honor, I fail to see the relevance of this line of questioning."

Judge Atwood raised an eyebrow my direction, inviting a response.

"I'm ready to move on anyway," I said, then turned back to address the witness. "When you arrived at the house, did Adrianna let you in?"

"No, I've got a key."

"The door was locked when you got there?"

Sheila Barlow licked her bottom lip. "It locks automatically when shut."

"How about the sliding glass door that opens onto the deck? Was that locked?"

She hesitated. "I don't remember."

"And Adrianna was in her room, is that correct?"

"Yes. I'd told her on the phone to go there and wait for me."

I weighed the moment, then let it pass. "So you found Adrianna in her room," I said. "And then the two of you went into the den, where you read to her and held her until the police arrived, is that correct?"

"I don't believe we read until after the police arrived, but in general terms it's correct."

"Did you check the rest of the house?"

"What do you mean?"

I gave a casual shrug. "To see if there were other signs of disturbance."

Sheila shook her head. "I guess I never thought about that. My main concern was comforting Adrianna."

"So you didn't go into the kitchen?"

"Correct."

"You didn't turn off the oven?"

She hesitated and glanced again in Madelaine's direction. "I don't remember."

"But you couldn't have turned off the oven if you didn't go into the kitchen, could you?"

She seemed to search her memory. "No, I guess not."

"Your sister was in the midst of baking cookies when she was killed. Yet when the police arrived, the oven was off. Who do you suppose turned it off?"

Sheila Barlow looked at me a moment, and then cleared her throat. "I don't know. Maybe I did it without thinking."

"But you just said that you hadn't gone into the kitchen. Are you changing your testimony?"

She took her time answering. "No. To the best of my recollection, I didn't go into the kitchen."

I turned for a moment to let my eyes roam the courtroom, drawing it closer. "Your sister was lucky to have such a conscientious killer, wouldn't you say? It's not often you find someone who commits murder and then carefully turns off the oven before leaving."

Madelaine jumped to her feet. "Objection, Your Honor. Defense counsel is badgering the witness."

"I don't think we've gotten to the badgering stage yet, Ms. Rivera."

Madelaine spread her hands, and added, "I also fail to see the merit to this line of questioning."

"If you'll give me a few more minutes, Your Honor, I think the importance of these questions will become clear."

Judge Atwood nodded. I suspected she was already catching a glimmer of the bigger picture. "You may continue."

There was a murmur from somewhere at the back of the room.

"Let's return to the kitchen," I said, handing the witness a photograph that had already been admitted into evidence. I pointed to a collection of baking supplies on the counter. "Can you tell me what you see there?"

"Flour, sugar, some spoons, a cutting board." Sheila's shoulders were hunched, her voice stiff. "An empty egg carton and a box of oatmeal."

"What about the brown plastic container next to the oatmeal."

Sheila chewed on her bottom lip. "It looks like chocolate syrup."

"Do you suppose your sister was using the chocolate syrup in her baking?"

A fractional shrug. "Adrianna likes chocolate."

"In oatmeal cookies?" I managed a tone of incredulity and didn't wait for an answer. "Does Adrianna like to eat chocolate syrup by the spoonful?"

A curt nod. "Yes."

Before I asked the next question, I sent a silent prayer to the heavens. "Is that how she takes medicine?"

There was a small change in Sheila's expression. "What do you mean?"

I could feel the tension in my temples. "Kids sometimes wash down bad-tasting medicine with chocolate syrup. Does Adrianna do that?"

Sheila's expression was pinched. "She might."

"She *might?*" My voice swelled. "Didn't Adrianna live with you for much of her life? I should think you would *know* how she took her medicine."

"Sometimes she takes it with syrup," Sheila said, making no attempt to hide her annoyance. "It depends on the medicine."

I breathed deeply. It was the answer I'd hoped for. "It depends on whether the medicine is flavored, you mean?"

"That's a consideration."

I took a step back. "Your sister had a prescription for Restoril—a sleeping pill that comes as a gel capsule. Do you happen to know whether the powder inside the capsule is flavorful?"

"Objection." Madelaine was on her feet again, her arms flying in the air. "The witness isn't a drug expert. This whole line of questioning is preposterous."

"I was asking about Ms. Barlow's personal knowledge only."

Madelaine snorted. "What does the witness's personal knowledge about the flavor of *any* medicine have to do with the question before this court? Your Honor, I—"

"Never mind," I said turning to Judge Atwood. "I'll withdraw the question."

I walked back to the defense table and made a pretense of checking something in my file. In truth, I was gathering my courage. My pulse beat so rapidly I could hear it pounding in my ears.

The courtroom was quiet with expectation. Grady sat stock-still, his eyes facing forward. He didn't look at me, only at Sheila Barlow.

I looked up from the page, took a breath, and addressed the witness. "Miss Barlow, would you be surprised to learn that your fingerprints were found on that bottle of chocolate syrup?"

"My . . ." She opened her mouth and shut it again, obviously caught off guard. Yet she made a quick recovery. "Not at all. Only the day before, I'd been at the house and made Adrianna a glass of chocolate milk using that same bottle of syrup."

"So it doesn't surprise you?"

Madelaine huffed in exasperation. "Asked and answered."

I nodded and called the court's attention to section IV(a) of the lab report concerning fingerprints found at the scene.

"Actually, Miss Barlow, your initial reaction was on target," I said. "There were no fingerprints at all found on the bottle of syrup. The rest of the kitchen was rife with prints—baking is a sticky business. But the bottle of chocolate syrup had been wiped clean."

Sheila's face was flushed. She gave me a venomous look, then shrugged elaborately. "Deirdre must have cleaned it up. As you said, things get sticky."

I glanced at Grady. He was now watching me intently.

Abruptly, I swiveled to face the witness. "Isn't it true, Ms. Barlow, that you were at your sister's the night she was killed?"

Sheila recoiled as though she'd been slapped. "No."

"Isn't it true that Adrianna's 'dream' about the chocolate syrup wasn't a dream at all? You gave her the syrup with the powder from one, or more, of your sister's sleeping pills because you didn't want her to wake up and find her mother's body."

"No, that's not true." Sheila's voice had a thin, scratchy quality it hadn't before.

"Isn't it true that you were outside on the deck on a winter's night because you wanted to smoke and Deirdre wouldn't let you do so in the house?" That would explain Xavier's red-eyed evil force.

She shook her head.

"Isn't it true," I said, picking up the beat, "that you killed your sister by pushing her over the railing, then turned off the oven out of concern for Adrianna's safety?"

Sheila was shaking her head vehemently. So vehemently that her whole body trembled. "You don't know what you're talking about."

I softened my tone. "You and Deirdre were once in love with the same man, weren't you? The man who became Adrianna's father."

Sheila didn't answer. She rocked silently in the witness stand.

I was playing a hunch. I remembered the photo of the three of them, taken the day Sheila had introduced Frank and Deirdre. I remembered Nina's comment about Sheila's failed romance and I thought about the glow of reverence that colored Sheila's expression whenever she mentioned Frank's name. Looking at her face now, I knew I was right.

"You were both in love with him," I said, "and he chose your sister over you, didn't he?"

Sheila jerked forward, grabbing the edge of the witness stand tightly with her hands. "No, we were *not* both in love with him." Her voice spiraled. "*I* was in love with him; Deirdre stole him from me by getting pregnant. All she wanted was someone to support her. She never cared about him the way I did. Never."

The courtroom was silent. No shuffling of feet, no muted whispers. The full attention of everyone present was riveted on the witness.

"Frank was one of the most generous human beings I've ever known," Sheila said softly. "Deirdre milked him for every cent she could get her hands on, forcing him to spend more than he could afford. She drove him into debt."

"And ultimately," I added, "to suicide."

"She was responsible for his death. As much to blame as if she'd pulled the trigger herself." Sheila spat out the words in contempt.

"Is that why you killed her? To even the score?"

For a moment Sheila said nothing. Then she slumped forward, covering her face with her hands. "I didn't mean to," she wailed. "I was angry. I didn't mean to kill her."

There was a collective gasp from the courtroom, followed by a wave of murmurs.

Sheila rocked forward. "I didn't even realize what I'd done until I heard that awful thump of her body hitting the ground. I was angry. I wanted to hurt her, that's all. Like she'd hurt me."

"Hurt you how?" I asked.

She ignored the question. "I went to the house to see if I couldn't talk some sense into her. That's all I wanted to do, talk. But Deirdre wouldn't listen. She wouldn't think of anyone but herself. She never did."

"Talk to her about what?"

Sheila glared at me, her expression filled with loathing. "This is your fault. You don't know what it's like to love a child. You've never experienced the kind of hold that has on you."

"You're referring to Adrianna?"

"Adrianna is Frank's child. She's all I have left of him. And she's the most important thing on earth to me."

I shook my head in confusion. "I'm not sure I follow. You killed your sister because of Adrianna?"

Sheila looked up at the judge and emitted a soundless cry. "Deirdre was going to move away. She was going to take Adrianna with her. All the way to Florida. She took Frank, and now she wanted to take Adrianna too. It was like I had no rights. No rights at all."

CHAPTER 48

Nina held the huge bouquet of yellow roses to her nose and inhaled their sweet aroma with obvious delight. She leaned closer to Grady, sitting on the bed beside her. "They're absolutely beautiful," she said. "But having you home again is all that really counts."

She was still reeling from the euphoria of seeing Grady walk unexpectedly through the doorway of their bedroom. She kept touching him to make sure he was real.

Grady kissed her forehead. "I love you, Nina. I've put you through hell, and I'm going to spend the rest of my life trying to make it up to you. I promise."

Briefly, Nina turned in my direction. "How did you know it was Sheila?"

We'd covered the main points of the morning's court session in bare-bones form already, and now that she was sure Grady was home to stay, she wanted the details.

"I didn't," I told her. "It was only a hunch. But it was also our only hope of dismissal."

"I'd all but given up hope," Grady said.

"So had I." My shoulders still ached with the tension of the last few days. "I saw a long shot and took it. But it might not have worked."

Grady draped an arm around Nina's shoulders. "There must have been something that alerted you to the possibility it was Sheila."

I nodded. "Emily told me that she ate chocolate syrup by the spoonful to cover the taste of medicine. When I heard Adrianna say she'd dreamed that Sheila have given her chocolate syrup,

Emily's comment flashed in my mind. There was chocolate syrup on the kitchen counter, yet the cookies Deirdre was baking were oatmeal."

Nina laughed. "This is the first I've heard that you know *anything* about baking, Kali."

"Well, I didn't know for sure. There was a chance that chocolate-oatmeal was all the latest rage. The real trigger, though, was the oven. The killer had to have been someone who cared enough to turn off the oven before leaving."

"But still, her own sister . . ." Grady shook his head in disbelief.

"I don't think it was something she planned. But when Deirdre told her she was moving to Florida and taking Adrianna with her, Sheila lost control."

"She's so devoted to Adrianna," Nina said. "It must have been difficult for her to leave Adrianna alone for the night."

"I'm sure it was, but she couldn't very well take the child home with her without raising suspicion. That's why she woke Adrianna briefly to give her the sleeping powder, to ensure that she'd sleep through the night. Sheila intended to get back to the house the next morning before Adrianna woke up."

Grady rubbed his cheek. "So that's why you asked her what time she'd gotten up Sunday morning."

"It struck me as curious that she got to the house so soon after Adrianna's call. And she never checked to see if Deirdre might be alive or if there was anyone else in the house."

"She was lucky Adrianna thought the whole episode was only a dream," Nina said.

"I suspect she may have planted that idea herself."

"She must have been ecstatic when she found out Adrianna had seen a silver convertible in front of the house," Grady added.

"Doubly so when the police locked on to you as their chief suspect."

"But why make up the story about the answering machine tape, then?" Nina looked to Grady. "She did make it up, didn't she?"

Grady nodded. "I'm not proud of the things I've done lately. But I never threatened Deirdre. Or even considered it."

"She wanted to avoid going to trial," I said. "For Adrianna's sake as well as her own. Now, tell me about Marc."

Nina had told me soon after we arrived that she'd talked to

him, but she hadn't been willing to say more until she'd heard the full story of Grady's release.

"Marc's in the hospital," she said slowly.

Foreboding shot through me. "Which one? Is he okay?"

"He's not hurt, if that's what you mean."

"Where is he, Summit?"

She shook her head. "In southern California. It's a special hospital."

"Special?"

She hesitated. "Drug rehabilitation."

The words hit me broadside. I felt as if I were suffocating. Anger and grief welled up inside me, pressing against my lungs.

Grady leaned forward. "What? Marc's a drug addict? Impossible."

"It's true," Nina said. "I spoke with him myself. He had me fooled too."

"Jesus, what was he on?"

"Cocaine mostly. Probably some other stuff too. We didn't get into the particulars."

Why hadn't I suspected? The signs were all there—if only I'd been willing to look. The lingering cough and sniffles, the erratic behavior and odd hours, the abrupt mood shifts.

But denial is like a pervasive heavy fog: it changes the landscape and makes it impossible to see anything but the single tree in front of your nose.

"So *that* was his connection with Tony Rodale," I observed, thinking aloud.

Hal had been right when he said he'd seen the two of them together. And Rodale was undoubtedly the link between Marc and Deirdre. No wonder Marc had left the ComTech party in a hurry once he'd noticed Deirdre was there. She was part of his other life, not his work life.

"When he found out the police were zeroing in on Rodale," Nina said, "he panicked. Instead of going to his regular sources, he went looking for drugs on the street."

"That's why he was beaten the other night?"

She nodded. "There never was any phone call from a guy with information about the case. That was just an excuse to cover up the reason he was out in that part of town."

"He was walking the streets, looking for a fix? How could he be so stupid?"

"He's an addict, Kali. One who hid it well, I grant you that. But poor judgment sort of goes with the territory, don't you think?"

Poor judgment wasn't the half of it. "How did he sound when you talked with him?" I asked.

"Sick, scared, filled with guilt. He realized after he was beaten how much his life had spun out of control."

My own felt as though it were still teetering. "He could have left word that he was okay," I snipped, feeling that I'd somehow had the wind knocked out of my sails. Against my better judgment I'd let myself begin to care about him. When he was hurt, I'd gone to help him—no questions asked. And yet it hadn't apparently crossed his mind that I'd be worried.

"He was ashamed," Nina said. "He was embarrassed to call you."

"He'd rather leave me wondering if he was hurt?"

Nina shrugged. "Don't judge other people too harshly, Kali."

There was the clatter of feet on the stairway, and then Emily burst into the room.

"Daddy." She flung herself at Grady and wrapped her arms around his neck.

"Hello, sweetheart. I missed you so much."

"We're so glad you're home." She looked at Nina. "Aren't we, Mommy?"

"Absolutely."

A few minutes later Grady and Emily went downstairs for hot chocolate. Nina leaned back against the pillows and exhaled loudly. "Whew. What a day."

"You're telling me? My stomach was so twisted in knots this morning, I don't think it will ever get back to normal."

Her eyes met mine. "Thank you, Kali. For what you did for Grady. For being my friend through all this."

"I only wish I could make . . . the rest of it better."

"Cancer. You can say the word in my presence." She closed her eyes a moment, her expression a mix of resignation and repose. When she opened them again, it was with a smile. "I've come to appreciate what's good and not dwell on the rest. Or at least I'm trying to."

"That strikes me as a remarkably healthy attitude."

"Along those same lines . . ." She smoothed the comforter with her open hand. "I know you know more than you're saying, and it bothers you. And I think it's likely that Grady was sleeping with Deirdre. But I don't know for sure." She paused to look at me. "And I don't want to know for sure. There's a lot of good in Grady, and that's what I want to focus on."

I nodded, and hoped for Nina's sake—for the sake of all three Barretts—that Grady meant what he'd said about making up for past wrongs.

The sky was turning dark by the time I reached home. I felt relief knowing that the charges had been dropped and Grady was free. Beyond that, though, there was little to celebrate.

I put my key in the lock and let myself in. The house was empty. I flipped on the light in the kitchen and found a note from Bea and Dotty saying they were having dinner with a friend.

Pouring myself a glass of wine, I went to sit by the living room window and watch the lights come on around the bay. When the phone rang, I decided to let the machine pick it up. I was in no mood to talk with anyone.

After the seventh ring, it became clear that the machine wasn't turned on. Finally, I reached for the receiver.

"Kali?"

I took a breath. "Hello, Marc."

He hesitated. "Have you spoken with Nina today?" His voice was thin, his tone tentative.

"She told me about your drug problem, if that's what you're asking."

A pause. "Just like before. I screwed up again, didn't I?"

"You have so much going for you, Marc. How could you risk losing it all?" Sadness pulled me in its wake like the receding tide.

"I tried not to. I hated myself for it. But the more I hated myself, the more I screwed up. The break-in at our office scared the shit out of me, Kali. But I still couldn't stop."

"You think that was drug related?"

"I'm sure it was. Rodale was nervous about being busted. When we started looking at him in connection with Deirdre's murder, I guess he put two and two together and got five." There was a moment's silence. "Also, I recognized the guy who came after us as someone I'd seen with Tony."

"What? Why didn't you tell the police?"

"How could I? Not without coming clean about my own involvement."

"Oh, Marc. How did you let yourself get into such a mess?"

"When I think what might have happened, Kali, how you might have been hurt. How you might have been killed even . . ." His voice faded for a moment. "I don't know how I got to this point. I can't believe this is really me. That I've fucked up so totally."

"You can still turn your life around, you know. It isn't too late."

"Yeah," His tone lacked conviction. "That's what they say."

"It's true, Marc. It's in your hands."

"Not very capable hands, from the looks of things."

"You can change that."

He gave a bitter laugh. "Maybe." Another moment's pause. "I'm sorry, Kali. Truly sorry. For everything."

"Marc, you can—"

He cut me off. "I'm not sure I can, that's the problem."

"You've taken the first step by getting help."

Silence hung between us. "I wanted things to turn out different," Marc said finally. "I wanted us to have a future."

"Me too," I whispered.

"Maybe . . ." He paused. "Well, you never know what tommorow holds."

"I'm rooting for you, Marc. Remember that."

EPILOGUE

Nina and Grady have a son. He weighed in at a healthy seven pounds three ounces and has been gaining steadily ever since.

Nina is halfway through the prescribed course of chemo. She's lost her hair but not her spirit or resolve. There are times, like the two days early on when she was vomiting so heavily, she had to be hospitalized, that she wonders if she has the strength to continue the fight. But those times are remarkably few and fleeting. Grady has been a diligent husband and friend to her, surprising me, and I think Nina as well, with his sensitivity and support.

I've spoken with Marc several times but only over the phone. He's fighting demons too, and holding his own. But I'm not sure his resolve is as strong as Nina's. Only time will tell.

Both Nina and Marc would like me to stay on permanently. It's an offer I'd have jumped at a couple of years ago but I'm less certain now.

We are making our way, each of us, a step at a time.